SILVERHAND

5k

MORGAN
LLYWELYN

SILVERHAND

THE ARCANA, Book 1

MICHAEL SCOTT

SILVERHAND: THE ARCANA, BOOK I

This is a work of fiction. All the characters and events portrayed in this book are fictional, and any resemblance to real people or incidents is purely coincidental.

A Baen Books Original

Baen Publishing Enterprises
PO Box 1403
Riverdale, NY 10471

ISBN: 0-671-87652-X

Cover art by Gary Ruddell

First printing, April 1995

Distributed by Simon & Schuster
1230 Avenue of the Americas
New York, NY 10020

Library of Congress Cataloging-in-Publication Data

Llywelyn, Morgan
        Silverhand / by Morgan Llywelyn & Michael Scott.
            p.   cm. -- (The Arcana : v. 1)
        ISBN 0-671-87652-X
        I. Scott, Michael, 1959-   . II. Title. III. Series:
    Llywelyn, Morgan. Arcana : v. 1.
    PS3562.L94S57   1995
    813'.54--dc20   94-44443
                                                    CIP

Printed in the United States of America

for Micaela,
a book of her own

What is the nature of evil?

And good — define for me its nature.

Then explain to me how we can tell one from the other. We judge darkness in comparison to the light. We recognize evil by contrasting it with good. But are such judgements easily made? Can good be put to evil uses, and evil used for good?

This I have learned: There are no absolutes, nothing stays the same.

from the Journal of Caeled Silverhand

THE SPOKEN ONE

PROLOGUE

The feathered sidewinder twisted across the noonday sand, leaving a distinctive trail in the dunes.

The serpent paused, tongue flickering, alerted by the faintest trembling on the desert air. Its tongue flickered again, sorting through various smells: acrid silicate, hot stones baking hotter in the sun, the oozing waxy sap of spiny succulents. Familiar atmosphere, nothing alarming.

The snake curled and twisted its body, muscling its way forward across the rippled surface of the dunes. Then it realized the sand was actually burning its skin.

The sidewinder hesitated again.

Movement.

A slight shuddering of the air, vague, indistinct.

Odor.

Sweet and cloying, bitter and repellent.

The forked tongue of the serpent danced and its head swayed from side to side as it tried to detect the source of the movement, the origin of the scent. It reared upward with its multicolored feathered frill vibrating in alarm.

The sand began moving, shifting, twisting, patterns distorting, symmetrical ripples dissolving into chaos.

The serpent was deaf; it could not hear the sudden scream that tore through the sky. A scream without emotion, without shape or color. The White Scream of something that had never lived, a wordless howl that blotted out the normal desert noises. Gone was the hiss of blowing sand, the sighing of the wind.

Then the scream itself ceased.

The silence that followed was the silence of ice and death, of some terrible, unimaginable emptiness.

The sound of nothingness. Negation.

The snake's limited vision could not encompass the cloud that suddenly appeared above the desert. The cloud convulsed, forming and reforming. Swooping from the sky, it rolled across the desert sand like some sentient predator, hunting.

When the sidewinder's primeval brain alerted it to danger, the snake began trying to escape. Frantically it hooped itself across the sands in search of shelter.

The cloud fastened upon the living creature.

The scream returned, but at a different pitch. It shrilled higher and higher, rising until it was felt rather than heard. Sound tore through flesh like a knife.

The snake thrashed briefly, then snapped rigid as its muscles locked. The cloud shrank in on itself. The serpent's flesh began to split, fluids and pale blood leaking from the tears in the skin.

The cloud vanished. The scream stopped. The sidewinder exploded into ragged meat.

Where the serpent had been was a gleaming sheet of blue-green glass, sizzling, still molten. In the air above the glass a single, multicolored feather circled lazily on an updraft.

CHAPTER ONE

The tower was strictly forbidden to the youngsters of Ward Point. A ruined pillar of stones jutting upward from the remains of a keep, the structure resembled a broken finger rising from a clenched fist. Caeled, who loved old stories and legends, listened with fascination to tales of a long-ago time when the tower had been part of a defensive network protecting the borders of the South-lands from the savage northern tribes.

Once these stones had witnessed violence and terror in full measure. Now the fortification was nothing more than a dangerous ruin, but lingering superstition still kept people away.

Caeled was not afraid of the tower, however. In his few short years he had experienced real fear and deprivation; tales from the ancient past could not intimidate him. They merely stimulated his curiosity. A thin, wiry boy, long-legged, with knees perpetually skinned, he enjoyed clambering through the ruins and exploring the echoing chambers, and had encountered nothing more sinister than a pack of dog-rats breeding in the cellars. He managed to kill one with his slingshot and drop it onto the heads of a gang of young rowdies at the foot of the tower, giving them a fright which made him chortle with glee.

He often sought refuge in the tower when the local bullies pursued him. They swaggered and boasted, but the tower's bloody history had so far discouraged them from following Caeled up the dark well of the spiral stone stairs.

His tormentors were local youths no older than
himself, boys on the brink of manhood exploring male
aggression. They delighted in attacking anyone who
seemed different, and Caeled was a favorite victim. He
was quiet where they were loud, gentle where they were
brutal. Even his looks set him apart.

Of all the boys in the town, only he had a swarthy
complexion, coarse dark hair, and night-black eyes. Such
coloring indicated origins in the far south. Natives of
Ward Point where Caeled and his mother now lived were
fair and pale-eyed. They needed little pigment to protect
them from the weak sun that rarely shone in the border
districts. Thick mist hovering over the marshlands created
an almost perpetual gloom.

Caeled assumed his looks were a gift from his father,
though he knew little about the man. He had stopped
asking about him a long time ago, when he realized such
questions tended to bring on one of his mother's bouts of
drunken melancholy.

On one of the rare days when a watery sun broke
through the mist, Caeled climbed to the very top of the
tower to enjoy the view. In his ragged knee-length cloak
and tattered tunic he made his way through shells of
rooms and along roofless corridors, feeling gritty debris
crunch under his feet, teetering with outstretched arms
across a jagged spar which was all that remained of an
upper floor. A moment's lost balance made his heart race
but he quickly recovered, thrilling with the shudder of
delight that follows a danger survived.

The boy let out a whoop of exhilaration — then
laughed at the startled scuttling of rats in the walls.

In the tower Caeled could be a child. There had been
little opportunity for childhood in a hard life that forced
him to mature before his time. One would have to look
very deep to discover the unextinguished twinkle lurking
in his eyes.

The tower was in slightly better repair closer to the top. Legend had it that a creature of fire and air had once erupted from beneath the cellars and claimed every living soul, but for some reason failed to rampage through the upper reaches of the tower. It was a believable story. Scorch marks on the stone walls and charred timbers showed evidence of once having endured terrible heat. These were enough to fuel Caeled's imagination. He would visualize the tower intact as it must have looked long ago, then dream up fire-breathing monsters and play at defending the stronghold against them.

In such games he was always fearless — and victorious.

Closer to the top the air was sweeter. A damp wind off the marshes swept away the smells from the town, odors of grease and cooking, of wood and turf fires, of excrement and urine and the indescribable stench of too many people huddled together. Seen from the tower, Ward Point became less squalid. Distance blurred its weatherbeaten timber houses and shops into a pleasing pattern, neat as the town itself could never be. The majority of the townspeople existed in filthy, cramped conditions, struggling to eke out a living on the brink of poverty. Their lives were devoid of beauty.

But Caeled in his tower could imagine beauty for them.

Sitting in the crumbling arched window at the very top of the tower, the boy breathed deeply, filling his lungs as he gazed out across the marshlands to the north. This was his favorite place, his private sanctuary. Here he could let his dreams take wing.

"I will be emperor someday and give every one of my subjects a palace to live in!" he proclaimed. "And a fertile field to farm," he added with a sense of practicality. Shading his eyes, he scanned the landscape in vain for suitable farmland.

His attention was arrested by an area where desolate swamp disappeared into the gray nothingness that marked a pocket of the Void.

Void. He shaped the word with his lips, silently.

From the moment his mother had brought him to this tiny border town, Caeled had been fascinated by the proximity of the Void. In the Southlands of his earliest memory, Voids were considered little more than myths. But in the years he and his mother had spent moving ever closer to the border and the north, fleeing debt collectors and magistrates, they had learned that the Voids were more than legend.

Some day, when he was old enough, Caeled planned to investigate this nearest Void.

His dreaming eyes fixed on the dull, pale-orange disc of the sun, almost obscured again by a bank of swift-moving clouds. Then for no particular reason, he glanced back at the marshlands. The earth was a drab gray-green, monotonous and depressing. Suddenly a shaft of defiant sunlight broke free of the clouds and illuminated the earth beneath. The marshlands exploded into color. Sunshine turned the water to mirrors reflecting the heavens. Sparkling pools of yellow light danced amid myriad tiny islands of vivid green moss.

With sunlight washing over the fens, the boy could see the Void quite clearly. Its edges were sharply delineated against the marsh colors, as if an artist had rubbed away a section of a painting, erasing the paints, leaving bare canvas beneath. The Void was an absence of light and life, a negation of the visible world. A terrifying emptiness.

Caeled gazed at it, wondering . . .

Abruptly, color sparkled at the very heart of the Void.

Caeled blinked.

For a single instant, startling hues — blood red, bruise purple, bone white — had burned in the center of the emptiness.

Caeled shook his head, telling himself it was nothing more than the afterimage of the sun on his eyes.

Yet as he watched, disbelieving, new and different colors appeared. An eerie blue-green, a leprous yellow, a sullen and angry scarlet. Then the clouds recaptured the sun and the marshlands were plunged back into their usual somber tones. But the colors remained in the Void. Pulsating colors throbbing in the very center of emptiness.

Caeled deliberately closed his eyes and looked away. He counted to five before he turned back.

The colors were brighter. Nearer.

And a figure seemed to be moving in the heart of the Void.

Not only moving, but coming closer.

Part of the boy was frightened and longed to look away, yet he was drawn by the hypnotic lights. They were so beautiful. His mother once had a pendant set with glass jewels. She had stolen it from an Amorican merchant and spent three days in the stocks as a result, but Caeled never forgot that pendant, and the way the colors — reds, yellows, blues and greens — had sparkled like so many stars.

The lights in the Void reminded him of that pendant.

The sun escaped the clouds once more, flooding the marshlands with radiance. The colors in the Void faded by contrast, only to blaze anew when the clouds reclaimed their prisoner.

And a figure seemed to step out of the Void.

Startled, Caeled leaped to his feet. He swayed dizzily for a moment. Those sparkling lights had carved patterns onto his retina. When the youngster looked toward the Void again his stomach churned with such violence he gasped. Sudden cramps knotted his insides.

At that moment a terrifying sound split the air. It was a sound composed of every possible noise all whirled into one, a sound like the world tearing apart. A White Scream.

Caeled slid helplessly to the floor, overcome with nausea. He was shivering yet he could feel icy sweat gathering in his armpits. Perhaps the sound was part of his sickness.

Must have been something he'd eaten, he told himself, though he'd had nothing but a crust of oil-soaked bread since breakfast. Maybe the bread was mouldy again, or had maggots in it. He hated bread with maggots, though he knew some people ate cheese with maggots crawling through it and were thankful for the nourishment they provided. At the thought, his stomach heaved and he vomited his meager breakfast.

When his retching finally ceased he realized the scream had ceased also. He was so exhausted he could only curl up in a ball on the stones, all interest in the Void forgotten. A dizzy darkness claimed him. Caeled awoke.

He lay unmoving, trying to remember where he was. Directly in front of him a carrion-spider was picking through his crusted vomit. He could see with frightening clarity the long red hairs on its legs and fat round body, and the pincerlike jaws masticating its meal. When it realized the boy was watching it in horrified fascination the spider turned toward him and reared up, waving its forelegs threateningly.

With a cry of terror, Caeled jumped back. The carrion-spiders were not deadly, unlike many of their species, but their bite could cause painful pustules for days afterwards.

The boy got slowly to his feet. He was grateful that the spasm, or whatever it was, had passed. But he groaned aloud when his painfully tender stomach protested his movements.

Leaning on the window ledge, he gulped great lungfuls of clean marsh air to clear his head and wondered how long he had slept. Not very long, judging by the light in the sky. He glanced toward the Void, then immediately looked away as his stomach heaved in memory. He fought own his nausea and tried again.

No lights flickered and pulsed in the Void. Nothing moved there.

Had he really seen what he thought, or had his eyes

been playing tricks on him? Cradling his sore stomach with his arms, he began the long descent to the street below. He hoped he would not run into any of his tormentors. He was too weak to outrun them and they could easily throw him into the midden again.

As he neared the ground level, Caeled became aware of a puzzling silence. There was no hum of insects, no scurrying of rats in the walls. He stopped and turned his head from side to side, listening, then deliberately spoke aloud, just to hear his voice and be certain he had not gone deaf. "Hello?"

The sound echoed reassuringly from the stones around him.

He took another few steps down, head tilted to one side, ears intent. Though the tower walls were thick, and muffled noise, he knew he should be hearing some sounds from the nearby town: carts rattling over the cobbled approach road, hawkers crying their wares, the high-pitched squealing of pigs being driven to market.

But there was nothing.

Absolute silence.

He came to the bottom of the steps and waited. Now he could only hear the hammering of his heart in his chest.

Drawing a deep breath, the boy made himself step through the ruined doorway and out onto the road.

CHAPTER TWO

The road was empty. Caeled followed it around a bend, into the town . . . and the town was empty too.

The boy stopped and stared. The High Street which ran the length of Ward Point should have been bustling with activity both human and animal. Whistles and squawks from the bird market should be mingling with wails and curses from the slave pens, with the shouts of hawkers selling their wares and the greetings called from friend to friend, from door to door.

But the only sound was that of wind moaning dismally around the chimney pots. A large ball of spiked roller-weed bounced past Caeled and he drew back instinctively. Some rollerweed spikes were poisonous. There seemed to be more toxic plants appearing all the time, with a corresponding diminution in the number of beneficial plants. Farmers were complaining. But farmers always complained.

Caeled looked down the street in the direction the weed had come. How did it get into the town? Usually one of the beggars at the gates caught the weeds and turned them in to the town fathers before they could do any harm, collecting a minute bounty as reward.

Caeled hesitated as he approached the fruit stalls. From the nearest issued an appalling stench that made his eyes water. Drawing his woollen cloak across his nose and mouth the boy hurried past, wondering what could have happened.

When he reached Fat Mattoc's stall, he discovered a reason for the smell. The fruitseller's awninged stall was awash with a gelatinous liquid, a brown sludge that reflected no light. The nauseating substance had dripped onto the ground beneath the stall and partially congealed there, though in places it continued to bubble thickly, viscous bubbles that burst with a disgusting pop to release a foul gas. But where had the fruit gone? And where was Fat Mattoc, whose broad and smiling face was always beaming above his wares?

Fat Mattoc had been kind to Caeled and occasionally found an extra piece of fruit for him and given it without charge. His was the most popular stall in the town. He specialized in exotic fruits from the warm Southlands, great orange globes whose skin was bitter, but whose flesh was as sweet as summer. And tiny black grapes, so rich that a handful could make a man drunk. And clusters of yellow fruit that grew in a shape like a human hand, and melted deliciously in a human mouth.

Gone, now. Replaced by that sickening substance that smelled so awful. Caeled pinched his nostrils closed with his fingers and walked on, fearing what he might find.

Red Roly had the next stall. He too was missing, his stall drenched in vile liquid. Because his trays were tilted forward to display the assortment of grains and legumes he offered, most of the liquid had flowed off onto the ground in front of the stall. There it was hardening into a crust like a scab on the earth.

The Yam Man's stall was the biggest in the market. A copper-skinned native of one of the barbarian islands that lay to the east, he had come to town penniless and in less than four cycles become one of its wealthiest merchants. All because of yams. When he arrived none of the townspeople ate yams, now they were part of everyone's diet. Most people professed to love them, but Caeled disliked the stringy texture of their flesh.

The enormous pyramid of yams that was a feature of

the Yam Man's stall had vanished. The gelatinous sludge was thickest here. Crouching on his haunches, Caeled prodded the sludge with a stick. As the crust broke apart, the smell that enveloped him burnt his eyes and seared the back of his throat. But he fished out a dissolving yam rind. Dropping the stick into the liquid, Caeled looked wildly around. Suddenly he was very cold, and very very frightened.

The produce had putrefied. Fruit and vegetables which had been fresh when Caeled passed through the town that same morning had rotted in an impossibly short time, dissolving into rancid sugars and foul liquid.

What could have done such a thing? What in the name of the gods had happened here?

And where were the people?

Caeled found the first body in one of the slave pens. It was, to his horror, someone he knew — or almost knew. He had been watching the girl for the last few days, pitying her captivity, idly wondering how he could help her to escape, knowing he wouldn't dare try. Her coloring attracted him. She had an olive complexion, black eyes and hair reminding him of his own. She had been held apart from the others in a pen with metal bars, and doubly secured with leather thongs around her wrists and ankles. She was either especially valuable or had tried to escape. The latter, Caeled felt, from the hotly defiant look in her eyes.

She had obviously tried to escape this time, to flee whatever had entered and defiled the town. Caeled caught sight of her feet protruding through the metal bars. Her ankles were rubbed bloody and raw where she had struggled against her bindings. But the leather itself was gone.

The boy approached the pen cautiously. Even from a distance he could see to his horror that nothing remained of the girl above the knees . . . except more of the slime, shot through with sparkles. Caeled was baffled by the sparkles until he realized they were the polished metal of the chains that once connected the leather shackles, now gleaming through the viscid mess. As he stared at the horrid puddle on the ground, Caeled found himself wondering why her legs remained. Was it because they were touching the cold metal? Possibly whatever had consumed the girl was not able to digest metal.

Fear ran through him like blood, turning his extremities to ice. He longed to run but where could he run to, where would he find safety? It was better to try to discover the source of the horror, he reasoned. Then he might know how to protect himself from it.

Now that he knew what to look for, the signs were obvious. Puddles of slime on the street marked the positions of people. Tarag the itinerant peddler had stood on that corner, selling oddments from the Seven Nations. Noxious filth, speckled with thimbles and needles, was slowly draining into the gutter.

Messalane, the whore, had plied her trade on those steps. Once she had been beautiful, until a rival cut her face with a blade. Afterwards she covered her scars with a yashmak decorated with hundreds of southern coins. Where she had been standing when the nightmare descended on her, putrid corruption now trickled down the steps, brightened with numerous tiny coins with holes in their centers.

His mind reeling from what he had seen, Caeled raced along the High Street and turned into the narrow laneway leading to the tenements where he shared a single room with his mother. The reek which permeated Ward Point was appalling. His eyes and throat burned; his hair seemed to be crawling on his scalp. He longed to wash, to scrub away the stink and sights of the ruined town — though he already knew they would never leave him.

Most of all he longed to find his mother.

The town was dead; he was forced to admit that to

himself. Every living thing — from the birds in their ornamental cages to the stray felines that roamed the alleys — was destroyed. Nor had he found any surviving humans. Occasionally tiny portions of flesh and bone remained, but only where they had been touching cold iron.

When he came to the end of the lane he paused warily in a doorway, looking across a deserted square to the tenement which was his home. The square should have been swarming with noisy children playing, couples arguing, women gossiping, some hopeful musician practicing off-key. Instead there was silence. Even the self-important pigeons that usually strutted along the cobblestones were gone.

Caeled looked up toward the fourth floor of the tenement. Only the very poorest lived in the leaky attic apartments. He had known that he and his mother were poor, but he always hoped things would someday, somehow, get better. He vowed he would make them better when he became a man, though in his heart he knew it was only a dream, a straw to clutch at during the cold hungry times when he could hear his mother sobbing in the night.

There was an ache in Caeled's throat now as he stared up at the window of the room he and his mother shared.

He was afraid to imagine what must lie on the other side of that window.

He did not want his mother to die that way, in poverty and squalor. If she was dead, then all his dreams, all his futures had died with her.

Steeling himself, the boy darted from the doorway. As he ran across the square he made a futile effort to keep from thinking anything. He did not want to go into that building, up those stairs — he already knew what he would find — and yet he had to go, just in case. He had survived. Maybe his mother had survived too.

The stairs were coated in slime. He tried to avoid

stepping in it, but it fouled the bottoms of his boots in spite of his best efforts.

He found the source of the slime on the first landing. There was nothing recognizable in the bubbling pool in the corner. On the next landing, he discovered the entire floor covered in reeking foulness. A tiny metal chain attached to two studs perched atop the sludge, and he recognized Serana's nose chain. She usually carried her twins in two pouches, one on either hip. The boy turned away with a sob, suddenly understanding why the puddle was so big.

The door to his mother's room was open — but that was not unusual. The top floors of the house were always stifling and the odors of the tenement accumulated, clinging to the ceiling and coating the walls with a pervasive smell.

But there was another, stronger smell in the building now.

"Mama?" Caeled called fearfully, approaching the open door. "Mama?"

The silence mocked him.

He tried to call again but his voice failed him. Pressing his hand flat against the door, he pushed it open. "Mama?" The word came out as a whispered croak.

The dingy room with its broken bits of furniture was home, yet he already knew it would not be home to him any more. Even as he stepped through the doorway he knew he was looking for the last time at the peeling paper, the stained ceiling, and the smeared windows. His world had changed, changed irrevocably.

He found her on the bed. Her shape was clearly visible where it had soaked into the straw mattress, leaving the black shadowlike outline of a human body. Liquid was trickling out from beneath the bed.

Now that he had found her and knew the worst, Caeled felt . . . relieved. The emotion confused him. He was angry, yes, and frightened too, sickened body and soul by what had happened here, but at least now his mother was at peace. Probably for the first time in her life.

She had suffered, he knew, in ways he could not imagine. Her suffering had left her scarred and bitter. There had been walls between the two of them that were not of Caeled's making, though he had dreamed of the time he would do something so wonderful that the walls would dissolve and she would hold out loving arms to him.

As it was, her attitude toward him was puzzling. There were days when she had looked at him with an expression akin to fear in her eyes, though Caeled knew himself to be a gentle boy at heart. His tough and independent exterior had been forced upon him by the lives they lived, as a form of defense. He would never have hurt his mother.

But did she detect some unsuspected and frightening quality in him that reminded her of someone else? His father, perhaps? Caeled had often wondered, yet not dared ask. Now he would never know.

He made himself take a long last look at her body — if the mess on the bed could be called a body. Something shiny caught his eye. Holding his breath against the smell, he leaned closer.

The leather thong his mother had always worn around her neck had dissolved with her flesh, but the trinket she carried on the thong remained. Caeled's earliest memories were of sitting on her lap and trying to play with that trinket. She invariably pushed his hand away; he had never been allowed to touch it. For some reason he had come to believe it once belonged to his father, and was all his mother had of that vanished man.

A ring. A simple, heavy metal ring, so large it could almost have been a bracelet for a little boy. A ring without a stone, for where one was meant to be, with prongs to hold it in place, there was only a gaping oval. The ring was incomplete. Yet his mother had cherished it as she cherished nothing else.

With a terrible effort, Caeled forced himself to reach into the jellied ruin and extract the ring, which he hastily dropped onto a table. The touch of what had been his mother's flesh made him shudder; he wiped off any traces from his fingers, fighting down returning nausea.

Then he went to the battered cupboard that held their few clothes and took out his other homespun tunic and woollen trousers. His "best" clothing, they were nominally newer and less patched than the ones he wore. He changed into them and pulled on his only pair of soft leather boots again, cross-gartering them to hold them on his legs.

He wrapped the long strip of worn leather he used for a belt twice around his waist, fastened it securely, and wedged the handle of his slingshot beneath it. Then he gazed around the room, wondering if there was anything else he should take with him. Firestrikers, of course! The only knife their household had possessed, with a dull blade and broken handle. Still it *was* a knife; his mother had not liked for him to handle knives but she could not object any more. Finally he picked up a bent tin spoon that had served as a toy soldier in his childhood fantasies. With the faintest of smiles, he added it to the collection.

From a piece of coarse sacking they had used for a towel he fashioned a pack for his back to hold his few possessions. Then he found himself staring at the ring on the table by his mother's bed. He reached for it; drew his hand back; finally picked it up.

With a piece of twine he hung the ring around his neck, thrusting it down inside his tunic so no one would notice it and try to rob him.

If there was anyone. Anywhere.

Perhaps in the ruins of the town he would find some hidden hoard of coins or a few valuable trinkets, though he doubted if there was anything that remained edible. He would take whatever he could find; why not?

Caeled squared his thin shoulders resolutely. From his

mother he had learned the art of survival. He would go scavenging and then leave the town forever. There was nothing for him here anymore. Wrapping himself in his only cloak to try to stop the shivering that wracked him, Caeled took one long last look around the room.

By the time the boy left the tenement, the fire he had set beneath his mother's bed had taken hold. The ancient wooden structure was engulfed in flame as he walked away from it, not looking back. Tears were pouring down Caeled's cheeks but he was unaware of them. The horrific experiences of the day had left him numb. He could only walk, setting one foot ahead of the other, toward an uncertain future.

His final act before leaving Ward Point was to build up piles of wood and rotten timbers in various places along the High Street and laneways and set fire to them, too. By nightfall the whole town would be cleansed, burned to the ground. Caeled thought it a fitting pyre.

CHAPTER THREE

In his youth he could have felled the tree with a single mighty swing of the axe. But his youth was long gone, and age and experience had taught him to conserve his energy. He now used half a dozen carefully placed blows to bring the stonewood crashing to the earth. Setting aside his felling axe, Papul took satisfaction in the knowledge that although he was nearing his half century, he could still do the work of two ordinary men.

Pulling a trimming axe from his belt, the huge man began lopping off the branches and piling them on a roughly made sledge. He labored methodically throughout the afternoon, taking pleasure in the simple repetitive work.

By the time the light began to fade the sledge was heaped with wood which he had trimmed to even lengths. He secured it with stout cords, checking each knot as he drew it tight. He worked swiftly, unwilling — despite his size and strength — to be out in the forest at night. He would return with the dawn and continue chopping up the tree. The task should be done by nightfall, and then he would have firewood for the next three days; more, if the weather was kind.

Shouldering his big felling axe, Papul dragged the sledge behind him along the rough pathway he had hacked through the forest, heading back to the cave he now called home. The noise of his passage disrupted the woodland tranquillity but he considered that a blessing:

The noise should keep away all but the most curious.

A sliver of crescent moon was caught in the clutching fingers of the trees. Papul raised his axe in salute; the Lady Lussa would protect him.

The big man smiled at the irony. Less than a year ago he had been burning Elementalists . . . and now he supposed he had become one. Once he had been Papul, High Priest of Duetism. Then he had become Papul, the Heretic — and all because of the love of a woman. He had been prepared to give up everything for her . . . then she betrayed him. Now he was simply Papul, sometimes called the Hermit.

But at least he was safe here in this remote forest, and in time, he knew, civilization would forget him. Maybe even the twins would forget him. Initially, he had been surprised that they did not come after him, but then he realized they would probably consider a life spent in exile punishment enough.

Once — only a cycle ago, two seasons: warm and cold — he had been one of the most important men in one of the most powerful cities in the world, with servants beyond number to do his bidding. He had slept on silk sheets, eaten the finest of foods, worn the most costly apparel. Now he grubbed for survival in the forest.

And he was happier.

Here he had rediscovered his love of nature and the beauty to be found in simplicity. His great strength, which had withered in the effete court, had gradually returned to him. He had established a sense of being in touch with his true deity. God was all around him: pulsing in the earth, fragrancing the air, singing in the waterfalls.

God was everywhere.

Except in the Voids.

Papul stopped, peering through the trees. One of these mysterious flaws in the landscape lurked in the center of the forest, a pocket of desolation.

Void.

Throughout his life he had pondered the existence of the Voids. There were a hundred theories, another hundred "true explanations," and not a day went by without yet another discovery being announced by some self-styled expert. But in truth no one knew . . . because there was nothing to know about the Voids. They were simply emptiness. As dark is opposite to light, they were the reverse of being.

He gazed toward this Void now, torn as usual between curiosity and the repulsion the Voids engendered. The latter won out as it always did.

Time to go home.

The big man was turning away when something sparkled in the heart of the Void. Papul stopped. Was there unaccustomed light in the emptiness, or was it simply his imagination?

He watched for a few moments, saw nothing, and was moving away when the light flickered again. Abandoning the loaded sledge, Papul hefted his felling axe in his two big hands and turned to face the Void.

Stars!

Tiny incandescent stars, red and yellow and green, pinwheeling within the emptiness.

Flames!

Streaks and sparks of blue and green fire spiralling in the distance.

The lights were beautiful, like oil on water. The colors were sinuous, almost liquid. The hermit knew he should be afraid, but instead he felt only irresistible fascination. Was he witnessing a natural but thus far unreported phenomenon, something which happened to every Void? Or was this an unprecedented event? He had read that the Voids constantly changed in nature through the years. There was one school of thought which held that the Voids were not meant to be empty holes at all, but doorways to another time and place. It was only through misuse that the nature of the Voids had altered — or so some said.

This particular Void no longer appeared empty. Papul took a step closer. There was something within, something that burned with cold fire. He turned his head, pulling thick hair away from his ear so he could concentrate on a sound that had no place in the forest. A note as of music, high and sweet, like the song of a boy soprano.

It was coming from the Void. Papul stepped out from the cover of the trees and cautiously approached the Void. He listened intently as the musical note altered and became something else, something strangely . . . *familiar.* It was a sound he had heard before, long ago . . . he could not quite remember where, but he would in a moment . . . something akin to a heartbeat, an oceanic roaring, a cadenced throbbing. It was the sound of . . .

White light flared at the core of the Void.

Growing.

And with the light came the Scream.

For Papul, the White Scream began with that high, musical note that at first beguiled, then besieged his head until it became a brutal invasion ripping through his brain. Sound magnified past the point of pain, it resonated in his skull and bones, threatening to pulverize them. No noise had ever been so excruciating. It seemed to come as much from within as without, a cacophony generated inside him and played on his own eardrums, battering them to a pulp.

Taking him over body and spirit.

The Scream, the White Scream! The big man writhed in torment.

Then his eyes were drawn to the light again — so cool, so beautiful and pure — and in his dissolving brain he thought he might escape the Scream by entering the light.

Papul was reaching toward the light when the Scream vibrated through the bones of his hand, taking control. The axe rose of its own volition. Its wood handle dissolved into slime; the metal head crashed to the ground. But Papul saw none of this. His bulging eyes were fixed in disbelief on the disintegration of his arm. His flesh was turning into a stinking jelly that promptly liquified and poured from him like dirty water. He tried to cry out but he had no breath.

He died with the White Scream in his ears; the Scream born from the sound he had almost recognized.

CHAPTER FOUR

He had no idea where he was going, no idea what he was going to do. He was cold, so cold . . . and empty, bereft of whatever warmth had once sustained him.

When the realization finally struck Caeled he stopped and wrapped his arms around his chest, hugging himself in a vain attempt to find comfort. He felt hollow. Everyone he had known was gone. All those people, all those lives, snuffed out. His mother too was gone, and with her his past.

Eventually he forced himself to walk on, keeping to the road and heading south. No matter how far his mother had brought him — and they had wandered through most of the Seven Nations — she had always promised that one day they would return to the flower-fragrant Southlands of his birth and start afresh. He had ceased believing in that particular dream by the time of his eighth Naming Day, but he suspected his mother had never stopped believing. Sometimes, when she couldn't sleep or she had drunk herself sober, she used to sit wrapped up in her blanket and talk about her plans. She was going to return to the Southlands and establish a dancing school there.

She boasted of having once danced for Los-Lorcan, though Caeled knew that was untrue, one of the stories she made up to cheer herself in a cheerless existence. When her school was successful, she insisted, they would want for nothing. Absolutely nothing. His mother had sometimes wept as she spoke, but he never knew whether she was weeping for her vision of the future, or because she knew it would never be.

Now Caeled's feet carried him southward as if to fulfill a promise. When he got to the Southlands he would . . .

His thoughts crashed to a halt. He did not know what he was going to do.

He did not even know how far it was to the Southlands. They lay beyond the Seven Nations, once very dangerous territory for anyone to cross. The Seven Nations were reputed to be at peace now for the first time in many cycles, but his knowledge of their geography was based on the fading memories of a young child. There were some forests. And some mountains. And a vast plain under a sweeping, empty sky, with no roads or trackways, just a wilderness of windblown grass. Could he find his way through to the Southlands?

Even supposing he made it, what then? He was nearly fourteen summers and unskilled. If he survived the journey, he would end up a slave or a soldier.

But they were worries for another day. Right now he was cold and hungry and he simply did not care.

Trying to fight back emotions too powerful to deal with, the boy continued down the road. One foot after the other. He hardly noticed the landscape on either side, the stretches of swampland, the occasional stands of un-healthy vegetation, leaves lost to giantism, too thick, too lush, so they drooped on their stalks and lay on the earth to rot. The encroaching forests pressed close to the road, as if to smother any life that came along.

When the rain began to fall, needle-thin and chilling, he tilted his face up, letting the downpour dilute his tears and wash the grime from his skin and hair. He filled his mouth with fresh water then spat it out, ridding himself of the taste of death that had coated his tongue ever since Ward Point.

The shock of the icy rain roused him and he realized night was drawing down; purple and black clouds were massing on the horizon and flickering with lightning. He had to find shelter soon; these forests were reputed to harbor ancient evil. Creatures of nightmare that had assumed legendary status in the Southlands were commonplace here.

But where was he going to find shelter in such a lonely, unfamiliar place? The road on which he stood was his only link to civilization, but there was no protection out in the open.

The roadway, a badly maintained portion of the King Road, supposedly ran all the way to the High Gate of Barrow, capital of the Seven Nations. Caeled and his mother had come north to Ward Point along this road, travelling with a caravan of grain merchants. His mother had paid for their passage by cooking for the caravan drivers. He recalled sitting on a splintery plank seat beside a heavily armed wagon driver, as an endless dreary countryside unfolded around them. Much of it was scrubby marshlands, bracketed east and west by the mountain ranges of Spine and Skull.

To alleviate his own boredom, the driver had taught Caeled the names of the constellations that wheeled overhead in the night sky. He had also regaled his young passenger with stories of the creatures that lived in the marshes, creatures that had once been human but were now no better than beasts, beasts who retained a dangerous degree of human intelligence.

Caeled had not believed him then, but now, standing alone on the same road with night falling, he could almost feel the eyes of those beasts watching him balefully, hungrily.

He recalled other stories he had heard in Ward Point: tales of travellers who rode out and never returned — at least in human form; of whole caravans which had simply vanished; of a contingent of the Watch, ten heavily armed men who had gone in search of what they thought was a rabid dog. But the mad dog had turned out to be one of the Clan Allta, the werebeasts. About the time they realized this the hunters had become the hunted. Four of them were torn apart and another three fatally savaged before the creature was slain. The three badly mauled survivors had been burnt alive in the town square so they would have no chance to spread the infection.

Caeled knew that if he remained on the road, he would not survive to see the dawn. Even if the werebeasts missed him, the beasts of flesh and blood which lived and hunted in the marshlands would not. There were wolves aplenty, murderous wild boar and savage marsh lions. On this cold air the salt tang of his sweat and fear would carry for a great distance.

He hurried on down the pitted roadway, looking left and right, thankful to have something to occupy his mind. He was looking for an outcropping of rocks, perhaps a cave — *no, not a cave* — a clump of bushes, a place to hide, rest and think.

Dusk was descending by the time he found a doubtful haven.

The temperature had fallen dramatically. His fingers were so stiff he could hardly feel them, so he crossed his arms over his chest and tucked his hands into his armpits, seeking what little warmth he could find. In the distance a wolf howled. It was immediately answered by a marsh lion's ragged cough. The nearness of that cough startled Caeled and he inadvertently stepped off the road, only to sink ankle-deep in sticky mud. Off to his right he spotted a stand of needlefern trees crowning a grassy knoll, appearing like an oasis in the swale. Needlefern trees were far from his first choice as sanctuary, but with marsh lions about he had little choice, he had to get off the ground.

Pulling himself free from the mud, he ran to the knoll and scrambled up it. Brittle bones cracked and snapped underfoot as he scurried toward the trees. Caeled crouched and picked up a tiny bird's skull that glimmered like ivory in the fading light. No scrap of leathery flesh or feathered skin clung to it; almost immediately the skull crumbled to powder beneath the pressure of his fingers. He tilted his head back and looked up. In the twilight he could just barely see the numerous pathetic remains of birds that had become impaled on the trees' poisonous needles. During daylight the trees looked like innocuous giant ferns, but at night finger-length, razor-sharp spines sprang open amid the dense foliage, turning every tree into a deadly trap. In this barren countryside, the carnivorous trees survived on the creatures they speared.

Rain had made the bark slippery, and Caeled climbed with infinite care into the lower branches of the nearest tree. If he touched one of the spines within its concealing tracery of sensitive fronds, the rest would attack him. Their virulent poison was capable of killing a human. It was claimed that some of the barbaric tribes beyond the Forests of Thusal sacrificed criminals on needlefern trees, condemning them to a lingering, excruciating death.

The tree was beginning to awaken as Caeled gingerly settled into a saddle-shaped crotch among the branches. He pulled off his belt and looped it around a branch before retying it around his waist. He did not expect to sleep, but if he did doze off, at least he would not fall into the foliage.

His backpack served as a pillow; his cloak became his blanket. When he had made himself as comfortable as possible he nestled down and watched with wide eyes as the fern fronds around him unfurled like opening hands, disclosing deadly weapons. By the time darkness filled the trees and he could see no more, Caeled was secure behind a protective barricade of thousands of poisonous needles.

The rustling of the foliage eventually lulled him into a doze. He was vaguely aware of wolves howling in the distance, and there were other, less distinguishable cries, hunter and hunted in the surrounding marshlands, but in spite of this he sank further and further into sleep. At last there was nothing, only blackness, only peace.

He awoke with a start. Something was thrashing in the branches in front of his face. Hot salty liquid spattered across his mouth. Then the trapped creature ceased to struggle and Caeled heard the dripping of blood. A pungent meaty odor made him aware that he hadn't eaten in a long time. He was reaching blindly for the bird — he assumed it was a bird — impaled on the spikes, when he heard the distinctive sound of hooves on stone.

Caeled twisted his body so he could peer around the trunk of the tree, but he could see nothing through the foliage below. Only by looking up was there any view. Clouds raced across the sky, skimming past the Lady Lussa in her phase as a slender curved maiden.

The hoofbeats were coming nearer.

There were stories of Dullahan who haunted the King Road, headless horsemen on headless horses, who whipped out the eyes of passers-by with metal-tipped whips.

Through the branches of the tree Caeled caught a glimpse of blue sparks being struck off the stones in the road by iron horseshoes. Then the solid thud of hoofbeats stopped, replaced by a liquid squelch. A horse snorted at unfamiliar footing. Caeled realized the horseman had left the road and was approaching the stand of trees, riding toward the knoll through deep mud.

Maybe it was just another traveller, seeking shelter like himself. But what would any sane person be doing on such a demon-haunted road at night?

Then a random fragment of breeze brought Caeled the smell of the horse, a sweaty odor that reassured him; at least the horse was real, so its rider was no ghost. A brigand then, a road bandit? A cannibal?

Caeled's eyes were of little use in the darkness; he was thankful that he had other sharp senses. His nostrils flared as he attempted to sort through the odors of the night. He identified the scents of needlefern trees and marsh mud, the smell of blood and feathers from the dead bird nearest him, and, faint but growing stronger, the metallic tang of armor and a whiff of clean human flesh.

A human rider, then: someone who had recently bathed. A noble, a huntsman. But there was poor hunting in this region.

Leather creaked as the rider dismounted. Heavy feet crushed the litter of bones on the ground. Metal rasped as a sword was drawn. An armored cuirass scraped against the trunk of Caeled's tree.

He tried to make himself as small as he could; invisible, melting into the needlefern. Its dangers at least were known and understood.

The voice, when it came, was muffled by a helm. "I'll wait for you here, boy. You can come down when the sun rises."

CHAPTER FIVE

Breast to breast and lip to lip they lay together in the tall grass. Their tongues played a tender game: lick, taste, caress, seek more deeply. They exchanged breath.

Hot wind whispered through the grass.

They whispered promises, murmured phrases intended to excite as fingers stroked, teased, fondled.

The wind sighed into silence. The sun blazing overhead briefly darkened, as if a cloud crossed its face.

In tall grass, small creatures that hunted and slew one another felt the whisper of gathering power and fled.

The pair lying together in the grass soon forgot their surroundings. The summer meadow, the distant snow-capped mountains, the azure sky were nothing more than constructs from their imagination, a dreamscape for passion.

Their bodies pressed closer, striving for the ultimate union. The woman straddled the man and controlled her own emotions while she worked to heighten his. This was the oldest magic in the world, the first magic . . .

She bent over her lover and trailed her long hair across his naked chest. Her mouth closed on his; she murmured a single word around his questing tongue. A word of power.

The sound of the word in their joined mouths inflamed him.

The air around them trembled as if disturbed.

In the distance the mountains faded to shadows.

Patches of gray began to appear through the delicate eggshell blue of the sky.

He pressed closer to her, demanding, but she laid her fingers across his lips. "Wait." The command burned like a hot coal.

The woman resumed the rhythm of the ritual, mind and body working as one, senses heightened to an almost painful degree. This was the most delicate moment, when passion and power trembled on the brink and could so easily be destroyed.

She repeated the word. The single syllable tore a tiny hole in the fabric of space between the two lovers.

The world darkened perceptibly. All their concentration was now on one another.

When the woman said the word a third time her passion leaped inside her, refusing to be restrained any longer. She plunged against him and the man felt the quivering of her tissues, the clenching of her muscles. Gasping with ecstacy, he allowed his own passion to take him then.

The air around them boiled, the atmosphere charged with the coming of a mighty storm.

Stilled, they remained unsatisfied. The desire for union did not abate but became even greater, tantalizing them with promises of an unreachable paradise where fragments of an ultimate pattern coalesced out of the shadows.

As they struggled anew to weld their bodies into one body, one inseparable unit, the lovers writhed in a gray dreamscape. The images they had so carefully created were now all washed away. Only their personal auras remained, pulsing prismatically.

The pair shuddered in unison as another orgasm rippled through them. Their joined aura turned opalescent with heat. It expanded, rainbow colors blending into a mindless force fed by the magic of the pair at its center. Then with the sound of something tearing, it pulled free.

A swirling ball of cold light appeared in the air between the lovers, close enough to brush their lips with its icy surface. Their moist hot breath imbued it with life.

For a third time, passion convulsed them. This time they cried aloud together, shouting the ancient word into the heart of the sphere.

The word stabbed into the shimmering white ball that was not a ball but a ravening emptiness, a terrible rapacious vacuum. Gathering force, the sphere began to whirl until it spiralled outward on a wave of desire. Voracious. Devouring.

Only life — rich, vibrant, bloody life — could assuage its terrible hunger.

"You were right, little brother. We've done it. Come back to me now so we can celebrate together."

Lares fixed on the sound of his sister's voice. In the sere and shifting dreamscape it was a beacon of solidity, anchoring him, calling him, pulling him home.

"Squeeze my hand if you can hear me."

Lares concentrated on the sound, listening to the words, and as he deciphered their meaning, he grew increasingly conscious of his body, of the weight of flesh and muscle and bone that pulled him down and imprisoned his incorporeal being.

"Squeeze my hand."

Using her voice to guide him, he dragged himself out of a pit of exhaustion. He had been gone from his physical body for so long that the ties which bound body and spirit together had become dangerously weak.

The pounding of his heart threatened to shatter him.

"Squeeze my hand."

Flesh. Cold flesh encased his naked body, constricting, confining. Lares became aware of the discomforts of having skin, the itch of hair on his skull and cheeks, the raw agony of pressure on his elbows and heels. Air blew across his sweat-damp forehead, its touch burningly cold. He lay suffering, unable to move until the painful acuity of heightened senses faded.

Then he recognized silk sheets covering his body and warm fingers clasping his.

"Squeeze my hand."

Lares exerted all his strength. His forefinger twitched.

Relieved laughter filled the room. "So you are alive. I thought I'd lost you this time." Sarel's voice was light and bantering, but he could detect her concern. Still unable to open his eyes, Lares visualized his sister's face, identical in every feature to his, like looking into a mirror. Their subjects could not tell the twins apart, could not distinguish male from female, so lately Sarel had taken to wearing her amber hair long and flowing, while Lares worked his into two tight braids.

Now the corners of her violet eyes were creased with concern, and her lips drawn into a bloodless line.

She continued speaking, murmuring softly, using her voice as a lifeline to draw him back to his body.

"I've been so worried ever since you failed to return from the Aethyra with me."

"How long . . . " he mumbled.

"You've been gone three days now. You've lost a lot of weight and . . . " Her fingers traced the line of his ribs. "This is a danger we must be aware of. We must stay closer together, not allow anything to separate us."

He heard her moving around. Then water, tasting faintly of perfume, was dripped between his lips. Lares regained enough strength to open his mouth and extend his swollen tongue, letting the liquid flow down his parched throat. Its taste was as sweet as nectar.

"The desert experiment was a success, and now we know we can duplicate it." Sarel continued. "We can control the Voids and move them from place to place in the physical world — though the cost is great in terms of our energy. We must find ways to counter the debilitating effect on us. But once a Void locates life it feeds, and its own power grows."

Lares finally summoned the strength to open his eyes.

The chamber was filled with a radiant light that came from no identifiable source. Sarel's face swam into view; his face replicated, yet infinitely more dear to him.

"The heretic," he croaked, and watched as Sarel's lips drew back from her teeth in a smile of pure pleasure.

"Papul the Heretic. Aaah, but that was sweet, so sweet," she said softly, leaning forward to kiss her brother. "The lights in the heart of the forest Void drew him closer — that was a master stroke. The ruse used practically no energy and it excited his curiosity without frightening him away. And when he was close enough . . ." Sarel laughed. "The look on his face! Horror; dismay. Thus end all heretics. But, and more importantly, the experiment proved that the Voids can be controlled with precision, plucking a single man from a forest without touching any of the other forms of life around him."

Drawing the sheet away from her brother's naked body, Sarel began to cleanse him with warm scented towels. "But the town was the triumphant conclusion of the experiment," she went on. "An entire town, twelve hundred souls, devastated in less than a dozen heartbeats. And again, with practically no effort. Once the Void was enlivened, no one could stand against it!"

Sarel cupped her hands around her brother's gaunt face and looked into his eyes, seeing herself mirrored in them. "Think of it, Lares, think of it. We have proved that the Voids can be controlled . . . and if we control the Voids we control the world!"

Lares caught his twin and pulled her down on top of him, feeling warmth and energy from her body soak into his, replenishing him.

"We can make and remake the world . . . " he whispered.

"Shaping it in our own image!"

CHAPTER SIX

Shon'sen was Madra Allta, of the Clan Allta.

Unlike many of those who wore the dog form he felt no bitterness, no anger at the quirk of fate that had turned him into one of the werefolk. There were times when he thought it was actually preferable. He had been a beggar in Ward Point for most of his human life, constantly hungry, frequently cold, stealing what he could, when he could, to survive. He realized now that he had only been surviving, not living. But now — now he was living!

When the dog bit him, at first he had been unconcerned. He had survived the bites of rats, snakes, and spiders without contracting so much as a fever, and had once found the corpse of a cat which died shortly after biting him. He boasted that his vermin-infested beggar's flesh had poisoned the feline, so he expected to suffer no ill effects from a mere dog bite.

But the bite proved more dangerous than he expected.

He had been bitten in the silent hour before the dawn, when in his sleep he rolled over onto a stray canine that had crept into the crawl space beneath the tavern. By noon he felt sick and dizzy, but he blamed hunger, and the change in atmosphere occasioned by an approaching storm. By evening he was burning with fever, his flesh so hot that the flakes of the blizzard exploded into steam when they touched his skin. His last clear memory was of falling — which had seemed to go on forever — but his landing was cushioned by a snowbank.

Later he would wonder if he had actually died that night.

When he awoke the following morning at first he thought himself blind. Then he discovered he was buried in a snowdrift. His open eyes gazed into a darkness that gradually became luminous, until he realized he was seeing distant daylight through snow. Snow over his head, over his face, pressing against him, making breathing difficult but not impossible. A small air space existed in front of his nose where the ice had been melted by his breath. But he could not stay there long; a man would freeze to death in a snowbank!

Scrambling out of the drift, he had found himself near the middens at the edge of town. The odor of dung and refuse should have been blanketed by the heavy snow-fall, yet surprisingly he could smell the middens clearly. But the scent was not disgusting; he was astonished to find it intriguing, even pleasant. He wrinkled his nose in appreciation.

It was only as he crawled away that he had discovered he was walking on all fours. The hair on his arms and legs had coarsened and lengthened; the flesh and bones of his hands and feet had melded into misshapen paws. When he eventually found a puddle of melted snow and gazed into it, the mask of a beast looked back: a frighteningly canine visage, yet with some of the characteristics of a human face still visible beneath the fur.

Shon'sen knew then what he had become: Madra Allta, werecreature, condemned to wear the form of a beast except for the brief period when the Lady Lussa rode round-bosomed through the heavens. Only then he could regain a shambling semblance of his human form.

The first few days had been hardest as he struggled to come to terms with his new identity, but soon Shon'sen, formerly a weak and miserable beggar, discovered the advantages of his new body.

For the first time in his life he felt truly alive.

He was stronger than he had ever been, and fast. His senses were extraordinarily keen. He ate voraciously, slept snug inside his shaggy coat and rutted without inhibition among females of his new clan.

There were other werebeasts in the wilderness beyond the towns, mostly boar-folk and dog-folk and those of the wolf kind. He even heard stories of weresnakes deep in the marshlands. In time his human consciousness would fade and he would become more like an animal, but while he retained human intelligence and cunning, he used them to the fullest to facilitate his hunting.

He had come upon the spoor of the horse two days earlier. A well-fleshed beast, carrying either an overweight or a heavily armored rider. The latter, he learned by scouting the horseman's camp when the man halted to take a midday meal. As he crouched in the undergrowth the werebeast observed a big man wearing a leather cuirass reinforced with bronze bosses, and a helm that he only took off his head while eating a sparse meal of smoked fish and dried fruit. The horseman was equipped with a bladed weapon of some sort in a scabbard, and a boar spear was strapped to his saddle pack.

Shon'sen bared his teeth in a feral grin. A horse and rider would keep him in meat for a ten-day. His mouth flooded with saliva as he thought of fresh food still warm with life: horse meat and human flesh. The last flesh he had eaten had been dead for four days and he'd had to fight a jackal for it.

The werebeast stalked the man patiently, staying well out of sight, content to allow his senses of smell and hearing to keep him informed. He felt certain he knew where the horseman must be heading. Ward Point was the only town in this direction.

The beast had been pleased when the rainstorm began; it meant the rider would be forced to break his journey, and there were few places along the road that would offer any shelter. But there was a grove of trees. . .

The werebeast was waiting, submerged in a pool of stagnant marsh water with only his nose and the tips of his ears showing, when the rider arrived at the stand of needleferns fifty paces off the King Road.

The immobile Shon'sen controlled himself with inhuman patience, allowing the horseman time to make himself comfortable and lower his guard.

When enough time had passed the werebeast raised his head cautiously. Golden eyes flared, adjusting to the night, the world in monochrome hues. The horse, a chunky gray gelding, was hobbled well away from the needleferns, while the man was barely visible sitting with his back to one of the trees, head slumped on his chest.

Shon'sen's mouth gaped open. Ropy tendrils of saliva dripped from his lips into the marsh water.

The man had built no fire, erected no physical barriers or magical wards; he obviously believed he was safe in this wilderness. The werebeast retained enough of his human intellect to appreciate the tactical advantages of the location the horseman had chosen for himself. Any approach would be difficult. Even a creature like Shon'sen would be unable to move through the sticky mud that surrounded the knoll without his feet making small sucking sounds that betrayed his presence.

Shon'sen sank back into the water, making plans. Soon it would be dawn and the needleferns would close their spines. The resulting sounds of crackling and rustling could be used to mask his approach.

Shon'sen would have fresh meat in his belly before noon.

Caeled leaned out of the tower window, watching beautiful lights flickering in the core of the Void. But the crumbling stone beneath him gave way, pitching him forward and down. . .

The boy awoke with a violent start. When he realized where he was, he was astonished to find he had actually fallen asleep, and appalled to realize he had slipped out of the crotch of the tree. Only his belt had saved him from tumbling face first into the deadly needles. With an effort he pulled himself up again, then leaned back against the trunk, heart hammering.

"Are you all right, boy?"

The voice startled Caeled still more. In his dazed and exhausted state he had forgotten about the man at the foot of the tree. He realized now that this was the second time the horseman had called him "boy" . . . but how did he know Caeled was a boy? Had he seen him? Followed him?

Without replying, Caeled shifted into a more comfortable position and resettled his pack in the small of his back. A sharp object dug into his spine. He reached over his shoulder, fumbled in the pack, and pulled it out. It was the crude toy soldier he had fashioned from a warped tin spoon. He had once imagined himself a soldier, a brave, proud warrior out of legend, riding a magnificent stallion, doing battle with monsters and werecreatures while his mother looked on in admiration.

Then he had learned that the worst monsters wore a human form, and many of these were soldiers. He had been ten when he and his mother fled Harald's Creek three days before the Marocan army stormed through on their way to the coast to put down some Island Corsairs. They had watched from the safety of the hills as the lines of soldiers, so grand and fine in their crimson and alabaster uniforms, had raped and looted the neutral town. Caeled had put away his toy that day and never played with it since.

Leaning forward, he peered down through the branches and wondered what sort of man crouched at the foot of the tree.

Caeled started as the needlefern creaked in a rising wind, and his former toy tumbled from his fingers. He heard it ping off metal below, followed by a grunt of surprise from the man.

The tree grew more agitated. The wood crackled, the leaves whispered hungrily to themselves. Fragile bird bones snapped, flesh tore like old cloth as the tree finished devouring the night's catch. Caeled could now see leaves and branches appearing before his face, gradually assuming shape and definition.

"Sunrise, boy. The needlefern is sheathing its claws. You can come down now."

Caeled looked down. He could make out the outline of the man below, the details becoming ever clearer. A heavy cloak was thrown back from the horseman's shoulders, revealing his metal-studded cuirass. A naked sword rested across his knees as he sat on the ground examining a battered piece of tin. Without looking up, he called, "You dropped this. What is it — a spoon?"

"A soldier. I mean it used to be . . . I mean it was a toy," Caeled stammered.

The stranger nodded. "A toy soldier. I can see that now. When I was younger I had a set of toy soldiers. I had an army for each of the Seven Nations," he added softly, turning the spoon over and over in his gloved hands.

"What happened to them?" Caeled inquired as he was stealthily untying his leather belt from the tree and refastening it around his waist. He dug into his pack and found a gold coin he had taken from the ruin of a merchant's shop in Ward Point.

Experience had taught him that those with gold could buy their way out of many things. If all else failed, perhaps he could bargain for his freedom.

But he had rather run, and keep the gold.

"I'm not sure," the man below was replying. "I played with them for many seasons, then I think they eventually passed to my brother."

"I always wanted a set of soldiers," Caeled said. He needed to keep the stranger talking while he slid down the opposite side of the tree and ran off into the marsh. The heavily weighted man would not be able to follow.

"I once wanted to be a soldier myself," he added. "Are you a soldier?"

"No," said the stranger, surprising him. "Many years ago I followed that trade, but no longer." Caeled slid down the tree as silently as he could, holding his breath until he reached the ground. Dawn mist was coiling up from the marsh; the air smelled of rank vegetation. Crouching, the boy surveyed his possible escape route. The thickening mist made his path uncertain, but he knew he had to avoid the bright green patches.

"Come down now, boy. We have a long journey ahead of us."

Caeled straightened and darted down the side of the knoll, racing for the marsh . . . and almost immediately sank to his waist in a pool of numbingly cold water.

With a cry, the horseman lurched to his feet.

Caeled grabbed a tuft of grass with one hand and hauled himself out of the pool. His other hand stubbornly continued to clutch the gold coin.

"Boy! Don't be a fool! Come back here."

Caeled stood erect, his heart pounding from his escape.

And the beast reared before him.

The boy had a brief glimpse of fur and fang and yellow knowing eyes before he felt the pain in his left hand; white-hot agony that numbed his entire arm. The werebeast growled and slung its head from side to side; then something pale and bloody was dangling from its jaws. The creature hurled itself upon Caeled, solid weight striking him in the chest and stomach, and he was falling . . . falling . . . falling. The creature was on top of him. He smelled its stinking breath as it prepared for the kill . . .

Fleetingly Caeled wondered if he would see his mother again, in whatever kingdom Death ruled.

Then bone cracked and blood exploded in every direction.

CHAPTER SEVEN

Caeled opened his eyes to find himself confronted by the blank featureless head of a monster.

"Easy, boy, easy."

His vision swam, then cleared, and he realized he was looking at a metal-studded leather helmet. Gloved hands appeared at the shadowy borders of his vision, gripped the helmet, pulled it off.

"I'm Armadiel," said a voice Caeled had heard before. The boy glimpsed a blurred face surmounted by a gleaming bald pate, then he lost consciousness again.

Pain stabbed him awake.

Hot ice and cold fire tore through his body, pulsing in waves that surged up his arm and into his chest, paralyzing his muscles until it was impossible to scream.

He dragged open gummy eyelids and tasted blood in his mouth. The bald man — Armadiel? — was crouching before him. For a few moments Caeled could make no sense of what was happening. One of his arms was stretched out straight, tightly held in Armadiel's grip . . . and the man was gouging at ragged flesh with a short-bladed knife, peeling back skin . . .

Caeled opened his mouth to scream but the pain had robbed him of breath; the pain that rose in a solid black wave then came crashing down to engulf him.

Some sort of pad soaked with cold water bathed his

eyes, applied with gentle, confident strokes that worked outward from his nose, then upward to smooth his forehead. He relaxed to the touch, letting it wash him away from the shores of pain.

More deliciously cool water was poured between his lips. He gasped, choked, then swallowed gratefully, keeping his eyes closed. He did not want to see any terrifying sights; he wanted only to concentrate on the peace and the coolness.

"It's time to wake up, boy."

He heard a snap; an acrid odor filled his nostrils, making him sneeze violently.

Caeled's eyes flew open.

The bald man was kneeling in the mud, facing him. "I thought I was going to lose you, boy." He stretched out his right hand, moving it before the boy's face, and Caeled winced at the bitter smell emanating from the broken stick between his fingers. But in some strange way the fumes cleared his head and enabled him to start thinking again.

"We have a decision to make, you and I," the man continued in a conversational tone. Caeled stared at him. Incongruously, although the man's face was heavily lined, with deep grooves along the sides of his nose that pulled down the corners of his mouth, his bald skull was as smooth as an apple and almost as rosy.

Caeled licked dry lips, attempted to speak, swallowed hard and tried again. "Who . . . ?"

"I'm Armadiel."

"What happened?"

"A Madra Allta got you." The bald man grinned without humor, revealing crooked yellow teeth. He drew the thumb and forefinger of his right hand together until they almost met. "The beast was this close to your eyes when I blunted my sword on its skull."

"Ma . . . Madra Allta?" Caeled whispered in horror. "Weredog?"

"Aye. But it died a man," Armadiel said, turning his head slightly to look at something.

With an enormous effort Caeled twisted to follow the direction of the man's gaze. Crumpled on the ground was the dismembered and decapitated body of an unremarkable middle-aged man. The head lay nearby, sightless eyes staring. There was a vaguely familiar quality about the face, but it was difficult for Caeled to identify the features. They were distorted by terror and blood.

"Madra Allta," Caeled said again. Something nibbled at the edge of his consciousness, *something* . . .

"It bit me!" he cried.

Armadiel nodded. Keeping his eyes fixed on Caeled's face, he lifted the boy's left arm into view. The movement sent white-hot pain through Caeled's body, but the agony was so intense it became almost an abstraction, something separate and apart from his real self. Caeled found he could look at the ruin of his left hand as if it belonged to someone else.

The last two fingers and half of the palm had been torn away. An impression of the beast's teeth was clearly visible on the remaining flesh, which was already swollen and turning black. Colorless ichor seeped from the wound. A leather strap had been bound very tightly about the wrist, and another was cinched just above the elbow. The area between them was also beginning to swell from the pressure.

Caeled stared, trying to understand. Trying to remember.

"My hand. I had . . . a coin in my hand. Gold . . ."

No coin now, and not much of a hand, either.

"Did the beast take my coin?" he asked, sounding aggrieved. His brain could only fix on one thought at a time, and it was easier to grieve over the loss of gold than the loss of . . . of . . .

"You have a choice, boy," said Armadiel in a matter-of-fact voice. "The Madra Allta bit you. I don't need to tell you what that means, do I? The corrupting poison is in your hand. I think I've prevented it from spreading into your arm, but I can't be certain." He looked at the mangled hand, then back into Caeled's horrified eyes. "Unless we do something, you will become one of the Madra Allta. The only sure remedy is amputation." He touched the boy's forearm just below the elbow. "Here I think, to be safe."

"No." Caeled's voice was a ragged whisper. Summoning all his strength, he shrieked, "No!"

Ignoring the cry, Armadiel took a short-bladed skinning knife from the sheath on his belt. "There are many ways to die. The werechange itself might kill you, or leave you neither man nor true werecreature but something in between, more horrible than either.

"The pain of twisted bones and warped muscles would likely drive you mad even if you did survive. You would end your days as a monstrosity, hated by all. Other creatures would hunt you down, young and inexperienced as you are. You would not survive one season. I cannot allow that.

"But as I said, you have a choice. Three choices, in fact. Where shall I cut? Wrist, arm, or neck?"

There was a long silence. Then, "Wrist," Caeled hissed through clenched teeth.

"What's that, boy?" The man bent closer. "I can't hear you."

"Take it off . . . at the wrist."

Armadiel frowned. "I'd prefer to cut higher, just to be certain."

"Wrist."

"If I take off only your hand and the werechange comes over you anyway, I will kill you at once," Armadiel assured him.

"My choice. You said. Just do it."

The bald man nodded. "As you wish."

Armadiel had built a fire in a circle of stones, and now

he added wood until the flames were leaping high. With his knife he cut a large rectangle of bark from the trunk of the needlefern. He then wrapped the moist bark around Caeled's arm, bending the material to form a sleeve. "The sap of the needlefern causes a degree of insensibility," he explained. "It will help dull the pain." Armadiel pushed a piece of wood into the boy's mouth. "Here, bite down on this. The sap will also numb your mouth and tongue, but there's no harm."

Using the point of his knife, the man marked out the position of Caeled's wrist on the bark. Then he plunged the blade of the knife into the heart of the fire and held it there for several heartbeats.

"Stand up," he commanded at last.

Caeled came shakily to his feet.

"Stretch out your hand, rest it against the tree trunk."

Caeled extended his arm until his remaining fingertips were touching the needlefern. The pain in his hand became a riptide of agony that threatened to sweep his soul from his body. Colored spots danced before his eyes, and there was a high, buzzing sound in his ears. He was certain he was going to faint and longed for the escape.

Metal rang as Armadiel pulled a short hacking sword from a scabbard affixed to his saddle.

"If you hold very still, I can cut clean. Move, and I'll sheer into the bones at an angle and they may splinter. Ready?"

Caeled managed a single nod. He felt as if all the blood in his body had drained into his stomach. Why did he not faint?

"I'll count to four," Armadiel said. "One . . . two . . . three . . ."

The sword flashed through the air, whistling, and crashed into Caeled's arm like a bolt of lightning. Shock jellied the marrow in his bones. Blade bit through flesh, severed muscle and bone with a sound he would never forget.

Caeled toppled forward as what was left of his hand fell, twitching, to the ground. Armadiel caught him in strong arms.

"What happened to four?" the boy managed to whisper as the world spun around him and the buzzing in his ears became a mighty roar.

He almost escaped into unconsciousness, only to come screaming back when Armadiel cauterized the wound with a white-hot knife blade.

CHAPTER EIGHT

"I bring extraordinary tidings, brothers! The prophecy is fulfilled."

The library fell silent as the monks watched Brother Maseriel tap his way down the central aisle, blind white eyes roving over their faces as if he could see them.

Brother Maseriel, Hieromonach of the order, seated himself in his gilded wooden chair before the Cabinet of Forbidden Books while the senior members of the Order of the Way ranged themselves around him, white-robed Seekers and red-robed Scholars, faces deferential, hands tucked into sleeves.

"The boy is found," the old man announced. From long practice he could pitch his stentorian voice to the raftered ceiling high above; lesser members of the Order lined gallery rails on three levels, listening intently. "The boy is found," Maseriel repeated. "Found god-marked and beast-touched as prophesied. And not a moment too soon."

A low murmur ran around the galleries until the old man rapped his staff on the flagstoned floor.

"Now is the time of our greatest danger," the Hieromonach continued. He raised a long-nailed forefinger to touch the red-rimmed edge of his eye. "Sixty cycles ago I sacrificed my human sight in return for the ability to see beyond this physical realm. It is a decision I never regretted . . ." the old man drew in a breath that was almost a sob, "until now. Now I have witnessed visions that would have destroyed a lesser man.

"I tell you, these are terrible times indeed, with the Rule of Law but a memory. The Duet have begun experimenting with the Voids, and recently they have had some success manipulating and controlling the Dead Spaces for their own purposes. I am convinced they intend to enlarge the reign of disorder, to allow the humankind and beastfolk and all of nature to run riot!"

Some of the monks gasped.

The old man appeared to gaze sightlessly around the long room, then raised his face to include the brothers in the galleries. "We cannot stand against the Duet. Not now. But in time, when the expansion of their power inevitably causes them to grow arrogant and careless, we shall undertake the restoration of order. We must work toward that day, brothers."

Maseriel sat taller in his chair and lifted his arm, the edge of his robe sliding back to reveal tattooed spirals encircling his wrist. "Five hundred generations ago, the first Hieromonach founded this library. Now it houses the sum total of human and inhuman knowledge. The help we need has to be here."

He turned in his chair to point to the Cabinet of Forbidden Books behind him. "You all know that somewhere within these millions of pages is recorded the location of the Arcana. Generations have sought the secret, but now that we have the boy, we *must* find it. Redouble your efforts. The survival of myriad races depends upon you."

CHAPTER NINE

Caeled sat with his back to the trunk of the needlefern, cradling his throbbing arm in his lap as he watched Armadiel saddle the gray gelding. The horse was tense, skittish, snorting in explosive bursts, flaring his nostrils until their glistening pink lining showed, flicking his ears rapidly back and forth. His hooves danced in a tight circle; he tried to look in every direction at once with his slit-pupilled eyes.

"I know, I know," Armadiel murmured to the animal while keeping firm hold on the bridle reins. "I know the predators are coming." He ran a soothing hand down the horse's neck, which was damp with nervous sweat. When he had calmed the gelding enough to trust it to stand still, he lifted his saddle of hand-tooled Galloway leather and positioned it carefully on the red leine saddle pad that protected the horse's back. The saddle, Caeled noticed in spite of his pain, was of curious design. A number of attachments were affixed to every available surface save the seat itself, including woven reed panniers, buckled leather bags, a canteen hanging from a thong, pouches and scabbards to contain the appurtenances a man might require for a long journey through dangerous territory.

Marooned in the center of all these supplies like an island in a sea of debris, the saddle seat was split in half, keeping the rider's weight from pressing on the spine of the horse. With a very high pommel in front and an equally high cantle at the back, the saddle would hold a rider snugly, with unusual security.

It looks like a chair, thought Caeled dizzily. If I had a saddle like that, I could ride a horse.

The boy had never been on a horse; such a mount seemed as far above him as the stars. But in his dreams of heroic deeds he had always imagined himself bestriding just such a beast as this — and riding magnificently.

So he tried, in spite of a coldness that was gradually creeping over him, to pay attention as Armadiel drew tight the leather cinch that held the saddle in place, then doubled the end back and gave it a final yank to be certain it would not slip. There was a smooth professionalism about the operation that betokened the experienced horseman.

Opening one of the panniers fastened to the cantle, Armadiel withdrew a leather breastcollar and a crupper which he fastened fore and aft to keep the saddle from slipping. Both were set with metal bosses like those on the man's cuirass and helm.

Lastly, Armadiel fitted a sort of leather cap onto the top of the horse's head, over the bridle, pulling the animal's ears through two earholes. The leather was heavily padded to protect the skull, with a sharp metal spike projecting from the center of the forehead like a horn. Thus caparisoned and helmeted, the gelding looked very much the war horse. He arched his neck with new pride, his former nervousness giving way to an air of confidence.

Keeping a firm hold on the reins, Armadiel walked over to the needlefern and squatted before Caeled. His voice was gruff, but his eyes were sympathetic as he said, "I know this is hard for you, boy, but we have to leave this place. Torc Allta and Madra Allta are gathering; the scent of blood draws them. I've heard a marsh lion cough not very far away. If we stay here letting you rest for much longer, they'll surely attack when night approaches again.

"We could make a fight of it, but this position is not invulnerable. While you and I might take refuge in the tree, they'd feast off my horse . . . and I've no wish to sacrifice such a fine animal. It would be too painful to have to explain his loss. Besides," he added, only half in jest, "if werebeasts eat the horse we'll have to walk, and I hate walking."

Caeled said nothing. His eyes were blank and glassy.

Reaching out, Armadiel brushed the back of one hand down Caeled's face. The boy didn't even blink. Armadiel wondered if he was dangerously deep in shock. During the time the man had spent in the Healing Chapel in the College at Baddalaur, he had seen life-threatening shock following serious injuries, but he had neither the medicines nor the experience to cope with such complications. The best help he could give the boy now was to get him to Baddalaur as quickly as possible.

He kept talking to Caeled as he wrapped his own warm cloak around the unresponsive boy. The important thing was to try to hold some fragment of the boy's consciousness and keep him from slipping away too far to retrieve. "We might head south," Armadiel speculated aloud. "I know where there are some useful ruins, easily defensible, with enough of an association with the Old Faith to help keep the beasts at bay. Or we can head north to Ward Point and . . ."

Caeled's eyes suddenly focussed. "No," he said softly. Then his voice rose to a shrill scream. "No!"

The scream sent a nearby flock of silvertails spiralling upward in alarm, while deep in the marsh Madra Allta howled and Torc Allta grunted and squealed. Then, ululating across the bleak landscape like the last voice left in an emptied world, came the unmistakable baying of wolves.

Armadiel patted Caeled's uninjured shoulder. "South it is, then." Stooping, he lifted the boy and carried him to the horse. Caeled roused enough to clutch the pommel with his right hand and hold himself steady as the big man climbed up behind him with a clanking of metal and creaking of leather. He lifted the panniers and tucked his thighs under them so he could give Caeled the saddle seat, while he straddled the horse's rump. Armadiel took a length of rope out of one of the panniers, looped it around the boy and then tied it to his own waist. The binding would restrict him if they were attacked, but if he were overcome then the boy's life was forfeit too.

Armadiel clucked to the gelding, and the animal picked its reluctant way through the gooey mud and standing water separating the knoll from the road. When they reached the solid surface the man turned to glance briefly toward the north. Ward Point lay just up the road in that direction, no more than a short gallop.

But obviously something terrible had happened at Ward Point, something that had driven the boy into the dangerous wilderness and made the very mention of the town enough to break through his pain and the effect of the narcotic sticks.

Armadiel turned the horse resolutely south, away from Ward Point. He relaxed and allowed his mind to go questing, ranging across the marshes, locating and identifying the peculiar flavors of werebeast and marsh lion minds; rank, brutal, concentrated on killing. With ease he read the cold passionless thoughts of the serpents in the weeds along the verge of the road; at a greater distance he sensed a herd of normal wild boar, not werebeasts, their primitive desires like splinters of stone.

To Armadiel's highly trained senses, each individual mind had its own taste and color.

Blanking out the beasts of the wastelands, he sought the shining spark of a human soul . . . but found nothing.

He twisted on the horse's rump and looked back to the north one more time, a longer, more searching stare. Then his brows knitted into a deep frown.

Armadiel had been told that Ward Point had a population of over twelve hundred people, so the Aethyra should have been roiling with their thoughts and emotions. The sky above the town should have shimmered with the aura of their spirit lives, detectable to one like himself from miles away. But there was nothing. Armadiel realized to his horror that nothing lived there at all — not even an animal.

Caeled lay back against the man, a small weight against his broad torso. The injured boy's mind had slipped into a fuzzy darkness where pain did not reach him.

Armadiel picked up random fragments of the boy's unconscious thought and examined them with interest.

There were images of a woman no longer young, face lined and tired, eyes empty and lost, but her resemblance to the boy was marked. Mother? Sister? Mother, Armadiel decided.

As always when he encountered some trace of a woman in someone else's mind he felt his heart begin to pound with that tender excitement no amount of self-discipline could erase. She did not have to be young, or beautiful. She need only be a woman. They were all beautiful to Armadiel, who was not allowed . . .

With an effort he dragged his thoughts back to the business at hand, the investigation of the boy's mind. There were fleeting glimpses of towns and landscapes: He recognized the spires of ancient Barrow and the enormous caverns of the City of the Dead, the cemetery beyond the capital, where the destitute made pitiful homes for themselves in a moldering necropolis.

Next came a succession of towns, some by the sea; Armadiel recognized the reef-locked villages of Kern and Skerries, which meant that the boy and his mother were moving northward in his memories. There were faces too, usually men, flavored by the boy's disgust and loathing.

And then Ward Point. The images clearer now. Armadiel recognized the town from the description Brother Maseriel had given him. Just another squalid northern town, home — refuge — for the lost and the dispossessed, the detritus of the Seven Nations.

A change of scene, of mood: pulsing colors danced in the boy's mind and his body began to twitch in rhythmic response.

Armadiel recoiled from the flickering lights now haunting Caeled's feverish memory. They made him feel so cold, so lost; they soured his stomach and brought a rush of bile to his mouth. Where could the boy have seen them? And from whence came that disgusting smell?

Of course! Surely what the boy was remembering was the horror that had overtaken Ward Point. But it would have involved more than flickering lights and an appalling stench. They must have been precursors of something infinitely more awful to which Caeled had been unwilling witness.

Was that why Brother Maseriel had sent Armadiel out to find the child? The Hieromonach had not explained his reasons and the man had not dared to ask. Those who followed the Way swore complete and absolute obedience to the Hieromonach, the chief of the Order.

Standing before the old man, Armadiel had felt the weight of the Hieromonach's personality battering him as irresistibly as a mighty wind. He had received a clear image of the boy's face as Maseriel was speaking. "You will find this boy in the town of Ward Point at the northernmost point of the King Road, and you are to bring him here to us at once. Let nothing stop you. Do you understand?"

Armadiel had nodded.

"Guard him well, Brother. I have walked the lines of his future. It is a dark and twisted pattern, one of the most complex I have ever seen. And like most complex patterns there are breaks in the strands. There are a score of places where his life might end. But if he survives to manhood, then his future will be entwined with the survival of the Seven Nations."

The Hieromonach read the unspoken question in Armadiel's mind. "No, even I am not sure if he is the one,

Brother Armadiel. In my lifetime, twenty boys have been brought to Baddalaur. Each time, we believed we had the child. Twenty times we have been disappointed . . . though perhaps disappointed is too strong a word. All the boys stayed with us and proved of value to the Order in one way or another." The old man smiled faintly. "Why, I believe you were one of those boys," he said as if only just remembering, though Armadiel knew that Maseriel never forgot anything.

"I was," he acknowledged. His parents, impoverished fisher folk at the edge of the Eastern Ocean, had sold him to some leather-clad warriors for a handful of coins. Strange indeed was the odyssey that had eventually brought him to Baddalaur and the Order . . . and in time, to undertake another odyssey, to find another boy . . .

Caeled groaned. The movement of the horse had set his wound bleeding again. When they made camp for the night Armadiel would take another look at the wound. If telltale black streaks were starting up the arm he would have to cut off another portion of it while the boy was still strong enough to endure the operation. He knew the dangers of leaving the amputation too late. If he misjudged the time, corruption would have spread through the boy's body and he would die.

Cradling Caeled's unconscious body to cushion it from the impact as best he could, Armadiel urged the horse into a faster gait. They could not reach the next town before nightfall, so he was making for the ruins he had mentioned to Caeled. When his horse settled into a steady, ground-eating canter, Armadiel allowed his thoughts to roam. With his trained senses he pinpointed the location of the creatures who were now very deliberately tracking them.

A small pack of Madra Allta were keeping pace with the horse from a safe distance. Farther behind but closing fast was a Torc Allta, a wereboar, which retained the mindless savagery of the wild boar and would kill for pleasure, even if it did not need to feast on flesh. One raking thrust of those curving tusks could transmit sufficient poison to turn those of their human victims who "survived" into wereboars like themselves, doomed to an existence of homicidal madness.

As often before, Armadiel regretted that his horse was not taller. The animal was big and strong for its species, but books in the Great Library at Baddalaur depicted horses in the past who had been both rangier and more powerfully built, with horizontal pupils to their eyes rather than vertical catlike slits. In spite of careful breeding by the ranchers in western Galloway, the species as a whole seemed to be shrinking and growing weaker.

They could not even run as fast as the books claimed they once had run. Sometimes Armadiel puzzled over this.

The road stretched unbroken toward the horizon, a gray thread through a verdigris landscape. In the distance Armadiel could just make out the ruins of some ancient structure, silhouetted against a rapidly darkening sky. He squinted at the heavens, gauging the amount of daylight left. At this pace, they would not reach the ruins before night fell.

Armadiel gave his horse a violent kick, pushing it into a full gallop. The wind whipped its mane so that the coarse hair lashed his fingers as he held the reins.

He caught a flicker of alarm from the Madra Allta. That part of them which was still human recognized his intention. He must not be allowed to reach the relative security of the ruins. An unspoken command from the spotted leader of the pack sent the weredogs racing toward the road at an angle to intercept the galloping horse. Only the younger dogs yapped and barked. The others ran in grim silence, their thoughts red and bloody. *Meat. Soft meat. Fresh meat.*

Armadiel counted nine of the beasts as he drew his sword from its sheath. Three were running well ahead of the others, racing with bellies low to the ground and yellow eyes gleaming. Their human features were almost discernible beneath coarse hair and altered muscle. They were the dominant beasts in the pack; they would choose when and how to bring their victim down. The other six had formed into a semicircle on the road behind the horse. These were experienced hunters guided by almost-human minds; they rarely failed to make their kill.

A sword would not be sufficient against them. While he might strike down one animal, Armadiel would surely be attacked by another. And if he died the boy would die with him only to awake into a worse existence. Thrusting the sword back into its scabbard, Armadiel pulled a flail out of its sleeve fastened at the base of the pommel and slid one hand through the wrist loop. The weapon resembled a leather whip, but with seven lashes, each tipped with an iron spike.

The man could feel the tension in the horse between his legs. The gray gelding was as aware of the danger as he was. Its every instinct was to panic and bolt, but it had been well trained and maintained the rhythmic gallop the rider demanded. "Steady, boy, steady," Armadiel whispered. "We need a tiny advantage."

Then suddenly the first of the Madra Allta was upon them. With an almost human snarl it attempted to leap onto the horse's back. Armadiel waited until the last moment before lashing out with the flail. The seven metal spikes tore into the weredog's face, ripping away skin and muscle, destroying its eyes. The creature whirled in the middle of the road, snapping and rending its own haunches. The horse skidded to a halt, whirled, and pounded the creature with furious hooves before turning again and galloping on. Immediately the two nearest Madra Allta abandoned their pursuit to devour what remained of their erstwhile leader. But the six in front closed in, preparing for the kill.

Armadiel prayed the boy in front of him would not

regain consciousness just in time to experience an agonizing death. He dropped the reins and gave the horse its head. It surged forward. The oldest weredogs soon fell behind and were forced to give up the chase, turning back to join in devouring their fallen leader. The three who remained were strong, determined beasts, however. Human flesh was sweet. They would not give up easily.

As they closed in on the racing horse, Armadiel twisted in the saddle and lashed out with his flail to the left and the right, temporarily driving them back. But they came on again.

Meanwhile the horse, under its double burden, was tiring.

Realizing this, one of the dogs struck off at an angle. Armadiel tried to read its seething thoughts. Beneath the red lust for killing and blood he caught a monochrome impression of a boulder overhanging the road, and a Madra Allta leaping from the boulder onto the back of a running horse.

Armadiel smiled to himself as the road twisted to the left and he saw the overhanging rock ahead.

When the werebeast launched itself off the boulder onto the rider below, it was impaled on a waiting sword. The man used the beast's momentum to toss it onto the ground, where it writhed, disemboweled, as the two remaining Madra Allta ran up to feast on its dying body.

Toward the end its screams sounded quite human.

A weary Armadiel rode into the ruined shrine as the last rays of the setting sun broke through the clouds, gilding the tumbled stones like a benediction. He had outwitted the Madra Allta, but he was all too aware that other beasts would soon prowl the night. He prayed the residual magic of the holy place could keep them at bay.

CHAPTER TEN

The lovers writhed on silken sheets, limbs entwined. Their passion was not entirely spontaneous. Though roused by each other's bodies, they moved with as much control as if they were following the steps of a dance, carefully gauging pulse and tempo, assessing their passions until just short of the ultimate ardor . . . and there they stopped.

Eyes dreamy with lust, Lares gazed at his sister. Sarel ran her fingers through her hair, combing it aside so she could see the expression on her brother's face which so exactly mirrored her own.

They felt in equal measure the power that flowed through them, around them, that crackled in the air between them. Raw energy to be channelled.

Lares pulled back slightly, allowing a measure of air into the space between their bodies. With his fingertips he approached his sister's bosom. Waves of heat flowed between his fingers and her flesh.

Sarel ran her palm in slow, smooth strokes up her brother's thigh. The caress caused the fine hair to rise on the surface of his skin.

"Hold the image," Lares commanded, his voice thickening. "At our moment of greatest passion, hold the image."

"The image of the Void," Sarel whispered, spreading her legs to receive her brother. She could see the twisting grayness ever more clearly; over his shoulder she watched it coalescing out of the air. Colors began to sparkle in the heart of the Void, brilliant reds and yellows that throbbed in time to her passion and her brother's pounding lust.

"*Hold the image*," Lares commanded.

"I see it," she cried in ecstacy. "I see it!"

The web of energy around them brightened in intensity. Coruscating lines of power danced from the twinned flesh to the metal objects in the chamber, blackening buckles, singeing buttons, boiling wine in silver goblets.

"See the Void," Lares said.

"I see it."

"I see it!" he echoed.

"Make it grow," she groaned.

"It grows!"

"Now . . . almost . . . now . . . " Sarel murmured — then her voice rose to a scream — "Send it!"

"Where?"

"South, south, south . . . to Brethany!"

The twins collapsed in each other's arms while all around them flames danced and sparked and hissed, leaping from surface to surface. The chamber smelled of ozone.

And in Brethany, a Void formed.

CHAPTER ELEVEN

Gwynne slowly straightened, pressing muddy hands to the small of her aching back. The band of muscles at the base of her spine was burning; darts of agony ran up into her neck. The leather straps holding the babysling were biting painfully into her shoulders. Silan had spoken of padding them for her, but he had so many demands on his time that she hated to ask for something so trivial.

To add to her discomfort, she could feel sticky moisture oozing down around her heavy breasts. It might have merely been sweat — but it might have been blood. The straps could have rubbed her shoulders raw. She resisted pulling open the neck of her gown and looking. If she was bleeding, there was nothing she could do about it right now. The day's work must be finished.

If her shoulders were bleeding, Silan would kiss them well tonight.

Gwynne smiled, taking such pleasure from the image that she was able to forget how cold her feet were, ankle-deep in black water.

The tall, weathered woman turned to look out across their small farm. From left to right she could see the rest of her family, bending over in the deliberately flooded field, gathering the golden stalks of the long grains. Four of her surviving children were old enough to help with the planting and the harvesting. Even Bevan, the youngest aside from the baby, was almost seven summers.

As she gazed at her children Gwynne smiled again,

crinkling the network of wrinkles at the corners of her green eyes. "Laugh lines," Silan called them fondly when she complained about them. "They make you more beautiful . . . to me. It means I'm not growing old by myself."

Gwynne shifted again in a vain attempt to ease the weight on her back. Baby Derfyl had surprised them all by surviving, in spite of last year's famine and a protracted, agonized labor that took far too long. "You should never have conceived another child at your age," the old women had warned Gwynne, shaking their heads and clucking their tongues.

But they did not know how sweet was Silan's embrace in the night, how comforting the heat of his body next to hers. How irresistible his continuing desire for her, affirming the youth she felt inside.

This Naming Day, Gwynne would count forty summers. She had borne ten children, five of whom survived. The Goddess had indeed smiled upon her. When she and Silan were bent with age, they would have children and grandchildren to look after them.

Shading her eyes with a mud-caked hand, Gwynne looked for her husband's familiar figure. There. After all these years, it still gave her a jolt of pleasure to catch sight of him. Silan was at the far end of the field, dragging a bulging cloth sack to the wooden-wheeled cart they had parked in the early morning when shadows lay long across the still water. By squinting she could just make out four similarly-filled sacks on the back of the cart, though they had only harvested half the field.

At least they wouldn't go hungry this year. Maybe there would even be another child, another girl, a sister for Derfyl.

As if she could read her mother's mind, the baby on her back cooed. Smile deepening, Gwynne returned to her work. As she pulled the tough stalks out of the mud and pushed them into the sack tied to her belt she was dreaming of another child. Another gift from the Goddess.

When the shadows had completely disappeared and the sun had long legs, Gwynne straightened and clapped her hands. The sound echoed across the standing water in the field. Derfyl, who had been dozing peacefully in her babysling, awoke and began to cry at once in a demanding tone.

"Time to eat!" the four older children shouted eagerly.

Gwynne was doling out thick broth from a pot set on dry ground beside the cart when Silan at last left his work to join them. "It's going to be a good harvest," he announced with satisfaction. Collum, the eldest boy, was red-faced from heaving his last sack up into the back of the cart. He stepped to one side to make room for his father, who tousled his head affectionately.

"We'll be finished by nightfall," Silan told his wife. He accepted a wooden bowl from her but declined a spoon. Putting the bowl to his mouth, he tilted his head back and swallowed in great hungry gulps. The four boys were about to follow his example when their mother's glare stopped them.

"Will I ever teach you manners?" Gwynne asked as she reached out to pluck shreds of meat from Silan's red beard.

He caught her hand and kissed the palm. "Never," he promised. "Aah, but if you could have seen how I ate when I was a soldier . . . "

"How did you eat, papa?" Bevan asked.

The man crouched on the soft earth and his four sons, each of them marked with his red hair and brown eyes, gathered around him. "Why, sometimes we ate very well," he told them, repeating an old story they never tired of hearing. "I was with the emperor's army when it took Galloway Fort. The people there were wealthy beyond measure. We slept on their feather beds and ate from their silver plates.

"But less than a single moon later," he continued, lowering his voice, "when we were returning through the Spine in the depths of the Cool Season, we had nothing to eat. We were forced to subsist on dog-rats. Raw," he emphasized.

The boys stared at him wide-eyed.

"Of course that was where I met your mother."

The boys elbowed one another and exchanged winks. They knew what was coming.

"There we were, the remnants of one of the most powerful armies ever to march across the Seven Nations, lost and starving in icy mountains." Silan's voice was hushed as he remembered the friends and comrades he had lost to a monarch's stupidity. For a brief moment, Los-Lorcan had held the world in his hands . . . and had thrown it away to indulge in a rampage of wanton savagery which unified his enemies against him.

Silan had shed no tears when he learned that the twins had slain their tyrannical father and assumed power in his place. Anything was preferable to Los-Lorcan, who could sit in his silken tent gobbling roast meats with both hands while his warriors were starving a few paces away.

Forcing himself to set aside such terrible memories, Silan looked into the eyes of his sons and felt his heart swell with pride. Blessed with such children, he counted himself richer than the emperor at the height of his power.

"Your mother rode with the Snowscalds then," he said to the boys, continuing his narrative. "They were fearsome mountain bandits."

"Don't listen to your father," Gwynne said quietly. She had opened the neck of her gown and held the baby to her breast, smiling down at the eager little face pressed against her flesh. The times they were speaking of seemed long ago. Fourteen summers had passed since she rode with her kinfolk in the high mountains. "The Snowscalds were all women who had no menfolk. Many had lost fathers or husbands in the wars. Banditry was the only way they could survive."

"Well, those helpless women attacked us in one of the long passes. They blocked up both ends with boulders and rained spears and stones down on us. There was an army of thousands up on the cliffs . . . "

"Ninety women," said Gwynne, shifting the baby from one breast to the other. "Widows and orphans, mostly."

"So we surrendered," Silan grinned. "They were a terrifying sight, those women on their grotesque mounts."

"What was grotesque about them?" Marik asked eagerly, hoping for some new and deliciously frightening detail.

His father told him, "They had freakish feet. No hooves at all, but a cluster of toes."

"They were peries," Gwynne explained to her sons.

"Huh?"

"Peri is short for perissodactyl, which means having an odd number of toes. Some people call peries 'new horses' because the first ones were discovered in the mountains within my own lifetime. They aren't grotesque at all; aside from their feet they look like ordinary small horses, but they are more agile and as surefooted as cats."

The boys gazed at their mother in open-mouthed admiration. She had lived a whole other life they could hardly imagine, and knew things far beyond their own experience.

Collum asked, "Where did you learn all those big words? Like peri . . . perissowhatever?"

Gwynne chuckled. "Perissodactyl isn't a big word, it's made up of little words put together, words that come down to us from ancient times. There used to be books about such things. I read some of them when I was in school. I was orphaned, you see, when I was twelve cycles; too young to ride with the Snowscalds, though I had kinswomen who did. My grandparents had also recently died, so there was nothing to be done with me but to send me to the Sisterhood of Lussa for raising and educating. Then when I reached sixteen cycles they tried to make me take the Vows of Lussa. Instead I ran away to the mountains and became one of the Snowscalds myself." With a mischievous wink at Silan, she added, "You see what rebellion got me!"

The boys were more impressed than ever. Sensing he was losing his audience, Silan cleared his throat loudly and resumed his narrative. "The Snowscalds agreed to allow us out of the pass one at a time if we paid tithe to them. They took everything we possessed. Even our clothes!"

Small Bevan burst out laughing.

"When it came my turn, I found myself facing this terrifying warrior wearing a leather breastplate and carrying a barbed sword in her hand. Aaah, but she was magnificent! 'What do you have?' she demanded. 'Nothing,' I said. 'You must have something to give me,' she replied, and I thought she was going to run me through with her sword. 'Only a kiss,' I said. And she took that." He shook his head, laughing at the memory. "Six moons later I returned to the mountain, and we found each other. We were handfasted that same day."

Gwynne removed the baby from her breast and held it over her shoulder, gently rubbing its back. "Don't believe a word your father says. I have to . . . " She stopped, suddenly tense, and looked anxiously around.

Silan reached for his curved sickle. "What's wrong?"

Gwynne was frowning. "I thought I heard something."

Silan cocked his head to one side. "Rustling," he said decisively. "I hear something rustling."

Gwynne agreed. "Rustling." She settled the child in the sling on her back.

"Rats? Serpents? What do you think?" Silan asked her.

The woman stepped back from the wooden cart. "No," she whispered. "No. Look there, Silan." She pointed to the bed of the cart. One of the sacks of long grains had opened, spilling its golden contents onto the bed of the cart. As they watched, each stalk was shifting, causing a peculiar rustling noise.

Silan stooped and placed the flat of his hand on the ground. Brethany was not noted for earth tremors, but the weather patterns had been unstable recently and that was usually a portent of trouble.

But the earth was quiet to his touch.

"It's in the air!" Gwynne gasped. Just then the baby started to cry, a high-pitched wail of pain. They all heard the alien sound then, a distant moaning like the night wind across the moors that rapidly escalated into an agonizing screech. Silan groaned at the ache it caused in his teeth. The boys clapped their hands over their ears and clustered around their mother like chicks seeking safety beneath the hen's wings.

Then briefly, very briefly, the air was filled with a multitude of odors. Some were foul, others pleasant; some bitter, others sweet.

The entire cart was shaking now, each individual grain on the stalks buzzing with a life of its own. The branches on the trees bordering the field were whipping violently as if blown by some tremendous gale, though there was no wind. If anything, the air was too still. Yet leaves were torn from the trees to blow in verdant clouds across the field before dropping at last onto its flooded surface; a surface already shuddering with a million tiny ripples.

The woman was just turning toward her husband for reassurance when the unearthly screeching exploded into an even more terrifying scream. "Run!" shouted Gwynne. But her voice was lost in the sound.

Air warped and a gray whirlpool materialized out of nothing, bringing nothingness with it.

The Scream turned white-hot with passion.

Silan grabbed the two oldest boys. Gwynne caught Bevan's hand and shoved him and Nole away from the amorphous shape suddenly hovering over the cart, just as the long grains turned black and slimy. The air filled with the stench of putrefaction.

Silan and Collum caught the corner of one sack and pulled, desperate to save their harvest. The gray nothingness shifted and flowed around them. Collum saw it settle onto his father's face, saw the features melt and run, but before he could scream, the bloated Void settled over him.

Frenzied with terror, Gwynne ran, pushing her two youngest sons ahead of her. Once she glanced over her shoulder. She could not see Silan or Collum or Marik; then the Void twisted and for an instant — a single heartbeat — she caught a glimpse of red hair, brown eyes pleading and lost, and then the image vanished. The devouring Void moved on past the cart and swept across the field, leaving oily pools of fetid waste on the water.

Gwynne was frantic to get herself and her remaining children to safety. She was determined to reach the shelterbelt of trees; perhaps it could not follow them there. Running, stumbling, sobbing, she splashed across the field, herding her sons in front of her.

She dare not look back again.

Suddenly it was upon her. The shapeless shape swooped low and snatched little Bevan before her eyes, absorbing the child into nothingness. Gwynne grabbed for Nole just as the Void reached for him. Her disbelieving eyes saw gray cloud sheer away the top of his skull. Then the Void closed over him entirely, mercifully concealing his fate from his mother.

Numb with loss, driven only by instinct, Gwynne staggered toward the trees. Her brain had ceased to function rationally, although she was dimly aware that the White Scream had stopped. The only sounds she heard were her own gasps and flounderings, and the whimpering of the baby on her back.

Something hit her. It was not a physical blow, but a

chill so total, so encompassing that it drove her to her knees. A moment more and she toppled face first into the mud. The cold settled over her with crushing weight. Derfyl! she thought. *My baby!*

Then she heard the Scream one final time, fading yet triumphant, and knew her baby was gone.

When Gwynne finally managed to sit up the field was deserted. The only evidence of the Void's passing was a few black oily patches on the surface of the water, and a burning coldness in her back and shoulders.

CHAPTER TWELVE

"What is this place?" asked a faint, drowsy voice.

Armadiel stood up. The firelight washed over his thin face, highlighting the broad cheekbones and deepening the hollows of his eyes beneath his leather helm.

He was still wearing his armor.

"A Way Shrine, or at least what remains of one," he told the boy who lay on a pallet of musty straw beside the altar. At the sound of the man's voice the caparisoned horse looked up hopefully from the other side of the chamber, ignoring the nosebag fitted over its bridle. "Eat the grain I've given you, good friend," Armadiel advised the animal. "It's a small enough ration and I apologize if it's not what you get at home, but under the circumstances we make do with what we have."

The horse listened as intently as if it understood every word, then sighed and began munching the contents of the nosebag. The rhythmical sound of its chewing competed with the crackling of the small fire Armadiel had lit on the broken flagstones.

Caeled struggled to sit up. "I dreamed that . . . Oh!" he gasped in sudden pain when he moved his left arm. His face went white and sweat broke out on his forehead.

"That part, at least, was no dream," Armadiel told him. "I am truly sorry."

Caeled leaned against the altar, pressing the back of his head against the worn stone. He squeezed his eyes shut and felt something wet gather in their corners and trickle down his cheeks.

Armadiel leaned over him to brush the tears away with the ball of his thumb. He rubbed the moisture against the boy's dry lips, saying, "Take these tears back. Cry only for others. Never for yourself." Turning away, he knelt by the fire again, feeding it with twigs and dry moss. "I am Armadiel," he called over his shoulder.

"My name is Caeled," the boy began, and then stopped, suddenly remembering there was no one left alive who would know him by that name. Everyone who had known him — his mother, friends, neighbors — were all gone, victims of whatever evil had stalked through Ward Point. His eyes threatened to fill again. "I seem to remember we were chased by wolves . . . " he said hoarsely, forcing himself to think of something else.

"Madra Allta," the big man corrected him. "Weredogs." As he spoke the flames of his fire cast grotesque shadows on the walls. "But there are wolves out there tracking us, and a marsh lion has been following our trail. In truth, however, they are not our greatest worry. I have always found the beasts which walk on two legs far more dangerous than any furred creature."

"They'll smell the smoke," Caeled warned.

"They won't need the smell of smoke to find us, and I would rather have the light and warmth of the fire than sit here in the darkness waiting. It's the odor of blood that draws the beasts, and we have shed enough blood recently to call the entire marshlands to us."

Caeled attempted to stand, levering himself upwards against the altar. The ruined building shifted and swam around him and he clung to the altar with his one good hand. He breathed deeply, trying to forget about the pain by concentrating on his surroundings.

"What is this place again?" he asked through gritted teeth.

"A Way Shrine," Armadiel repeated. "I do not know which

god or goddess it's dedicated to, though. The statue which surely stood in that niche over there is long gone. When the Katan rode through the Nations two generations past, they destroyed all the shrines they could find. They considered it sacrilege to raise an image of a deity."

"The legends say the Katan desecrated all the holy places and butchered the priests in ways too terrible to describe."

"There is some truth in that," Armadiel confirmed. He glanced sidelong at the boy, one side of his face gilded by the fire, the other in shadow. "Do you know much of legends?"

"Some," Caeled replied. He was holding onto the altar as he edged slowly around it, making his way to the warmth of the fire blazing cheerfully in the center of the chamber. "Do you?"

"Some," Armadiel said, bending his head to hide a smile. "I am a Seeker of the Way."

"A holy monk!"

"Not holy, merely one of the Order. We study and we seek." Armadiel was faintly embarrassed by the term some outsiders applied to himself and the other brothers.

Caeled leaned against the scarred altar, wincing when his injured arm touched the stone. "Are you a Lawgiver?"

"There are no more Lawgivers," Armadiel said quietly. "None have been trained in Baddalaur for generations."

"I know the legends of Baddalaur!"

"Most people do. But some of the stories are, I'm afraid, just that: stories. Many of the tales of fearless Seekers riding to the rescue of some besieged town or kidnapped maiden were created in Baddalaur by Seekers who had never stepped outside the College. Baddalaur has always attracted its share of, ah, creative minds. Some of them find everyday reality boring."

"I think I prefer legends myself," Caeled murmured, haunted by his own recent reality.

"Most people do," Armadiel said again.

Holding his left arm cradled against his body, Caeled moved slowly around the room. It was a single circular chamber that rose to a high domed ceiling. The original design was windowless, the only opening being the door which faced the altar, but time, the elements, and human agency had broken a gaping hole in the ceiling and another opening in the wall to the left of the door.

At last reaching the fire, swaying slightly but triumphantly independent of support, Caeled carefully tilted his head back so he could look up. For once the night sky was clear; he could see stars far above like pinholes in black cloth. Fancifully, he imagined beings — gods? — on the other side of that cloth, peering down at the world through the tiny holes.

Suddenly a real shape flickered across the sky; then another and another. "Something's moving up there!" he whispered.

Armadiel rose to his feet to stand behind him, placing a steadying hand on the boy's uninjured shoulder. They stared into the starry vault together. "Flying devils," the man said after a moment. "There must be a nest nearby."

"Will they attack us?"

"Their name and reputation are worse than the actual creatures. Flying devils live off the blood of cattle. They cannot feed on human blood, it's poisonous to them. But if they are attacked and frightened enough they will bite and claw humans. Like so many creatures, the flying devils are only made dangerous by fear."

As he spoke, Armadiel went over to the still-saddled horse and took a blackened copper pot from one of the panniers. From other pouches and pockets he extracted meal, flour, a bottle of water, and mixed a sort of porridge which he cooked over the fire.

Since the man had his back to him, Caeled allowed himself to return to the altar and lean against it once more. Soon the smell of the porridge began making the boy's stomach rumble in spite of his injury. He was young and growing and it had been a very long time since he ate anything.

When the meal was ready, Armadiel beckoned him. "Sit here by me, boy. Conserve your energy, there's no need for you to stand. You might need all the strength you can muster before this night is through."

Caeled eased himself to the ground, sitting cross-legged beside the fire with his bandaged arm resting in his lap. "You saved my life," he acknowledged, "and I must thank you. If you hadn't been there, the Madra Allta would have killed me."

Armadiel's lips twisted in a wry smile. "It's a moot point. The Madra Allta was tracking me originally, so if I had not been there, it would not have been there to attack you. The important thing is, our meeting was predestined."

"My mother says — *said* — there is no such thing as destiny, and that all fortune tellers are frauds."

"She's right to a certain extent. There is no one future. The threads which comprise the tapestry of any person's fate are constantly shifting and twisting, presenting a variety of possibilities. Occasionally a very gifted seer will be able to trace one particular line of a man's future to its logical destination, and foresee an outcome that ultimately proves to be true. But there are some points in every life which are immutable; knots in the string.

"Our meeting was such a knot."

"Can you see the future?" Caeled asked, leaning forward. As he did so, the firelight gave him his first clear look at the man's face and he blinked in astonishment. "You have no eyebrows!"

The big man chuckled deep in his belly. Reaching up, he pulled off his helm. Firelight gleamed on his bald pate. "Seekers have no hair. None at all," he elaborated, pushing up his sleeve to reveal an unnaturally smooth arm. "People say the members of our Order are hairless because shaving is a way of imposing order upon the undisciplined growth of hair. According to the legends, we deliberately remove every hair from our bodies simply to exert control over random nature.

"But shall I tell you the truth? The truth is, the brothers choose to be hairless because during the Warm Season, Baddalaur is infested with lice."

The boy burst out laughing. Armadiel's eyes twinkled. "Now there's a sound I like to hear. I'll wager it's been a long time since there was any laughter within these walls." Withdrawing a knife from his belt, he used it to hook the pot out of the fire, and then thrust a wooden spoon into Caeled's remaining hand. "Take my spoon, boy. Your own is too bent to use."

"Are you not joining me ?"

"I shall eat later," Armadiel lied. There was barely enough food for one. He had been travelling light to make speed, trusting that he and the horse could forage if the need arose. "I'm not hungry at the moment. Eat and then sleep. I'll keep watch."

"Will the beasts come after us tonight?" Caeled asked nervously.

"Perhaps." Armadiel returned to his saddle and took up his sword. "But before anything can attack you it must get inside these walls. And that will mean getting past me."

In the world of men Brother Maseriel was a blind, rheumatic oldster who had seen seventy summers, but in the Aethyra he was once again in his prime; powerful, strong, with the sharply chiselled features that had given him his nickname — Hawk. Sometimes when he travelled in the Aethyra he assumed the shape of a hawk and soared up through the dreamscape, or hung in space on outstretched wings to read the patterns and auras on the land beneath him as one might read a map.

Only initiates could make use of the Aethyra, the fabled Thirty Realms inhabited by beings not at home on the World Below or in the Sky Beyond. Ordinary folk with mortal eyes could not see the Aethyra, though it loomed over them in thirty shifting, shimmering layers traversed by forces they could not imagine. Modern philosophers debated its existence, but an exceptionally sensitive person might occasionally catch a glimpse of something glimmering and strange, like heat waves rising.

Maseriel preferred it to all places on earth, for in the Aethyra he was young.

High above Baddalaur he swooped and soared effortlessly on the Timewinds, seeing the ancient edifice carved into the living stone of the mountain dissolve into a tapestry of emotional colors. Most of the brothers emitted somber hues of brown and gray, but there was an occasional fiery red or bright yellow, the telltale aura of an exceptional consciousness. Each of these was like a jewel to the proud Hieromonach.

Reluctantly, Maseriel at last turned away from his contemplation of Baddalaur. He had an all-important task to accomplish and little time remaining. He had lived beyond his years; only his indomitable will and a magic that was not entirely benevolent had kept him alive this long. But he had sworn that he would live until the promised one — *a boy, god-marked, beast-touched* — had been found. Now he was spending the last of his energy in an attempt to discover if this indeed was the boy.

Leaving Baddalaur, he flew in search of the aura that would identify Brother Armadiel. Maseriel relished this opportunity to assume the familiar and beloved hawk shape. How good it was to feel, just once more, the rush of air across his feathers, the strong downbeat of his wings as they lifted him through the Aethyra! All the limitations of his aged body were forgotten in sensual delight.

But responsibility called him back to the task at hand. Sloping northward on the Timewinds, he saw, faint and faraway but distinct to his spirit eyes, the shimmering silver aura of a particular Seeker. Maseriel concentrated his vision.

The silver was surrounded by deadly black.

The wolves had arrived.

For some time Armadiel had been aware of their stealthy reconnoitering of the ruined shrine. He tasted their minds: wild, but clean, and detected no werecreature among them, yet intuition told him some agency beyond themselves was directing them. A Tire Allta, a Wolf Lord, possibly. Few humans survived the werechange into wolves, the most complex and intelligent of all werebeasts, but those who did were exceptionally dangerous.

Armadiel was standing by the door with his sword in one hand and his knife in the other when the night shadows shifted, assuming fur and teeth. His sword slashed through the forelimbs of the first creature; he swung it free to drive the blade deep into the neck muscles of a second beast. The wounded animals fell snarling and snapping at each other, blocking the door.

On his bed of straw, Caeled came awake with a scream.

Another wolf launched itself over the bodies of the first two. Dropping to one knee, the big man tore open the creature's belly with his knife as it attempted to leap over him. It fell twitching to the ground.

His pain forgotten in the excitement, Caeled darted forward intending to drive his mother's blunted kitchen knife into its heaving chest. The wolf's eyes locked on his; the boy recoiled from the agony in them.

Armadiel put the two creatures in the doorway out of their misery, then swiftly dispatched the third and added its body to the pile.

A lupine head appeared at the break in the wall to the left of the door. The horse saw it before Armadiel and gave a squeal of anger. Charging forward, the gray gelding thrust his head into the gap and plunged the metal horn on his helmet into the snarling mouth of the creature. When the horse shook his head violently from side to side, the impaled wolf choked on its own blood as it died.

"Four down," Armadiel said mildly.

"How many are left?" Caeled wanted to know.

The Seeker hastily sorted through the minds of the animals milling outside until he had differentiated among more than two dozen wolves.

"How many?" Caeled asked again.

"Enough," Armadiel said flatly. He quested again, until at last he found a protectively cloaked consciousness at the very rear of the pack — *packs*, he reminded himself; there were at least two packs and possibly more.

The wolves began howling then, a long drawn-out ululation that echoed eerily around the walls of the shrine and raised the hair on the back of Caeled's neck. The horse whinnied and pawed the ground.

"The next time they come they may well break through," Armadiel warned. "Let the horse block the opening with his body, and you stand beside him. There is a flail in that bag. Use it on anything that gets into the shrine."

"I've never heard of wolves attacking like this," Caeled remarked as he examined the flail curiously.

"A Tire Allta is controlling them. A Wolf Lord."

"But why?"

Armadiel glanced over his shoulder. "Are you a virgin, boy?"

Caeled felt his cheeks bloom. "Yes."

"So am I, and I never regretted it more than at this moment. It is claimed that the pure blood of a virgin can return one of the Clan Allta to its human form. Individually we might not have been enough to excite him, but rising together, our auras must have blazed into the Aethyra and alerted the Wolf Lord. Tire Allta have gifts not unlike some of those possessed by the Seekers. But he's taking a great gamble, coming after us like this."

"Why?"

"Controlling so many wolves will be costing him dear in energy. If the creatures don't overwhelm us soon, they will turn on him. True wolves hate a false leader."

The baying stopped.

"Seeker." The voice from outside was a deep and chilling growl. "Seeker," it repeated.

"I hear you," Armadiel called.

"Do you know what I want, Seeker?"

"I know." Armadiel risked a quick glance through the doorway. The night revealed nothing, but by concentrating on his hearing and smell he detected the footfall of heavy paws and the musky odor of wet fur. "Get ready," he said in a low voice to Caeled.

Then Armadiel was all but overwhelmed by the reek of the alien mind.

"I will trade you, Seeker. Your life for the boy's. He's crippled, good for nothing. Give him to me and you can go free."

"No."

"A worthless child against your life. Think of all your years of training, Seeker. Are you going to throw them away now, sacrifice them uselessly?"

"You sound tired, wolf-man!" Armadiel shouted. "You don't have much time left, do you? Are your reluctant followers getting restless?"

"You will never leave this place alive, Seeker." The voice was softer now, more menacing.

"That may be so. But I'll not feed a child to you."

"Then I'll have to take you both. I'll enjoy feasting on your flesh before I lap your blood."

The wolves attacked then, filling the doorway and surging against the break in the wall. Armadiel hacked and slashed, piling up wolf bodies, while the horse thrust and hammered with horn and hooves. Caeled tried to use the flail, but in his inexperience he only succeeded in wrapping its strands painfully around his own good arm. He threw it aside and snatched a brand from the fire to use as a blazing torch. When a wolf got past Armadiel Caeled sent it yelping with scorched fur and burned face.

But still they came on, guided by the Wolf Lord. Claws scrabbled on the walls, seeking purchase on the rough stone so they could climb to the opening in the roof.

"*Adur . . .*"

The word shimmered in Caeled's mind.

"*Adur . . .*"

He caught the image of a hawk. Golden winged, with blind white eyes.

"*Adur . . .*"

The word was meaningless to him, but he shouted it at the top of his lungs. "*Adur!*"

The Seeker gaped at him, then dropped his weapons abruptly and pressed both palms against the stone walls of the Way Shrine. Concentrating all his energy he called, "Adur, Lady Adur, aid us now. Light our way!"

Wolves swarmed through the doorway in such numbers that for a moment they jammed themselves in the opening like a cork in a bottle. "Lady Adur!" Armadiel cried beseechingly. "Do not let those who pray to you become victims of the darkness! Help us now and candles shall burn in your honor in Baddalaur!"

The tiny stone shrine lit up like a beacon. Lances of light stabbed out into the darkness and set ablaze the fur of the wolves trying to get in. They yelped in terror and fled, the bonds that held them broken.

Only one did not run. At the edge of the gaping hole in the roof a lone wolf rose on its hind legs like a man, silhouetted against the stars. The grim dark shape stared down into the shrine at virgin flesh and blood, and licked its lips. It paused for only a moment to savor the feast to come . . .

. . . and the light rose to envelop it.

The Wolf Lord teetered on the brink of the hole, screaming with a human voice. His figure was haloed with fire. Caeled and Armadiel looked up, appalled, in time to see him claw at the sky, then slowly topple forward as in a dream, wrapped in flame. He hit the flagstoned floor with a thud, but what lay there was no longer alive, merely a charred and smoking sacrifice.

For a single instant the shrine was whole again. Murals painted around undamaged walls told the old sacred stories anew, with the symbols of wheel and sun picked out in gemstones. A heavy cloth-of-gold blanket covered the altar, where glowing alabaster lamps burned scented oils. In a niche a statue stood with arms outstretched. Somewhere voices were chanting an ancient hymn of praise.

Then the image faded. In the stunned silence that followed, Armadiel and Caeled stared at one another.

"The name . . . " Armadiel began. "How did you know this place was dedicated to Adur?"

"I didn't." Caeled felt exhaustion rising over him like a sea. His legs were trembling and he no longer cared if anyone saw his weakness. He longed only to lie down.

"How did you know the name of the Lady of Light?"

"I heard it."

"Heard it?"

"There was a voice in my head. I saw the image of a hawk."

Armadiel smiled a slow, strange smile. "I see. Of course." Raising his head, he gazed toward the stars through the broken roof. "Thank you, brother."

CHAPTER THIRTEEN

Sarel came running into the room, her diaphanous gown billowing behind her.

Lares was standing by the cavernous stone fireplace with his hands locked behind his back as he stared intently into the flames.

Green flames.

"Did you feel it?" the young woman demanded to know.

Her twin grunted.

"Old energy!" she exclaimed. "So intense, so . . . primal!"

Without looking around, Lares nodded. "One of the old gods woke briefly, fed and then slept again."

Sarel stood behind her brother, pressing her body against his back as she wrapped her arms around him. "But why, and how? Can we go and see?"

He shook his head. "The Aethyra is too disturbed for us to travel in right now; the sudden release of energy has sent shock waves through it." He pointed into the fire. "But I did manage to catch these images before the wash pushed me away."

Sarel looked over her brother's shoulder. Woven into the dancing flames were the faces of a boy, a hairless man, a slavering wolf and a white-eyed golden hawk.

"Interpret these signs, sister?" Lares invited.

"The man is a Seeker — see, he has no eyebrows. They remove all their body hair. As for the others . . . I don't know yet, but I sense something . . . "

Lares shrugged free of her embrace and then pulled her around to stand in front of him. Now he gazed at the flames over her shoulder as she said, "I think we should destroy this Order, brother. Wipe it from the face of the world and pull Baddalaur down."

Lares shook his head, setting his pigtails aswing.

"The Seekers present no threat to us now. Perhaps if the Lawgivers were still alive we might consider moving against them. But the Seekers are nothing but tired old men, spinning tales of their former glories."

"One of those 'tired old men' was present when this explosion of energy rippled through the Aethyra," Sarel reminded him.

Lares rested his chin on her shoulder, violet eyes brooding as they watched the flames. The faces so briefly glimpsed had disappeared but he could still see them in his memory. The hairless one looked strong, and the boy . . . "Yes," he said abruptly. "You're right sister, you're always right. I shall look into it, track this Seeker." He moved his hands, running them down Sarel's sides until they came to rest on her hips with a gentle, insistent pressure.

The look in her eyes mirrored his desire.

"We must practice our magic," she said.

CHAPTER FOURTEEN

Armadiel gently shook Caeled's shoulder. "Wake up, boy, you're about to see one of the wonders of the modern world: Baddalaur."

"Baddalaur," Caeled mumbled, cracked lips splitting. He licked them but that only made them sting. "Baddalaur," he repeated vaguely as if the name meant nothing to him.

Armadiel squeezed the boy's shoulder again, attempting to transmit a little of his own energy to him. But Caeled was very weak by now; the little strength he had left had been exhausted by their long and arduous journey into the mountains. Though it had not proved necessary to remove his forearm, over the past days he had burned with a fever that gradually increased until he was incandescent with heat.

Armadiel had done all he could for the boy. He had now decided to abandon caution and simply ride for the Healing Chapel as fast as he could. If the boy did not receive the attention of a Healer soon, nothing could save him.

"What do you know of Baddalaur?" Armadiel asked in a sharp voice, trying to fix Caeled's attention and keep him awake. If he sank into a coma he would tumble all the way down into death.

"The College," the boy whispered. He made an effort to raise his head, but then let it fall back like a dead weight against the man's chest. Armadiel could feel the heat from Caeled's body even through his leathers. He drew his cloak tighter about the boy, hugging him close. The mountain track they were following had brought them through several layers of low clouds and the oiled leather was beaded with moisture. He didn't want the boy to succumb to the Shivering.

"Do you know how Baddalaur got its name?" Armadiel asked Caeled in an effort to keep the boy's mind working.

"Bardal's Lair," Caeled replied in a slightly stronger voice, surprising the man. "Bardal the Lawgiver."

"The first Lawgiver, creator of the Seekers of the Way."

"He was a hero," said the boy, twisting in the saddle to look up at Armadiel with fever-bright eyes.

"Aye, he was a hero," Armadiel agreed. "He was a warrior from the ice fields of Thusal, who marched south with an army of savages and swept everything before him. In less than ten seasons he controlled the land from sea to sea."

"And then he gave it up," Caeled said. He struggled to rouse himself further just as the horse came to a wide, cuplike depression sloping down the mountainside. A slide of shale had obliterated the trail they were following. The gelding hesitated but Armadiel gave it an impatient kick in the ribs so the animal started forward again, picking its way across the scree.

The horse's solid hooves were too clumsy for the unstable surface. The slide shifted; the gelding scrambled wildly to keep its footing, then in one prodigious bound reached the trail on the far side just as the entire mass slid on down the mountain.

Caeled cried aloud with pain.

"Nearly there," Armadiel lied. Baddalaur was at least another half day's ride. "We were speaking of Bardal, I believe?" the man resumed as if the incident had not set his own heart to pounding. "He grew tired of the avarice and lawlessness that surrounded him. He had brought chaos in the form of fire and sword and ravening warriors who were more beast than men, but when he tired of conquest and wanted peace to enjoy what he had won, the chaos continued to expand.

"Bardal came to realize that the lives of men require order. So he formulated the Laws and established the Lawgivers, who were not only highly trained warriors but both judges and executioners when need be. In less than six seasons he had imposed order upon the lawless land, and the Nations entered an era of prosperity that has never been equalled."

"Why did he give it up?" Caeled asked, teeth chattering. The mist was rolling down the mountain. He was aware of thick cold air in his lungs and fever burning his body, but curiously, there was no feeling in his left arm. He found himself looking down just to make sure it was still there, not lost to him like his hand.

Armadiel was replying to his question. "There are many reasons. First the Island Peoples rose against him, then the Katan began raiding into the Nations, and the countries beyond the Spine rebelled and refused to pay tithe. Bardal crushed the rebellions and drove out the Katan, but at a terrible cost to himself and the Nations. It is then he grew tired," the Seeker said softly. "He was born in an ice house in Thusal, and though he became Emperor of the Known World, in his heart he remained a creature of the primitive northland. He preferred simplicity and loathed the complexities of so-called civilization. That is why his Laws and Lawgivers were so successful: There was only one truth, there were no shades of gray to confuse people."

They were climbing ever higher, following a zigzag trail that almost doubled back on itself as it wound up and up, circling stark outcroppings of gray rock that glittered with quartz; cutting through masses of low, spikey mountain shrubbery; skirting the edge of a precipice above a gulf of empty space; dropping down into a narrow valley lush with grass only to find themselves climbing another mountain, a higher mountain, riding on and on. The air grew increasingly thinner, making them yawn. They began to hear a faint, faraway ringing, and found themselves swallowing repeatedly in an effort to relieve the pressure in their ears.

The pain in Caeled's arm returned, throbbing in rhythm with his laboring heartbeat.

At last the mist began to dissolve and a watery sunshine burned through. The boy stirred restlessly and turned his face to the light. Looking down at him, the man noted that his eyes were deeply sunken in their sockets, his bloodless skin translucent with fever.

"Almost there," Armadiel assured him. He raised an arm. "Look, Caeled, look. Baddalaur!"

The boy's eyes followed his pointing finger. For a moment he saw nothing but a procession of mountain peaks rising into an eggshell-blue sky. Then clouds drifted before the face of Nusas the Sun; their shadows fled across the panorama, pursued by rays of slanting light that threw the scene into stark relief.

Caeled found himself gazing across the next valley at a vision that made him forget his pain.

Once the rock shoulder of the mountain on the other side of the valley had vaguely suggested the front half of a crouching lion. Generations of builders and craftsmen had reinterpreted and refined the image. Now Baddalaur was shaped like a warrior sitting tall and proud in a high-backed chair, forearms stretched along the arms of the chair, feet planted solidly on the ground.

The cloud dissipated. The full brilliance of Nusas blazed across the mountains, destroying shadows, wiping away the impression of the seated man.

Caeled squinted in astonishment. All he could see was a bald mountainside with polished cliff faces riddled with dark holes. Insects appeared to be crawling in and out of the holes.

"The seated man is supposed to represent Bardal,"

Armadiel said. "There is evidence that the mountain was worshipped in antiquity. A thousand men now live in the mountain, in a series of caverns."

"Are they all Seekers?" Caeled wondered. His eyes were still wide and staring as he sought details on the mountain. He realized now that what he had first taken for insects were actually people going in and out of caves and moving along walkways carved into the mountainside.

"Less than half are Seekers. An almost equal number are Scholars of the Order, and the remainder are visiting scholars and priests from a dozen different religions. Baddalaur has one of the finest libraries in the world."

"What do you do now that you are no longer Lawgivers?" the boy wanted to know.

"We study, we teach, we heal. Some of us are poets, some keep the histories."

"Why? Why are you a Seeker?"

Armadiel bent his head to hide a smile. It was question he had asked himself. He was not a natural scholar, he lacked the patience, as he lacked the prodigious memory required of a great teacher. He knew he had been a disappointment to the Order, which once had high hopes that he might be the Spoken One. Yet he retained a certain prestige. He was one of the few Seekers who was encouraged to leave Baddalaur to gather information from the towns and villages. Whenever the Hieromonach needed a courier, Armadiel was invariably entrusted with the messages. He was reliable and relied upon, but that was not enough. He did not know why he was a Seeker . . . yes, he did know, if he had the courage to admit it to himself. It was because he had nowhere else to go.

"I am a Seeker so I can collect knowledge," he said in answer to Caeled's question.

"Why do you want knowledge? What do you do with it?"

"We gather it, record it, cross-reference it . . . " His

voice trailed away as he realized just how trivial it sounded. He said with a sigh, "Nothing stays the same, boy. The world you see around you today is not the world of tomorrow. We need information to enable us to plan for the morrow."

The twisting trail they were following was suddenly enveloped in thick mist. The horse stopped, reluctant to move forward blindly. The experience with the shale slide had made the gelding wary.

"What can you see now?" Armadiel asked Caeled.

"Nothing."

"But you know we are on our way to Baddalaur?"

The boy nodded.

"The future is a little like this path," Armadiel told him. "We know it is there, at the end of our journey. We're simply not sure how to proceed."

"No man knows the future," Caeled said. The mist was not only thick, but bitterly cold, making his teeth chatter in spite of Armadiel's cloak around him.

"There are many futures," Armadiel continued, urging the horse to pick its way forward because he felt the boy shivering. "Some are more likely than others. Baddalaur's finest Scholars agree that there is one potentially great future, and say the Seekers have a role to play in the shaping of that future. We are working towards that end. Mankind advances through order and knowledge. The Seekers are dedicated to both."

"The mist is clearing," Caeled remarked thankfully. At that moment two shapes materialized beside the trail. Caeled gave a start, setting his injured arm to aching again.

"Hold up, Seeker-man!"

A man completely enveloped in a shaggy cloak loomed out of the fog. A hood was pulled forward down over his brow and a scarf wrapped across the lower part of his face.

Armadiel reined in his mount. The horse stopped with

his muscles bunched as if expecting to flee from danger.

A second hooded man stepped forward holding a heavy black crossbow at the ready. The barbed bolt was pointing directly at Caeled's chest.

"What do you want?" Armadiel demanded.

The first stranger lifted a crossbow of his own, taking aim at the man on the horse. "I want you to keep your hands where I can see them."

"I am a simple Seeker," Armadiel protested. "I have nothing to give you."

"Oh, you can give us plenty, Seeker-man." The hooded man came closer and Caeled's nostrils quivered at the foul smell of him. "Warm clothes, weapons, the contents of your bags — and of course your horse. Good eating in that."

"I am taking this sick boy to the Healing Chapel at Baddalaur," Armadiel said evenly. "If you follow me, I will ensure that you are given food and clothes."

"Is that the same promise your lot made to Moban?" snarled the second man. He stepped up to the horse's head and threw back his hood to reveal a skeletal-thin face. His skull was covered with old scars. He jabbed Armadiel in the leg with his crossbow. "You remember Moban? He came begging at your postern gate and you turned him away. And when he crept in that night and stole some food and a blanket to keep alive, you Seekers impaled him as an example."

"I remember the man. Thickset, he was, with a scruffy beard and beady eyes. He killed a Scholar," Armadiel replied.

"If you had given him bread, he wouldn't have killed anyone. Now give us the horse, your clothes and weapons, and you can go."

"You're condemning us to death! We'll freeze here."

"It took Moban three days to die," the hooded man snapped. "I just offered you a much kinder death than impaling."

He suddenly lifted the crossbow and fired.

❖   ❖   ❖

Later, much later, Caeled recalled the sequence of events clearly. He had heard the wet snick of leather as the crossbow fired. Almost simultaneously there was a sharp clap over his head. He had expected Armadiel to topple off the horse's rump, shot through the heart, but when he looked back at him the Seeker was holding the crossbow bolt in his gloved hand. He had snatched it out of the air when the head was barely a finger's breadth away from his chest.

Then almost as if time had slowed, Caeled watched as Armadiel reversed the bolt and drove it point first into the second man's scarred skull. The force of the blow and the internal pressure it caused distorted his face, bulging his eyeballs from their sockets. Before he could fall Armadiel had snatched the already loaded crossbow from his hands. The Seeker pulled the bolt from the dead man's skull as he pitched sideways and fitted it into the weapon. Astonishment paralyzed the other man long enough for Armadiel to shoot him through his gaping mouth. The blow sent him spinning off into the mist.

Neither man nor boy spoke for the rest of the journey to Baddalaur.

Caeled awoke as he was being lifted off the horse and laid on a thick blanket on the ground. There were people all around him and he was momentarily terrified until Armadiel took his hand and squeezed. "You're safe now, boy. The Healers will take you to their chapel and . . . " He stopped as an old man appeared, carrying an elaborately carved staff. The gathered crowd — all male, all bald — moved back as the old man approached.

He's blind, Caeled realized, looking up at eyes like polished white stones. Strangely familiar eyes.

"You have done well, Brother Armadiel." The voice of the Hieromonach was strong, powerful, belying his frail figure.

"Thank you, Brother Maseriel."

"I understand you had a problem with the bandits on the mountain."

Armadiel shrugged. "It was nothing."

"Rest now, and on the morrow, take twenty Seekers and eradicate them. They must trouble us no more."

With an effort that made his joints creak, the old man knelt by Caeled's side and placed a hand on his chest. The boy stiffened, feeling energy flow into him. Then the old man began to shudder, a trembling that started at his fingertips and ran through his entire body. Waves of heat poured from him into Caeled, thunderous waves like surf beating upon the shore. The feeling was so intense the boy writhed, trying to escape, but Maseriel grasped his shoulder and held him with a grip of terrifying strength.

"Do not move," hissed the white-eyed man.

He bent lower, as if peering into Caeled's face with his blind eyes. "Is it you?" he murmured several times. "Is it you?"

Then he flung himself backward with a loud cry that reverberated through the mountains. "Aaaiii! Our prayers are answered!"

Two Seekers came and lifted the old man to his feet, and Caeled saw that he was weeping.

"What's wrong?" the boy asked as Armadiel crouched down beside him.

"Nothing."

"Why is he so sad?"

"He isn't. Brother Maseriel has waited a lifetime for this moment. He weeps for joy."

CHAPTER FIFTEEN

. . . addendum to the History of the Day.
There is now no doubt. The boy is the one, the Spoken One, and I am honored that I should be Hieromonach at this most auspicious of times.

This is indeed a joyous day for the Order, a day which emphasizes the importance of acknowledging and understanding the ancient lore. One hundred generations ago, Ekezial walked the lines of the future and saw the coming of this boy. In the Collected Writings, he tells us that the boy will be "a cripple, sick and close to death," and that "his condition will mirror the condition of the land." According to the records, two hundred boys have been brought to Baddalaur, twenty of them in my own lifetime, but none have been so obviously identified with the prophecy.

The boy is indeed a cripple, and sick unto death. None can deny that the Seven Nations are equally ill — sick with depravity, their health destroyed by the excesses of the Duet. Likewise, the Nations and the border lands are crippled — crippled by debt they can never repay, crippled by the Duet's increasingly dangerous misuse of elemental forces. There can be no doubt; the Duet are stripping the energy from the earth.

If the boy survives we will train him to be our instrument to use against them. He will make the Nations great again. He will inspire the Seekers and restore the Lawgivers. He will bring Order to the world.

Dictated by Brother Maseriel, written down by Brother Rasriel

CHAPTER SIXTEEN

There was no pain.

He awoke to an almost forgotten sensation of comfort and lay floating blissfully for a measureless time, in that misty downy space between dreams and full consciousness, until he realized with a shock that he felt no pain.

The relief was enormous, as if a huge boulder that had been crushing his entire body had been rolled away. He could breathe again.

There was no pain!

His physical distress had begun when he first stared into the Void and was sickened by its flickering lights. Misery had intensified until he felt as if his heart was going to burst when he discovered his mother's remains. He had experienced actual physical pain when the beast bit him, but that was nothing compared to the agony when Armadiel cut off his ruined hand.

From that point on, pain had become a constant part of his every waking moment. Every breath, every movement sent darts of torment through his body. Later, when the fever took hold of him and added its fire, he had longed to die simply so he would stop suffering.

There was no pain.

Caeled eased himself into a sitting position, afraid to move too suddenly lest he set it off again. He discovered he had been lying on a large stone slab in the center of a vast room. The walls were completely hidden by shelves and cabinets, each neatly labeled with a white card in a metal plaque. A glass dome set at an angle in the wall slanted sunlight to lave his naked body, and strategically placed mirrors throughout the chamber caught and reflected that sunlight, making every part of the chamber equally bright. Dry, warm air flowed around him; he detected the dusty scent of herbs.

The boy lifted his left hand and looked at the neatly bandaged stump. Armadiel had severed the hand just below the wrist bone so that only soft tissue had met the sword's edge. For the first time, Caeled could think clearly enough to consider his future as a cripple.

He had seen men, former warriors most of them, who wore hooks or spikes or sicklelike blades in place of missing limbs and he had often wondered how they managed.

Throwing his legs over the side of the slab, Caeled cautiously rose to his feet . . . only to have the room shift and sway around him. He automatically reached for the edge of the slab with his hand and knocked against the stone with his bandaged stump. The return of sudden intense pain cleared his head.

"Now, why would you want to do that, boy? Do you want to undo all my work?"

Caeled stared as an enormously fat man appeared out of the shadows, wiping his hands on the front of his green robe. With no apparent effort he scooped the boy up and laid him back on the slab, then lifted the bandaged hand and examined it critically.

"I don't think you've started it bleeding again," he decided. Seating himself on the edge of the slab, he cupped Caeled's chin with his hand and tilted the boy's face up to the light. "I'm Nazariel, the Senior Healer," he said, "and I want you to open your eyes wide for me . . . now your mouth, let's have a look at your throat . . ." He continued chatting as he made his examination. Caeled detected an educated southern accent. "Your eyes are clear, so is your throat. The fever has gone and your glands are no longer swollen, I'm happy to tell you. You're a very lucky young man. Offer up a special prayer to whatever gods you reverence; someone was definitely looking out for you. Either the werebeast bite, the amputation or the fever could have killed you. But you're strong. A fighter."

From some unsuspected depth, Caeled summoned a radiant smile that caught the Healer off-guard. "Thank you, sir," he whispered.

A lump rose in Nazariel's throat. Such a dreadfully injured child, and yet . . . "You'll be fine," he assured the boy heartily. "Just fine."

The smile faded. "My hand," Caeled said.

"Your hand." The big man's eyes saddened. "Yes, you have lost it. But the amputation saved your life, you know — and you *can* learn to adapt. You are right-handed?" he asked, turning over the boy's palm, sliding his big thumb across the ridges and calluses. "Yes, right-handed," he answered his own question. "So the loss is not as crippling as it might have been." He stood up. "And now you must rest. Sleep when you can, and as long as you wish. Sleep is healing."

"Wait . . . sir?" Caeled called as Nazariel stepped away from the slab.

"I know you have many questions, but there will be time for talking later."

"I am in Baddalaur?" Caeled insisted.

"In the Healing Chapel in Baddalaur, yes. The chapel is part of the College of the Way. Brother Armadiel found you and brought you here."

"Could I speak to him, please?"

"Brother Armadiel is attending to the remainder of the band of thieves who waylaid you. He left three days ago, but he should be back by nightfall. I can tell him then that you want to see him when you're strong enough."

"I have no coin to pay you," Caeled apologized.

The big man looked surprised. "We do not ask for payment . . . not in coin, in any case."

"How then are you paid?"

Nazariel flashed a gap-toothed smile. "By what our patients teach us in the process of their healing. We will add your personal and medical histories and whatever scraps of useful knowledge you possess to the College records: That is our payment." He placed the palm of his hand flat against the boy's forehead. "Now sleep," he commanded.

Caeled was asleep before his head touched the herb-stuffed pillow.

A tiny, oval-faced man came into the chamber and took up a position on a stool at the end of the slab, behind the boy's head. The newcomer had a sheaf of pressed kenaf leaves in one hand, a hollow, dye-filled reed in the other. "Very resistant, was he?" he enquired with professional interest.

"Resistant enough; he's a strong boy. But I wish you'd let him rest a little longer."

The small man shrugged. He settled a single polished glass circle into his eye and lifted the first sheet of kenaf. "The Hieromonach has scheduled a meeting of the Twelve Seniors at dusk. He is expecting our reports then, so I could not wait."

Maseriel turned his head, blind eyes seeming to linger on the faces of the dozen Seniors gathered around the table. They were the upper echelon, veteran members of the Order who stood at the pinnacle of their respective professions.

The Hieromonach stopped at Nazariel. "Report from the Healer?"

"The boy is making excellent progress. He is strong, stronger than he knows, and in the four days he has been here he has shaken off the fever. Furthermore, he shows no signs of Allta infection, for which we can be truly grateful. When he came to us he was undernourished, but he has already gained a little weight and there should be no difficulty in building meat and muscle."

The Healer paused to draw a deep breath. "The amputation presented the most serious problem, of course. The wound was infected, but the cut was clean, bone, muscle and tendon sheared through with a single stroke. Brother Armadiel is to be congratulated. If we had the original hand — the remains of the hand — we might have tried to regenerate it . . . " He shrugged, then, realizing that Masariel could not see him — though one could never be sure. He concluded, "We cannot regrow his hand."

"What did you learn, Brother Tarkiel?" the Hieromonach said, turning his head to where the small man was sitting, a bundle of sheets covered in minute writing on the table before him. "Given the boy's condition and the experiences that must have befallen him, we expect a fund of information from our Recoverer."

Tarkiel fitted the glass bowl into his eye and lifted the first sheet. "These notes I took from him as he slept, so we can be assured of their veracity . . . or at least we can be assured that he believes them to be true. He is called Caeled nam Myriam. He wears his mother's name and has no knowledge of his father, save the vaguest of memories. However, it is impossible to distinguish the actual memories from dreams. He has a blurred mental image of a tall, dark-haired man, dressed in a flamboyant fashion reminiscent of the officers of Karfondal."

Tarkiel dislodged the glass bowl from his eye and gazed at the faces around the highly polished table. "It seems likely that his mother was nothing more than a common camp follower and the boy a mercenary's get. There is one interesting item, however."

From a pocket of his unadorned white robe, Tarkiel produced a ring. It was not a complete ring, merely an empty setting hanging from a piece of twine. "The boy was wearing this around his neck and believes it originally belonged to his father. The ring is solid gold; obviously it was set with a seal at one time."

The men around the table leaned forward, peering at the ring with interest.

"If the boy survives, you will return his property to him," Masariel said coldly.

"Of course I will. But there is every likelihood that the mother stole it in the first place. She was a thief; the boy has clear memories of seeing her branded and whipped in the stocks for picking pockets. Curiously however, the woman never sold or pawned the ring even when they were in desperate need. Caeled remembers finding his mother late at night weeping in her sleep, with the ring clutched tightly in her hand."

Tarkiel paused with a memory of his own, that of Caeled crying as the Recoverer extracted the images from the boy's unconscious mind. Moved by the tears, Tarkiel had brushed them away though in so doing he had to endure the stinging sadness of the child's pain on his own flesh.

He cleared his throat and went on. "The boy's earliest memory is of a large coastal town that resembles Barrow more than any other. He remembers himself as being about six seasons of age at that time, three cycles. And the images in his mind are very definitely images of warm and sunny places, so perhaps he and his mother came from the Southlands."

"His coloring does suggest southern blood," Nazariel agreed.

"Tell us about the boy himself, his character, his qualities," insisted Maseriel. The Hieromonach had planted his staff on the flagstone floor and was leaning forward, his hands folded over the head of the staff, his chin propped on his hands. His sightless gaze seemed firmly fixed on Tarkiel.

Tarkiel leafed through his notes, selected one particular sheet of kenaf, and fitted his glass back in his eye. He read aloud, "The subject is a dreamer, well-versed in legends and folklore. He is unlettered, without formal education of any sort, but he has an innate grasp of both reason and ritual."

At this there was a pleased murmur from the other white-robed Seniors around the table.

"The boy's memory is good, his dreams are vivid and he possesses a powerful imagination. I also detect a rather formidable amount of willpower for one so young. His spirit is extraordinary, and is undoubtedly the reason he has survived thus far."

"I agree," Nazariel interjected. "Healing involves the spirit perhaps even more than the body. If a certain hunger for life is not present, the flesh will fail no matter how skilled the Healer."

"Does the boy know what happened to Ward Point?" Maseriel asked.

"He has a vivid memory of seeing peculiar lights swirling within a Void. Looking at them made him desperately ill and he fainted. So strong is the boy's sense of imagery that I, a veteran Recoverer who has encountered many horrors, was nauseated myself. When Caeled revived he found every living thing in Ward Point had turned into liquid rot. He is convinced the Void was in some way responsible."

Maseriel lifted his chin and tapped the head of his staff with one long-nailed finger. "Were I to believe in destiny I would consider it significant that this particular boy was witness to one of the earliest manifestations of an obviously expanding evil."

"He will never forget the horror," said Tarkiel. "His mother was one of those who died in Ward Point."

"Nor should he be allowed to forget," the Hieromonach responded. "Remind him of that imagery, use it, let it fuel his hate." Maseriel paused. "But we are getting ahead of ourselves." The blank eyes moved from face to face. "Do we accept the boy as one of us?"

"He has not asked for admittance," said Rasriel, a slim man of chiselled features who sat to the immediate right of the Hieromonach.

"What else is left for a crippled orphan?" his superior challenged. "If he goes on the road he will survive a couple of seasons — at most. Even if he does survive, all he can look forward to is a brief hard life of disease and beggary." The old man's lips curled in the merest suggestion of a smile. "We can make Baddalaur seem like paradise to him. He will beg for admittance to the College."

"He is blemished," Rasriel stated flatly. "We cannot accept one who is incomplete."

"Even if that person might be the Spoken One?"

"It is a basic tenet of our order, laid down by Bardal himself." Rasriel habitually spoke in clipped tones as if every word was inarguable.

"And yet Bardal himself was not without blemish," Maseriel gently reminded him. "Did he not lose an eye in the Battle of the Mire, and a foot defending the Causeway?"

"In later years," Rasriel had to admit. "But he was whole when he formulated the Rules of Order!"

"Brother Daniel . . . ?" the Hieromonach turned to the man on his left, an elderly individual with a fleshy nose and a pendulous red underlip.

Daniel shifted in his seat. He was the Senior Librarian in Baddalaur, and his breadth of knowledge was legendary. "There is precedent for an imperfect Seeker," he said, tenting his fingers. "Tamariel, Astariel and Isiniel were all marked in one way or another."

"We represent order," Rasriel snapped. "Our brothers are whole in mind and body. Chaos marks its victims by disfiguring and crippling them. We cannot allow the boy to join us."

"We are all marked," argued Nazariel, his fat cheeks reddening. He was keeping his anger in check with difficulty. "Not one of us is unflawed as we sit around this table, no matter what our condition when we originally entered the College. I am Senior Healer, I know the blemishes that afflict each of us. Do you wish me to speak of your imperfections, Rasriel?"

The other man half rose, his face suffused with anger. But he sat down abruptly when the Hieromonach brought his staff down on the table with a crash. "Enough of this bickering! Nazariel is correct. None of us is perfect. However, we aspire to perfection, and perhaps that is enough. Brother Daniel, be so good as to continue."

"The loss of a hand presents peculiar problems to a Seeker," the Librarian reported. He lifted a leather-bound book from the floor beside him and placed it on the table, blowing away a cloud of dust before reverently leafing his way through pages which crackled with age. "Hamel, writing nearly one hundred generations ago, tells us that he is writing his History of the Day with his left hand because he lost three fingers of his right to severe frostbite."

Rasriel opened his mouth to speak, but the Hieromonach brought the staff down across his hand, painfully rapping the knuckles. "Listen," the blind man hissed.

Daniel glanced up. "This was the time of the Great Cold. Eight generations of Seekers recorded only snow and ice, and when Nusas did shine, he shed no warmth." Looking down at the book again, he continued, "After that first injury, Hamel unfortunately froze his other hand, necessitating its amputation and making writing all but impossible for him. Yet he persevered with only two fingers, though his script was appalling.

"Then here he tells us that Losriel the Craftsman is making him a new hand of metal and leather. When it is ready, Atiel the Healer will fit the artificial hand to the stump, fastening it to the bone and connecting the tendons with those in the forearm."

Daniel turned the brittle pages very carefully, releasing an odor of musty kenaf; tiny flakes broke away in spite of his best efforts and scattered on the surface of the table. "And here we are, a few days later, and his writing is perfectly legible," he pointed, showing where the writing had gouged into the leaves, "if a little too forceful."

The Librarian closed the book, sneezing as a small cloud of dust arose. "I have gone through the library and found the Histories of the Day kept by both Losriel and Atiel. Their notes are precise and very instructive. We can duplicate their efforts, even improve upon them. For this boy Caeled, we can create an artificial hand not unlike the one Hamel wore." Daniel smiled, a flash of yellowing teeth. "Do you know the Spoken One's oldest name, the first name in the earliest prophecies?" His eyes swept the Seekers sitting around the table.

Maseriel was sitting rigidly upright. "Silverhand," he whispered.

"Silverhand," Daniel agreed. He quoted, "Lo, I have seen him wielding the Blessed Arcana with the silver hand of justice and order . . . "

" . . . and chaos fled before him," the Hieromonach finished.

"Written two hundred generations ago in the darkest hour of the Seekers, when chaos ruled and the gods fought in the heavens, raining fire upon the earth."

Maseriel turned his face toward the Senior called Casriel, who had so far remained silent. Bull-necked, with broad meaty shoulders and thighs like tree trunks, the heavily muscled man looked out of place among the other Seniors.

"What say you, Brother Casriel?" the Hieromonach asked. "Can you make this boy a hand?"

The Senior Craftsman held up his own hands, surprisingly small, with long delicate fingers, and studied them thoughtfully. "I will read the accounts," he replied. "And I will try."

"You must do more than try. You must succeed." The Hieromonach turned toward the healer. "And you, Brother Nazariel, can you fit this creation to the boy's arm?"

"I too will read my predecessor's history. But I fear we have lost many of the techniques he knew."

"And we have perfected many others," Maseriel snapped. His staff thudded on the floor. "Go now. Attend to your duties. But you wait here," he added in an undertone to Rasriel as he stood to file out with the rest.

When the two men were alone in the room, the Hieromonach said to the younger man, "You are not in agreement with this plan." Although he could not see Rasriel's face, he could read the emotions sparking around him. "You think I am an old man desperate for the immortality of having discovered the Spoken One."

Rasriel said nothing.

"I have lived my entire life waiting for this moment. Do you deny the portents, the fulfilled prophecies?"

"No, Brother Maseriel."

"But you are unhappy."

"What choice does the boy have?"

"Choice? The boy has none. He is an instrument in the same way that you and I are instruments. Choice leads to chaos. Humans are comfortable when choices are made for them, as a benevolent father orders the lives of his children. For many hundreds of generations we, the Seekers of the Way, made the choices for mankind. Now men live lives of chaos, but we will redress the balance and impose order on this world again. Not in my lifetime, but in yours."

Maseriel reached out, finding the younger man's arm unerringly and giving it a deliberate pat. "You will succeed me, you know that. You will be the Hieromonach of the most powerful institution in the world. Kings and emperors will bow their heads to you."

"That is not what I seek," Rasriel said quickly.

"Like Caeled, you have no choice. When Armadiel found the boy, he set in motion a series of events that will change our world."

"For good or evil?" Rasriel wondered.

"For ever."

CHAPTER SEVENTEEN

"She is the most beautiful woman I have ever seen," Pelotas nam Crucas exclaimed, running a fingertip over his oiled moustaches. "She is truly a goddess made flesh."

Tinos nam Crucas sniffed. "I knew her when she was still a snivelling child . . . of course that was before the cult of Duetism rose in the days following Los-Lorcan's disappearance."

"Such talk is deemed heretical in Galloway," Pelotas said softly, glancing over his shoulder.

"It is considered so here."

"Woman or goddess, she is still beautiful."

"Do not even think about it, nephew. Hers is the beauty of the spider," Tinos nam Crucas warned under his breath. But the younger man ignored him. Remaining at attention, he watched the Duet approach. As they drew nearer, the nobleman could see the astonishing similarity of the pair, whose only visible difference was a matter of hairstyle.

Their eyes — which his people maintained were the mirror of the spirit — were identical: a pale, liquid violet. They looked to be no older than children, eighteen cycles perhaps, with the wide-eyed innocence of the very young.

He had always suspected that many of the stories circulated about them were exaggerations, rumors created by the dead emperor's allies who resented their loss of power when Los-Lorcan died, eight cycles previously. Murdered, some said, by the twins themselves. But

Los-Lorcan had been a bloody-handed despot who deserved no better. Killing him had been a mercy.

As the Duet passed, Pelotas, his uncle, and the rest of the minor nobility bowed deeply, a habit ingrained in them since the days of Los-Lorcan. They remained on their feet, however, unlike the commoners who prostrated themselves at full length on the ground.

Pelotas did not bow so deeply that he could not peer at Sarel from under his eyebrows as she passed. She swayed delicately when she walked, like a lily stirred by the breeze. Pelotas' mouth went dry.

The twins continued down the Grand Gallery and ascended the Stone Thrones that were older than Barrow. There was complete silence until they were seated and attendants had arranged their robes, then Carazell the Chamberlain rapped his staff on the bronze plate set into the floor and the audience began.

Pelotas stood in line as a stream of courtiers and nobles approached the Duet. Some pleaded cases, others begged favors. Some, like himself, were merely there to be presented formally by a relative already at court.

Occasionally the Duet found a position for someone who piqued their interest. There was a rumor — now strongly denied — that Carazell had been a beggar on the wharves of Barrow until the twins elevated him to his present position. Making a former beggar one of the most respected men in the Seven Nations was no more than a childish amusement for them, it was whispered. When they tired of Carazell they would dispense with him just as quickly.

Eventually Pelotas found himself at the head of the line. Smoothing the looped braid adorning his short-waisted satin doublet, he stepped forward with his uncle. The Duet waited impassively on their thrones, beneath a blue silk canopy spangled with golden stars. Somewhere a lute was playing, and the fragrance of sweet wine hung heavy on the air.

"Tinos nam Crucas begs leave to present his nephew," Carazell intoned. His voice was a harsh rasp, his accents those of the dockside. His bandy-legged body wore the embroidered robe of office with ill grace. Pelotas suspected that the bulge on his hip was a dagger concealed beneath his clothing, though the carrying of weapons in the presence of the Duet was forbidden.

Tall, gray-haired Tinos stepped forward and bowed deeply. "Your Majesties. My nephew, Pelotas, eldest son of my younger brother, hearing of the splendor of your court, has travelled from Galloway to present his compliments." He bowed again and backed away, at the same time propelling Pelotas forward with a hand on his elbow.

Pelotas imitated his uncle's bow. When he raised his head, he met — and held — Sarel's wide-eyed stare. "I bring you greeting from your loyal Gallowans, Majesties," he said loudly. A singer of no mean reputation, he knew how to project his voice. Murmured conversations at the end of the Grand Gallery ceased as people looked in his direction.

Pelotas drew himself up to his full height. "As a humble gift for your Majesties, I have brought you ten of the finest Galloway steeds — all twins," he added with a smile. "And single-hoofed, of the old line."

The woman Sarel returned his smile and then dropped her eyes, but he could feel her watching him through her lashes. In that moment Pelotas rejoiced, thinking his position at court was assured. Few women had ever resisted him; this one would be no exception, and prove his greatest conquest.

Lares said, "We thank you for your gift, loyal Pelotas, and . . . "

"Is there anything we can do in return?" asked Sarel.

"Majesties, I wish nothing in return save the opportunity to serve you."

"In what capacity?" Lares responded.

"Are you skilled?" his sister asked. Though the words

were innocuous, the look in the girl's eyes was full of mischief.

"I have numerous accomplishments," Pelotas said, speaking directly to her. "With bow and sword, with horse and hawk, in singing and in dancing. I can do anything you require of me, and do it very well indeed."

"A proud boast," Sarel remarked.

"It is no boast, I assure you," Pelotas replied. Her eyes emboldened him, her perfume intoxicated him. He threw caution to the winds. "I have an extensive education in all the arts, which I will match with any man's." He beamed at Sarel, convinced that he was dazzling her.

Lares leaned back on the white marble throne worn smooth by many monarchs over many generations, and plucked at an invisible thread on one of his flowing sleeves. "A poet came to us a season ago," he said mildly.

Sarel suddenly smiled.

"He claimed he could recite the entire Leabhar Staire, the great history book of the land. You know the work?" he asked with perfect innocence.

Pelotas tensed, aware he had overstepped himself. The Leabhar Staire was a history in verse comprising twelve volumes, each book containing a thousand stanzas. He had never read it; he had only glimpsed it once, on the bookshelves of a fellow nobleman whose wife he was trying to seduce. "I am of course familiar with the work, Majesty," he said with a sinking feeling in the pit of his stomach.

"In Book Eight, stanzas five hundred and two and seven hundred and twenty-three are remarkably similar. Have you made this observation yourself?" Lares continued pleasantly.

"No, Majesty, I admit that I have not. But then I do not possess Your Majesty's literary acumen," Pelotas said carefully. He was beginning to sweat.

Lares slouched on his throne, looking bored, as if he had initiated an interesting game and his hoped-for opponent refused to play. "At least you admit your shortcomings. The poet I mentioned did not. Because he had made an idle boast and then could not prove it true, we removed his tongue." Lares yawned.

Pelotas was chilled by the icy realization that his life hung in the balance, at the capricious whim of this indolent young man. He glanced sidelong at his kinsman, but Tinos was keeping his head lowered and his eyes studiously fixed on the floor.

Sarel leaned over and rested her slim white fingers on her brother's arm. She whispered something to him; he nodded, a spark of interest returning to his eyes. Then she spoke aloud. "If Pelotas nam Crucas hails from Galloway, and brings us horses as a present, am I right in assuming he is skilled with such animals?"

"Yes, Majesty," he said, grateful that the subject had been changed from poetic history. At least, when it came to horses he really did possess knowledge. He was able to keep his voice steady, though there was still a knot in his stomach to warn him he was not yet out of danger.

"Then you will attend us in the forenoon," Sarel said. "My brother and I are fond of riding." For some reason Pelotas did not understand, Lares chuckled at his sister's words. Sarel went on, "Demonstrate your knowledge of horses satisfactorily and we may have a position for you."

Pelotas bowed as low as he possibly could. "It will be my honor, Majesty." He backed away from the Stone Thrones, only looking up when he heard Carazell announce the next in line.

Tinos gripped his arm and dragged him from the Grand Gallery into a small side chamber. "You fool! You arrogant fool! You could have got us both killed."

Pelotas started to protest, but Tinos' hand cracked across his face with a slap that made his eyes water.

Holding tightly to his arm, the older man dragged him down a narrow corridor and out into the herb garden. The sweetly scented air could not quite disguise the underlying smell of the manure used to fertilize the beds.

Tinos maneuvered his nephew into a corner behind a globe-shaped linsom bush, where no one could overhear them. "Listen to me, you crowing cockerel. This is not Galloway, where our family has ruled for generations. This is Barrow and the Duet rule supreme. No one here knows or cares that ours is an ancient and honorable family; here the Duet judge men by words and deeds, and make no distinction between a nobleman and a guttersnipe.

"They simply want to know if a person is gifted; if he or she will be an addition to their court. Your thoughtless words out there were ill-advised to say the least, and revealed you as a fool and a braggart. They might have killed us out of hand, and when that was done, wiped out our whole family line for good measure. They have the power."

"Surely," said Pelotas, "a woman so young and lovely would not be so cruel. You must be mistaken. Now that I have seen Sarel I cannot believe the stories told of her."

Tinos shook his head. "The poet they mention, the man who was uncertain of a few lines of verse? He was Alvear, the Poet of the Isles. I counted him as a friend. He was my age, and had spent his life as a minstrel poet. He had brought pleasure to untold hundreds." He paused to glance over his shoulder, as if afraid of being overheard. "And yet they killed him for a simple error."

"I thought they took his tongue," Pelotas said.

"He was a poet! Without his tongue — he hanged himself from a singing cedar."

Pelotas started to say something else, but the look on his uncle's face silenced him.

"That same day the Duet passed a decree that all suicides' property was forfeit to the crown," Tinos continued. "Alvear's son protested — and was summarily executed for daring to question the twins. Beheading is in fashion this season. Last season they preferred strangulation."

"But this is monstrous," Pelotas whispered.

"You think so? I assure you, the twins are not as bad as their father, not by half. *His* favorite method of execution was impaling — did you not notice that long row of huge iron spikes across from the palace gates? Those are not some new form of sculpture, Pelotas. They have served a more sinister purpose in their time."

The younger man was staring at him. "Are such beings mad?"

"The world is mad," Tinos replied. "And growing madder every season, one way or another.

"You may recall I tried to warn you about Barrow, and the court. But you wanted to come here."

"I'll return to Galloway at once!"

"It is not that easy. First you must ride with the Duet. Fail to keep that appointment, and your next appointment will be with the executioner's axe, I assure you."

"Did you breed these mounts yourself, Gallowan?" Sarel asked, running her hand along the russet mare's silken neck. They were standing in the hallway of the royal stables, with large stalls on either side, holding fine horses. But none so fine as the animals Pelotas had brought, including the mare Sarel was admiring. An identical mare in the next stall hung her head over the half-door and whickered softly.

The female half of the Duet was dressed in a butter-soft leather riding coat that emphasized her graceful figure. With her hair tied back, and wearing neither paint nor lip dye, she looked older, however. Pelotas saw a wealth of experience lurking in her eyes; far too much for the young girl she had at first appeared.

He watched with a combination of fear and fascination as she gently blew into the mare's nostrils, teaching the horse her scent. At least Sarel knew horses. "This is a fine animal," she observed. "Wide between the eyes. And both these mares are obviously in excellent condition."

"They are from my father's stables," Pelotas told her

with a pride he could not conceal. "This pair was sired by Windlord out of Stardancer — the most courageous stallion in Galloway, and the swiftest mare."

"They are taller than our usual mounts," Lares commented as he joined them. He too was dressed in leather, with tight-fitting breeches and gauntlets reaching to his elbows. Sarel promptly put on her own gauntlets.

Pelotas blinked; seeing them standing side by side, they were mirror images.

"In the distant past," he told the twins, hoping to impress them with his knowledge, "horses were taller, their withers as high as an average man's head. They were deeper through the loin, broader across the rump, and they had longer necks with an arch to them.

"There are many accounts of these original animals. Some were bred for speed, others for strength and stamina. Some were extremely docile, but other lines required expert handling. In old books I have seen pictures of horses bred exclusively for beauty, with great dark eyes that could break your heart and tiny little muzzles that would fit in a lady's palm.

"My family has devoted itself to attempting to recreate those early steeds. We seek out those horses which come nearest to having the old-fashioned characteristics, and breed the best to the best, reinforcing strengths and eliminating weaknesses. We cull their offspring scrupulously, keeping only the finest for our breeding program. Already we have succeeded in producing taller, stronger horses, as you see here. In another two or three generations we may have a horse that is identical to its ancestors, and a vast improvement over the degenerate modern animals."

"Proud beasts. Handsome," Lares murmured. "And you say they are strong?"

"Stronger than any mount in your stable," Pelotas said, and then, realizing that he was boasting, added hastily. "At least, so I have been told."

Lares walked along the row of stalls, peering critically at the horses inside. "These are the only sort of animals we should have in our stables," he told his sister. "They make all others look inferior. Have you bred many of them, Gallowan?"

"We have another twenty — though none so perfect as these."

"Send them to us at once; we shall make do with them until you can supply more."

Pelotas was dismayed. "But Majesty, if we send you all our stock we cannot continue our breeding program."

"Are you refusing?" Lares asked in a deadly cold voice.

"Don't refuse him," murmured Sarel.

"No. Of course not!"

"Then send them. We will continue the experiments for you," Lares told Pelotas in that same icily serene tone.

"Of course, Majesty."

"And you must come with them," Sarel added. "We will have need of your expertise." She moved so that she was standing directly in front of Pelotas, and just a hair's breadth too close to him to be casual. He inhaled her perfume, a blend of flowers and spices with a musky undertone, heady and exotic but somehow not sweet at all. It reminded him, curiously, of warm blood. Her eyes were wide and compelling. "Tell me, Gallowan, this method you use to breed horses, does it hold true for other species?"

"We have bred hounds and deer in a similar fashion."

"Humankind?"

Pelotas almost laughed. But she was serious. The question, with its implications, chilled him so that he could not reply.

"Could humans be bred in such a fashion?" Sarel persisted. Her twin came and stood behind her, his right hand resting on her right shoulder, his chin on her left. It was like looking at a two-headed creature.

"I'm . . . I'm sure humans could be bred so," Pelotas said eventually.

Sarel rewarded him with a dazzling smile. "Then you will do that for us also."

Shaking his head, Pelotas backed away from the Duet.

"We shall give you a fine title," Sarel promised. "The Breeder."

"I will do nothing so . . . "

They stared fixedly at him in concert, four violet eyes expanding and encompassing him until he felt as if he was tumbling into a deep pit with walls the color of bruises. Sick with vertigo, Pelotas dropped to his knees in the hallway of the stable. He did not feel the cobbles under him; his blank eyes did not see the twins watching him, assessing his reactions with a vast, dispassionate curiosity.

The stable was filled with the placid, contented sounds of horses munching grain or rustling straw as they moved about their stalls. The air lay quiet, disturbed only by tiny dancing dust motes in beams of light streaming through the open doorway.

Tiny dancing dust motes, whirling chaotically . . .

Sarel and Lares separated to stand one on either side of the blindly kneeling nobleman.

"He is perfect," said Sarel, "skilled in matters we as yet know nothing about, but replaceable when we have learned all we need from him. Hmmmm . . . I wonder if . . . "

She did not have to finish the thought. The Duet understood one another perfectly. "He seems relatively intelligent," Lares commented. "Remember, up until now the technique has only been applied to those who make little effort to use their minds."

"So now we will take it a step further! I want to see if it will work on someone like this, someone who might have enough mental strength to fight back. Will he not be more of a challenge, and his conquest more of a triumph?" Sarel's eyes sparkled.

"You do it then," her brother said. "I will feed you."

Sarel knelt in front of Pelotas and placed her hands on

either side of his face. Lares crouched behind his sister, resting his hands on her shoulders as he concentrated on gathering strength from the pit of his stomach, drawing it up through his arms and passing it into her body.

Sarel closed her eyes and looked deeply into the young man from Galloway.

She had discovered the technique while she and Lares were first experimenting with the Voids. Exhausted one evening, they had stopped long enough to eat, but everything they touched rotted before they could put it in their mouths. At first they had feared they would starve to death, but then the residue of corrupting power faded.

Yet knowledge of it remained, tempting Sarel to explore its potential.

While Lares sought to control the greater Voids, Sarel had experimented with narrowing the focus of mindless destruction until she was able to control something akin to a miniature Void. Such areas were no bigger than the head of a pin, but, carefully controlled, they were devastating. At first she had experimented with fruit, moving her consciousness deep into the core of yellowhands and orange globes and planting the tiny gray seeds of destruction. Within moments the fruit turned to black putrescence.

When these early successes lost their novelty she had gone on to experiment with animals. Here she found that healthy living cells fought the miniature Void, so she learned to locate areas within the body already damaged or weakened by natural causes, and target her seeds of chaos there.

She had experimented on Barrow's imprisoned criminals next, choosing only the strongest and healthiest of the brutish band. No doubt they had considered themselves lucky when they were delivered, freshly washed and shorn, to her chambers, to find a naked Sarel waiting for them invitingly on her silken bed.

The look on their faces was part of the fun.

None had left whole. Some she blinded, placing Voids in the soft tissues of the eyes. With others she corrupted various organs, curious to see the effects on the whole body. In some men she introduced her minute Voids into the bone.

Thirty men had come to her; thirty men had ultimately died from these experiments, until she began to lose interest.

Then Sarel undertook to introduce a Void within the living brain. Sixty-two men died in agony while she perfected the technique, but in time she made a fascinating discovery: she found the tiny area at the core of the brain which controlled conscience.

"I will make you free," Sarel whispered, delving deep into the Gallowan's brain. In her mind's eye it was a house with many doors and corridors. Some doors were open, most were shut. The door she was seeking was deep in the cellars of the house.

"Free to do what you will, without conscience, without regret," she whispered as she searched.

Sarel found the door, opened it and planted the Void.

Unlike the criminal brutes, Pelotas fought back — for less than a heartbeat, and then Pelotas' concepts of right and wrong, good and evil, the lessons of his youth, culture and religion, were stripped away. A great darkness flooded through his mind.

"Breeder," Sarel said, naming him.

Lares lifted her to her feet. "Let's go riding," he said.

CHAPTER EIGHTEEN

When Lu-shi stretched out her hand, the hovering peist folded its glittering, rainbow-hued wings and settled onto her palm. Blowing gently on the enormous insect to calm it, she noted the single yellow spot daubed on its back.

Someone had entered the high passes, then.

One solitary traveller, on foot.

Lu-shi gently eased the peist into the wicker basket where five more of the long, sticklike insects waited to be used for carrying messages to and from the sentries.

She slid the side of the box shut as quickly as she could, but even so she had an unpleasant whiff of the charcoal substance which coated the inside of the container and kept the peist docile.

"Anything?" Moiren asked, nodding toward the peist box. As she spoke the buxom yellowhaired woman lifted her leather breastplate off the table and began strapping it on.

The tiny Katan warrior shook her head. "Yellow spot."

"Do you want me to check it out?" Moiren's voice was briefly muffled by the baldric as she slipped it over her head. She adjusted the wide leather belt across her body at an angle, from her right shoulder to her left hip, then ran a swift thumb over each of the ten flat throwing knives as she inserted them in their slots in the baldric. It was a coolly professional performance to which she seemed to be giving no conscious thought, but Lu-Shi knew Moiren would detect the most minute flaw on any blade instantly. If she found one she would hurl the knife across the room with language that would turn the air blue.

"Let the sentries handle it," Lu-shi told the big blonde. "It's just one person, not worth your effort." She poked at the fire smoldering sullenly on the hearth, and was rewarded with a pall of acrid black smoke that billowed through the hut, driving both women out into the cold morning.

Fifteen huts of stone and timber nestled into the sides of the narrow mountain valley. Spirals of smoke rose from fourteen. "Look at that," Lu-shi grumbled. "Every chimney draws but ours. We have to get it fixed, we're being smoked like fish in our own house. In my country it's possible to have a blazing fire on the hearth and not a wisp of smoke in the room."

"Stop complaining, you're not in Katan now," Moiren reminded her. The blonde woman edged back inside the door and retrieved a fur-lined cloak from its peg. She swirled it over her shoulders, tied it at neck and waist, and picked up a short-handled boar spear. "Beyond the Forests of Thusal my people live in ice houses and burn dung. A little of the smoke escapes through a hole in the roof, but most of it stays inside. Everything, including the people, smells of smoke and dung."

"I can see why you left," Lu-shi retorted.

Another peist came floating down through the clear air, wings vibrating, to alight on Moiren's shoulder. She craned her neck to get a look at its back. "Another yellow spot."

"So whoever it is is coming nearer," said Lu-shi. "I wonder what's made the sentries so nervous about a lone traveller?"

"Could be one of the Duet's scouts. And the Marsh Lords have increased the bounty on us again. Perhaps this is a bounty hunter?"

Lu-shi said calmly, "I wonder just how much I'm worth now?"

The northern woman smiled, showing irregular yellow teeth. "'The reward for Lu-shi the Katan, leader of the Snowscalds, is one hundred pieces Old Metal,'" she recited, "'plus two oxen and a square of land.' Outsiders believe you command an enormous band of female warriors."

"We used to be an enormous band. When I first joined the Snowscalds we numbered over a hundred."

"Well, there's only a score of us now," Moiren reminded her. "And the authorities want to wipe out those. They obviously hope to entice the hill farmers with the cattle and land."

"What about the rest of the band, what reward for them?"

"Ten pieces in New Coin for the head of any member of the Snowscalds, or for information leading to her capture. I heard it in the village from a Duet priest who was spreading the word. I kept my cloak on so he didn't recognize me. None of the villagers betrayed me, they're too afraid of us."

"You're lucky he didn't know who you were."

"He's the lucky one. I would have had to slit his throat."

"Then they would have sent an army up here after us."

"We've defeated armies before," Moiren said with grim pleasure.

"That was then and this is now. Now we survive because of our reputations," Lu-shi reminded her. She stopped suddenly as a young girl came racing up the valley. She wore the gray and brown of a sentry, designed to be invisible among the rocks.

Lu-shi and Moiren hurried to intercept her.

"What's wrong, Seanne?" Moiren cried, holding out her arms to catch the girl who appeared on the point of collapse.

"Some. . . something strange in the pass," the sentry

panted. Her eyes were wild, her face drained of color.

"Soldiers?" Lu-shi demanded. "A beast?"

"No. A traveller."

Lu-shi frowned. "We saw the peist. A single traveller, is that the one?"

The sentry nodded, pressing a hand to her heaving chest.

"A man? Woman?"

The girl shook her head. "Don't know."

Moiren reached under her cloak and produced a flask wrapped with leather. Pulling out the cork with her teeth, she pressed the flask to the girl's lips. "Take a drink of this," she ordered.

Seanne drank and then burst into strangled coughing as the fiery alcohol burned its way into her stomach. Tears flooded her eyes.

Lu-shi glared at Moiren. "Did you give the poor child some of that appalling liquid fire you distill yourself? Shame on you! That drink will melt rust off a sword."

Ignoring her, Moiren said, "Start again, Seanne. Speak slowly. What did you see?"

"A statue. A walking statue!"

Armor, Lu-shi concluded, settling into position in a wind-gnarled cedar that clung to the mountainside above the barely visible trackway. The child must have mistaken some form of armor for stone.

In her own land, the finest armorers specialized in creating suits to an individual's form. The armor was based on an ancient design, the metal shell mimicking the contours of the muscle beneath. Only the helmets deviated from the human image, being cast to resemble beasts or demons. The armor was light enough to wear without excessive discomfort because the Katan had mastered the technique of folding thin sheets of steel. When they first raided into the surrounding lands wearing the new armor, the natives had fled terrified from "the metal men."

Seanne might have seen someone wearing Katan armor. Unpolished steel might have been mistaken for stone in the early morning light. But what would someone wearing Katan armor be doing walking the high passes?

Unless . . . The Katan were among the deadliest fighters in the world. It was not unknown for the younger men to undertake solo quests of honor into barbarian country to prove their mettle and hone their killing skills.

Well, this was one questing Katan who would not be returning home to boast of his victories . . . and his armor would fetch a pretty price in Old Metal.

Cautiously raising her head, the leader of the Snowscalds scanned the surrounding terrain, but she could see nothing out of place. She had fifteen of her band well concealed among the rocks. When the traveller reached the center of the trackway, the Snowscalds would attack. Even a highly trained Katan could not withstand the fury of sixteen warrior women.

A flicker of movement caught Lu-shi's eye. Someone was coming up the path. The small woman squinted, trying to make out details.

Something was obviously wrong. The traveller was moving slowly, weaving from side to side.

A trap? A trick?

Holding her breath, Lu-shi waited as the figure drew closer. Beneath its hooded travelling cloak, the Katan woman glimpsed something that might be armor, though the helmet had been molded to resemble a human face. The detail was incredible, the work of a master craftsman.

The traveller was leaning on a stout quarterstaff, but that did not explain the stiff, awkward movements he made, or his unnatural gait. Everything about him was peculiar, including the long knife strapped upside down atop his chest in a way no normal warrior would wear a weapon.

The Katan woman felt the small hairs on the backs of her hands rise. She dry-washed her hands. She knew that feeling of old: the unmistakable tingle of magic.

A magician, then? A sorcerer?

The figure stopped just short of the center of the path. Raising one hand, it pushed the hood back off its head and shook out a mane of long gray hair.

Lu-shi stifled a gasp. She was looking at a woman!

The traveller lifted her head and Lu-shi's surprise turned to incredulity. Green eyes glittered through what might be holes in the helm, and the lower part of the faceplate moved, taking the form of a pair of stone-gray lips that shaped words.

But what helmet could be constructed to so mimic a human face?

"When I rode with the Snowscalds, we often used this spot to ambush travellers." The voice, which appeared to be directly addressing Lu-shi in her hiding place, was harsh, rasping. Sexless.

The Katan woman froze, praying her followers would do the same until they knew what manner of being they faced.

"I've been watching the peist fly," the inhuman voice continued. "They were daubed with a single yellow spot. If I had been a raiding party or a war party then the code would have been three red spots. A merchants' caravan, a single yellow line. At least that was the code in my day, when I rode the high passes with Lilith, the Dark Lady, and we harried Los-Lorcan's army to its desruction."

Lu-shi slid to the ground, dropping lightly to her feet before the traveller. At once fifteen Snowscalds materialized from among the rocks to stand behind her, bows and blowpipes levelled.

"Who are you?" Lu-shi demanded.

"A sister."

"Let us see you. Take off your helmet."

"This is not a helmet." The figure stepped closer, giving the other woman a clear look at her face.

The Katan hissed. She was not looking at a metal mask,

but at human skin: skin the color and texture of stone, covering the woman's visage from forehead to chin. The green eyes and the pink interior of her mouth when she opened it to speak provided the only color in that ashen face.

Wordlessly, the woman dropped her cloak to the ground, then undid the ties of her tunic and pulled it over her head. Naked, she turned slowly, letting them look.

Much of her body appeared to be petrified. Cracked granite spread from between her shoulders and down along her spine, tracing her ribs around to the front of her torso where a gritty grayness covered most of one breast, leaving a portion of the nipple pink. The adjacent arm was as gray as the breast. Her belly and upper thighs looked like solid stone.

"Nine days ago I was harvesting with my husband and five children in Brethany," she told her horrified audience. Her eyes glittered in their granitic mask but did not weep. Could not weep. Stiffening facial muscles had closed the tear ducts.

"Something fell upon us out of nowhere, a gray Void that consumed my four sons and snatched my baby daughter off my back. I think it took my husband too." The woman's voice was a monotone, devoid of emotion. "But it did not take me. Gorged, it departed, leaving me for dead.

"When I awoke I could not feel the skin on my back where the baby had been riding in her sling. Since then this creeping disease has spread over me to the extent you see, turning my flesh to stone." Bending with an abnormally rigid back, she retrieved her knife from its scabbard and slashed savagely at her gray arm. Sparks danced off the blade. "Stone," she repeated wearily. The part of her body which still appeared human was shivering.

Moiren threw off her own fur-lined cloak and stepped forward to wrap it around the woman.

The stranger sighed gratefully. "I once rode with the Snowscalds," she said to Moiren, "and now I've come back because I have nowhere else to go."

"What is your name?" Lu-shi inquired.

"Gwynne."

"Welcome home, sister."

CHAPTER NINETEEN

A sudden yelp of anguish woke Caeled. "If you move again," the Senior Healer was saying to someone nearby in dispassionate tones, "you'll rip it off entirely."

"I'd swear it didn't hurt so much before you got your hands on it!" the patient replied with feeling.

Recognizing Armadiel's voice, Caeled opened his eyes. He slid off the hard, narrow bed and padded barefoot across the floor of the tiny sleeping chamber, his damp feet leaving fleeting patterns on the polished stone.

He discovered Armadiel sitting slumped on an examining slab in the central chamber of the Healing Chapel. Nazariel stood over him, doing something to one side of the Seeker's face. A bowl on the slab beside them held water stained pink with blood. As Caeled entered the chamber the Healer turned toward him. "Curiosity, eh? A sure sign you're healing."

"Hello, boy." Armadiel attempted a smile which crumpled into a grimace of pain as Nazariel resumed his work.

"What happened to you?" Caeled wanted to know.

The stout Healer said over his shoulder, "A mountain brigand tried to slice off this man's ear with a rusty knife. I'm attempting to sew it back on, but he's whimpering like a child. Stay here and talk to him; make him put on a brave face in front of you."

"You look a damn sight better than the last time I saw you," Armadiel remarked to Caeled, trying not to flinch as Nazariel sewed his ear with sturdy thread. The Healer gave the needle a flourish, knotting the line, then tugged at the most recent stitch.

In spite of himself, Armadiel gasped. "You did that on purpose!"

"Of course I did. You wouldn't want the knot unravelling, would you?"

Caeled hooked one leg over the edge of the slab, perching so he could watch. The Seeker's ear looked like mangled meat; he wondered how the Healer could hope to restore it to normalcy. "That's a bad wound," he told Armadiel with a certain amount of boyish admiration.

Armadiel grunted. "I was lucky. A finger-length the other way and he would have destroyed my eye."

"Or he could have cracked your skull," Nazariel remarked, peering critically at his handiwork.

Caeled said, "You could have saved his eye or fixed his skull, though, couldn't you, Nazariel?"

The Healer shrugged modestly, but he was pleased.

Caeled asked Armadiel, "Did you kill many bandits?"

The reply was succinct. "All of them."

"I know we had to make the mountain passes safe again," remarked Nazariel, "but I confess to having a certain sympathy for those men you killed. Poor fellows, they were mostly refugees left over from Los-Lorcan's border wars. They had spent years hiding out, struggling to survive with every person's door barred to them. Their past was a shameful nightmare and they had no future. What a waste of lives," the Healer sighed.

Armadiel replied coldly, "They were bandits."

"Were there many?" Caeled wanted to know. He had forgotten the pain in his arm in the excitement.

"When we raided their camp in the high mountains we found and killed twenty-two. However, before we razed the camp we discovered thirty bedrolls, so we knew there were eight still out there, somewhere.

"We were heading back here to eat and rest before going after them again, when this happened." He reached up to touch his ear, but Nazariel slapped his hand away.

Armadiel continued for the fascinated Caeled, "We were ambushed in a narrow pass where those eight bandits fought like men possessed."

"They had nothing left to lose," the Healer reminded him.

Armadiel looked as if he was about to say more on the subject, but thought better of it. "You've made good progress since I last saw you," he commented instead to Caeled.

The youngster nodded. Then he blurted, "I don't remember saying this to you on the way here, but . . . thank you! You saved my life I don't know how many times."

"I would have dishonored myself if I had failed to try to help you," Armadiel replied.

Nazariel finished a second row of stitches and snipped off the last of the thread. "You'll have a scar, but when the swelling goes down your ear will look somewhat like an ear again. Go now, get some fresh air and keep your hands off the wound until it's had a chance to heal. If you have a lot of pain come back to me, though the worst of it should be over now."

Armadiel eased himself off the slab and helped Caeled down. Putting an arm about the boy's shoulder, he guided him toward an arched doorway on the other side of the chamber. "Tell me how you feel?" he asked as they walked.

"My hand is sore. . . ." Caeled began, then shook his head. "Not my arm, my *hand*. I can feel my fingers." He raised the bandaged stump. "Sometimes I wriggle them."

"It will take time for your body to adjust to the loss," Armadiel said gently. "I once spoke to an Island Corsair who'd lost his leg above the knee, yet he swore he could feel his toes." He stopped, blinking in the sunshine as they stepped out onto a narrow terrace. Leaning on the rail, he turned his face up toward the sun and closed his eyes. Light shone bronze and gold through his eyelids.

"Nazariel makes me come outside for a while every day and it's always so warm here," said Caeled, "yet I seem to remember that it was cold in the world beyond Baddalaur. Is this warmth some sort of magic?"

"No. Well, perhaps natural magic," Armadiel amended. "We're in the belly of a fire mountain, a volcano. You know the word? This entire mountain is hollow, riddled with caves and caverns. The surrounding countryside is far colder, of course."

Caeled's eyes widened. "Aren't you afraid the volcano will explode some day?"

"No. It has been dormant for so long it will never awaken now."

"Are you certain?"

"There are no certainties, boy. I've sought them all my life and never found them.

"But look," he said, gesturing. "Look down at the Central Courtyard on the level below us, at the heart of Baddalaur. Can you see that the paving is actually a bed of solidified lava?"

At its widest the Central Courtyard stretched a thousand paces across, its center occupied by an enormous sculptured fountain of complex and intriguing design. The fountain had not worked in living memory, though in some of the oldest records it was described as shooting a column of steaming water into the sky at regular intervals.

The sloping interior walls of the hollow mountain were studded with innumerable caves. Terraces cut into the stone ran in front of elaborately decorated cavemouths carved and painted to simulate the gaping mouths of beasts. Some of the beasts bore no resemblance to any known creature; they were the products of myth and nightmare.

When Caeled tilted his head back and looked up he could see a network of gossamer-thin aerial walkways like spiderwebs connecting the highest caves, those nearest the rim of the volcano and the blue sky far above.

"I want to walk up there," Caeled said, pointing with his remaining hand. "Are they safe?"

"They're safe enough, I suppose," Armadiel growled.

He disliked the high walkways; he had an inexplicable fear of heights. "They enable the brothers to cross from one side of the mountain to the other without having to come down to ground level. When I joined the Seekers half a lifetime ago, there were wicker and metal baskets that could convey people to the highest caverns. But they don't work any more," he added.

Caeled was about to ask why not when he realized Armadiel's attention had wandered. Following the man's gaze he looked over the railing and down. A group of white-robed Seekers was crossing the courtyard. When he recognized the old man in their midst — Maseriel, the Hieromonach — a shudder ran across the boy's shoulders as he was swept by a vivid memory of Maseriel standing over him, staring at Caeled with blind white eyes.

Maseriel stopped below the terrace and called up, exactly as if he could see them, "Brother Armadiel, bring that boy down here!"

With one hand on Caeled's shoulder Armadiel maneuvered him along the sloping terrace and down to the courtyard to stand before the Hieromonach. Once he was close to the old man, Caeled was surprised to discover that Maseriel was no taller than himself. The Hieromonach's eyes fascinated the boy. The iris and pupil appeared to have been washed away, leaving only the white eyeballs. But the white was shot through with jagged lines like a broken mirror. And when Maseriel turned his face towards them, Caeled was convinced he could see.

"You did well, brother," Maseriel congratulated Armadiel as the other Seekers ranged themselves in a semicircle around them. "I understand none of those brigands survived."

"None."

"And you razed the camp?"

"Yes, brother. We burnt the bodies and stuck the heads on poles around the site. It will not be used again."

"I am told you were injured."

"A minor injury," Armadiel said quickly.

"It should not have happened."

"We were surprised in a narrow pass and someone jumped onto me from an overhanging rock."

"You should not have let that happen. You should have been prepared."

"Yes, brother."

Caeled looked from one man to the other, feeling tension in the air. Armadiel's grip on his shoulder had tightened almost painfully.

"Do you need instruction, brother?" Maseriel asked.

"I do not think so," Armadiel said cautiously.

"How then do you account for your error?"

Armadiel took a deep breath. "I make no excuses. Possibly my journey into the Northlands in search of . . . my journey exhausted me. Perhaps I should have rested more before setting out in pursuit of the bandits."

Maseriel took a step forward. Armadiel's fingers dug into Caeled's shoulder until the boy almost cried out with pain.

Then the Hieromonach stopped and nodded to himself. "Perhaps you are correct," he said. "The error was mine in allowing you to go without sufficient rest. I will consider my mistake should a similar situation ever arise." Turning to Caeled, he reached out unerringly to place the palm of his hand against the boy's cheek. "And you, Brother Armadiel's find, how are you?"

"Well," Caeled murmured.

"Well? Is that all you have to say?"

"I am well thanks to the courage of Armadiel who rescued me and the skills of Nazariel who is healing me. And also thanks to your kindness for allowing me to stay here while I am being treated."

"Well said," Masariel approved.

"I will move on as soon as I can," Caeled assured him.

To his surprise, Maseriel turned and began to walk away. The other Seekers remained where they were, but Armadiel gently pushed the boy forward so that he fell into step beside the old man. As they crossed the courtyard together Caeled, looking down, noticed a faint pattern etched in the surface of the lava bed, as if to convey a message. He tried to decipher it but the meaning eluded him, worn away by the feet of countless generations.

"Where will you go?" Maseriel was asking.

"I don't know," Caeled replied. "To Barrow possibly, maybe south to Karfondal."

"And then?"

"I don't know," Caeled said again.

"You have family you could go to?"

"No."

"You have skills then?"

"None."

They paused beside the fountain in the center of the courtyard. The old man sighed. "I fear your options are limited. You can become a beggar — your disability would prove an advantage there. You would want to go to Karfondal, in that case, where the populace is sympathetic to beggars. Beggars have an unfortunate habit of disappearing off Barrow's streets.

"Or you could become a thief, though pickpockets and cutpurses really need two hands. However, in time you might adapt — if you survive and avoid the gallows. Alternatively, you could become a whore. There is a lively trade in Barrow in young men, and your deformity might render you desirable to those of perverse tastes." Maseriel bent his head toward Caeled like a snake approaching a rabbit. "You really have no other choices, you know."

The boy turned his gaze toward the disused fountain, trying to distract himself from the old man's almost gloating tone. He was determined not to weep in front of the Hieromonach.

The ancient fountain, he now observed, was sculptured from an enormous chunk of Old Metal that must have been worth a fortune. It took the form of a beautifully balanced cascade of geometric shapes, squares and balls and triangles.

At second glance Caeled noticed what appeared to be hands; long fingers were clawing their way between the abstract shapes as if someone buried inside the sculpture was trying to get out.

"Or you could stay here from now on," said Maseriel.

Caeled was wondering why no one had bothered to repair such a magnificent fountain right in the center of Baddalaur. . . .

"What did you say?" he gasped as his mind tardily registered the Hieromonach's words.

"I said you could stay here."

Caeled looked at him blankly.

"We will give you a home, an education, a future. At the end of your training, if you have applied yourself sufficiently and fulfilled our expectations for you, you may choose to take the vows of the Order and remain with us always as a brother."

"And in return?" the boy whispered, his heart thundering. "What would you want in return?" Everything costs, his mother had told him wearily, more than once. Everything costs.

"While you are training, we demand nothing more than your obedience," Maseriel replied. "If you remain with us, then your unswerving loyalty." The old man turned his head as if to survey the Central Courtyard. "There are currently no others of your generation training with us, so you would be assured of the finest education with a great amount of individual attention. When you're finished you could find employment at any court in the land. It is just a suggestion, of course," he added innocently. "Perhaps you would like to think about it."

"No. I mean, yes! Of course I would like to stay!" Caeled felt a vast relief sweep through him. He would have a home, an education — even a family, of sorts. It seemed too good to be true.

"Very well," said Masariel with a wintry smile. "We will do what we can for you. If you are as bright as I think you are, you may rise through the ranks of the brotherhood. You might, for example, someday become a Scholar . . . "

"Or a Seeker like Armadiel?" Caeled interrupted excitedly.

Maseriel said in a stern, cold voice, "Only those complete in mind and body can aspire to be Seekers of the Way."

Caeled glanced at the bandaged stump of his left wrist. The sight no longer made him feel queasy as it had done at first, but filled him with a vast hopelessness that would have bordered on despair, had he possessed a less sturdy spirit.

He raised his eyes again to Maseriel and met the blank white gaze that saw nothing.

Yet the Hieromonach knew Caeled was looking at him. Knew, and widened his strangely chilling smile.

CHAPTER TWENTY

By the time he had climbed the first one hundred steps, Caeled was exhausted. The muscles in his legs were burning and his stump was throbbing in time to the pulse in his temples.

"A moment, please," he panted. He sank down on the step with his back to the wall.

The short, sly-looking Recoverer — whom Caeled had instinctively disliked on sight — returned to stand a step above the boy, tapping his foot impatiently. "I don't have all day," Tarkiel grumbled.

Ignoring the man, Caeled took advantage of the opportunity to gaze out over Baddalaur. He stared bemused at the grotesque yawning mouth of a dragon surrounding the entrance of the cave opposite, and grinned when he glimpsed men moving back and forth inside the dragon's mouth.

When he looked down from this height he could more clearly make out the pattern incised into the lava floor of the Central Courtyard below. What had appeared to be random lines made more sense now. He could distinguish faded threads of green and gold, black and silver in an intricate spiral design that drew the eye toward the fountain.

Caeled wondered what the effect would have been when the colors were new and bright and the fountain in working order, spraying water almost as high as the mouth of the volcano.

"Are you ready to go on yet?" the Seeker demanded.

Caeled glanced up at the man, trying to remember his name. Tarkel . . . Torkeel? Tarkiel. "Have we much farther to go, Brother Tarkiel?"

"To the top," the Recoverer replied. "There are six hundred and seventy stone steps from the Central Courtyard to the highest levels where the student quarters are. As the brothers progress through the Order, they move to lower quarters, until they eventually return to the courtyard. The Hieromonach and the Seniors have their quarters there, together with the Great Library and the Halls of Study."

"Maseriel told me . . ."

"Brother Maseriel," Tarkiel snapped, "or you may use his title, the Hieromonach."

"Brother Maseriel told me," Caeled amended, "that there are no other students my age in Baddalaur." Having caught his breath, he got to his feet and moved onto the next step. Tarkiel turned his back on him and proceeded upward. "I was wondering why that was?" Caeled called after him.

The Recoverer climbed on in silence. Just when Caeled was beginning to doubt he had heard the question, the man said over his shoulder, "We represent order." He went a few steps more, then added, "We stand for the dignity and perfection of the old ways. These new generations, however, prefer the tumult of chaos. 'Do what thou will' is the modern credo.

"That is not our way. We believe in stringent discipline, the dignity of suffering, the nobility of self-sacrifice. People are not meant to enjoy, but to endure, as we have always taught. But our beliefs are not . . . *fashionable*," he mouthed the word as if it burned his mouth.

"In Barrow, for example, the Duet rule a court of unbridled licentiousness. They encourage the people to live from day to day without thought of the morrow. If they continue to promote debauchery they will destroy the capital and beggar their subjects in less than ten cycles. Or turns, as you southerners might call them."

The remark disturbed Caeled; he wondered how this strange, cold-eyed Seeker with the unusual title of Recoverer knew he was from the south. Any accent he possessed he had long since outgrown.

"In twenty seasons," Tarkiel continued, "Barrow will be a ruin, the army in disarray, the fleet dispersed, disease and crime rampant. Then the invaders will come: warriors from Katan, Brethans and the savage Shemmat and Island Corsairs." Drawing a deep breath, he made a visible effort to control his emotions.

"In such a chaotic climate, what use is there for learning and knowledge? Young men now dedicate themselves to the pursuit of pleasure. There are schools in Barrow, for example, which offer instruction in lovemaking! And command a high price for their instruction!" Tarkiel sounded scandalized. "The gladiatorial schools have been revived, and assassins are teaching their skills to anyone with a purse full of coins. Even the healing arts have been perverted; I am reliably informed that one can purchase instruction in poisoning and maiming."

The Recoverer shook his shaven head. "Proper schooling, on the other hand, is no longer compulsory as it was under Los-Lorcan. A generation is growing up without the benefit of reading skills, without any knowledge of the past. That is how the Duet keep control: through ignorance." Tarkiel paused at last and looked back; Caeled was several steps below, struggling to follow him but finding it increasingly difficult to raise his aching legs.

Tarkiel was unexpectedly touched by the wounded boy's valiant effort. "Rest," he commanded more kindly than was his wont. "Sit for a moment before we go further."

Caeled promptly slumped onto the step, but with his one hand he continued to cling to the rope guardrail that prevented his tumbling into the Central Courtyard far below. "How high are we?" he wheezed.

"Five hundred and ten steps."

Still clutching the rope, Caeled leaned forward to peer down. He quickly drew back. The height made his head swim. He tried looking up instead, at the blue inverted bowl of the sky which seemed closer now. Much closer. As if he were about to tumble into it.

He swallowed hard and pinned his eyes on Tarkiel. "What am I going to learn up here?" he asked anxiously, wishing he had the nerve to turn around and go down again. How could he live here and learn here when he felt so suspended in space, so lost in the sky?

"You will receive the most important part of your education upon which all else depends," Tarkiel told him. "While you are on this level you will be taught to read, to write and to reason. Those abilities will give you access to the knowledge of previous generations which is contained in the Great Library. Armed with knowledge, one can rule the world. Knowledge is the ultimate power!" Tarkiel raised one fist and brandished it like a weapon, an incongruous gesture on the part of so small a man.

Caeled laughed before he could stop himself.

"You doubt me," Tarkiel snapped. "Tell me, who is the greater: the warrior or the scholar?"

"The warrior," replied the boy quickly.

"And yet without knowledge from the past, which is carried into the present by the scholar, the warrior is useless."

Caeled shook his head. "I don't understand."

"If his armorers have not been trained in the ancient skills of metal working and leather tanning, a warrior will be defenseless. He will have neither arms nor armor. Without knowledge of successful tactics and stratagems used by great warriors of the past, he will stand no chance against his enemies. And if farmers know nothing of raising crops or husbandry, they will not be able to produce the food that will keep the warrior strong and enable him to win."

Caeled's forehead crinkled into a frown as he followed the man's reasoning. "I think I understand," he said.

"In order for this society to survive and grow," Tarkiel went on, coming back down to sit beside the boy, "all important knowledge must be recorded and passed on. But who is to say which things are important, or will be necessary to someone in the future? No one knows, so we gather and guard all the accumulated wisdom of the past, even the most seemingly insignificant detail. How many eyes does an ant have? From which direction did the wind blow on a given day five hundred cycles ago? That information is somewhere in the Great Library of Baddalaur, Caeled.

"But the twins are attempting to render all our work useless. They want to reduce this world to chaos."

"Why? Why would anyone want to do such a thing?"

"It is their nature," Tarkiel said simply.

The cave was situated just inside the rim of the volcano, the highest point in Baddalaur. It was long and narrow, cool to the point of chill in its deeply shadowed interior, and innocent of any furniture. A low shallow slab which had been cut into the wall close to the floor took the place of a bed, while a series of grooves in the rockface served as shelves and held a supply of foodstuffs. A single coarse blanket was neatly folded on the bed; a cask below the shelves contained fresh water.

The cave was at the end of the narrow walkway, and accessible through a single low door carved to represent the half-open beak of a bird.

Two perfectly circular windows, the bird's eyes, looked out toward the snow-capped mountains in the distance.

Tarkiel left Caeled in the cave and began the long walk down by himself. When he was sure the Recoverer had gone, the boy sank onto the cave floor and massaged his aching leg muscles with his remaining hand. He hoped Tarkiel's legs ached too.

They had passed many empty caves on the way up

here; he was sure Tarkiel had deliberately brought him to the coldest, loneliest one in an effort to make him feel helpless. What Tarkiel did not fully appreciate was that Caeled had spent his life travelling from one slum to another, surviving rat-infested ghettos where death and disease were rampant. He and his mother had even spent two cycles in the City of the Dead beyond Barrow. The ancient cemetery housed a huge population of the poorest of the poor, who fought for possession of the crypts with dog-rats, carrion-spiders, serpents, and, it was rumored, some of the Sith, the blood drinkers. A sweltering sinkhole during the day, the necropolis became a place of terror during the hours of darkness.

Even the room they had occupied in Ward Point had been little better, a cramped cell in a lice-infested tenement with neighbors who would slit their throats for the food in their mouths.

So this cave, cool and clean, the air sweet and invigorating, bigger than any room he had ever shared with his mother and her succession of lovers, was luxury.

Caeled lifted his stump and examined it. Maseriel had said something about the brothers making him a hand. What could that mean — a hook, a claw? A spike?

He was unfamiliar with the term, yet instinctively he felt the irony of his situation. It was only because he had lost his hand that he was in Baddalaur, and he lost his hand because he fled Ward Point, and he fled Ward Point because of the *thing* that had destroyed his mother.

His mother. Myriam. He felt a surge of guilt; he had not thought of her for days. Now his throat burned and tears filled his eyes as he recalled her face. His mother had died, and as a result he was in Baddalaur to receive an education.

An education! Caeled nam Myriam, who was nothing, the son of a nobody, would have a finer education than the richest man in Ward Point. Out of his mother's death was born a new life for him.

He laughed, a bitter sound more like a strangled sob that echoed around the stone walls.

The boy went to the mouth of the cave and gazed out at the orange disc of Nusas, sinking toward the distant mountains. Spots of color danced before his eyes, reminding him of the colored lights that had danced in the heart of the Void.

Caeled narrowed his eyes. Had there been anyone to see, he would have looked suddenly mature, his face set in hard lines. *Tarkiel said all knowledge was contained in the Great Library. Surely that would include knowledge of the Voids.*

As he lit his mother's makeshift funeral pyre he had promised her that she would be avenged. Someday. Somehow. A childish vow, at the time it had amounted to nothing more than words whispered to comfort himself amid the crackle of the flames.

But now . . . his mother's death had brought him a new life. And that life would contain knowledge of the Voids.

Knowledge *was* power.

Power to destroy the Voids!

CHAPTER TWENTY-ONE

He could see the stars through the round windows, sharp as splinters of ice against the night sky. The stars had always fascinated him. He knew most of their names and the legends associated with them, but he had never seen them so clearly before. They looked close enough to touch. Close enough to walk into, like walking into a forest of lights.

Caeled swung his legs off the bed and wrapped the blanket around his shoulders. A few steps took him to the mouth of his cave. He hesitated in the doorway, however, reluctant to venture out onto the narrow balcony in case he lost his footing and tumbled to the courtyard below.

The Central Courtyard and the lower portion of the hollow mountain were illuminated by a number of torches in iron holders affixed to the stone. Their flames outlined the mouths of the caves, throwing the carving into stark relief so that grotesque and improbable creatures appeared to be crouching within the volcano, vibrating with fiery life. Further up, however, there were fewer torches. The last of these — a solitary flickering flame — was well below the level where Caeled stood. Its warmth and light might as well have been as distant as the stars.

The boy shivered and looked away from the torches. It was a trick he had learned while still very young: If he did not look at food, he would not feel as hungry. If he turned away from fire, he would not be aware of the cold.

Raising his head, he gazed at the stars instead.

The Lady Lussa was missing tonight, leaving the sky ablaze with stellar patterns without the distraction of moonlight. Almost directly overhead the Horned Hunter pursued the Fawn, while below them the Hooded Scorpion raised its barbed tail over the coiling Viper. The Swans were just coming into sight at the rim of the volcano, though the Barge they hauled was still below the horizon.

Caeled recognized the broad swath of the Salt, a great spill of stars bright enough to obscure nearby celestial bodies. But his favorite performers in the night sky were the Dancing Fires, which shimmered on the northern horizon in certain seasons, or pulsed across the entire width of the heavens looking like watered silk in shades of rose and violet and emerald.

Caeled was familiar with silk. A childhood spent travelling across the Seven Nations, begging rides with merchants' caravans, sneaking around the fringes of wealth while his mother looked for ways to feed them both, had exposed him to many luxury items he could never expect to have for himself.

But when the Dancing Fires rippled across the sky their beauty was his; a beauty greater than any emperor could command. Unfortunately the Fires were not dancing tonight. Had they been, they could have made him forget the cold.

Caeled drew his blanket tighter around his shoulders. The wind had come up, sighing, whispering, moaning across the mountain tops. The boy frowned. The sounds reminded him of the noises his mother made when she was . . . *entertaining.* He had always pretended to be asleep, but in truth he used to gaze out the window above his bed at the stars then, too, seeing them through a rainbow of tears. Trying to find the distraction of beauty as he sought that same distraction tonight.

When he was too chilled to continue stargazing he

reluctantly turned to go back to his bed. But he had only half-completed the movement when he froze, alerted by something seen out of the corner of his eye. The skin on the back of his neck began itching as if an insect were crawling up his nape. He whirled to face the sky and caught another glimpse of the faintest flicker of movement, the merest disturbance in the air beyond the narrow strip of balcony.

A bird? A bat?

No, something much larger that had momentarily seemed to be directly in front of his cave . . . but that was impossible. The nearest solid place to stand was the Central Courtyard far below.

Must have been a bird, Caeled decided as he slid back onto his stony bed and pulled the blanket up to his chin. He waited for his body to generate enough heat under the thin covering to allow him to stop shivering.

No doubt Brother Tarkiel had expected he would find the bed uncomfortable, but the boy preferred cool, dry stone to wet marshland or flea-infested straw.

While he lay waiting for sleep he looked toward the nearest window in time to see the stars disappear and then reappear, as if something moved across them. He was reminded of the flickering he had glimpsed as he stood in the cave mouth.

Caeled knew the sky well; this was not a familiar phenomenon. Were such things common in the vicinity of Baddalaur? he wondered. Everything was so different here, far outside his experience.

Perhaps the education he was going to receive would explain it. Education seemed to him to be a wonderful thing, as rare and precious as the Dancing Fires. A great longing swept over him for his new life to begin, and in the dark the boy hugged himself, not for warmth or comfort this time, but in anticipation.

He was still lying thus when he fell asleep, with the faintest of smiles on his lips.

❖   ❖   ❖

"For a moment I thought he saw us," Brother Rasriel said, his voice a ghostly echo on the Aethyra.

"He almost did," Maseriel replied.

Rasriel turned his head, swivelling his neck in the fashion peculiar to owls.

When he rode the Aethyra on his own he usually assumed the form of a golden hawk, but as that bird was the Hieromonach's chosen persona, Rasriel opted for the form of a great snowy owl when they flew together. In truth, he enjoyed the sensation of gliding silent as a whisper on the outstretched wings of the night predator; the lack of sound heightened the sensation of flight.

"How could he see us?" Rasriel now wondered aloud. "We stayed well clear of the light."

Maseriel's hawk shape spiralled upward and Rasriel hurried after him, feeling a twinge of annoyance that he lacked the other's speed.

"He didn't see us," the Hieromonach called back to him. "I think he sensed us."

"A natural talent?"

"One we shall develop and train, honing it until . . . "

"Until?" Rasriel prompted, putting in an extra down-stroke so he could catch up with the soaring hawk.

"Until we unleash it."

The monks rose higher and higher on the Aethyra. From time to time they glanced down at the world below them, automatically observing the varied auras emitted by every form of life. They had long ago learned to ignore the tender colors of the living earth, lovely though they were, and concentrate on the more vibrant hues of men and beasts. But as they continued to climb these auras also faded into the distance.

Baddalaur, however, still glowed like a beacon, warm reds and gleams of bronze radiating from the intense concentration of brothers at prayer or study. The country-side surrounding the mountain was mostly dark, flecked with only random dots of colored light as humans or beasts fought, made love or died, their auras briefly flaring.

Maseriel rose ever higher and Rasriel struggled to stay with him. He was beginning to suspect the Hieromonach was doing this on purpose, a subtle form of intimidation to emphasize his own superiority in the Order. It would not be the first time.

Left to their own devices, Seekers rarely ventured this high into the Aethyra. It required an enormous expenditure of energy in addition to considerable courage; they had now entered one of the most dangerous levels, inhabited by disembodied spirits and some of the malevolent lesser gods.

"Look," Maseriel commanded, briefly assuming human form for one heartbeat in order to point with a bony finger. It was a gesture of overweening confidence, the gesture of a man who had no doubt he would become a hawk again before he could fall.

Rasriel remained an owl, knowing he had no energy to spare.

"What do you see when you look below and to the southeast?" the Hieromonach demanded of him.

"Nothing," Rasriel replied.

"Nothing?" Maseriel mimicked cruelly. "That is no answer for a Seeker! Where is the information which should be contained in your every statement?"

"I see nothing," Rasriel said quickly, "because the Aethyra is deeply shadowed . . . " He stopped. There were no shadows on the Aethyra. "There are no colors," he amended, "no spots of consciousness. No auras to be seen in the direction you indicate."

"Oh, but they are there," insisted Maseriel. "Look closer."

As the younger monk strained to see, a cluster of tiny, brightly colored sparks rose into the Aethyra but immediately vanished into a roiling cloud which absorbed them completely, extinguishing their beauty.

Maseriel groaned as if he witnessed children being slaughtered. "You are looking at Barrow," the Hieromonach told Rasriel. "Observe the dark cloud of selfishness the Duet have unleashed there, overwhelming every spark of decency. Lust and greed run riot. People behave with less sense of obligation than the lowest form of animal life. Nothing is planned, nothing is ordered. They live only for the moment, they snatch up one pleasure after another and discard them as quickly. Seize, grab, take! More, and more, and more, nothing is ever enough! Meanwhile children abuse their parents and parents abuse their children because all restraint is abandoned. How can anyone concentrate in such an atmosphere? You see for yourself how the few noble thoughts remaining are devoured and destroyed almost as soon as they appear.

"I have walked the lines of Barrow's future, and they are all the same. Consider that, Rasriel. An undisputed future. In the history of the humankind there have been less than a handful of futures beyond the ability of anyone to change them. Barrow's ultimate descent into savagery is one."

"But what about the boy?"

"The Spoken One? Not even he can prevent it. Better for him — and us — if he were to destroy Barrow altogether before the contagion can spread and engulf the world. When he has overthrown the Duet he can lead the Seekers back to their former glory, with you as their head, Rasriel.

"You must promise me this: You must swear to me that the boy will receive the best education possible. Stint on nothing, withhold nothing he might require. See that he has everything he needs . . . to remake the world."

Hawk and owl hovered far above the dark earth. Night wind sang through their feathers. Below them the world slept; the damaged, chaotic world.

"Just what does he need, brother?" Rasriel asked the Hieromonach.

"Knowledge. Courage. And the Arcana."

CHAPTER TWENTY-TWO

Scholar Nanri had come to Baddalaur as an illiterate boy of ten cycles. He thought he recalled being sold as a scivvy to the kitchens by a coarse-faced woman who might have been his mother, but as time eroded images of the past he had become uncertain whether this was an actual memory or a dream. Perhaps it was even a false history he had compiled for himself unconsciously, borrowing the idea from someone else's recounting. Not that it mattered.

Nanri had spent sixty-two full cycles in Baddalaur. He never regretted having remained there once he worked his way out of the kitchens; never dreamed about the life he might have had beyond the mountain. Baddalaur was his life. Here he had learned to speak and write twelve languages fluently, had acquired a working knowledge of another ten and had deciphered four of the Elder Scripts. A candle burned in his cell long before cockcrow, and another candle illumined his desk with its constant stack of books and papers when the rest of the College was asleep. No fact was too small for him to ferret out, no scholarly pathway too obscure for him to follow to its conclusion.

But his obsession with facts had made enemies, even among those who were supposed to be equally dedicated to the pursuit of knowledge. There had been a most unpleasant incident when he was still a young student and insulted a contemporary by daring to contradict him in class. Nanri had been correct, his fellow student wrong. But the man he embarrassed publicly never forgave him. That man had been Maseriel.

When Nanri concluded the second stage of his education and formally requested acceptance as a Seeker, his application had been refused. Maseriel, who had become Seeker before him, successfully blocked his admittance. Nanri had remained a Scholar while Maseriel went from strength to strength in the ranks of the Order, eventually becoming Hieromonach.

But through diligent effort Nanri grew to be one of the most respected men in Baddalaur in spite of the limitation imposed upon him. He never openly expressed resentment; cycle after cycle he continued to pore over his books, constantly adding to his fund of knowledge. One could ask him anything on any subject and expect an informed answer. His knowledge of the Elder Times was second only to that of Brother Daniel, the Senior Librarian.

Occasionally even Maseriel was forced to come to him with a question.

Quietly, without discussing it with anyone, Nanri had devoted the last thirty cycles to the task of discovering the whereabouts of the Arcana, the ancient symbols of power and order. When he began his studies in his youth only two of the brothers had been engaged in the task, and he had been assigned to assist them in their researches. One had died; then the other. The information they had compiled remained with Nanri.

In the last few cycles, especially since the Duet had taken control and the Seekers had lost power in Barrow and Karfondal, the hunt for the Arcana had intensified. Eventually everyone in the College was involved in the task of discovering the whereabouts of the Arcana.

Now the search had been given even greater urgency by the appearance of the boy called Caeled.

From a vantage point three levels above the Central Courtyard, Nanri had observed Armadiel's arrival with the boy. The Scholar's eyes had grown dim with time and he disdained the use of glass eyepieces, so from such a height he had been unable to make out the boy's features.

But he saw Maseriel's reaction. It was obvious the Hieromonach desperately wanted this to be the Spoken One.

With the ending of Los-Lorcan's despotic reign, the Hieromonach had lost his position as spiritual adviser to the royal court and with it the last vestiges of his personal influence beyond the walls of Baddalaur. But Maseriel was ambitious, and determined that the Order he headed would once again be the preeminent power in the land.

The Hieromonach was realist enough to know that he could not live forever. But he could mold those who survived him so they would fulfill his ambitions. To strengthen his own prestige, Maseriel wanted the College records to show that the Spoken One had been discovered during his Hieromonachy. Even entombed he would not be forgotten. If the prophecies were fulfilled, the name of Maseriel would forever be linked in glory with that of the Spoken One.

Typical, thought Nanri. Typical.

Sitting in the mouth of his cave, the old Scholar watched the flickering Aethyra shapes of Maseriel and Rasriel distort the stars. Tilting his head back, Nanri allowed his fading eyes to follow their progress upward along paths he could never take.

Seekers could explore the Aethyra. Scholars must content themselves with exploring the written word.

Nanri was unaware of the sadness in his sigh. Had anyone asked, which no one did, he would have said that he was content.

He now asked himself a question: *Was* the boy the Spoken One?

The Prophecies of Ekezial, Maliel and Effelial had each spoken of a one-handed individual who was marked for death, but represented an extraordinary opportunity for mankind. Bardal, in his Letters, wrote that he had seen the future grasped in the silver hand of a cripple.

There was now talk of preparing a silver hand for the boy.

But was this a prophecy fulfilling itself, or Maseriel making certain the prophecy was fulfilled?

Meanwhile all the monks of Baddalaur, no matter what their rank, were frantically searching for clues to the location of the Arcana.

Nanri took some small amusement from the frenzied activity. He watched without comment as they went over ground he had abandoned cycles ago, carrying their researches down blind alleys to dead ends. The body of folklore surrounding the Arcana was immense and contradictory, and a combination of extraordinary scholarship, intuition, and a certain amount of blind luck was involved in researching such documents successfully.

But no matter how hard the current searchers tried, they would never unravel the mystery . . . because Nanri had removed all clues five cycles earlier, when he had discovered the whereabouts of the Arcana.

CHAPTER TWENTY-THREE

Pressing himself against his sister's back, Lares wrapped his arms around her and peered over her shoulder. Her skin was soft to the touch, but the muscles beneath were, like his own, firm and strong. Holding her was like holding himself, only better. The heat of her body burned through the silk of the robe he wore.

"I have something very interesting to show you, my brother," Sarel murmured, gesturing toward the pit in front of them. "A present for you."

"You have, ah, perfected the process?" Lares enquired, nuzzling his chin into her shoulder. His voice was strangely distorted by the metal with which the walls of the chamber, and the pit in its center, were lined.

"Perfected it and more," she replied. "While you create huge Voids of absolute destruction, I prefer the more intimate touch." Though Lares could not see her sudden smile he felt it, knowing her body as intimately as his own.

Sarel leaned forward to get a better look at the naked blond man waiting below in the pit.

She gazed at him for a few moments, then closed her eyes in concentration. Lares could feel her body gather itself into a hard knot of focussed will; the vibrations ran from her flesh into his, thrilling him with their raw power.

The blond man was quiet now, though when he was first brought to Barrow's infamous dungeons he had screamed his throat raw.

The structure was ancient, a meandering maze of

chambers and tunnels that honeycombed the earth beneath the city. Some of the chambers were lined with silvery Old Metal as highly polished as a mirror; others were walled with enormous stones too massive for any known technique to have cut and placed so precisely. Nitre formed repellent stains on the stone, glittering with an eerie life of its own in certain lights.

Some historians claimed the dungeons predated Barrow itself, perhaps being all that remained of an earlier city on the site, one of the lost civilizations of Elder Times. Legends abounded but no one cared to investigate the bowels of Barrow too thoroughly. Even the privileged and protected Duetist priests found excuses not to go into the depths.

What was known for certain was that once someone disappeared into one of the metal chambers, that person was never seen again.

In the beginning the blond man had struggled wildly, futilely, out of his mind with terror. When his panic wore off it left him exhausted. Now he simply waited. There was nothing else he could do, the pit was too deep to leap out of, the walls too smooth to climb. He waited like an animal in its pen at the slaughterhouse, with his head hanging.

"He seems vaguely familiar," Lares remarked, peering down at him over his sister's shoulder.

"He served us wine on several occasions."

"Now I remember! He splashed wine onto your gown three nights ago. Clumsy."

"It was my favorite gown," Sarel pouted. "I had it designed just to please you. Then that barbarian ruined it the first time I wore it, before you had even had an opportunity to appreciate it properly.

"I intended to have him simply put to death as a warning to the other servants, but when I came down to observe the execution, it seemed a pity to waste so fine a body. Strong young men are not that easy to find." She gave a delicate sigh, as of one vexed with some inconsequential trivia.

She stepped forward to the very brink of the pit, followed by Lares, who clung to her like a cape across her back. The shadow of their joined bodies fell across the man below.

He had been standing slumped, seeming almost unaware of his surroundings, but now he raised his head. Lares could see the sunken hollows around his eyes and the terrified pallor of his cheeks. His cracked lips parted and his mouth worked as if he was trying to say something, but no words came.

Sarel spoke instead. "Your punishment is at an end, Asten," she said softly.

Lares had heard that tone, which sounded so gentle, before, and was not deceived. But the man in the pit looked up with a terrible hope on his face.

He bowed, the metal walls of the pit reflecting a distorted parody of courtly manners. "My lady, you are generous indeed," the prisoner croaked.

Instead of replying to him, Sarel turned her head to address her brother. "Previously it was necessary to be in physical contact with my subject," she told Lares. "Now, however . . . " Her body tightened again with that intense concentration of will, and she fixed narrowed violet eyes on the form of the man in the pit.

Asten stared up at her, hope draining from his face like a candle sputtering out. His broad shoulders hunched as if he expected a blow. "My lady? Of your mercy. I have a wife . . . three young children . . . "

"The lower classes breed like rats, don't they, brother?" Sarel commented in a voice heavy with distaste.

Lares felt her grow even more rigid in his arms.

Abruptly, all expression vanished from Asten's eyes. His face grew blank, masklike. His posture stiffened.

"What have you done to him?" Lares asked his sister, intrigued. He knew she was controlling the man by force of will, but surely his twin would not have distracted him from his own researches for such a simple trick. There must be more.

Sarel produced a thin-bladed knife and tossed it casually into the pit. Then she slipped out of her brother's arms and crouched down at the edge of the pit, locking eyes with the prisoner.

"Plunge the knife into your belly," she commanded.

Lares watched in fascination.

The young man lifted the knife from the slimy metal floor, reversed it, and without hesitation drove it into his stomach. He grunted with the effort of forcing the blade through the powerful webbing of muscle.

"Tear your flesh open," instructed Sarel's dispassionate voice.

With a savage jerk, the man called Asten wrenched the knife to the left and then back to the right. His face was expressionless, but blood spurted across the pit.

"Drive the knife into your left arm now."

Asten pulled the knife out of his stomach and stabbed it deeply into the muscle of his left arm.

"Now back into your belly, make that wound deeper."

Asten obeyed.

"Remarkable!" Lares exclaimed. "He's disemboweling himself, yet doesn't seem to feel a thing."

"Can you guess how I did it?"

"Introduced a Void into the brain and destroyed the pain centers?"

Sarel laughed delightedly. "Very good, brother! I have indeed. With my miniature Void I've destroyed all the higher functions. Of course, the technique needs a little further refinement." She frowned as Asten's legs began to tremble from loss of blood. "He looks human, but I have taken away everything that makes him human. Now he is less than a beast."

"A beast which feels no pain," Lares pointed out.

"A beast who will obey your every command," said Sarel.

In the pit, Asten fell into a pool of his own blood and convulsed in his death throes.

"Think of the possibilities, brother . . . I told you this was a present for you. Is he not a useful toy?"

Lares was grinning as he threw his arms around his sister and pulled her hard against him. "An army of warriors who feel no pain!"

"Unstoppable," she murmured.

"Invincible!" he exulted.

CHAPTER TWENTY-FOUR

"I am Brother Daniel," the stout, sweating man in the crimson robe announced, "the Senior Librarian." He tented his fingers and rested his elbows on the enormous desk that separated him from the boy who stood fidgeting before him. "Brother Maseriel tells me you will be joining us."

The boy nodded silently, shifting from one foot to the other.

"There are certain things you must know," Brother Daniel said, then interrupted himself to fumble in one of the full sleeves of his robe. He extracted a limp linen handkerchief and mopped his brow. "Once you begin your training here, you will be bound by our rules. Indeed, the first lessons you will learn are the rules. Failure to abide by even the least of them will be punished immediately. All punishments are severe, but there are some transgressions which merit death, so be scrupulous about obedience. Never break any law of the Order, for any reason whatsoever."

Daniel wiped his face again, then tucked the handkerchief back in his sleeve. After leaning forward to take a hard look at Caeled, he gestured toward a highbacked chair opposite his desk. "Sit," he commanded.

Caeled sank gratefully into the chair. He had been in Baddalaur only six days and while he was healing fast, he still felt weak. As he stood before the Librarian, he had become aware of a ringing in his ears and the muscles in his legs had begun to tremble.

The Senior Librarian got up from behind the desk to proffer a tumbler of water, then waited while the boy drank.

"You will be my student," he continued, making a conscious effort to soften his tone. The child was obviously still far from well. "However, some of the other brothers who have specialized knowledge will also instruct you. Have you any questions?"

Caeled licked his lips, tasting the residue of the water. It had a strange metallic taste he was not sure he liked. "Am I your only student?"

"Alas, you are." The big man stretched his arms wide, as if to encompass the circular chamber. "Once this room would have contained a hundred students in addition to the members of the Order reading or studying here. There was a time when we were actually turning young men away. We could pick and choose from among the best, and almost every morning there was a line at the gates seeking admission."

"Do you not take women?" Caeled wondered. "I have seen none here, but surely . . . "

"Women who are inclined to the monastic life take the Vows of Lussa or follow the Silent Path," Daniel answered brusquely, making it obvious the subject held little interest for him. "Their disciplines are somewhat similar to ours, but they have their own mysteries."

"What will I have to do here?" the boy asked.

"Do? Here you will learn. You will ask questions. Always question. Mankind advances through questioning. And in turn I will question you. I may occasionally punish you if your answers are incorrect, and I shall certainly punish you if your replies are impertinent. You will accept your punishment in the knowledge that it is instructive. In time we will discover your speciality, that particular branch of learning which best utilizes your talents, and we can begin to concentrate your efforts in that direction. Do not despair if your speciality does not manifest itself early, or if you are attracted to divergent interests. Many brothers master two or more courses of study. I, of course, have a working knowledge of them all," he added with a slight smile.

"When do we begin?" Caeled asked.

"We already have."

The library was enormous, rising ten floors up into the walls of the extinct volcano. Caeled had never imagined there could be so many books in the world. The more modern works were on the shelves on the lower floors, Brother Daniel explained, while the older books, some of which were written on leather or wood or thin sheets of metal, were kept on the higher shelves. On the topmost floors were texts from the Elder Times which had so far proved indecipherable.

As Caeled stood in the middle of the ground floor and looked up, the shelves of the higher levels vanished in shadow. It was impossible to tell the exact size of the tremendous room, or guess at the number of books it might contain, even if he had a good knowledge of numbers. But like most of the poor, Caeled's ability to count was limited only to enumerating necessities. He could count his fingers, or eggs, or fruit. He had never thought that someday he might count books.

The library was filled with Seekers and Scholars. Numerous small alcoves encircling the central area were occupied by brothers examining books in relative privacy, with leather curtains drawn. Enormous tables in the center of the room were surrounded by still more members of the Order poring over charts and maps, or leafing through various journals and making copious notes. The brothers jostled one another in their search for information, and the smell of their closely packed bodies filled the warm room, large though it was.

The monks observed the rule of silence in the library, or at most, whispered. Yet the entire facility seemed to vibrate with suppressed sound. Caeled found himself straining to catch the occasional word, as if a hum of knowledge had soaked into the walls and could somehow be recaptured if one just listened hard enough.

The only distinct sounds, however, were the shuffling of slippers on the stone floor, the whisper of pages turning, and the scratching of bone pens or bamboo quills on sheets of parchment or kenaf.

"You are standing in the heart of the Great Library of Baddalaur," Brother Daniel whispered to Caeled with proprietary pride, "which began with Bardal's personal trove of twelve books. From that humble beginning the library has grown until we now have a collection that runs into hundreds of thousands of volumes. Some say the entire knowledge of the world is contained in this building — and I like to think it is true. If a man were physically able to read every one of these books and absorb their information, he would surely become a god."

"Has anyone ever read all of them?" Caeled wondered aloud.

"It would be quite impossible, I fear. Although," Daniel added with a smile which attempted to be modest, "I myself have read very many of them, and Scholar Nanri has read even more." As a sudden thought occurred to him, the Senior Librarian put his hand on the boy's shoulder and turned Caeled around to face him. "Can *you* read?"

When the boy nodded, Brother Daniel heaved a sigh of relief. "I was afraid we might have to start at the very beginning and teach you to read and write, which would take up a great amount of valuable time."

"I can read and write my own name," Caeled claimed.

"Your name," Daniel repeated dubiously, recognizing a potential problem. In the Southlands, those unable to read and write their own names — signs of education — were refused entry to the cities. It was not uncommon for beggars to have memorized the shape of their names so they could scrawl them on kenaf and satisfy the guards at the gates. Such an accomplishment could hardly be called literacy, however.

"But what about other words?" Daniel asked. "You can read and write your own name, but do you know any other names? Spell Daniel, for example?"

The boy's eyes went wide with panic. Such beautiful eyes, Daniel noticed for the first time: dark and bright as a starry sky, framed by thick black lashes. Intelligence lurked there, buried under the anxiety.

It was a pity such a boy was disfigured, especially as other brothers had already spoken of his courage and unexpected courtesy. There seemed an innate nobility about him — surprising in one of his background — which made his terrible wound more poignant.

Caeled seized the Librarian's sleeve with his remaining hand and said quickly, "My mother taught me some of my words. I know the alphabet — the Southlands script — and I can speak three languages. I can read signs and large letters, though I've never had my hands on a book. Please don't tell Maseriel. He won't let me stay if he discovers how ignorant I am."

Daniel patted his thin shoulder comfortingly. "He won't throw you out because of that. Many have entered Baddalaur with much less education than you have. However," and his glance fell with a certain distaste on the bandaged stump at the end of the boy's arm, "speaking of having your hands on a book — there is another problem."

Caeled's eyes followed the Librarian's. "Only those complete in mind and body may become Seekers," the boy said. "I know. Brother Maseriel told me."

"It's more than that, boy. Such a handicap might limit you in a number of ways."

"It wouldn't, oh, it wouldn't, I promise!" came the instant reply. Caeled's face glowed with intensity as he strove to convince the Senior Librarian. "I can learn to do everything one-handed, I know I can. Even if I can't be a Seeker I can turn the pages in books." Caeled cast a quick, envious glance at the Scholars around the room, devouring treasures with their eyes and their minds. *Reading books!*

"Besides," he went on eagerly, "I've seen men with metal hooks or wooden claws who were able to care for themselves very well indeed, sometimes better than men with flesh and blood hands. There was a chestnut seller in one of the villages we passed through who fished the roasted nuts out of the fire with his metal hook. He could reach into the hottest flames and not get burned. You should have seen him, it was like magic. Everyone bought his chestnuts because they were piping hot.

"If I had a metal hook, or even a wooden peg, my arm would not look so . . . so bad," Caeled finished hopefully.

The Senior Librarian replied, "A metal hook, is it? That would make you happy?"

Happy. Caeled tasted the word. It had little meaning for him; happiness was not an emotion he had often experienced. But at least with a metal hook at the end of his arm he would be complete again, after a fashion.

That was all he could hope for; more than he might have expected.

He swallowed hard and gave Brother Daniel a brave smile.

Caeled lay on the stone, the smooth surface chill beneath his naked back. His eyes were closed against the glare of Nusas, the light of the sun that poured through the circular window to be reflected throughout the Healing Chapel by polished metal mirrors.

He felt no fear now. The bitter liquid Nazariel had given him was numbing his emotions and blurring his mind. The words of an obscene Corsair shanty frolicked through his head. Some sailor at some dockside had taught it to him; some sailor waiting for his mother's attentions . . . he pushed the thought away. At the time he learned the song he had not understood the words, but he was older now. As the drug coursed through him he had to bite his lips to keep himself from singing them aloud and shocking the brothers working over him.

Caeled lay as in a soft gray mist, drifting. He was only vaguely curious about what Nazariel and the others were going to do to him. It did not seem very important. Nothing was very important. There would be pain, the Healer had said, but Caeled was familiar with pain. Nazariel had assured him the results would be worth it, though exactly what those results might be he would not say in spite of Caeled's insistent questioning. But that did not seem to matter either, now.

Lights shifted and twisted behind his closed lids, swirls and splashes of gold and bronze and brilliant crimson. He sank into them, unresisting, surrendering the last of his will . . . .

Dark memories gathered like predators at the edges of his consciousness. Caeled veered away, trying to concentrate on something bright, something light . . . and the colors swooped and swirled and changed, pulsing as they had done in the heart of the Void. The familiar nausea wracked him once more and he fought a grim, desperate battle against the clouds in his mind, trying to regain some control over his thoughts and memories. He was aware of his helplessness. He was aware that the drug, in cushioning him from pain, had opened him to something worse, and he pitted all the strength he could summon against it.

He became aware of movement around him, of shadows coming between him and the light that shone down onto his closed eyelids. He tried to open his eyes but could not, the lids were as heavy as stone. From a great distance, he heard the voices of the brothers talking among themselves.

He clung to those voices. They were lifelines to lead

him away from the pit into which he had fallen.

He began trying to pick out individuals, struggling to identify them by accent or inflection.

First he recognized Nazariel and then Daniel. He knew those voices well, they were easy to identify and comforting in the darkness. And that was surely the voice of the one they called the Recoverer, Brother Tarkiel. Although they did not speak, he remembered that there were others in the room also: a big, broad-shouldered man wearing a leather apron had been waiting in the Healing Chapel when Caeled arrived, together with several Scholars — one very old and gray and bent — and two younger monks clad in green, Nazariel's assistants.

"Is all in readiness?"

With a start, Caeled recognized Maseriel's croaking voice coming from the other side of the room. In the silence that followed he heard the Hieromonach's staff tapping its way across the chamber. Caeled was abruptly aware of the sour odor he associated with sick old men. He had run messages for an elderly shoemaker who lived beside them in Ward Point; that man had exuded a similar odor not long before he died.

"The boy looks fit enough," commented Maseriel.

"He is young and his will is strong," Nazariel replied. "He passionately desires to be well, so we can trust that his mind will take an active part in mending the body."

"Is he strong enough to undergo this procedure?"

"I would prefer to leave it for a little while, but the timing is critical. Already his body has begun to make allowances for the loss of his hand. The flesh is healing fast. If we don't do it now, it would mean opening the wound again."

The meaning of the words slowly penetrated Caeled's mind. They were talking about doing something to him, something that must be important . . . what?

The Hieromonach enquired, "Has Brother Casriel brought the artifact?"

Artifact? Caeled puzzled over the word. It had no meaning for him.

"I have." The voice was deep and powerful. Instinctively Caeled knew it belonged to the Seeker wearing the leather apron.

"Will it work?" Maseriel demanded to know. "Can you guarantee success?"

"I cannot give such a guarantee, brother, much as I would like to. I have worked with Brother Daniel and Scholar Nanri, following the ancient instructions to the smallest detail. But some of the techniques have not been used for many generations and some of the skills are lost to us, so I was forced to improvise."

"Am I hearing the self-serving excuses of a man anticipating failure?" Maseriel enquired. His voice had a hard edge, sharp and threatening as a knife blade.

The Senior Healer tried to placate him. "It is an untried technique, but we must accept that. Brother Casriel and a team of craftsmen have worked in shifts night and day to prepare the artifact. They have followed the old texts to the letter, and where the information has been insufficient they have made decisions based upon their skill and knowledge, which are without equal as you know. If this does not work they cannot be held culpable."

"Then the fault will be yours?" Maseriel snapped.

"I'm not saying that," the Healer replied coolly. "If it does not work, we will try something else."

Caeled forced his eyes open. Light blinded him.

Immediately someone bent over him and raised his head. Another poured a trickle of bitter liquid between his lips. He swallowed, choked, swallowed again.

"Lie back," said a voice.

He did not want to obey, did not want to be flung back into that darkness where the Void waited for him. But the drug was too strong to fight. It soaked into the cells of his body, melting their defenses. Colors and shapes swirled through his brain once more and a wild, strange music swelled. He found himself trying to hum along with it. Somehow the music was preventing the colors from disintegrating into the Void he feared . . .

He was dimly aware of pressure on his left arm, the arm being lifted, cloth tearing as the bandages were cut away. Nerves which had led to his severed hand twitched in protest.

The music grew louder. He kept humming, trying to remember the less obscene verses of the Corsair shanty so he could sing them for the brothers . . . the brothers who were going to make everything all right . . . his new family . . . the monks of Baddalaur . . .

Metal clinked.

Caeled smelled something burning . . . like old leather . . . like scorching meat.

And then the pain!

CHAPTER TWENTY-FIVE

Pain.

The pain vanished like a bubble bursting and Caeled found he was looking down from above at a large and well-lit chamber.

It took him a few moments to make sense of the scene below. A man in a green robe and several Seekers wearing leather aprons were working over something on a stone slab, while more Seekers and a red-robed Scholar watched from the side. As the men shifted positions, the naked body of a boy was revealed lying on the slab. His handless left arm was a cylinder of blackened skin and purple bruises.

With a shock of recognition, Caeled realized he was looking down at himself.

He was dreaming.

Nazariel the Healer was bending over the bloody stump of his arm, dexterously employing a flensing knife to remove the skin. Caeled saw the ivory gleam of bare bone.

He was dreaming.

This had to be a dream. He was dreaming about what the brothers were going to do to him and imagining the worst. Of course.

He turned away from the sickening sight of his ruined arm, and unthinkingly glanced at the high circular window . . . only to find himself moving toward it. His body — but it could not be his body, that was lying below on the slab — was gliding with silken ease through space.

He wanted to laugh aloud at the simplicity of it, thinking he had made a great discovery and would never forget how it was done. He hurled his thoughts forward and his incorporeal being followed until he was perched on the window rim looking out over the Central Courtyard.

Wonderful! The merest wish, and there you were.

Grinning with delight, Caeled willed himself upward into the brilliant noonday sky.

Now he was floating over the College, looking down into the maw of the extinct volcano. Seekers and Scholars moved like white and red ants across the Central Courtyard. From this height the pattern in the cold lava was clearly discernible. Caeled recognized a stylized snake attempting to swallow its own tail. In his dream he understood the symbolism. It was perfectly obvious. The snake represented . . .

Distantly, he became aware of someone screaming. A boy's voice, high and torn with agony. He tried to focus on the snake and its meaning but the scream came nearer until it seemed to resonate through his body . . . his body?

His hand hurt terribly.

In his dream he still possessed his left hand and the pain was intense. He lifted it, stared at it, flexed the fingers. An icy light bathed them with a metallic sheen.

Hoping to escape the pain Caeled soared higher, floating as a bubble floats, insubstantial — except for the hand, the cold hand that hurt so badly, that felt so strange.

Looking down, he saw the landscape spread below him like an intricate Kathan carpet. He had once stood barefoot on a Kathan carpet in a big house where his mother worked as a cleaning woman until they caught her stealing some bauble. She had told Caeled the carpet was priceless, and it felt as soft as moss beneath his calloused feet, but the edges had been frayed and mud had obscured part of the pattern.

Now when Caeled turned his eyes toward the south, he saw that the pattern of fields and trees and serpentine river was similarly blotched by a stain like rot on ripe fruit. Impelled by curiosity, Caeled drifted in that direction until he recognized the blue rim of the sea. The location of the stain must be the coastal city of Barrow.

The boy frowned.

The discoloration did not affect the city itself but seemed to float above Barrow, forming sullen clouds around the fluted minarets of the Royal Palace. Repelled by the stain, Caeled sought to turn toward the sea instead, redirecting himself to soar over the waves and swoop down to feel the blown spume on his face.

Yet he was still being drawn toward the city!

He redoubled his efforts to fly as he chose. A few moments before it had been easy. Now, no matter how hard he tried, the city loomed inexorably closer. He was helpless to control his fate.

This was turning into the sort of dream that had tormented his childhood, a repetitive dream in which he attempted again and again to pass beyond a certain door. But no matter how often he stepped through the door, he found himself back where he started. The dream had the quality of a nightmare although nothing bad ever happened; just a sense of futility, of doom.

Even as he recalled the dream, the sky and sea and distant Barrow disappeared and were replaced by the door!

A simple arched wooden door in a stone wall, rough planks held together by stout metal rivets. Horrifyingly familiar. There was a metal grill in the door and a metal loop set into the wood. The boy knew that door as surely as he knew his own face. He would walk up to it, open it and step through . . . and find himself still facing the same door.

Unable to stop himself, Caeled opened the door.

He found himself in a chamber flooded with opalescent light. The walls were polished stone as white as porcelain, trapping some of the light within their depths.

On a low table inlaid with onyx and pearl, decanters held jewel-like wines, while other tables offered baskets of fruit and platters heaped with cheeses and sweetmeats. A tiny apelike creature with a silver chain around its neck sat in a corner, unself-consciously picking through its fur for fleas.

A naked couple was locked in love on a bed of silken sheets. One was male, the other female, though the difference in gender was not immediately apparent. They were identical; as they rolled and twisted together, amber hair coiling around their bodies, Caeled found it impossible to distinguish one from the other.

Curiosity took him closer to the bed. He was not floating now but walking barefoot, and his feet slipped on polished flagstones slick with blood.

He could smell the thick hot smell of gore, like the odor emanating from a slaughterhouse on a summer's day.

A bloody arm protruded from under the bed on which the twins lay. Twins. Duet.

He recognized them now.

. . . and realized they were daubed with blood. It was smeared across their upper bodies and faces and encrusted around their mouths . . . as if they had drunk . . .

They were looking at him.

Eyes wide with alarm, they were disentangling, rolling off the bed. Standing up. Coming toward him. Slipping on the stones, falling . . . rising again, fully clothed in shining armor, with shimmering swords in their hands. Their mouths opened and he knew they were speaking to him, they were saying things of great importance.

Yet he could not hear a word.

Pain.

The pain in his hand cancelled out all other thought. He looked down to find an enormous Madra Allta was chewing on his hand, tearing away the flesh and muscle to reveal gleaming bone beneath.

Caeled opened his mouth to scream, but he had no

breath left. The twins were almost upon him, swords raised. When the woman slashed at him he raised his left hand instinctively. Metal struck metal. Sparks exploded. With a loud cry, the woman staggered backwards.

Agony burned across Caeled's shoulders as razor-sharp talons sank into his shoulders. He was lifted clear just as the man swung at him with a huge two-handed sword. Twisting to look up and see what had so painfully saved him, Caeled found himself in the grip of a giant golden hawk, bigger than an eagle, more terrifying than any creature of nightmare had ever been before.

Below him the twins were dissolving into mist, into white smoke, into a pair of identical white crows, each almost as large as the hawk. The crows leaped into the sky in pursuit of the hawk, but when Caeled felt the thunder of the hawk's wings shatter the air he realized the crows could not catch them. He did not know whether to be glad or sorry, for the monster hawk could be taking him to an even worse fate.

This had ceased to be a dream. He knew one did not always recognize dreams while they were happening, but Caeled had the firm conviction that this was hideous reality.

He did not dare struggle for fear the bird might drop him. When he tried to get a better look at the hawk it cocked its head so that he could see one eye.

One blind white eye.

Carrying the helpless boy in its claws, the golden hawk sped through the Aethyra toward Baddalaur. When they were directly over the volcano, with the Central Court-yard far, far below, the great bird opened its talons.

Caeled fell and fell and fell, sickeningly, down through space and walls, down through time and memories and hope and horror. Back into the body of the boy on the slab.

Caeled awoke screaming. Blood was pouring from the puncture marks on his shoulders.

CHAPTER TWENTY-SIX

The crows soared into the Aethyra, indifferent to the patchwork landscape below. It was only earth, with earthly limitations.

The skies were different. The skies were interpenetrated by the Aethyra. A watcher on the ground would have observed only a peculiar shimmer, the explicable phenomenon known as heat waves disturbing the atmosphere. Human eyes would never have detected the albino crows who rode those waves.

Calling to one another as they flew, the twin predators searched in vain for the fleeing shape of a golden hawk. Swift as they were, the hawk was swifter.

At last, with great reluctance, the white crows spiralled back through the Aethyra toward the ugly stain that identified Barrow. They were as indifferent to the stain as to the earth; the byproduct of their actions did not matter to them.

As they dove toward the royal palace the foremost crow began to change shape, flickering into a vaguely human form, an amalgam of white feathers and pink flesh. Sarel's shocked voice exclaimed, "What *was* that?"

"I'm not sure," replied her brother, following her toward the open window of their tower. Before entering he used the residue of Aethyra energy to transform himself into his latest personal art form, a man-shaped creature of crystal and brass.

For once Sarel paid no attention. Usually she gave him

the applause he sought, but she was too distracted now.

"Whatever it was, it was powerful enough to find a way in here and watch us," she said in an aggrieved voice. "I thought you said our tower was impregnable."

"I'm as surprised as you are. Priests of the Duet consider it an honor to stand guard in the private corridors, and the lower floors are held by the palace guards. I have strewn the Aethyra with traps and mazes. I would not have believed anything could get through to us."

"There were two of them, Lares. Two . . . things. One had the spirit form of a youth, and another appeared as a bird. They are obviously creatures who understand the potency of the Aethyra and know how to use it. I demand an explanation!" Sarel exclaimed vehemently as she finished regaining her human form. A few white feathers still clung to her small breasts and flat belly.

"I thought your sword struck one of them," Lares commented as he handed her a robe. Portions of his crystal skin were flooding with color, blood red, muscle pink.

Sarel wrapped her naked body, still damp from their recent exertions, in yellow silk, then flung out one arm in a flowing sleeve. In her hand a flaming sword material-ized. The fire hissed and crackled, yet gave off no heat.

She gazed at the weapon, bemused. "The youth blocked my blow with his hand, Lares. With his hand! The shock of it knocked me backward." She frowned; the sword faded.

Lares sat down on the edge of their bed, carefully avoiding the stiffening blood on the sheets. "A threat to us, then," he surmised.

"I agree. Anyone that powerful is a threat. We must know more about them."

"Could we track their wake through the Aethyra?"

"You saw how easily they escaped us. The hawk figure had carried the boy into the upper reaches of the Aethyra almost before we completed our own change. Did you see which direction they took, Lares?"

He shook his head. "It all happened so fast. I have an impression that they fled north and east, though."

Sarel drew in her breath with a hiss. "North and east? Toward *Baddalaur*?"

"Baddalaur," Lares repeated huskily. "Seekers? But surely not. The brothers haven't the spine to defy us."

Chilled by unfamiliar fear, Sarel put her hand on her brother's arm and squeezed. She needed the touch of flesh that was her flesh; she needed reassurance. But when her cold fingers closed on cold crystal she shuddered. "I've told you before, brother: Destroy these cursed priests."

"You're right, my sister. But if what we just saw was a demonstration of their power, we must not move against them yet, we are not prepared. Fortunately, however, you with your clever experiments have given us the very weapon we are going to need." Putting his hand over hers, Lares attempted to give Sarel an affectionate squeeze, then realized he could not feel her skin. At once he frowned, concentrating; crystal melted into flesh.

When the transformation was complete, Lares put both arms around his sister, his other self. "We will let the Breeder grow us an army," he murmured, his lips against her hair. "Then you can work your special skills and bind them to our will. When the time is right, we will send a huge Void deep into the heart of Baddalaur . . . and our new army will cut its teeth on the Order as they flee!"

CHAPTER TWENTY-SEVEN

Caeled awoke to a feeling of some great weight pressing on the left side of his body. It was as if his arm, shoulder and chest had a massive boulder atop them. Yet there was no pain.

He knew at once where he was. He lay on a stone slab in Baddalaur's Healing Chapel, surrounded by the rich, thick odor of melted tallow.

When he opened his eyes at first everything was hazy, but his vision soon cleared. The usual flood of sunlight in the Chapel had been replaced by the soft glow of numerous candles. It was night, then. A glance upward at the window confirmed this with a view of stars that just might have been reflected candle flames on the glass.

The boy breathed deeply. The air was chill and sweet, but he winced as his lungs filled because it made his chest ache.

"How do you feel?" Nazariel bent over him, wearing an expression of professional concern leavened with genuine fondness.

When Caeled tried to speak his tongue was swollen and his mouth too dry. The Senior Healer moved away, reappearing moments later with a flask. Placing an arm beneath Caeled's head, he eased him into a sitting position and pressed the flask to his lips. The drink was blood warm, herb-scented, and the boy drank gratefully. When he could manage a whisper he croaked, "My ears are ringing."

"That's from the residue of drugs in your system; it's nothing to be concerned about. Here, take another drink and then you can lie back and rest." When Caeled sank back and closed his eyes, Nazariel perched one hip on the edge of the slab beside him. "I think you're strong enough," the man said, "to learn what's been happening to you. To begin with, you have been asleep for four days and four nights."

Caeled's eyes flew open in surprise and the man smiled reassuringly. "Sleep is the greatest ally of the Healer," he explained. "In that time your body has done most of my work for me."

Caeled's lips moved. Nazariel leaned forward, putting his ear almost over them to save the boy effort. Then his smile widened to a grin.

"What have we done? Look!" he said. He gently lifted Caeled's left arm and held it up in the wavering candlelight. "We've given you a hand."

The boy's eyes were huge and dark, blank with incomprehension.

Nazariel promptly supplied a small square lamp fueled with fragrant oil. When he slid aside the metal disc that shielded the flame, an outpouring of yellow light made Caeled blink. The Healer adjusted polished mirrors inside the lamp to direct a beam of concentrated light onto the boy's arm.

Caeled's eyes followed the beam, expecting to see a hook or metal claw.

Instead he found himself staring at a perfect hand of gleaming silver.

When the boy gasped, Nazariel's grin grew even wider. He was thoroughly enjoying the moment.

Wonderingly, Caeled raised his arm until he was holding in front of his face a fully articulated metal hand that replicated flesh and blood in extraordinary detail. The fingers were long and slender, with oval nails; when he rotated the hand on his wrist he discovered a palm creased with lines like those the wise women read.

He rotated the wrist again, suddenly aware of the wonder of its jointing. There was a little knob on the outside like the knob of bone that had been there . . . before. And his knuckles were wrinkled, just as he remembered. And there were tendons clearly visible in the back of the hand, as well as subtle wormlike veins.

All of it silver as finely wrought as a queen's jewels.

Caeled imagined the hand closing — and thought he saw the fingers curling into a fist.

He gasped again.

Nazariel was watching him intently.

The boy dug his heels in and pushed himself up into a sitting position. Bent double, the metal hand resting in the puddle of light, he concentrated on moving his fingers individually.

Nothing happened.

He threw a panicked look at Nazariel, who simply smiled and kept watching without offering help or advice.

Caeled began to doubt that the hand had made a fist at all.

His imagination had tricked him, surely. This was nothing more than a piece of metal; cunningly wrought metal, but no real substitute for flesh and blood.

Still, it was better than anything he had hoped for.

In his excitement he forgot about the ringing in his ears and the lingering discomfort in his shoulder and chest. They were nothing compared to the miracle of having a hand again — and such a hand! "Will I be able to use it?" he asked Nazariel eagerly. "Even better than a hook, maybe?"

The Healer's eyes twinkled. "That's up to you. But I must say, those of us who worked so hard to create it for you expect great things. It looks like silver, but the silver is alloyed with other metals to make it incredibly strong, so it should be able to perform many functions for you."

Lower lip caught between his teeth, Caeled studied his

new appendage, trying to understand how it worked and why.

The metal hand seemed to be set directly into the bone of his wrist. A cuff of some soft material he did not recognize was fitted at the end of his forearm, like a brace, above the point where metal fused with flesh, and above this was a broad band of leather to give added strength and support. But the hand did not look weak. On the contrary, as it glittered in the lamplight it looked extremely strong, surpassing anything of flesh and bone.

Suddenly the fingers twitched as if they were alive. This time it was no trick of the imagination.

With a growing sense of awe, Caeled studied them. On close inspection he saw they were jointed at each digit by some tiny hinge mechanism concealed within the wrinkles that mimicked flesh. When he placed his right hand beside the left, he discovered that the new hand was slightly larger, though otherwise it might have been a mirror image.

Watching him, Nazariel affirmed, "It is larger, but that's because you're still growing. There was no purpose to be served in giving you the hand of a child when you won't be one much longer, so we estimated the size your hand should be in adulthood and made this one accordingly."

Caeled licked dry lips. "It moves. Like a real hand. Is it magic or am I dreaming?"

The Healer fumbled through his clothing and produced a metal coin. Wordlessly, he flipped it toward Caeled's left hand. The boy snapped it out of the air without thinking, then gaped at the metal fingers that now clutched the coin.

This time Nazariel laughed aloud. "You learn very fast indeed, boy; even faster than I'd hoped. That hand is part of you now, it will do exactly what you will. Your mind sends it messages and it obeys, if you can call that magic. It is the magic of flesh and blood, modified by following the instructions handed down from ancient times.

"Forget that your hand is metal. Start thinking of it, simply, as your hand. In fact, it will be easier if you do not think of it at all, just use it. You are whole again."

Caeled opened the silver hand. It was easy; he thought the thought and the fingers followed. There was no pain, no sensation at all. Merely thought and response.

Whatever Nazariel might say, it *seemed* like magic.

Within the palm of Caeled's new hand lay a bright metal coin. For a long time he stared at it, then he slowly closed and opened the fingers over it as if he were watching the greatest miracle in the world.

The silhouetted heads of the twins on the coin were magnified by his tears.

CHAPTER TWENTY-EIGHT

Lashed by stinging sleet, the woman threw back her head one more time to scream her agony of flesh and spirit.

In their huts the Snowscalds huddled beside their fires and listened to the terrible keening as they had done on so many nights before. The voice was stronger than the storm, and more chilling. None who heard it ventured out; they knew there was nothing they could do to help their sister.

With Gwynne, they had watched the creeping disease as it crawled across her body, and they had shared her horror as her flesh continued to harden to a stonelike consistency, then cracked and fissured like weatherworn rock. Now only the upper portion of her face and the tips of her fingers remained recognizable as flesh and blood.

At first the Snowscalds had tried to help by smearing her with salves and plastering her with poultices. None of it did any good. While her flesh was in a state of flux, the slightest touch hurt unbearably. As the skin hardened, it gradually became impervious, but until the final petrification, she suffered. She could not bear the weight of clothing. Only the wind blowing across her body seemed to bring her any relief, so every night found her outside, enduring the elements. Crying her grief aloud.

There was no doubt in any of their minds that the Duet was somehow to blame for Gwynne's affliction. For many moons, travellers from Barrow had been whispering rumors that the twins had learned to control the Voids, and Gwynne's description of the horror that had destroyed her family and brushed over her was all too clear.

But other strange tales were issuing from Barrow. There were accounts of a deformed man who scoured the capital for the strongest men and women and bred them like cattle. There were witnesses who claimed to have seen a new band of bodyguards in the royal palace, blank-faced, dead-eyed warriors who had no normal human responses.

No one knew where it would end.

When the Snowscalds emerged from their huts at dawn, they discovered Gwynne in the center of the compound. Granules of sleet blanketed her head and shoulders, glittered on the slope of her capacious bosom, lay heavy on the curve of her buttocks. She was sheathed in ice.

But she no longer suffered; at least, her flesh no longer suffered.

The other women gathered around her in a grim and respectful silence. The transformation was complete. Gwynne's skin had become stone, yet still she lived and moved. Somewhere within that granitic facade a heart beat, lungs breathed.

Blazing in the rigid mask of her face, her anguished eyes betrayed her humanity.

CHAPTER TWENTY-NINE

Caeled pressed too heavily with the bamboo quill and the point snapped as it gouged a hole in the thin sheet of kenaf. Scholar Nanri leaned over to rap the boy's knuckles with a switch. Striking metal, the willow switch rebounded harmlessly. Caeled tried in vain to suppress a grin. Swifter than the eye could follow his instructor lashed the switch across the boy's flesh and blood hand, leaving a red weal.

"You handle the quill as if it were a shovel. You're not digging earth now," the old man snapped.

Caeled raised his head to look at Nanri. For a moment his dark eyes blazed with an anger so intense it startled the old Scholar. Then the boy lowered his lids enough to screen his anger with his eyelashes, smoothed the leaf of kenaf with his metal hand and selected another quill from the box by his side. The stone floor beneath the desk was scattered with broken quills. Chewing on his lower lip, he began once more to inscribe the simple lines of Modern Script, digging them just deep enough into the kenaf to allow them to be read by sensitive fingertips as well as by eye.

The boy labored in a small, windowless cubicle somewhere in the labyrinth that was Baddalaur. Such cells were reserved for students, being fitted out with plain wooden desks battered by generations of use. Unshaded oil lamps provided merciless light. Unadorned walls offered no distractions.

Caeled would have welcomed a distraction. Intense

concentration was giving him a thumping headache.

From his position in a high-backed chair beside the desk, Nanri watched the boy intently. Was he the Spoken One, the prophecy fulfilled? In the few days he had been with the Senior Scholar, the boy had displayed no outstanding qualities. He was intelligent, but at an age when new concepts were becoming increasingly difficult to assimilate, making the breadth of his intelligence hard to assess. He struggled with his letters, apparently uninterested in them, yet showed some aptitude for simple mathematics. His knowledge of geography was rudimentary, being principally confined to the east coast where he had travelled with his mother. He knew little of the history of the Seven Nations and practically nothing about the Elder Lore. However, he showed marked enthusiasm for both and his knowledge of common folklore was considerable.

There was also a deep pool of reserve in the boy surprising in someone so young, as if he were holding back, concealing, perhaps even from himself, certain aspects of his character. No one knew what inheritance he carried in his blood, or what shape his experiences had wrought upon his spirit. Yet Nanri had begun to suspect there was a great deal more to Caeled than met the eye.

The Scholar found himself gazing at the metal hand. The boy was now beginning to use it unconsciously, unthinkingly, and it was responding better than any of them had dared hope. When on occasion Caeled concealed the silvery contrivance within a flesh-colored glove the craftsmen had made for him, it seemed like any normal hand. But Nanri speculated that it might prove symbolic of Caeled himself: hidden resources beneath an ordinary exterior.

Scholar Nanri appreciated the effort that had gone into creating and attaching the artificial hand. Seekers and Scholars had painstakingly extracted the necessary information from the vast collection of arcane knowledge in the library, but even the wisest of them had not understood everything they read. They could only mimic the techniques of a forgotten age.

Once it had been possible to restore the entire human body, if the ancient texts were to be believed, rebuilding it piece by piece after the most horrendous damage.

The Scholar picked up his own fine bone writing instrument and scrawled a quick note to himself: Was there ever a point when such creatures — an amalgam of flesh and metal — ceased being human? Search the texts.

Another quill snapped and Nanri lashed out with his switch, catching the boy across the tips of his fleshly fingers. Caeled shot him a look of such sudden, blazing resentment that Nanri drew back. In that moment the Scholar saw in memory the image of a wild-haired kitchen boy who had been sold into slavery in Baddalaur's kitchens more then sixty cycles ago. A boy seething with resentment, anxious to settle scores.

"Put down the quill, boy," Nanri said softly, "and let me see your work. Pass me the sheet with your left hand," he added.

Caeled's metal fingers closed over the flimsy sheet and handed it across the desk. Nanri held it up to the light. The kenaf was torn where Caeled had cut through it with the nib of the quill, but his metal fingers had not damaged the delicate fibers.

"Does your hand bother you?"

"At night," Caeled admitted, turning the hand palm upward. "It aches then." Suddenly he chuckled. "Last night I thought I felt a splinter under my nail."

"Your brain is making the hand part of you. Brother Nazariel tells me you've made remarkable progress in the past eight days. If only you could master your letters with equal proficiency," he added, sighing.

Caeled confessed, "I cannot seem to make the shapes of the letters match the words in my head."

Nanri nodded. "I remember what that was like."

"You do?" the boy asked in surprise. "How did you learn, then?"

"You have seen the Great Library?"

Caeled nodded. "Brother Daniel took me through it."

"I wandered into it one day — when I should not have been there — out of simple curiosity. So many stacks of books, so many shelves and levels and staircases. They must contain something very important. I wandered around with a sense of awe, unable to understand because I could not read. But I wondered . . . . I wondered.

"Do you realize there are books in the library that date back to the dawn of time, books of Elder Lore that tell of a time when the gods themselves walked this earth — books actually written *in* that time?" Nanri spoke as if the wonder of those early discoveries had never quite left him.

He stood up and Caeled rose with him. They walked around the desk and out through the open door into the hallway leading, after many twists and turns and changes of level, to the Great Library. When they entered the huge central room some of the brothers glanced curiously at the red-robed Scholar and the tousled boy in his gray tunic, his silver hand forgotten at his side.

"As I looked at all these books," Nanri murmured in a very low voice so as not to disturb the silence, "I realized they were like men struck dumb following great adventures. All the details of their adventures were locked away inside them. The only way I could share the excitement was to learn to read. So I began teaching myself, refusing to accept failure, struggling and cursing my stupidity and trying even harder until at last one of the brothers discovered what I was doing, and began to help me.

"Now I speak and read twenty-two languages to a greater or lesser degree, and I have deciphered four of the Elder Scripts . . . and do you know why? Because I was curious. I wanted to know what those books could tell me. As simple as that.

"Are you curious, boy?" the old Scholar asked abruptly, fixing a stern eye on Caeled.

"I . . . I suppose I am."

Nanri's expression softened into a smile. "Good. Very good. Stay that way; stay curious always. No matter what else happens in your life, remain eager to *learn*. Learn what is in a book, what is in a head, what is around the next bend in the road. Seek and learn."

"Seeker," Caeled whispered.

When Nanri nodded, the boy read regret in his faded eyes.

Caeled followed the old man to one of the upper levels. "Do you have a favorite legend?" Nanri wanted to know.

"Sarafantis, the Lost City," Caeled answered immediately. "My mother told me the story once when I had a fever, and I've never forgotten it."

Gripping the boy's shoulder with bony fingers, Nanri propelled him along the corridor. "At the heart of every legend there is a grain of truth," he was saying as they turned left into a maze of shelving. At last the Scholar halted to pluck a book from a shelf and hand it to Caeled.

The boy turned the volume over and over, gazing at it. It was the first real book he had ever handled. The cover was dark and glossy, with a series of colored lines overlaid on an ornate chart. The pages were similar to leaves of pounded kenaf but with a slicker surface, and were covered in tiny symbols and pictograms.

"Do you know what you're holding?" Nanri inquired.

Caeled shook his head.

"A guide to the city now known as Sarafantis."

Caeled's mouth and eyes were three circles of astonishment.

"Sarafantis was real." The old man's finger tapped the design on the cover. "This is an image of the city seen from the air, these lines represent roads of stone and bridges of metal."

"But . . . " Caeled riffled through the pages, his mind

filled with legends of giants and monsters, of demons and spirits " . . . but, what does it *say?*"

Nanri plucked the book out of his hand and put it back on the shelf. "Learn to read," he snapped.

Armadiel grunted in pain as Caeled lashed out with his metal hand, catching him low on the ribs. From a fist of flesh and blood the blow would have been inconsequential, but the metal hand made agonizing impact.

"That's good," the bald man conceded, pressing his hand against his ribs and probing gently. Bruised, not broken, he decided. "But you lower your head when you strike. Keep your head up, your arms close to your body. Try again."

This time as Caeled moved in, Armadiel sidestepped, hooked a leg around the boy's and sent him tumbling.

"Concentrate," the Seeker growled. "Too much time in the library has made you sluggish. Try again."

Armadiel ducked a swinging blow and drove his open palm into the boy's diaphragm, forcing the air from his lungs. Caeled sat down with a grunt, gasping for breath, but in a moment he was struggling to his feet again, teeth gritted, both hands closing into fists — metal and flesh moving in unison.

"Try again," said Armadiel.

Taking a deep breath, his tongue protruding slightly between his lips, Caeled printed the alphabet. On the next line he repeated the twenty-eight symbols, making them smaller. By the time he reached the end of the sheet his writing was miniscule. He picked up a fresh leaf of kenaf and began again, frequently pausing to dip his quill into the thick purple ink made from berries. When his laborious writing covered ten sheets he gave them to Nanri.

The Scholar's nod of approval was reward enough.

✧   ✧   ✧

Armadiel repeated the graceful, dancelike movements of attack and withdraw, pivot and dodge, and Caeled mimicked him. "Not all the brothers remain here in Baddalaur," the Seeker was saying as he demonstrated the next bit of footwork. "Some venture out into the world for various reasons, on various missions, as you may. No, bend your knees like this, watch me.

"Beyond Baddalaur you will find that your status with us will not grant immunity from those who seek to rob or kill you, so we must prepare you to defend yourself. Keep your shoulders level now and stay loose through your body. No tenseness. Here, put your hand on my waist. Feel that, feel how supple I am, how easily I move? I bend, I twist like a willow in a gale if need be, yet no matter which way I pivot or leap I always keep my feet under me and my weight balanced over them . . . so . . ."

Trying to follow a particularly complicated movement of Armadiel's, Caeled got tangled in his own feet and took a hard fall. No sooner did he hit the ground than he was up again, however, resuming the position, his brow furrowed with concentration. He acknowledged neither pain nor embarrassment and made no excuses, Armadiel noted with approval.

"In your first cycle," the Seeker told him, "we shall develop your agility and stamina. One is no good without the other. Then we shall move on to make you proficient with sword and knife, spear and crossbow, flail and ax. Sharp to the right now, lead with your shoulder!"

At that moment Caeled tripped and fell again. But he got up laughing.

Nanri watched Caeled painstakingly copy the line of script from the book. When the boy grimaced the Scholar knew he had made a mistake. Without a word, he started again.

He had made remarkable progress in the past fifteen days. Nanri envied the boy his determination; he reminded him of himself, all those cycles ago, when he desperately wanted to unravel the riddles buried in the ancient texts.

Nanri read to Caeled from the Sarafantis book every day, making him mouth the letters as they went along. He encouraged questions, constant questions, and soon Caeled was revealing a limitless curiosity about almost everything that delighted the old Scholar. Nanri was coming to the conclusion that even if Caeled were not the Spoken One, he would make a fine Scholar and possibly a Seeker.

Twisting unexpectedly, Caeled stepped in close to Armadiel and slammed his metal fist against a particular point on the Seeker's thigh. The entire leg promptly went numb, as if ice water was coursing through the veins. An astonished Armadiel went down on one knee.

"I didn't teach you that," he grunted.

"I saw a picture in a book," Caeled replied with a smile.

The effort of concentrating was giving him a permanent squint, but Caeled persevered. As he hunched over the sheets of kenaf, his lips silently formed the words his hand was transcribing into tiny figures. When he examined his efforts he lost patience, tossed them aside, and began again.

"Everyone who has joined the Order since its founding has kept a journal," Nanri explained. "Not only do we record major events, but we also write down our important thoughts and elaborate on any meaningful discoveries. It was through referring to the earliest journals that we were able to recreate your hand."

"What happens to all the journals?"

"When a brother dies, his books are added to the library so others may profit from what he had to say."

"But what if I have nothing to say?" Caeled wondered.

"Nothing?"

The boy shook his head.

"You arrived here on the point of death having been

mauled by a Madra Allta, you wear a hand crafted through almost forgotten skills, and you have spent the last thirty days with me learning your letters. Your accomplishments in a short time are remarkable. Tarkiel the Recoverer informs us you have already undergone enough adventures to fill an ordinary life to the brim. And yet you suggest you have nothing to say?"

Nanri pushed a fresh pile of kenaf sheets across the desk to Caeled. "Fill these. Practice writing every day with either hand, you must use both equally. Never fail to make a journal entry. It doesn't matter how much you write; a single line, a whole page, but you must write. This brotherhood survives because those who have gone before us spent their lives keeping records."

The boy took up the quill in his silver fingers and wrote.

"I am Caeled nam Myriam."

Nanri nodded. "That is enough. For the moment."

CHAPTER THIRTY

I am Caeled nam Myriam.

Chewing thoughtfully on the end of his bamboo quill, the boy gazed at the words he had written so firmly they were incised into the surface of the kenaf.

I am Caeled nam Myriam.

Who is Caeled nam Myriam? he wondered. He looked up, sweeping his eyes around the stone walls of his cell.

Caeled, he knew, was a southern name, common enough in Karfondal. His mother's claim that he was the son of a Karfondal nobleman whose name he bore had been accepted without question when he was younger, but eventually he had discovered, quite by accident, that none of the Karfondali nobles had ever been called Caeled.

He could still recall how he felt that day: the sense of betrayal and of loss, the grief for a heritage that had never been his in the first place, but had helped to compensate for the misery of his existence.

Now he knew that the fact he bore his mother's name — Caeled nam Myriam, Caeled son of Myriam — was a sure sign he had been registered as a bastard birth.

Who am I?

The bastard son of a whore.

Myriam had not been a bad woman, she merely had done what so many other destitute women had done to feed and clothe their families. When she could find no honest work, she stole, or sold herself. Her fingers were light and her body female; they were the only resources she had.

Knowing what her life had been, her son could not blame her for seeking solace in drink. He could not blame her for anything, not for the lies she told to hide ugly truth, or for the humiliation and poverty of their days. He had longed to escape those things himself, so he understood her very well. Had she not died in Ward Point — his thoughts shied away from that particular memory — she would have drunk herself to death.

When he was younger — much younger — he imagined one day finding his father who would welcome them both home with open arms and restore Caeled to his rightful place as a prince. In his childish fantasy, Myriam would sit on a throne, dripping with jewels and laughing all the time instead of crying.

Caeled loved the sound of laughter, but try as he might, he could not remember his mother's laugh.

Perhaps he had never heard it.

Now he knew he was never going to find his lost father, the nobleman. Such a man did not exist. His father was no doubt some drunken sailor from the docks who would beat him if he showed up, and say cruel things about his dead mother.

Life was like that. Life was hard. Young as he still was, Caeled knew life was hard. And from that knowledge, so painfully acquired, the boy drew strength.

Had he not been able to do so, life would have defeated him already and he doubtless would have ended up like his mother, unable to face the day without a crutch.

The boy smiled briefly, bitterly. Why would he want a crutch? He already had an artificial hand.

I am Caeled nam Myriam.

Who was that now? An apprentice, an acolyte of the Order of the Way. His left hand was gone, but in return he had a future.

He put down his quill and stared off into space, pondering the exchange; the balance struck.

At last he lifted his left arm, peeled off the glove he was wearing, and surveyed the shining silver hand. The fingers flexed at his command. The hand worked perfectly now, responsive to his most unconscious thought. It seemed hardly different from a real hand except it was unnaturally strong. He still had a tendency to grip too tightly. Nazariel had him practice plucking grapes between thumb and forefinger, but no matter how careful he was or how delicate he tried to be he was crushing every third grape into pulp.

Nazariel let him eat them, though, crushed or not. "And someday, Caeled," the Senior Healer assured the boy, "you will become so skillful with that hand you will be able to peel the eyelashes off a frog."

Maybe he would study to be a Healer like Nazariel. When the Healers took away pain and restored health they made people happy, and that was no mean accomplishment. It would be good, thought Caeled, to make people happy. Perhaps he would research the medical lore of the Elder Days and apply it to the present, much as the brothers had done to make his hand.

Caeled gazed off into space and murmured dreamily, "Caeled nam Myriam, Healer."

His mother, who liked to pretend she had second sight, though in truth her only skill was one of observation, had claimed a great destiny awaited him. Perhaps it did, he thought for the first time — if he made it happen.

But she would never know.

Caeled blinked back tears. What had Armadiel said? "Cry only for others. Never for yourself." So perhaps it was all right to cry for his mother.

Myriam's greatest fear had been that she would die alone and forgotten. "Raise a marker to me, my son," she used to make him promise when she was very drunk and maudlin.

"You have done more than raise a marker."

Caeled leaped to his feet as Maseriel came silently into the stone cell. When the old man fixed his blind eyes on the boy, Caeled shivered. The Hieromonach had clearly read his last thought.

"Soon we will teach you to guard your thoughts, to wall them around with wards," Maseriel said conversationally. He crossed to the stone bunk and sank onto it, both hands clasped over the tall carved staff he carried.

Caeled busied himself with gathering up his quills and kenaf. He had not heard Maseriel approach, and the old man did not seem out of breath though this was the very highest level and a prodigious climb.

"I was not deliberately spying on your thoughts," Maseriel assured the boy, "but I could not help feeling your pain as I approached. The greater emotions — love and hate — travel easily through the Aethyra."

Caeled kept his head bent, unwilling to look into the blank eyes.

"You were regretting not being able to raise a marker over your mother's grave. Yet a marker would have warped and rotted within a number of turns. Now that you have written her name into your journal, perhaps you might write what you know of her story. By doing so you will be keeping her memory alive so that in future generations, Seekers and Scholars can look at your notes and think of this woman. It will be much more lasting than a grave marker."

Caeled swallowed hard and nodded. Then, unsure if the old man could see him, he said, "I understand."

"Sit," Maseriel commanded.

Caeled folded his legs beneath him and sat with his back propped against the wall. This was his first encounter with the Hieromonach since the day his hand was attached. He had caught glimpses of the old man on several occasions, though, and once or twice he thought Maseriel was watching him.

During the time he had been in Baddalaur, Caeled had become aware of the Hieromonach's formidable reputation, as well as whispered rumors of a power struggle among the Senior Seekers as to who would replace him. Listening to Nanri, interpreting both what he said and what remained unsaid, Caeled had decided the oldest Scholar had little time for the Seekers in general and Maseriel in particular.

"Your teachers speak highly of you."

"Thank you, Hieromonach."

"Nanri is especially impressed with your progress and Armadiel tells me you have the makings of a fine warrior."

"Thank you," Caeled repeated politely.

For a long time Maseriel sat with his white eyes turned toward the boy, saying nothing. Caeled shifted uncomfortably, aware he was under intense scrutiny, and increasingly conscious of an irritating crawling sensation in the back of his head as if an insect was moving through his hair. Yet Nazariel had cropped his head to little more than fuzz and he knew there were no lice in it.

"Your hand is comfortable?" Maseriel asked abruptly. His voice was harsh and dry, like the rustling of brittle pages.

"Yes, Hieromonach." Caeled raised the hand and waggled the fingers. "There are times when I'm not even aware of it."

"Good; that is as it should be."

Man and boy fell silent. Once again Caeled felt the crawling irritation at the back of his skull. Looking at Maseriel, he noticed beads of perspiration forming on his forehead and running into the deep vertical creases between his eyebrows.

Suddenly the boy understood. Rage erupted like a burst of flame. Squeezing his metal hand into a fist, he surged to his feet. "Stop it!"

The crawling sensation vanished. Maseriel rocked back on the stone bed.

"All I have left are my thoughts, but they are mine, they belong to me! I won't have them pillaged," Caeled said savagely.

The Hieromonach smiled, a mere twisting of thin lips. His flesh was very yellow and there were shadows like deep bruises under his blind eyes. "Very good," he whispered, "very good indeed. Now sit back down, boy. Sit."

Quivering with defiance, Caeled ignored him . . . then all feeling left his legs, dropping him heavily to the floor.

"Obey me," Maseriel said simply. "And listen to me, without question, without interruption." The old man's voice grew in strength, resonating from the stone walls of the tiny cell.

"You were wondering about your future, your destiny. It may be your mother knew more than she ever told you. Chance has not brought you here, chance did not place Armadiel in the wasteland outside Ward Point. He was riding there to find you."

Caeled opened his mouth, but the Hieromonach rapped the tip of his staff on the floor. "No questions. You cannot listen and talk at the same time.

"We are the Seekers of the Way, once the Lawgivers, men dedicated to learning and preserving knowledge and thus staving off the darkness of ignorance. This has been our mission since the time of Bardal the first Lawgiver. The more we learn, the more we discover about the old ways and the Elder Times, the more important we discover our role to be.

"A great civilization once ruled this world, young Caeled. A powerful civilization whom we refer to as the Elders. Their powers were beyond imagining.

"But in time they warred on one another, squandering their abilities on an orgy of destruction. The finest, most noble beings who ever existed, gods who had challenged the stars, forgot their wisdom.

"It did not happen overnight. Legends speak of a day

and a night of fire and flood, but in truth it took a hundred generations to complete the downfall of the Elders. During that time they surrounded themselves with cacophony that unwittingly destroyed their minds. They poisoned their own water and fouled their air until all manner of illnesses befell them. With mind and body degraded, they could not prevent the downward spiral.

"A few who retained some ability to think for themselves pondered their situation. They rightly identified the chaos descending upon them and endeavored to understand. It was they who formulated the Rules of Chaos. A paradox, is it not? That chaos has rules?"

Knowing the question to be rhetorical, Caeled did not answer. He was not following all of the Hieromonach's discourse, for the old man was using words unfamiliar to the boy.

Caeled privately resolved to memorize them now and learn their meanings tomorrow. Nanri would tell him.

"Another paradox," Maseriel continued. "Chaos is not random. This was one of the last and greatest discoveries of the Elders, but by that time their civilization was weakened past saving. If only they had known sooner that chaos has a pattern, a pulse, a heartbeat!

"And that heartbeat can be stilled.

"For this purpose, in their final desperation, the Elders created the Arcana."

As the name fell from his lips Maseriel seemed to gather himself. Trumpets rang in his voice. The Arcana.

Caeled's lips silently shaped the words. The Arcana.

"This we know about them," Maseriel told him. "There are four, representing the elements of earth and air, fire and water. The Arcana embody natural order, the forces which keep life in balance. Individually each has some power, but if conjoined, we believe they are capable of negating chaos itself.

"Do you know what the greatest irony was, boy? The Arcana were developed by four separate geniuses in four warring nations and even when the end was in sight, they refused to share their skills, to pool the Arcana.

"And so civilization fell and chaos held sway. This was the Dark Age when creatures that were like corrupted gods, and others more bestial than beasts, roamed the earth together with humankind. Some retreated to formerly inhospitable lands, the Ice Fields of Thusal, the Steppes, the Barbarian Islands.

"In time decent folk regained some strength and triumphed over the corrupt and the bestial. The wheel turned. Order was restored. Little by little civilization was rebuilt, using remnants of Elder Lore. The Seven Nations were carved out of wilderness and the jungle that had overgown long-forgotten cities."

Sarafantis! thought Caeled, his lips parting with excitement.

In an infinitely weary voice, Maseriel said, "Now the wheel has turned again. Once more civilization and order are being overthrown, and chaos reigns." The old man stopped, breathing with a curious rasping sound. His knuckles were white on the head of his walking stick.

Caeled wondered if the old man was ill.

With a visible effort, the Hieromonach roused himself and went on in a voice thick with phlegm, "It is possible to plot the cycles of order and chaos. Left unchecked, chaos becomes preeminent; the periods of order grow shorter, times of chaos last longer and come around more quickly. Unless something is done, soon chaos will rule forever.

"We have been seeking you — or someone like you, Caeled — for generations."

The boy started, eyes wild.

"Many stories are told of the Elders," Maseriel went on relentlessly. "Many lies. But what I tell you is truth. They were the greatest of the great, and although they are gone, we have not forgotten their achievements at the height of their glory. We of the Order are keepers of the flame. It is our duty to restore what was so tragically lost.

"The prophets spoke of you, boy. Hundreds — thousands — of likely candidates have been brought to Baddalaur over the generations, but none has ever come so close to the original prophecy as you."

The old man's white eyes blazed with a fierce light that made Caeled gasp in fear and awe. "You are the Spoken One!" Maseriel was almost screaming at him, "The Silverhand! Your destiny is to seek the Arcana and use them to restore order to this otherwise doomed world."

"No," Caeled whispered as a chill of foreboding swept over him.

"Yes!" cried Maseriel.

That final affirmation rang with savage strength through the stone cell, echoing off the walls, repeating itself over and over again until Caeled cowered under its weight. Even when he put his hands over his ears he could still hear the voice of the Hieromonach, condemning him to a destiny not of his own choosing.

Caeled did not realize for quite some time that the old man was dead.

CHAPTER THIRTY-ONE

Sponsored by Scholar Nanri, the Scholars of Baddalaur are proud to accept into their ranks Caeled nam Myriam, commonly known as Caeled Silverhand...

from the Scholars' Rolls

... addendum to the History of the Day...

Perhaps Maseriel was correct. In the cycles it has taken the boy to grow to manhood he has dedicated himself to his studies with a singlemindedness occasionally bordering on fanaticism. Even if history concludes that he was not the Spoken One, he will make a fine Scholar and eventually a dedicated Seeker.

However, his possible destiny as the Spoken One may never be fulfilled since, despite all our efforts, the whereabouts of the Arcana remain a mystery. Some of the most recent research casts doubts on whether the artifacts ever existed.

Rasriel, Hieromonach of the Seekers of the Way

Today I became a Scholar.

In my life there have been few real achievements. Formerly survival itself was an achievement, but when I came to Baddalaur a world of endless possibilities opened up to me.

I set out to read a single language: Now I can speak ten and have a working knowledge of another fifteen, including three of the Elder Scripts.

I have been trained in history, geography and

mathematics, yet these are but the grounding for the new schools of study which will open up to me now. My teachers, including Nanri, who has become more dear to me than I ever expected, will continue my education on the higher floors of the great library. There I will read from the Three Thousand, the body of learning each Scholar must assimilate before he can become a Seeker. And beyond that, there are the highest floors to investigate. I shall spend the rest of my life here, content in my studies. Perhaps when I reach Nanri's great age, I too will take an apprentice and pass on my knowledge.

There are times when he looks at me and I can see a great love in his eyes; perhaps I was the son he never had. I have set out to emulate Nanri, to make him proud of me by becoming an outstanding Scholar. Today I took the first step on that long road. Who knows what awaits me?

from the Journal of Caeled Silverhand

CHAPTER THIRTY-TWO

They arrived in the chill grayness before dawn, an enormous army prepared for battle. Only a few of their number were human.

Led by the savage man known as Kichal, most of the officers wore crimson cloaks and human form, though their blood-red eyes and expressionless faces hinted otherwise. The troops they commanded were like nothing seen in the Nations before.

They were roughly humanoid in shape but taller, broader, heavier than men. The massively muscled arms and thick necks of some were unnaturally long; others had overdeveloped buttocks and thighbones set at an angle that made them walk with a spraddling gait. The skulls of some creatures had little room for a brain pan, but many possessed a massive jaw and teeth like those of the greater carnivores. Along some backs the spines appeared to break through the flesh, throwing up a flange of bone that culminated in a crest rising above the nape of the neck to render it invulnerable.

They were the Bred.

The townspeople of Kathe lined the walls to stare in horror at the whooping, grunting warriors being assembled in a ragged formation on the hillside facing the town. There was only one question on everyone's lips: Why? Kathe was a fishing village, a day's journey from Barrow. It had no treasures, no strategic importance.

The town's gates were closed for the first time in a generation — no enemy had ever raided this close to the capital before — and every able-bodied man and woman had taken up a weapon for defense. Message-carrying peists had been released to warn Barrow of the impending invasion. But while the townspeople watched in dismay the finger-length creatures were shot out of the air by an almost impossible feat of archery performed by warriors with freakishly wide shoulders and short bandy legs. Then the archers shambled forward to snatch the irridescent corpses from the ground and tear them in two before sucking out their juices.

The misshapen army sat for most of the morning, simply watching the town. Within the walls rumor and speculation ran riot.

They are demons from beyond the edge of the world . . .
A new race from the Southlands . . .
Monsters from Thusal . . .
Devil spawn . . .
It is the end of the world. . . .

A fishing boat attempted to sail out of the harbor. It had reached the outer buoy when giant lizardlike creatures with rows of needle-sharp teeth rose out of the water beside the boat. When they finished and slipped back beneath the waves, only a spattering of blood and greasy gray matter remained in the small craft.

As the sun dipped toward the horizon the mayor of the town, a small stout fishmonger named Geede, was lowered over the walls in a wicker basket. Having bribed his way to the mayorality Geede had enjoyed several seasons skimming the taxes, enabling him to increase his personal fishing fleet from four to eight boats. Now he would gladly have traded all his wealth to be anywhere else in the Nations, or even just to be back behind the safety of the walls.

As the basket thumped on the ground, he discovered he had been clutching it so tightly that the woven sides had crumpled beneath his grip. Geede looked up. Faces peered down at him from the top of the wall. Implacable faces demanding that he do something. There was no chance, he thought sadly, of their pulling him back up again.

With the greatest reluctance he climbed out of the basket and walked on shaking legs toward the nearest beastmen, two hulking brutes whose naked torsos rippled with muscle like Gor Allta apes. Their faces were covered with leather masks revealing only red-rimmed eyes. He slowed as he neared the creatures but they ignored him, allowing him to walk past them and up the hill to the line of troops. The heavy metal chain of office, which he wore on any and all occasions, clanked dismally on his chest above his pounding heart.

This close to the massed army, Geede found their stench appalling: a mixture of rotten meat, urine and the metallic tang of magic. The man's eyes began to water. He was about to wipe them on the sleeve of his tunic when he realized that to his townspeople, it would look as if he were weeping in fear. Worse, the hideous army might interpret the gesture as a sign of weakness.

Blinking, he fixed his eyes on a human-looking warrior who wore a gleaming bronze helmet and a red officer's cloak. As Geede approached him the officer raised gloved hands to the helmet and removed it, tucking it under one arm. With the other hand the male half of the Duet smoothed his sweat-spiked hair.

Geede dropped to the ground, prostrating himself before Lares. "Majesty. We did not know! We did not realize! We merely thought that . . . "

There was movement behind him. From the corner of his eye Geede glimpsed a pair of tiny leather boots.

Sarel kicked him lightly just below the ribs.

"What did you think?" The voice was muffled. Geede dared not look up, but he guessed the woman was also wearing a helmet.

"We thought it was an army." He stopped, his mouth dry, and amended, "That is, we thought it was an enemy army."

Sarel kicked him again. "An enemy army so close to Barrow? Have you so little faith in us?"

"Yes, Majesty. I mean no, Majesty." Sweating heavily, more fearful now of the woman than the beasts, Geede babbled, "When we saw those creatures we were frightened, you must forgive us, we thought they might be an army of demons, or abominations from the Northlands."

"They are none of those," Lares said mildly. "Though they are an army. Untrained, it is true. Unblooded, certainly. But they are an army." Lares paused and turned to survey the mass of bestial forms. "Magnificent, are they not?"

"Yes, Majesty," Geede breathed.

"Each one bred to a particular specification. Some are designed for strength, others for speed or stamina. Each one is a killing machine. You are honored, for you are among the first to see the Bred, the personal army of the Duet."

"I am honored," Geede mumbled. "Thank you, majesty." His terror kept growing in spite of what seemed to be an effort to reassure him, and his bladder was achingly full.

"However, we have a problem," Lares continued. "We have an army which theoretically is invincible, but has never proven itself. Before we take our Bredi on a serious campaign, we need to observe them in action."

Geede twisted his head, looking up at the amber-haired young man. Suddenly the mayor began to understand what was coming.

"We need someplace close to the capital, sizeable, but unimportant. You should be pleased we chose your insignificant Kathe, which otherwise would never have distinguished itself. Now its name will go down in history because it made the ultimate sacrifice to further the experiments of the Duet. We shall raise a plinth in your memory."

"No," Geede whispered as his bladder betrayed him out of terror. A wet stain spread on the ground beneath him.

"Yes," insisted Lares.

"It is time," Sarel hissed.

Geede heard the soft hiss of a blade being drawn from its sheath and tried to scramble to his feet, but Sarel planted a booted foot in the small of his back and forced him down.

He screamed then. On the distant walls of the town, the inhabitants of Kathe shuddered at the sound.

Their mayor twitched as the stiletto entered — almost painlessly — between his third and fourth vertebrae. He was dead before Sarel withdrew the blade.

"Time to blood the Bred," she laughed.

CHAPTER THIRTY-THREE

Closing his eyes, Caeled ran the fingers of his right hand over the series of pinholes pricked into the long strip of bark. The gray-furred bat that had carried the message to Baddalaur clung to the front of the young man's robe, resting.

"Well?" Nanri demanded impatiently, leaning forward across his desk toward the young man who stood before him. The Senior Scholar's own age-numbed fingertips were no longer able to decipher the tactile messages scouts for the Order employed when they considered the usual methods too dangerous for sending reports back to Baddalaur.

"It says . . . " Caeled began, retracing the line of dots to be certain he interpreted it correctly. "It says that a town — Kathe, I think the name is . . . "

"A fishing town north of Barrow on the coast. Continue."

"Kathe has been destroyed by an army of grotesque warriors, monsters!" Caeled exclaimed, startling the bat, who took wing and flapped away in alarm leaving only a swirl of air behind.

Nanri bowed his head and chewed on the inside of his mouth for a moment. Then he looked up again. "Is there anything else to the message?"

"Three vertical slashes . . . "

"The code for speculation, unconfirmed rumor," the old man snapped. "Read on."

"Unconfirmed rumor says the army was under the command of the Duet." Caeled shook his head and read the last line again. "The Duet! There must be some mistake."

"Why?" Nanri asked mildly.

"Why would the Duet destroy one of their own towns, Master? What purpose would it serve? And what about this army of monsters, where did they come from?"

Stiffly, Nanri rose to his feet. His bony fingers clamped onto the young man's arm. "Let us walk."

Together Nanri and Caeled strolled out into the Central Courtyard, the younger man deliberately shortening his stride to accommodate the elder. They presented a study in contrasts: Nanri stoop-shouldered, becoming thick around the middle, hobbling with effort. Caeled erect, whipcord lean, his bones lengthened now into the stretch of manhood. The last childish roundness had melted from his cheeks to be replaced by a keen, sharp visage in which his black eyes sparkled with energy. His red robe barely concealed the symmetry of his body, spoiled only by the artificial hand he wore.

The season was turning; the air was chill, tart with the promise of rain. Clouds scudded across the face of Nusas and cast marbled shadows upon the pattern in the courtyard floor.

Using the technique Armadiel had taught him, Caeled breathed deeply to banish exhaustion. He had spent a sleepless night in the Great Library following an ultimately disappointing avenue of research into the location of the Elder Cities.

"The information we have received does indeed invite many questions," Nanri said. He stopped walking. He always stopped walking when he spoke. It gave him a chance to rest and he thought no one noticed. "And what is the Rule of Questioning?" he asked Caeled.

"One question at a time," Caeled replied, chastened. It was one of the first rules Nanri had taught him all those years ago when he was overflowing with curiosity and the queries came tumbling out of him faster than his tutor could reply. "Determine whether there is or can be an answer to a question before moving on to the next one."

"Indeed. Now let us begin with the first question that comes to mind. The destruction of Kathe. True or false?"

"True," Caeled decided. "There is no evidence to lead us to doubt the veracity of the message."

"The army of monsters?"

"Probably true also, for the same reason."

"Why was Kathe destroyed?"

"Impossible to answer without more information."

"Were the twins controlling the destruction?"

"Impossible to answer," Caeled replied again. He sighed. "We're no nearer the solution than we were moments ago."

"Not true." Nanri tapped the faded pattern on the ground with his walking stick. "Look down; what do you see?"

"Patches of color, red and bronze and gold."

"Yet you know that these colors are but part of a greater pattern that makes up the total design."

Caeled nodded silently.

"Now apply the same understanding to our questions. Consider this latest information as nothing more than additional colors in a pattern that already existed. What have you then?"

With the old man shuffling along beside him Caeled resumed walking, keeping a solicitous eye on the elderly Scholar. There had been a time during his second and third cycles in Baddalaur when Caeled's awe diminished through familiarity and he had played pranks on his tutor. He had delighted in pinning Nanri's robe to the chair while he dozed, or substituting salt for the powder Nazariel gave him to relieve a rash.

But that was in the past, forgotten and forgiven. As his body matured Caeled had become aware of Nanri's aging and the fragility it brought. A fiery spirit still burned in the Senior Scholar, but the flesh which housed it was wearing out.

Had he dared, Caeled would have put a steadying hand under the old man's elbow. Instead he contented himself with watching Nanri covertly while simultaneously scanning the pavement of the courtyard, seeking inspiration.

"Monsters," he mused aloud. "There was a report two seasons ago . . ."

"Three." Nanri stopped walking again.

"Three," Caeled agreed, pausing with him. "There was a rumor three seasons ago that the Duet were breeding some very peculiar creatures, ostensibly for their private zoo. They were said to have a collection of saurians unlike any ever seen before, some of them gigantic. One huge carnivorous lizard supposedly got loose and rampaged through the streets of Barrow, devouring people and crushing others beneath its feet before it was destroyed."

Nanri nodded. "Is that all?"

Caeled's eyes narrowed in thought. "No, there were also stories of beasts that looked like a cross between a boar and a wolf. And others that seemed to be a type of ape, but bigger, meat-eating."

Nanri nodded again. "Some thought the tales exaggerated at the time. But supposing they were true, how would you apply the fact to the message we just received?"

"If the Duet have been systematically breeding bizarre new forms for their zoo," Caeled speculated, "they might also have been conducting a breeding program for . . . other purposes. An army of monsters could be the result."

Nanri said nothing, merely listened with pursed lips like withered fruit and a glow of satisfaction in his faded eyes. Caeled's thought processes were clear, direct, unmuddied by rejecting what might at first seem impossible. To Caeled anything was possible.

In the years Nanri had known the lad, his initial

scepticism about his identity as the Spoken One had faded to be replaced with a deep and genuine affection for Caeled Silverhand. While many of the Order regarded the boy with an almost superstitious awe, Nanri treated him as just another of his students, which gave him a sense of acceptance. The old Senior Scholar had patiently guided the youngster's insatiable curiosity and harnessed his formidable energy, and was now rewarded with the knowledge that someday soon the pupil would surpass the master.

"Conclusion," Nanri demanded.

"The Duet have created an army of specially bred humans, or animals or werebeasts. Possibly all three. Then they unleashed this force on a defenseless town, one of their own. But why? It makes no sense."

"Bossur Dam," Nanri murmured.

Caeled remembered. Two turns ago, the twins had built a dam on the Bossur river to redirect the Bossur and increase the water supply for Barrow. The dozen or so villages and numerous farmers in the valley below the dam had assumed they would be warned and relocated before the valley was flooded. They had been mistaken.

Caeled said, "We have seen that the twins are quite indifferent to human life or the misery they may cause. They might have destroyed Kathe just to watch their new . . . " He hesitated, frowning.

"Their new what?"

"I almost said . . . their new toys in action."

"Toys." Nanri mouthed the word with disgust. He reached into one of the deep pockets sewn into all Scholars' robes and took out another strip of bark. "This message arrived yesterday, while you were at your studies," he told Caeled. "Brother Daniel read it for me. It seems the Duet have developed an army of monsters which they call the Bred, under the command of a particularly vicious human known as Kichal. Your conclusions are entirely correct, I am sorry to say."

They walked on in silence, almost completing the circuit of the Great Courtyard before Caeled asked, "What happens now, Master? Knowing what we know, is there anything we can do?"

"No," Nanri told him. "Rasriel will sanction no action against the twins."

"But there must be something! What point is there in knowledge without acting upon that knowledge?"

Nanri sighed. "You forget, I am a Scholar. We are not trained to be militant. Seekers who go out into the world are encouraged to action but we are not. If you become a Seeker you may someday . . . "

"Someday?" Caeled interrupted, although interrupting his tutor was strictly forbidden. "The danger is now."

Nanri overlooked his disobedience. "I have spoken of this to Rasriel who plans no response. He has reminded me that the Duet are the heirs of Los-Lorcan and the legitimate rulers of his kingdom. A town like Kathe is theirs to treat as they will."

"But if they wantonly destroyed it," Caeled argued, disregarding the rule of one question at a time, "what next? Some place larger, more of a challenge? And how long before they turn their attention to us? How long, Master?"

CHAPTER THIRTY-FOUR

Lares woke suddenly in a bed still warm with the heat of his sister's body, still musky with the odor of their lovemaking. Opening his eyes, he saw Sarel's beloved silhouette against the arched window. He rolled out of bed to stand behind her, pressing himself against her flesh. Her hipbones were like jewels beneath his palms.

"You're troubled," he murmured into her hair.

Sarel held up her left hand, letting moonlight paint it with silver and shadow. "I had another of those dreams."

"About the silver hand?"

Sarel closed her hand into a fist. "Is it just a dream, an image from the Aethyra that enters my sleeping mind? Or something else?"

Lares had no answer. His twin had been disturbed by a recurring nightmare for many seasons, a dream in which she was walking in procession with the nobility of the Seven Nations gathered in solemn lines on either side. The occasion was ill-defined, but Sarel thought it might be a coronation. She saw herself dressed in a gown of white silk and a dark blue sleeveless coat lined with satin, her slender form weighed down with the royal jewels inherited from elder times.

People were enraptured by her beauty and thunderous acclaim arose from every side. But as she knelt to receive the crown, a silver hand appeared out of the shadows and tore the clothes from her body. Her jewels were flung into the gutter like refuse, leaving Sarel naked before the assembly.

Without her finery her body was revealed as diseased and foul, with scabrous flesh and pustules festering on her thighs. Attached to her stomach as an obscene growth was a mannikin with her brother's features. The spectators cried out with revulsion.

Sarel always woke up just as the crowd began to attack her in homicidal fury.

"What can it mean?" she asked her brother for the hundredth time.

Lares squeezed her gently, aware that she was trembling.

"The hand strips me naked and reveals me to the world as something horrible! My own self revolts me!"

"It's just a dream," Lares assured her. "The excitement of the past few days and our success in Kathe have left you overstimulated."

"No, that isn't it. I've been standing here thinking about the silver hand and recalling the first time I saw it." Sarel turned toward her twin, her eyes seeking his. "Do you remember a night seven or eight cycles ago, shortly after we developed the Breeder? You and I were here, in this chamber, in bed, when we became aware of a presence watching us. Remember?"

Lares gathered her into his arms, trying to still her trembling. "I remember."

"We saw the form of a boy," Sarel continued, "spying on us. I created a sword with my mind and struck at the intruder, and he raised his hand to ward off my blow.

"It was his left hand he used, Lares. I can see it clearly now in my memory. His left hand looking as if he was wearing some sort of shiny glove. When my sword struck the hand there was a metallic sound and a blinding flash of light that knocked me backward. Then something snatched him away and he was gone. We pursued him through the Aethyra but could not find him, remember?" She was panting with her eagerness to secure Lares' agreement, his validation of her vision.

"I remember, my sister," he said gently.

"Tonight when I awoke from that terrible dream I realized the boy had not been wearing a glove at all. That boy we saw, we *both* saw, had a silver hand, Lares. A silver hand! And the hand that comes for me out of the shadows is a left hand, a silver hand. It is that boy who comes out of the shadows and strips me naked and . . . " Words failed. Sarel the strong and sure, the more powerful of the twins, clung to her brother like a child seeking comfort.

Lares looked over his sister's shoulder toward the sleeping city of Barrow beyond the window. The sky was the deep purple hue of a bruise. "We followed that boy and the giant hawk that rescued him toward Baddalaur before we lost all trace of them in the Aethyra," he recalled.

Sarel's acknowledgement was a whisper. "Baddalaur. The Seekers." Her mind made an instantaneous connection with the imagery of her dream. "Would they dare try to strip us of our power?"

Lares hugged his sister close. "Warnings should not be ignored."

CHAPTER THIRTY-FIVE

The first Void appeared deep in an enormous vat of cider, churning the golden liquid to putrid froth. The liquid swallowed the sound of the high-pitched White Scream as the Void fed off the molds and fermented juices inside the barrel. When it vanished, the only evidence of its presence was the disgusting odor of rotten apples.

The second, larger Void materialized in the latrines. They were empty; the ancient stone walls muffled the White Scream. The Void consumed the fungi that lived on human waste and destroyed a nest of dog-rats before disappearing. In the noisome depths of the latrines, the stench which remained went unnoticed.

The third Void, much larger still, spun shockingly into the heart of the Great Library. Another whirled into the Central Courtyard. A fifth was destined for the kitchens.

Then the Bred attacked.

CHAPTER THIRTY-SIX

At first it appeared as a black spark, a cinder lazily spiralling downwards, but as the Void descended on the Great Library of Baddalaur it grew, and as it grew the White Scream intensified.

High-pitched, exultant, the Scream vibrated with rage and pain, with lust and hunger. The unbearable sound drove the brothers working in the library to their knees as veins burst beneath their skin, dappling their cheeks with blood.

A Scholar writhed in agony, clutching his chest and left arm. Another fell with black blood pumping from his mouth as his lungs burst. On one of the galleries of an upper level a Scholar, reeling from the sound, pitched over the railing and tumbled down, mouth and eyes wide with terror, but the Void swallowed his shriek of horror so that he fell in silence. He brushed against the edge of whirling nothingness — and instantly his skin turned black and began to liquify. When he struck the floor what remained of his body exploded.

With terrifying speed, the expanding Void swept through the library. A white-robed Seeker attacked the intruder with a roar of fury and the only weapons he had on him — his two hands. The Void sheared through his hands, amputating them above the wrists. His agonized cry sent convulsions of pleasure through the ravenous emptiness, which promptly consumed what remained of his body. Whirling on, it exuded a filthy brown tar that briefly assumed a vague manlike shape.

Too frightened to think, an elderly Scholar hurled the book he had been studying at the advancing horror. The priceless volume vanished without a trace into the vortex. As the Void brushed by them, tables and chairs dissolved into filth; wooden shelving collapsed into rotting pulp; rare paper, leather bindings, vellum sheets and kenaf, all melted into a stinking sludge as the twirling, twisting, shifting Void grew and grew.

The monks fleeing the terror in the library ran into another Void in the Central Courtyard. The spinning horror stripped the ancient pattern from the ground and pulverized the stones supporting the fountain into sand, then fused the sand to glass. But it left the metal parts of the fountain untouched.

Some of the brothers shrieked at nightmare images they glimpsed in the heart of the Void. Others stood rooted, mesmerized by shifting patterns of light within the vortex. The patterns suggested different things to different people. One Healer ran forward with his arms flung wide and tears of joy streaming down his face, racing toward a memory.

The Void swallowed him whole.

Caeled was in the kitchens when a Void appeared there. As a Scholar he was expected to study not only texts but the life around him. This translated into practicality: He had to acquire a working knowledge of all the various functions undertaken by monks in the College, including the preparation of food. For this purpose he was apprenticed for a short period to the cooks and the bakers, and was spending this particular day helping to bake bread.

He first became aware of something wrong when he felt a slight buzzing in his artificial hand. The sensation was disquieting. Caeled peeled off the glove he was wearing and studied the hand curiously. It was such a part of him now that he rarely paid it much attention. Occasionally it seemed to ache if the weather was very cold, and when lightning stalked the ridges, thin blue lines of gossamar fire danced along its silver surface.

There was no blue fire now, but the hand was definitely tingling.

Shoariel, the red-faced, unfailingly cheerful Master Baker, clapped Caeled on the shoulder. "What's the matter, my young friend? Burn yourself? I would not have thought you could injure anything containing Old Metal."

"I'm not burned, but these fingers are . . . humming, sort of."

"From the heat?"

"Probably," Caeled agreed, replacing the glove.

Shoariel told him, "The batch in number two oven is ready to come out now."

"How do you know?" Caeled wondered. There were twelve huge ovens in Baddalaur, and Shoariel monitored them with an almost supernatural skill without ever looking inside.

"Practice," was the reply.

Grinning, Caeled pulled open the door to number two oven, taking care to stand well back and to one side, with eyes and mouth closed. This was a lesson he had learned on his first day in the kitchens. He had opened an oven without taking precautions and the initial blast of heat had blistered his face.

Now the young man lifted a long-handled bread shovel and, squinting against the heat, slid the implement under the first of the round golden loaves. He inhaled the heady aroma of yeast bread and wrinkled his nose with pleasure. Saliva flooded his mouth. But even as he withdrew the loaf from the oven the fragrance turned bitter, then nauseating. Caeled stared in dismay as the fat-bodied loaf on his shovel collapsed into a reeking black puddle.

Within the oven the remainder of the loaves were also melting into a tarlike substance that promptly ignited from the heat, sending a streamer of flame billowing outward. The fire licked across Caeled's apron and set it ablaze. He frantically ripped it off just as the first of the twelve ovens exploded.

Shoariel was struck in the chest by the oven door as it flew outward, the heavy iron punching deep into his body. Another baker was caught in the wash of flame and Caeled's dazed eyes saw the man's hair blaze like a torch.

A brother came running into the oven area from an adjacent kitchen just in time to disappear beneath a pile of bricks as number four oven was ripped apart by an explosion. Liquid flame roared from the hole, licking up to the timbered ceiling whose wooden beams were suddenly sagging with putrescent rot.

Without thought, Caeled dropped to his hands and knees and crawled toward the nearest exit. The bakery was open at both ends to allow the heat and smoke to disperse; now it also allowed the flames to breathe.

Another oven exploded, and blood and brick and black tar splattered across Caeled. He squeezed his eyes shut, instantly nauseated . . . and remembered the last time he had smelled that particular odor, seen that filthy tar . . .

A shape on the bed, clearly visible where it had soaked into the straw mattress, leaving the shadowlike outline of a human body. Black, tarlike liquid trickling out from beneath the bed.

And the smell . . .

Caeled knew then what had come into Baddalaur.

The floor beneath him trembled. He opened his eyes and looked up in time to see the oven to his left shuddering as mortar flaked away from between the bricks. He leaped to his feet with an incoherent shout of warning and flung himself forward. The explosion of the oven lifted him off his feet and hurled him out into the Central Courtyard.

Staggering to his feet, Caeled wiped blood from his lips and turned like an animal at bay to face the Void.

From his cell overlooking the Central Courtyard, Nanri saw the Void appear in the heart of Baddalaur. He knew then that the end had come, and was only surprised the College had not been attacked sooner.

Over the past twenty cycles the Senior Scholar had watched the Duet's exercises in absolute power with increasing alarm, and had kept the Hieromonach informed of his discoveries and misgivings. Despite their mutual animosity, Maseriel had listened to him and tried to prepare for the day when the Duet would become too dangerous to ignore.

Rasriel, his successor, was less prudent. Arrogant and ambitious, he had proved to be more interested in his own domination of Baddalaur than in the despotism of the twins.

Nanri knew of a dozen historical precedents for their increasingly tyrannical behavior. But though he condemned them, he did not view Sarel and Lares as the personification of evil. The Scholar recognized the unintentional good done by tyrants to be one of civilization's great ironies.

To withstand those who ruled through fear and brutality, people had often been forced to learn to work together in common cause. The highest ideals of humanity had been developed to counter the injustices of tyranny. It was a perfect example of the delicate balance of evil and good, chaos and order. One invariably led — sometimes slowly, often haltingly — to the other.

But the Duet were unlike any tyrants Nanri had ever studied.

Two who were one; two halves together forming a whole which was all the stronger because its parts were so alike, yet master and mistress of such different powers.

Nanri had no doubt the Duet dreamed of conquests greater than Los-Lorcan had ever achieved. Yet they were far more cunning than he, and more patient. A terrifying combination. They tempered their greed with the realization that some things were beyond their grasp.

For the moment.

So they learned what was necessary to extend their grasp.

Their breeding program, resulting in the misbegotten army they had unleashed on Kathe, was a case in point. The twins had created exotic pets for themselves, faster peris to ride, spectacular lizards to star in their zoo. It would have taken more skill and patience than the late Los-Lorcan ever possessed to build a war machine in that fashion, but for Sarel and Lares it was the obvious next step. And once the warriors were bred, it was inevitable they should be used.

Tyrants always used their weapons.

Nanri had long suspected from collating apparently unrelated reports that the twins had indeed learned to control the Voids. Once they achieved this the end of civilization was close at hand, unless they showed great self-restraint.

Never in their lives had the spoiled and willful Duet shown self-restraint, however. They had killed their own father rather than submit to him.

The concept of controlling the Voids was not a new one. When many generations earlier the philosopher and prophet Maliel wrote that the Voids were doorways for the soul, he was describing a physical doorway leading to the myriad worlds of the Aethyra. Some of the ancient magicians had thus utilized the Voids. One of the oldest legends claimed the gods had created the world out of a single fiery Void.

Debating with other Scholars, a more youthful Nanri had once put forth the theory that creation was the true function of Voids, from which matter could be drawn because they absorbed matter. If so, the secret had been lost, because now the Voids were nothing more than tears in the fabric of existence through which chaos could enter. Rather than being sources for creation, the Voids had become the ultimate destroyers, feeding ravenously off whatever life forces they encountered.

A perfect tool for the rapacious appetites of the Duet.

Maseriel had foreseen this, Nanri admitted to himself with grudging admiration. The old Hieromonach had hoped he would have time to train the Spoken One to use against them. Too late now.

A sudden detonation of sound made Nanri glance down. The massive timber gates of Baddalaur were crumbling to dust as a series of tiny Voids danced across them. He distinctly heard the sound of metal bolts and hinges, which the Voids could not digest, falling to the ground.

Then the army of the Bred burst into Baddalaur.

Armadiel lifted the heavy crossbow, steadied himself as if he had all the time in the world, then fired a bolt into the gaping jaws of a warrior who was somewhat less than human. The brute was knocked backward to be trampled beneath the indifferent feet of its fellows as the Bred swarmed forward.

Elsewhere in Baddalaur other Seekers were also fighting back. Those who could get to their weapons were the fortunate ones; many were caught, like the Seeker in the library, with nothing but their hands and feet to use against the enemy. But even then they were able to do great damage to the Bred.

Unfortunately, for every invader that fell there were two more to take its place.

Armadiel calmly reloaded and fired his crossbow again and again. Each shot brought down one of the creatures. He had killed five before the attackers fanned out across the courtyard to encircle him, as they were doing to other Seekers elsewhere. Dropping the crossbow, Armadiel drew his two swords from his belt and maneuvered until his back was to the nearest wall.

Like Nanri, he knew who had sent the monstrous army.

He had been urging Rasriel to move against the twins for the past four cycles as the Duet consolidated their power. They had stripped the wealth from the old families and undermined the influence of the guilds. With a combination of bribery and fear they had brought the people to their knees. Those who would not pay absolute homage to the twins were condemned as traitors.

"It is only a matter of time before they turn their sights on the College," Armadiel had warned, but the Hieromonach merely replied, "Nonsense, you start at shadows. They will probably offer us places at court, as Los-Lorcan did with Maseriel before me."

The Bred had not attacked Baddalaur to offer Rasriel a place at court.

There was only one hope now, Armadiel thought despairingly. A hope for the future. Gripping his swords and bracing his feet wide, he turned to look for Caeled.

As he stared at the Void, Caeled was simultaneously fascinated and repulsed.

The shimmering shapes he glimpsed within became beckoning figures that were strangely, beguilingly familiar. There was something disturbing about the shifting light through which they moved, yet he could not resist those figures.

Caeled took a step closer to the Void.

In a daze he walked unaware past a brother kneeling on the ground, staring wide-eyed in lust at whatever he saw in the Void. He had pulled his robe from his body and was straining forward with parted lips when the Void extended a flesh-colored tentacle. It caressed the naked body briefly, then insinuated itself into the man's open throat and dragged him into the whirling emptiness.

Caeled did not see this. Instead he was staring transfixed at a vision of his mother . . . her hair, the tilt of her head, the flash of her eyes, all captured within the Void. Dancing. Laughing. Beckoning.

The young Scholar stepped over the writhing body of an old man who was scratching and tearing at his flesh as if he were pulling off insects. He moaned, convulsed. Caeled walked on unaware.

The Void shifted, images changed into other images.

He saw an older man who looked much like himself, with dark hair and eyes and similar features . . .

He saw a friend from early childhood whose name he had forgotten . . .

He saw the first girl he ever kissed. They had hidden in the weeds of a vacant lot in Ward Point. She was no more than twelve and trembling with fear. He had trembled too, and she clung to him . . .

Maseriel. The Hieromonach stood alone in the center of the Void, gesturing to Caeled to come closer. Maseriel's face was youthful and hawklike and his eyes were clear. Caeled took an obedient step toward him just as a Seeker rushed past, screaming with excitement. The man knocked Caeled aside and hurled himself into the Void.

A mist of blood sprayed outward.

As Caeled jumped back to avoid it his mother appeared again, younger and prettier than he remembered, without the weariness and the cold calculation in her eyes. The dark man, now attired in noble clothing, stood beside her with one arm tenderly draped across her shoulders. Together they leaned outward toward Caeled, calling him home.

A feeling of incredible loneliness and longing washed over him. All he had ever wanted was there, just another step away. He had only to reach out and he would be reunited with his true family, never to be alone again!

Caeled hesitated. His mother smiled encouragement. He took the final step to the very edge of the Void and extended his outstretched hands toward her welcoming arms.

CHAPTER THIRTY-SEVEN

The fingertips of his left hand touched the amorphous edge of the Void.

The resulting explosion lifted Caeled off the ground, hurling him back across the Central Courtyard to crash into a company of the Bred who were systematically butchering defenseless Scholars. Three of the misshapen warriors were knocked to the ground. As Caeled struggled to get to his feet, one of the Bredi, a lanky figure whose reticulated hide kept changing color, lashed out at him with a weapon made from the jaw of some huge beast.

Caeled unthinkingly raised his left hand to protect his head — and the bone club struck it only to explode into ivory slivers. While the Bredi looked blankly at the ruined weapon, Caeled, still on the ground, punched him in the kneecap with the metal hand. Bone and cartilage exploded. The bizarre warrior fell forward, his inhuman face coming level with the Scholar's.

Caeled's second blow shattered the creature's forehead.

Alerted by movement at the edge of his vision, Caeled dived to one side as a spiked metal ball whooshed over his head. A spotted Bredi with the body of a huge cat and the paws of a bear raised the mace again, then stiffened and fell forward as the red light died in its eyes. A bolt from a Seeker's crossbow had sped across the courtyard and buried itself in the back of the Bredi. But while the bolt was still in the air two of the invaders grabbed the Seeker who had fired the shot and tore him to pieces between them, making gleeful gobbling noises as they did so.

The Bredi with the crossbow bolt in its back crashed on top of Caeled. For a moment he thought the creature was still alive, but when he pushed it away he felt the sticky wash of its blood pour over him. The body was already limp in death.

Heaving the dead invader to one side, Caeled staggered to his feet. At that moment a massive boarlike head loomed in front of him and he struck out with the edge of his metal hand. A single blow sheared the head from its neck and sent it bouncing away, just as Armadiel loomed out of a cloud of greasy black smoke. He was carrying a sword in either hand; the blades were dripping blood.

Meanwhile the body of the boar creature slowly collapsed like a deflated bladder.

"Are you hurt?" the Seeker asked anxiously. Armadiel was trembling with tension. The attack had come so fast he had merely grabbed up his weapons, not even taken time to don body armor.

"Nooo," replied Caeled, sounding none too certain.

Armadiel whirled. His swords lashed out in unison to disembowel a fang-toothed warrior that he left writhing amid its own intestines.

"Look out! Up there!" Caeled shouted, but his voice was lost in the sound of the aerial walkways collapsing. Rope and wood showered into the waiting maw of the Void below. High above the courtyard a red-robed Scholar hung, clutching desperately at a remaining segment of rope railing, but it disintegrated in his hands. With a despairing cry he tumbled downward. The lower portion of his body entered the Void and promptly disappeared. The upper body fell to the ground in a fine mist of blood and bone. The mouth was still gaping in soundless agony.

"Nanri!" Caeled cried frantically. "I have to find Nanri!"

At that moment a dwarfish figure ran up to him, grinned at the young Scholar . . . then leaped straight at his face with gaping jaws revealing triangular teeth and a tripartite tongue.

Armadiel's swords sizzled through the air between Caeled and the miniature monster, then angled to cut the creature's torso into sections. It fell spasming on the ground but the head and shoulders continued to scrabble forward, trying to get to Caeled.

With a shudder of revulsion he reached down and smashed its skull with his metal fist.

"Let's get out of here," Armadiel gasped, "while we're still alive."

"You go."

"Not without you, boy. I brought you here; I'll take you out of here."

"I'm not leaving without Nanri!" Turning, Caeled ran into the coiling smoke, heading for the ancient Scholar's quarters close to the Library.

"No time!" Armadiel shouted as he followed him. A female in body armor who appeared to be a normal human being rose in front of the Seeker. He hesitated for a heartbeat, confused until she reached for him with suckered fingers. His swords flashed; she fell.

Armadiel stepped over her. "Caeled! Wait for me!"

Caeled ran on. The Seeker could only follow, cursing under his breath.

The two fought their way across the Central Courtyard, leaping and twisting and spinning to strike at the enemy, Armadiel with his swords, Caeled with only his hands and feet. The creatures they battled were living nightmares, hideous amalgams of man and beast. A few showed human origins but most wore forms borrowed from the realms of wildest fantasy. This was the terrible army that marched, crawled, and hopped through Baddalaur, slaughtering the inhabitants of the College and feasting on their flesh. Around them whirled the Voids, doing their own damage but leaving the monstrous army untouched.

Scholars and Healers were slain like penned fowl. None of them had been prepared to deal with the world beyond Baddalaur, a world where a man might need finely honed fighting skills. But the Seekers had been trained to go out into that world, as had Caeled in anticipation of the day he too would become a Seeker.

Seekers did not die without a fight. They fought with a grim desperation that soon accounted for piles of cooling, grotesque bodies. Crossbows hummed, blades flashed. Men shouted encouragement to one another.

Yet the dreadful tide of invasion pressed inexorably forward. The savagery of the Bred was terrifying. Wounds made no impression on them. With a limb hacked off they attacked as enthusiastically as if they were unharmed. Only death stopped them, and the least strong of the Bredi was still harder to kill than a human being. They swarmed into pathways cleared by the Voids and threw themselves without hesitation onto the defenders of Baddalaur, rending and tearing them like beasts in a jungle.

The smell of blood hung hot and coppery on the air.

As the ranks of the defenders dwindled, the meekest of the Scholars began fighting back to back with the surviving Seekers in a desperate bid to stay alive. But the sheer numbers of the enemy soon overwhelmed them.

The end was never in doubt.

Three of the Bred were gathered around the entrance to Nanri's cell as Caeled ran up. Rage roared through him, finding expression in the furious cudgel of a silver fist. A porcine Bredi turned, tusks gaping, to stare at him and emit a high whinnying snort of warning to its fellows.

Caeled's fist pounded into the hideous face and drove splinters of bone into the thing's brain. Its gaping mouth spouted blood. A dog-faced woman snarled at him and adroitly caught his left hand in her jaws, meaning to grind it to pulp. But Caeled twisted the hand and closed his fingers around her upper jaw, then wrenched half her muzzle free of her face. The third Bredi was too stupid to be frightened. It grappled for Caeled with hairy, overlong arms which Armadiel promptly sliced through.

He and Caeled pushed past the dying warriors and into Nanri's cell.

The interior of the small chamber was ruined. Nanri's long rows of shelving, which the Senior Scholar had lovingly built for himself over the years, had been ripped from the walls. The floor was littered with books and manuscripts.

One dead Bredi lay amid the clutter, the front of its skull flattened by a heavy volume that lay beside it.

Another Bredi, a hairy ratlike humanoid the size of a large child, was busy at the rear of the cell. It was crouched over a bundle of clothing, ripping cloth . . .

And flesh, Caeled realized with horror. Flesh. The creature was tearing skin from the body of the Senior Scholar. As Caeled leaped forward the beast glanced over its shoulder toward him. A strip of bloody meat dangled from its lips. Gulping down the morsel, it hissed at Caeled and raised its taloned hands.

He hit the thing with such force it seemed to explode.

Caeled fell to his knees beside Nanri's body and groped for a pulse. He could find none. The ancient Scholar had fought for his life, however. His clenched fists were bloody and tufts of coarse hair poked from between his fingers. There was a purple-black bruise on one side of his head, another along the line of his jaw, and a gaping hole in the flesh of his thigh where the rat-boy had been feasting.

Crooning softly, Caeled cradled the old man's head in his arms. A sense of desolation closed over him like fog. He had not felt so alone since that long-ago day he walked away from the devastation that had been Ward Point.

Tactfully, Armadiel withdrew to stand guard at the doorway, leaving Caeled alone with his dead.

Nanri had come to mean so much to him. His relationship with his mother had been a difficult one in which he often had to be the parent to her child. And he had never known his father. Perhaps the old Scholar had not filled a father's role, but for Caeled he had been a stern yet loving grandfather, a model and guide as well as a trusted friend.

Grandfather.

Caeled had never said the word aloud to Nanri, had never even consciously thought it. Yet now it leaped to his lips.

"Grandfather," he murmured. A terrible burning filled his throat. He wanted to cry but it hurt too bad to cry. He could only hold the old man's head in his lap and stroke back the thin hair from the pallid forehead.

"Grandfather."

Nanri's eyes slowly opened.

Caeled stared down at him in disbelief. The Scholar was dead: no heartbeat, no breathing.

Nanri's lips moved. "I am dead."

Caeled's stomach knotted with terror.

"I am dead," the cold blue lips reiterated. "This fleshly shell has ceased to function, but I commanded my spirit to linger a while. I knew you would come."

"*Master?*"

"I have only a few moments before the jaw becomes fixed and I can no longer speak," Nanri said. The voice, though recognizably his, was strangely hollow, and the first whiff of decay emerged from the parted lips. "I am unsure how long I can force my spirit to remain here, Caeled. Already powerful winds tug it toward the Aethyra. Listen, my son. Listen.

"You have been the best of my students. You are, without doubt, the Spoken One." Nanri's open eyes were growing dull as their moisture dried. "Given another ten cycles, I could have brought you to your full potential, but we will not be allowed that time.

Now you must go forward on your own." The old Scholar's voice grew harsher as his will forced dead air from dead lungs and across dead vocal cords. "This world is slipping back into chaos for the final time. Once the process is complete there will be total destruction. Before it is too late, the Arcana must be used to force order onto chaos."

His flesh chilled with revulsion, but Caeled bent forward until his ear was pressed to the dead Scholar's lips. So intense was his concentration that he was unaware of noises coming from the doorway as Armadiel fought off more of the Bred.

"For generations the Seekers have sought the Arcana," Nanri was whispering. "But I discovered their where-abouts. I, Nanri, who was never allowed to become a Seeker!" Even in death, the old man's voice held an echo of pride and resentment. "I told no one, however, for fear certain ambitious members of the Order would use the great symbols for their own less than noble purposes."

"Where?" Caeled asked. He could feel the spurious life in his arms fading. "Where are they?"

"You know the legends, Caeled. Individually they are nothing; together they can reshape the world. Gather . . . gather the Arcana, use them . . . but hurry . . . hurry . . . chaos spreads . . . Void growing into Void . . . "

"Where, Master, *where?*" Caeled pleaded. He gripped Nanri's hand so tightly the bones ground and shattered.

The only response was the faintest hiss, then silence.

Caeled squeezed his eyes shut and concentrated all the power of his mind on Nanri. He visualized the living Scholar in every detail, recreating the man in his memory.

"You . . . hold me . . . " The voice was the barest thread. "Such is the power . . . of the imagination." There was another silence. Then, "Slippers," Nanri whispered. "Slippers."

"Caeled!" shouted Armadiel. The cry was urgent but Caeled could not respond. He was still caught in the grip of concentration required to hold Nanri's reluctant spirit long enough to extract that last, baffling word.

Slippers.

What could it mean?

The young man gently laid Nanri's head on the ground and closed his staring eyes. Frustration sickened him. To come so close! Nanri had known the location of the Arcana, but now that knowledge was irrevocably lost just when needed.

Could Nanri have been trying to say some other word, only to have it misshaped by his dead tongue? A book title, perhaps. Yet Caeled knew the entire contents of Nanri's private library and there was nothing that sounded even vaguely like "Slippers."

Armadiel shouted again, and this time the mounting desperation in his voice got through. But in the very act of rising to his feet to go to Armadiel's aid, Caeled's gaze fell upon the shredded remains of Nanri's bed. Peeking out from underneath were the shabby slippers the old man had worn every day of his life.

With an exultant cry, Caeled sprang toward them.

"Boy, help me! Now!" Armadiel sounded exhausted.

Caeled snatched up the slippers. Woven from plant fiber, with felt soles that made little sound, the slippers were the type preferred by brothers working in the Great Library. When they were worn out they were picked apart and the fibers reused in new slippers . . . except Nanri had always held onto his, mending them himself with substitute parts of his own devising. One of his inventions had been an unusual sole made of wood . . .

Caeled's metal fingers tore the slippers apart. Sandwiched between two thin layers of wood in the second slipper was a single sheet of kenaf inscribed with miniature sigils, the symbols used in the Elder Texts. When Caeled recognized the word Arcana he gasped, then smiled grimly, wondering how Nanri had felt as he walked around the College with the most sought-after secret in Baddalaur beneath his feet.

"You old fox," Caeled murmured in fond tribute. "You must have laughed to yourself."

"Caeled!" Armadiel's frantic scream was cut short to end in a bloody gurgle.

CHAPTER THIRTY-EIGHT

"No!"

The word plumed on the frosty mountain air.

The woman sniffed deeply, trying to identify the direction from which the smell was coming. She did not need an explanation of the odor itself; she had no trouble recognizing the battlefield stench of death. It was unmistakable. But she was surprised that it should be found here, so high in the mountains, staining the clear air. What could possibly . . .

All at once, Gwynne knew.

The nearest populated area of any size for which people might fight and die was Baddalaur.

With a stab of dismay, the woman realized she was smelling the death of the great College. She had made a hazardous and exhausting journey only to arrive too late.

Clambering with effort onto the nearest boulder she shaded her eyes with one hand and stared off across the undulating peaks. In a moment she had found the spiral of black smoke rising skyward. She gazed at it with a sense of helpless frustration, feeling hope die in her breast. For a while she could only stand there, wondering what to do next.

"Go on," she muttered to herself. "Just go . . . on." She was climbing down from her perch when the Bredi scouts attacked.

Two metal-tipped bolts hissed through the air. One struck Gwynne between the breasts, effortlessly penetrating her leather tunic. The second bolt from a crossbow hit her stomach.

Both shattered against her skin.

A creature that was neither man nor woman but something in between loped forward to slash at Gwynne with an iron-tipped flail. The metal points struck sparks from skin the color and texture of stone. Gwynne gripped the leather strands and yanked the creature toward her. Off-balance, it reeled forward. She closed her hand over its face and with granitic fingers pulped its bones.

The second Bredi wore the body of a man, but the head was far too small for its body, with elongated jaw and multiple rows of serrated teeth. The creature flung itself at Gwynne's arm and tried to bite it off, but its teeth shattered at the attempt.

She killed it by pounding both fists into the top of its head.

Wiping her hands clean on the forgiving earth, Gwynne set off again toward Baddalaur.

She did not know what she would find — if anything remained. But she must go; she could think of no alternative. At least she was well equipped for trouble.

At times like these she was forced to be grateful for the curse that had altered the very structure of her body. The impenetrability of her flesh had already saved her life several times as she made her way across country.

How ironic, she thought grimly, that I was coming to Baddalaur to find someone who could heal me of the curse!

CHAPTER THIRTY-NINE

A hairless Bredi with a retractable talon like a huge hook at the end of each of its arms had broken through the tiring Armadiel's defenses. One slash had torn open Armadiel's chest and upper belly. He managed to hew down the creature with his swords, but even as Caeled ran to him the Seeker collapsed.

"Armadiel!" Another of the Bredi was attacking the fallen man. A tentacled arm had wrapped around Armadiel's leg and was attempting to drag him out of the chamber, into the open. The young Scholar tore away the tentacles, then drove his left fist through the wall of the creature's chest and seized the living heart. One squeeze burst the organ. The octopoid Bredi joined the score of dead and dying that littered the doorway.

Caeled turned to Armadiel. The Seeker lay with his back to the wall, his swords beside him. Blood oozed between his fingers as he made a futile attempt to staunch his gaping wound. "So this is how it ends?" he whispered as Caeled bent over him.

"No! Nazariel can . . . "

"Dead," Armadiel replied. "A Void. In the Healing Chapel."

"No."

"It's over."

Caeled gripped the older man's shoulders and shouted into his face, "Not yet, Armadiel! Hold on, we aren't defeated. I have the location of the Arcana!"

The Seeker gazed at him blankly. Beads of sweat rolled down his forehead and into his eyes.

Reaching into one of the pockets of his robe, Caeled pulled out the two pieces of wood he had taken from Nanri's slipper. He removed the sheet of kenaf from between them and held it so Armadiel could see. "Nanri knew where the Arcana are."

"Nanri knew . . . " The Seeker's lips twisted in a faint, bitter smile. "How long, I wonder?" He shifted his body, trying to escape the pain.

In the Central Courtyard the surviving members of the Order were being rounded up and driven by the Bred into the largest of the Voids. They fought every step of the way but it was obvious they were exhausted. They only had moments to live.

Unnoticed by the enemy, however, a handful of Seniors led by the Hieromonach darted out of one doorway and into another, vanishing as completely as if the mountain had swallowed them.

Rasriel and his followers wound their way through narrow tunnels carved in the living stone generations ago against the possibility of attack. No matter what enemies conspired against them, the Seekers of the Way were obliged to try to keep the Order alive.

As they moved deeper underground a form of nitre oozing from the walls provided an eerie luminescence. They could see enough to keep from stumbling, but the air was cold and stale. Tarkiel the Recoverer shivered. "How far do we have to go?" he asked Rasriel in a husky whisper.

"Far enough," was the reply.

They ducked beneath a low doorway and down another tunnel, followed Rasriel to the left and went down yet another narrow corridor that terminated in a massive door of Old Metal dating from the Elder Times. Selecting one of the keys hanging from a ring on his belt, the Hieromonach inserted it into a lock rusty from disuse.

Next he turned his body so the others could not see what he was doing, and pressed the palm of his left hand against an embossed panel in the center of the door as he had been instructed. He waited, unsure exactly what to expect. His palm grew warm, warmer. Then deep within the door, huge bolts shuddered and slid back.

It groaned open on protesting hinges.

"Through here. Hurry." Rasriel cast an anxious glance back along the tunnel as the others passed him. Then he followed them and slammed the door behind him.

The clang of metal echoed through the tunnels.

Within the College smaller Voids had begun sweeping the open spaces, leaving nothing but an oily ash in their wake. Apparently no one was aware of Caeled and Armadiel inside Nanri's chamber but it was only a matter of time until someone — or something — would find them.

"We have to get out of here right now," Caeled decided. Rather than entrust the valuable sheet of kenaf to his pocket again, he paused long enough to fumble inside the neck of his robe and pull out the little oilskin pouch depending from a thong around his neck, in which he kept his journal and a few personal treasures. Nanri had long ago commanded him to keep the journal with him at all times, so no important day could pass unrecorded. Into this packet he slipped the kenaf, pushing it down between the slim journal and a ring with no stone. Then he thrust the pouch back into his robe.

Next he tore a strip from the hem of the robe and used it to try to bind the Seeker's wound and stop the bleeding. But the effort was futile. Almost immediately the crimson cloth was stained a deeper, sullen red.

"Save yourself," urged Armadiel. "I can't make it."

"I won't leave without you."

"Go!" The badly wounded man began to try to get up. "I'll stay here and cover your escape."

"You can't, you can't possibly. Lie back down, Armadiel, and I'll stay with you."

"Don't be a fool. You have no choice. Understand me, boy. I'm not doing this because I want to, but because I must." With a grunt of pain the Seeker lurched to his feet. He swayed dizzily. "My swords?"

With great reluctance, Caeled picked up the weapons and handed them to Armadiel. The man wiped the bloody blades on his equally bloody clothing as he said slowly, "I was little older than you when I learned to use the Aethyra. There are at least thirty layers . . . " He broke off, coughing, and a spasm of pain contorted his features, but he recovered and continued stubbornly, "thirty layers and planes in the Aethyra. The Dreamworld. Each layer has its own . . . meaning. One was strictly forbidden to me. Only the most adept were allowed to travel its paths, for it coils and twists through time.

"But I was young as you are, and curious. I defied orders and rose to that plane for a single heartbeat. And in that instant I saw my own death." The Seeker's eyes were bleak as they fixed on Caeled's face. "I've always known I would die like this, it is my destiny. Now you must fulfill yours.

"In your hand you hold the secret of the Arcana. Go, find them. Use them to prevent the Duet laying waste to the world."

Caeled hesitated, unable to leave his wounded friend.

"All your life has been moving toward this point," Armadiel said sharply, "and mine. I brought you here. Everything was ordained. Even the loss of your hand."

A group of Bredi started across the Courtyard toward Nanri's quarters.

Armadiel flicked a worried glance in their direction. "The well in the Healing Chapel is connected to an underground stream," he told Caeled, his speech rapid with urgency. "Get to the Chapel, hold your breath and drop into the well. Allow the water to carry you, don't struggle against it. Eventually you will emerge in a valley below Baddalaur." Armadiel coughed again. Caeled saw clouds forming in his eyes as he said, "Do this for me and for the Order. It is all you *can* do for us . . . now. Make our sacrifices worthwhile; it is the last thing I shall ever ask of you."

Caeled bowed his head, unable to argue longer. "I will do my best."

"Do better than that," Armadiel replied with a hint of his old forcefulness. "Now go, before that lot over there see you. Go and don't look back."

Sarel sat in a chair shaped from human bone. She appeared to be at rest. Her violet eyes were closed, her breasts rising gently, but closer inspection would have revealed that her naked body was sheened with sweat, and the knuckles of her hands white as she gripped the arms of the chair.

Lares sat in a chair facing her, his posture identical to hers except that while her head was thrown back, his was bent forward. A thread of blood drooled from his mouth where he had bitten into his tongue.

The twins were orchestrating the destruction of Baddalaur.

While Sarel maneuvered the army of the Bred, flitting from consciousness to consciousness, viewing the scene through the eyes of the monsters the Duet had designed, Lares manipulated the Voids. Gradually he was merging them into one ravenous sphere of destruction in the Central Courtyard. Of the ten Voids he had hoped to send to Baddalaur, eight had survived the chaotic process whereby Nothing was created from Something and the very fabric of the Aethyra was turned inside out.

Once unleashed into Baddalaur, the Voids were difficult to control. It was their nature to expand and they were gaining strength at a shocking rate with so much living matter to feed upon.

Sarel's task was easier. The Bred had a human commander and officers, but she had forced the humans to relinquish control to her once the army was inside the College. With only her will to guide them the grotesque army worked as a single unit, wreaking havoc. She fired them with the simple urge to kill and feast. Later, when they were sated, she would return their officers to them. The fun would be over then. In the meantime she peered from inhuman eyes, tasted with inhuman mouths, waded in blood for the sheer heady experience of slaughter.

A single Seeker burst from a doorway waving two swords and shouting hoarsely. The nearest of the Bredi flung themselves toward him. A brindled creature with sinewy arms tried to grab him, but Armadiel pivoted away, then back, decapitating the brute in one flowing movement.

Next a long-tailed saurian shape threw itself at the Seeker and was impaled on one of his swords. Its dull nerves were slow to transmit the message to its brain, however. Powerful belly muscles locked around the blade, holding it fast. As the beast moved it pulled the sword from Armadiel's weakened hands.

The Seeker slashed at the creature with his remaining sword in an attempt to free his other weapon, but the sword rebounded harmlessly from a collar of scaly protuberances that ringed the neck of the Bredi. It responded with a furious whistle and a lash of its muscular tail that knocked Armadiel's legs out from under him.

Other Bredi at once swarmed over his body.

Sarel was with and in them, savoring the joy of rending flesh, when she caught the flicker of movement off to one side.

A figure in red was running across the edge of the Central Courtyard. A Bredi warrior hurled a spear at him but the Scholar caught the spear and snapped it between his fingers without breaking stride.

At once he had Sarel's complete attention. She projected her consciousness into the apelike Bredi nearest him in order to get a look at him. He demonstrated remarkable strength and agility; it would be a shame, she thought, to destroy such a fine specimen. His talents should be introduced into the breeding program. Curiously, he was not heavily muscled. Tall, dark-haired — southern blood? — and quite young, nineteen or twenty cycles at the most.

Another Bredi of the saurian type rushed past the simian Sarel occupied and hurled itself onto the boy, driving him to the ground.

Sarel shifted her consciousness into its alien mind. She felt the passionless cold of saurian thought and perceived only monochrome, two-dimensional images. The young man beneath her was the alien now, a softskin with a mammalian smell that stimulated the appetite. Almost before Sarel realized it, the Bredi whose brain she occupied unhinged its jaws to bite off the head of its prey.

She tried to recall the impulse and save her valuable specimen, but someone was even quicker than she.

The young man in red twisted under her and freed an arm. A single hammer blow smashed the saurian's ribs, driving them inward to pierce the lungs. Then a viselike grip fastened on the jaw of the Bredi and ground bone and flesh to bloody pulp.

In the last fleeting heartbeat before the Bredi died, Sarel realized the hand grasping its — her — jaw was made of silver.

Her scream of terror sent her reeling from her bone chair in Barrow, breaking her contact with the Bred.

Caeled heaved the dead warrior off him and raced for the Healing Chapel. He was moving automatically now, numbed by the sights and sounds surrounding him. When one of the Bredi loomed in the door of the Healing Chapel, Caeled broke its neck with a single blow and no thought at all.

The chapel, thought by many to have been the most beautiful chamber in Baddalaur, was reduced to a shambles. The cool, faintly perfumed atmosphere had been replaced by the stench of bloody death. Piles of dried herbs and broken jars of spices littered the floor; the windows and mirrors were shattered.

Two tarry smears fouled the polished floor. Caeled recalled that two apprentices to Nazariel had been on duty that day.

There was no sign of Nazariel himself, however, and for that he was grateful. He could not bear to imagine what a Void might have done to the gentlest of the Order.

The well was in a tiny anteroom at the rear of the chapel. It comprised a circular stone pit in the floor, with a low curbing. Many times Caeled had drawn water from the well; it was said to be the purest water in the Seven Nations, capable of healing in its own right. Nazariel claimed the well was a thousand paces deep.

Without allowing himself to hesitate, knowing if he gave it any thought he might lose his nerve, Caeled perched on the stone curb and slid his legs over.

He could die, he realized. Die from the fall or drown in the icy black water. But Nanri had insisted death was not the end, simply a time of waiting until the new beginning. If that were true, and Caeled did die, at least he might be reunited with Nanri and Armadiel and . . .

An enormous Bredi warrior filled the door, two humanoid bodies seemingly fused into one.

Caeled drew a desperate breath and threw himself into the dark.

He fell for what seemed forever. As he plummeted he tried to keep his balance, to keep his legs straight, his arms by his sides, so he would enter the water cleanly without breaking limbs.

When he did hit the water the force of the blow was like hitting solid earth. He thought his body would smash to bits. Struggling against panic, he allowed himself to sink far beneath the surface until he felt a strong current take hold of him.

The water was cold, cold, cold. It stole heat and sensation from his extremities with terrifying speed. He tried to roll over on his back — but which way was up? — and reached out his hand, trying to touch the wellshaft.

He felt nothing but water. Water above and below and all around him, lightless water pressing down upon him like the earth of his grave.

The air had been driven from his lungs when he hit, and now he realized they were close to bursting. In a few moments his mouth would open in spite of all he could do and gasp in enough water to drown him.

A sudden eddying of the current spun him around and knocked him against something solid. When he did gasp he found himself inhaling air: stale, lifeless, but air all the same, trapped in some pocket among a wall of stones.

Clinging to slippery stone as best he could, Caeled refilled his lungs until the pocket was depleted. Then he let the current carry him away again.

In the rushing, freezing water, time lost all meaning. He attempted to count his heartbeats, but soon gave up. There were moments when he was not sure if he were alive or dead. He only knew he was cold, and moving. Being moved. Helplessly, with no sense of direction and no idea what the next moment would bring.

With increasing speed he seemed to be rushing through some long dark pipe. His body struck stone again but was swiftly borne away, tumbling, tumbling . . . pressure in his throat, behind his eyes, a ringing in his ears . . . terror he could no longer hold at bay. Not terror of dying but of this terrible formless blackness, this unworld through which he was speeding toward an unknown end.

In desperation he opened his eyes but there was nothing to see. In another moment he would open his mouth and breathe in the bitter water . . .

Light.

A glow, and then sudden, blinding light.

The current swept him forward. Encouraged by the light he began to flounder wildly. His head broke the surface of the river and he was gulping in great sobbing lungfuls of air . . . when a grotesque and unnatural arm reached toward him from the riverbank.

CHAPTER FORTY

Caeled struck out, determined to fight for the life that had just been given back to him. But in his weakened state he had no strength; his blow slid ineffectually off the warrior's arm. A hand closed on his wrist and he was being dragged from the water. He kicked and struggled but it did no good. Defeat was ashes in his mouth. To have come so far and endured so much only to . . .

" . . . lay still damn you!"

The words shocked Caeled. He thought he had been captured by one of the Bred, but the invaders of Baddalaur had made no human sounds, only inarticulate grunts and squeals.

His world turned upside down. He was being carried slung over someone's shoulder, a shoulder that dug painfully into his ribs. Then he was dropped face down onto damp earth. He turned his head to one side in time to see two stony knees — or was that a form of armor? — press into the soil beside him as his rescuer knelt. An agonizing blow landed in the middle of his back. He wanted to cry out in protest, but instead a stream of water gushed from his mouth and nose. Another blow to the back, another stream of water.

Then a firm pressure was applied to his ribs on either side, working them to simulate breathing, and he inhaled. The air burned all the way to the bottom of his lungs. With its ingestion came nausea. He lurched to his knees and vomited copiously, emptying his stomach of an incredible amount of water and bile.

When nothing remained but dry heaves he let his head hang for a moment, then summoned enough strength to wipe his face with his sleeve. Only then did he slump back to the earth and look up at his rescuer.

The body resembled a human female, but it was as if a stone statue had come to life. Her skin was roughened and pitted like granite long exposed to the elements. She had a domed forehead like a small boulder, yet below that forehead gleamed living eyes. Human eyes of green set in a gray stone face. And when she opened her mouth to speak, Caeled had a startling glimpse of pink tongue.

Across her shoulders this apparition wore a cloak of skins over a simple jerkin. Trews of leather, loosely stitched at the sides, covered her lower limbs. Her feet were bare. The viciously spiked head of a morningstar protruded above her belt.

Gwynne allowed the young man to stare at her. She had become accustomed to stares since leaving the Snowscalds. The community of women had accepted her, admired her extraordinary strength and even taught her that her disability was a gift of sorts, something which could be used to advantage. She was impervious to cold and heat and her skin was a natural armor that could withstand the blows of most weapons. Even a Steppe warrior wielding a Gallowan axe had only succeeded in chipping the surface, and after leaking a colorless, viscous fluid, the wound had swiftly healed.

She had been valuable to the Snowscalds. But in the greater world, Gwynne knew she was a freak. People stared. It was but one more thing to which she had become impervious.

"What . . . who are you?" the young man corrected himself.

Gwynne was not surprised at the question. Most people wanted to know what she was, rather than who she was. "I am Gwynne, sometimes known as the Stone

Warrior. But beneath the surface of what you see is a woman."

"I am Caeled, a Scholar of Baddalaur," the young man replied formally, getting to his feet. He noticed the woman's eyes lingering on his left hand. Looking down, he realized that sometime during this dreadful day he had lost his glove. He raised the silver hand and flexed the jointed fingers, pleased to see they were undamaged. "A werebeast took my hand," he explained. "The brothers at Baddalaur made this replacement for me."

"Did they really possess such marvelous healing skills, then?" she asked in a wistful voice.

"Yes." Suddenly Caeled understood. "You were coming to them? For healing from your . . . affliction?" He tried not to let himself look at her exposed skin.

"Seeking a reversal of this curse." Gwynne slapped herself across the chest with the hollow sound of stone striking stone. "What happened to Baddalaur?"

"The Duet sent Voids into the College. After them came a hideous army known as the Bred, who . . . who killed and . . . and devoured . . . " His face crumpled. To his own horror he heard himself begin to sob.

Gwynne watched Caeled with mingled pity and envy. She, who could no longer cry, knew the value of tears.

The Duet sent Voids into the College. . .

"Can the twins really control the Voids?" she asked incredulously as the possibilities dawned on her.

Caeled struggled to regain control of himself. "Yes. In fact, we believe they've been experimenting with control of the Voids for many cycles now."

"How many?"

"Seven, eight."

She nodded somberly. Seven cycles ago a Void had destroyed everything she loved.

Caeled straightened to his full height, surprised to realize she was not as tall as he was. Somehow she seemed taller. When he held out his right hand the Stone Warrior took it.

The coldness of her unyielding fingers startled him.

"Thank you," he said gravely, "for saving my life." The simple words seemed inadequate.

"What will you do now?"

"What I was . . . meant to do." Caeled raised his head to look back toward the mountain, the exterior of the ruined College. "I was being trained to be the instrument of the twins' destruction." He looked at the Stone Warrior. "And you? Where will you go? Some of the eastern teachers, or so I have read, are very skilled in healing techniques."

"Are the twins really so powerful?" Gwynne asked.

Caeled's laugh was bitter. "They have mastered the Voids; who knows what else they can do? Unless they are stopped the monks of Baddalaur believed they will destroy the world."

"Would they have the power to reverse what was done to me by one of their Voids, and make me a woman again?"

Caeled was appalled. "Surely you wouldn't consider . . ."

"You cannot imagine what it is like, being as I am. I would consider anything that could restore me to normalcy. If you are truly grateful to me for saving your life, answer my question."

He nodded hesitantly. "I should think they are capable of undoing the process if they wanted to. But I am sure they would not. There is no kindness in them. They would only use you for their own purposes."

"We'll see," said Gwynne. "I am not easily controlled. Without the sensations felt by nerves in the skin the mind has little to distract it. It can follow strange pathways and develop uncommon skills. The Duet might find me a formidable opponent."

Gazing at her stern face, Caeled had no doubt. Not only was this woman's skin unyielding, her very spirit was solid as rock. "The roads we mean to travel are similar," he told her, "but they lead to different goals. Shall we travel together for a time, however — and guard each other's backs?"

While Gwynne was considering her answer, the Bred attacked.

CHAPTER FORTY-ONE

Six of the misshapen creatures lumbered out of the undergrowth. No two were identical. Three were roughly saurian, with mottled greenish brown flesh and flat yellow eyes. Another bore simian features atop a lupine body, and was loping beside a thickset hairy brute with an upright mane running the length of its spine.

The most humanoid form had a face that was all but featureless, with a circular hole for a mouth and two sunken indentations the color of bruises that could have been either eyes or nostrils.

Gwynne reached across her chest to ease the morning-star from her belt. The haft was as long as her arm, the spiked metal head as big as a child's skull. Gripping the haft in both hands, she planted her feet and waited for the beasts to come to her.

Caeled breathed deeply, filling his lungs, allowing the pure sweet mountain air to invigorate his body. This was one of the first techniques Armadiel had taught him.

He stepped away from the Stone Warrior to give her room to swing the morningstar. It was a terrifying weapon whether used by the untrained, who handled it like a bludgeon, or the professional warrior, in whose hand it was more deadly than a sword.

Their opponents were armed, Caeled noted, with bladed weapons adapted to their various hands and paws. No spears and no crossbows, for which he was thankful. The creatures were further protected either with leather chestplates or a natural growth of scales or bone that shielded vulnerable areas.

In addition, the saurian types had long, muscular tails, talons, and teeth like needles. They looked the most dangerous by far.

The six Bredi spread out, attempting to encircle Caeled and Gwynne and trap them on the riverbank. They moved in silence as if obeying some unspoken command.

"Can you fight, Silverhand?" Gwynne demanded, her gaze following the enemy to read the tell-tale blink of an eye, the involuntary knotting of muscle that would warn of imminent attack. The thing that looked like a cross between an ape and a wolf would attack first, she decided. It fairly vibrated with tension.

"I can fight," Caeled assured her softly, maneuvering until his back was to hers. As he positioned himself he kept a close eye on the corresponding movements of the Bredi. The ape-wolf followed him. Ridges of muscle layered its shoulders and its eyes were overhung by bone ridges. Abnormally long forearms warned of an extensive reach. While Caeled was deciding how best to fight the creature, Gwynne murmured to him over her shoulder, "There is a knife in my belt."

"I don't think a knife is sufficient. Look at these things, they've been bred for fighting and given exceptional physical defenses."

Gwynne squinted at the encircling warriors. "Bred? Are these part of the army you described?"

"They appear to be."

"I've seen their kind before, then. I met a couple of them on my way to Baddalaur."

The ape-wolf squatted, wriggled, leaped. In one of its simian hands it held a shortsword. As it sprang the weapon flashed in the air.

Gwynne lunged forward. Her morningstar described a short arc and struck the Bredi in the face with a sickening sound. A twitching corpse fell at the Stone Warrior's feet with its fingers still clutching the sword hilt. "The Duet need to improve their breeding program," Gwynne coolly remarked. "These creatures are not as invulnerable as they look."

Caeled gave her a glance of astonishment. It had never occurred to him that a woman could be such a fighter.

His momentary lapse of concentration cost him. The maned monster flung itself on him and wrapped its forelegs around his body. Its vile breath blew hotly into his face as it tightened its embrace around Caeled, intending to crush him to death.

The Bredi's strength was awesome but its reflexes were not as fast as his. Before it could hug tightly enough to kill him, Caeled squirmed free and dropped to his knees. He drove his metal hand between the creature's legs, caught flesh, and exerted all his force.

The Bredi let out a deafening shriek and collapsed, mouth gaping in agony. Caeled snatched his hand free of the falling body and drove two silver fingers into the warrior's eyes and all the way to the brain.

As the creature was dying the featureless Bredi scuttled sideways towards Caeled, while the remaining saurians focussed their attention on the Stone Warrior.

Each of them carried two daggers. The one directly in front of her moved its weapons in tiny circles, endeavoring to hold her attention while the other two came at her from the sides. So, she observed for future reference, the saurians were at least intelligent enough to fight as a unit.

The Bredi on her right moved first, striking out with its knives. Metal sparked off the arm she raised in defense. Gwynne immediately lunged to her left and crushed the chest of the Bredi there with the morningstar, then spun in a half circle, smashing the weapon into the face of the saurian in the center.

A hasty glance showed her that Caeled was out of the way, so she rocked back, shifted her grip on the morningstar, and swung it through its deadly arc again, this time finishing the destruction of the three Bredi in one great sweep. For good measure Gwynne stamped one stone foot on the nearest Bredi as it fell to the ground and listened with satisfaction to the snapping of its ribs.

Meanwhile the thing with no face had edged closer to Caeled, separating him from the Stone Warrior by menacing him with a ripple-edged dagger crusted with gore. One glance told Caeled that if the wound it made did not kill him, the filth on the blade would. Nazariel had once explained the ancient belief that death and disease were carried by dirt, and subsequent reading in the Great Library had convinced Caeled he was right. The theory was no more bizarre than some of the other discoveries from the Elder Times.

Not being able to read the eyes of the Bredi who was about to attack him was a decided disadvantage, Caeled found. But Armadiel had taught him to interpret the subtle shifts of body weight and stance. When the Bredi gestured with his left hand but lunged with his right, Caeled ignored the distracting move and concentrated on the blade, bringing his left hand up, positioning it so the point of the dagger struck the center of his metal palm.

The blade snapped.

In the moment of indecision while the creature tried to understand what had happened, Caeled chopped its windpipe. At the same moment Gwynne struck the Bredi in the back with her morningstar, and the spine snapped with an audible crack.

Gwynne glanced at Caeled's metal hand. "A useful weapon," she murmured.

The Scholar rapped his human knuckles against her stony forearm. "Effective armor," he countered.

"I would trade it tomorrow for ordinary flesh."

Caeled surveyed the silver hand. "So would I," he admitted.

CHAPTER FORTY-TWO

Kichal moved through the remains of Baddalaur, slowly calling the Bred to order, dragging them away from the last bloody scraps upon which they feasted, forcing them into some semblance of a formation in the Central Courtyard so he could take a head count. Cleanup work.

Kichal was one of the few humans, and officially the Commander, of the army of the Bred. Plucked from a lonely guard post by Sarel herself, he had spent three nights in her bed . . . and on the fourth morning was placed in charge of her army.

He was almost certain that was the sequence of events, but his recollection of the time before Sarel was fragmentary. Memories of his nights of passion with the Empress of Barrow were vivid, however, and still had the power to arouse him.

Kichal knew he must have had a life before, but it had faded like a bad dream. He rarely thought about it except when he was very tired, or in the lethargy following battle. Then faces and images meandered through his mind. Some of them were surely people he had once known . . . and forgotten.

Once when he was marching down the High Way in Barrow a woman came screaming out of the crowd and threw herself on him, calling him by a name he did not recognize and pummelling him with her fists.

He flung her aside. Her head made a sickening sound when it struck the stone gutter.

After walking on a few paces, he looked back. A boy of ten or eleven cycles was crouched over her sprawled form, staring in his direction with eyes narrowed by hate. Kichal had shrugged at the time, indifferent to the emotions of small boys.

But sometimes the faces of the woman and the boy, maddeningly familiar, came back to haunt his darkest hours.

Kichal grabbed the ears of a boar-headed Bredi and pulled the warrior off the well-chewed remains of a corpse lying amid the shreds of his robe. The uneaten hand of the body still clutched a staff. The beast snarled at being dragged from its prey . . . then cowered in submission when it looked into Kichal's face.

Sometimes the commander of the Bred wondered what his warriors saw when they looked at him. He had stared at his own face in mirrors but could see nothing out of the ordinary. He was handsome, or so Sarel had said. His features were those common to men of the Steppes: broad cheekbones, a sensuous mouth, a deep strong jaw. But he was taller and better proportioned than most of his people. He wore his raven hair cropped close to his skull and went beardless in the Southern fashion.

When Kichal stared at his eyes in the mirror he could not recall what color they had been originally. Now iris and pupil alike were blood-red.

Is that what frightened his warriors?

If so, he was glad, for he needed whatever power he could get to control the bestial army of the Bred.

One by one his human officers joined him in the ruins of Baddalaur. Like him, their eyes betrayed the adjustments the Duet had made. Their eyes were milky and dead looking, however; only their commander had orbs of flame.

"Report," he commanded harshly.

"We lost sixty of the Bred. We found corpses for fifty-two. Eight scouts are unaccounted for."

"Does anyone survive here?"

"None have survived."

Kichal nodded. "Find the missing scouts," he said to one of the officers. "Take warriors whose sense of smell is highly developed. When you locate the missing, alive or dead, bring them back here. We will wait for you."

While he waited, Kichal ordered the corpses of dead Bredi laid out in the Courtyard. As they were being collected the Commander wandered around the College.

He felt he must surely know something about Baddalaur; the place was famous. But searching for the memories was like trying to hold water in a sieve. "Destroy it," Sarel had ordered, and Kichal had hastened to obey, never questioning. His task was made easier because the Duet had first directed Voids into this den of . . . insurgents? Rebels?

Why, he found himself wondering tardily, *had* it been necessary to destroy Baddalaur? What was here that was so dangerous?

Kichal had been looking forward to a pitched battle; he wanted to match his troops against worthy opponents. Instead they had encountered monks who offered pathetically little resistance.

Could it be that the brothers were sorcerers who had been plotting to overthrow the twins through magic?

Pondering the mystery, Kichal rambled on.

The Great Library lay in ruins. What the Void had not taken had simply collapsed as a result of structural damage. He entered warily, sidestepping a fallen timber, then crouched on the floor to leaf through debris, looking for anything of value.

His fingers touched sheets of kenaf . . . no, not kenaf. Paper. That was it, paper. He smiled to himself, pleased he had remembered the word. Paper, ancient and priceless.

Kichal stood up and looked around with renewed interest. This place had housed countless volumes; he had never imagined so many books in one place. All ruined now, but still . . . He shuffled his feet through tumbled manuscripts, flipping them over so he could stare down at the letters and sigils inscribed so painstakingly on page after page.

What did they all mean?

Like a feather from on high, a single sheet spiralled down through the air, planing on currents Kichal could not feel. He plucked it out of the air and held it to the light, frowning. For an instant the symbols on the page seemed to shift and sharpen and he almost understood them; then they blurred back into gibberish.

With a sense of disappointment he could not explain, Kichal balled the paper in his fist and tossed it into a corner.

When he examined the dead, Kichal made a thorough investigation of their wounds. As part of his report to the Duet he must explain the type, nature, and severity of all injuries, and determine what weapons had done the damage. This information would be given to the Breeder to ensure that the next generation of the Bred would be more resistant.

He was puzzled by several fatalities in which bones were not only broken but appeared to be mashed together. Incredibly powerful blows had hammered the slain Bredi, and Kichal could not identify the weapon capable of such damage. Some of the dead monks, those who had worn white robes, seemed to have attempted to use swords or knives, but no blade he knew would have inflicted the injuries he was seeing.

The next generation of the Bred must be prepared to face the unknown weapon. He would tell the twins.

One of his human officers came running across the Courtyard toward him. "We have found the missing scouts," he said breathlessly.

"So? Where are they?"

"We did not bring them back with us. We thought you

had better come see them just as we found them; two together, and farther on, the other six. Follow me and I shall take you to them."

Kichal read the signs of struggle on the disturbed earth.

Two broken bolts from crossbows lay where they had fallen. At first he thought they had missed their targets, until he discovered that the tips were blunted as if they had struck some impenetrable object.

One of the Bredi scouts lay a little farther on with a look of horror frozen on its inhuman face. Clutched in its paw was an iron-tipped flail with metal stars woven into the strips of leather. The stars were also blunted, some of the points broken off. No flesh adhered to the stars; they had not struck skin, then.

The second Bredi was lying almost on top of its companion. It had been killed by a massive blow to the top of its head, but the wound that interested Kichal was to its mouth.

Most of the creature's teeth were missing. Some were snapped off close to the gums, others broken and fallen back into its throat.

Kichal felt the faint, cold breath of an emotion he had not experienced in the three cycles he had commanded the Bred: fear.

The condition of the remaining scouts added another element to the puzzle. Although he felt the first two had been killed by a single opponent, it appeared that two working in unison had slain the six. There was evidence of two beings, one heavy enough to leave deep indentations in the damp soil of the riverbank, the other light and quick, with dancing feet that hardly damaged a blade of grass.

Two to kill six — and three of those six were the saurian stock for whom Sarel had such high hopes. "They are invincible," she had boasted.

They were dead, now.

As he followed the corpses back to Baddalaur, Kichal wondered how he was going to report his discoveries to the Duet. Someone or something apparently had escaped the destruction of Baddalaur and had killed a number of the Bred along the way.

Kichal felt the whisper of fear again; the twins had no tolerance for failure.

CHAPTER FORTY-THREE

This was the ultimate passion.

She had come close to it before with Lares yet never felt the union to be absolute; there was always flesh and bone in the way.

Until Lares with his ceaseless questing discovered another attribute of the Voids.

The Voids existed in the physical world but could be projected into the Aethyra. Building on this knowledge, Lares speculated that it would be possible to move from place to place through the Voids, as if through tunnels. His theory was as yet incomplete, but in forgotten manuscripts in the neglected libraries of Barrow he had uncovered fragmentary evidence that the ancients had used the Voids in a similar fashion.

Sarel wondered what it would be like to travel through a Void in the Aethyra. Asking the question was the first step in a process which inevitably led, for her, to demanding the answer.

First she experimented with prisoners and slaves, using her own servants when these others were in short supply. Drugged wines and meats or poisoned perfumes lulled them into the deep sleep of unconsciousness in which the spirit drifted from the body in search of dreams. Sarel would be waiting in the Aethyra to ensnare the unwary spirit and force it into a shape mimicking its fleshly shell. Then she pushed that shape into the Aethyra Void.

❖   ❖   ❖

Occasionally — though not always — the body would reappear in another place, though by that time it did not resemble human flesh.

Gradually she had refined the process, spending considerable flesh and blood. When she felt confident enough she projected her strong spirit into the Aethyra Void, willing it to travel to various destinations. She did not, however, consider the process trustworthy enough to risk her own vulnerable flesh.

She next experimented with shifting her consciousness into the miniature Voids she had sown within the living bodies of her servants. Initially some of their minds had disintegrated under the invasion, the brain unable to accept the intruder. But slowly, patiently, she had mastered the technique.

Now she possessed the ability to look through the eyes of others, to see what they saw, to feel what they felt. It was the ultimate passion, the ultimate experience.

Kichal moved stiffly.

He could *feel* Sarel within him. He could taste her perfumed lips, feel the silken caress of her hair, the moist heat of her flesh.

She was part of him, looking through his eyes.

He had made his report earlier, sent a peist message bearer soaring into the evening sky. His written observations had been to a minimum, no more than a list of casualties and the comment that possibly two had escaped from Baddalaur.

As he wrote the message he wondered, fleetingly, when and how he had learned to write. But he forgot the question almost at once.

Sarel entered him in the still hour before dawn, as he slept in the command tent surrounded by snoring officers. Kichal awakened abruptly, intensely aware of her.

Trembling, he threw a cloak over his shoulders.

She walked him from the tent and down to the field where the corpses of the dead Bredi awaited burning. Using Kichal's hands, Sarel examined each corpse carefully. She even pressed his fingers into the wounds to measure their depth.

Then she took him farther, to the river's edge where Caeled had emerged from the underground stream and met the Stone Warrior. She made Kichal's body kneel on the sodden earth and run the palms of his hands over footprints and crushed grass, charting the ebb and flow of the battle there.

Her anger burned through him, white hot, ice cold. He cringed in agony.

"Find these two, whoever they are," her voice thundered through his brain. "Bring them to me in Barrow, and bring them alive. Alive!"

Then the pain turned to pleasure as Sarel left Kichal shuddering on the riverbank.

CHAPTER FORTY-FOUR

"Will they follow?"

"Possibly," Gwynne replied, pitching her voice low. Sound carried in the clear air of the mountains. "When they find the warriors we killed they may decide to come after us. If it was their intention to destroy everyone in Baddalaur, I should not think they will want you to live."

"They have to find me first," Caeled said shortly. He turned his concentration to the winding trackway, picking safe footing amid rocks and shale as he trotted forward, followed by the Stone Warrior.

He knew where he was. He had run along this trackway every morning for the past six cycles, no matter what the weather. In the beginning the run had been agonizing: his lungs burning, his metal hand spoiling his balance. But Armadiel had insisted. "You must build up more stamina. Too much time spent in the Library makes you soft."

So Caeled had run until the pain became a pleasure and he completed the course in ever shorter time. At last Armadiel questioned if he was actually running the whole distance to the head of the trail which led to a valley below. Caeled had promptly challenged the Seeker to a race and left him far behind.

There was no pleasure in the run now. Every step hurt, not with a physical pain but something far deeper, the wrenching bitterness of cowardice. I should have stayed in Baddalaur and fought to the end, Caeled told himself. I could have killed more of the Bred.

And then? asked some layer of logic built into his brain by Nanri. Eventually they would have overwhelmed and killed you. That would truly be the end of all our hopes.

Inside his sodden robe Caeled could feel the oilskin pouch that held his journal and Nanri's last message to him. It lay against his skin, over his heart.

When Gwynne's stone fingers touched his shoulder he flinched automatically. She did not resent his reaction. Even the Snowscalds, her friends and sisters-in-arms, had been repelled by her touch.

Caeled halted and Gwynne, with pointing finger, directed his attention down the slope to their right, through a sparse scattering of trees to a small town on the bank of a river; the same stream, only farther down, that had borne him away from the College. Caeled had never ventured as far as the little community. He knew of one occasion when Nazariel had treated a plague that swept through the population, taking every third person, and he also knew that the locals supplied fish and vegetables to the kitchens at Baddalaur, but he had never heard the place referred to as anything other than "the Town."

Now as he gazed down from the hillside above, he wondered what had alerted the Stone Warrior. At first glance he saw nothing more than a huddle of houses and sheds protected by a palisade of pointed stakes designed to keep casual predators out and livestock in.

Then Caeled realized there was no sound.

No short black cattle lowing, no curly-horned sheep bleating.

No human sounds either.

He stiffened, recalling a similar silence.

Where were the children? The women on the river bank washing clothes, the men tilling the fields?

No smoke curled up from cooking fires into the late afternoon sky. The gates of the palisade gaped open: a shocked mouth. The track that led out of the village was churned to a sea of mud as if an army had passed through recently.

Almost with a sense of relief, Caeled realized the Bred had come through the town.

Standing beside him, Gwynne said, "They may have left guards behind, a nominal garrison." Her breath blowing past his ear felt like stone dust.

He started to suggest, "We could go around . . . " when he realized that would mean crossing open ground. The townspeople had cleared the surrounding fields for farmland. If any of the Bred were lurking in the village, it would be too dangerous to approach them across fields with no cover.

Then he noticed a few small boats moored at river's edge a few hundred paces from the palisade. Boats that could carry them away from the vicinity of Baddalaur, leaving no trail for their enemies to follow. Glancing at Gwynne, he saw that she was looking in the same direction.

He suggested, "We could stay right here and wait for nightfall, then try to get to the boats under cover of darkness."

Had it been possible, Gwynne would have given her head a negative shake. But the stiffened skin on her neck made such gestures awkward and she had schooled herself against them. Where her body was jointed she still had full mobility, but aside from her facial muscles, the lesser range of physical expression was lost to her. "Waiting here would waste too much time," she told Caeled. "Make it easier for pursuers to catch up with us." She narrowed her eyes and gazed thoughtfully at the town. "We need to know if they have left some sort of garrison behind — and if so, how large." Her teeth — still ivory, Caeled noted — flashed a surprising grin. "Only one way to find out!" she said cheerfully. "Come on."

The Bredi existed.

It had no concept of self or time, of past or present. It knew warmth and chill, hunger and thirst. And fear.

Always fear.

The female creature with amber hair — a creature like and yet unlike itself — filled the Bredi with terror. The male creature with eyes of blood was also frightening, though the Bredi did not know why. But the emotions were instinctive and powerful.

The Bredi could also experience pleasure.

The rapture of killing, of seizing smoothskins and rending them with teeth and talons, lapping up hot salt blood, devouring still-quivering meat . . .

Fulfillment. Beyond the nagging physical hunger that was always there — together with the fear — lay a sense of fulfillment that could only be achieved by killing. At the moment of extinguishing life in some other being the Bredi felt a dim sense of having accomplished something very important.

On a day when there was no killing its existence seemed futile and wasted.

There were other creatures like itself. Their forms were different, but their skills and desires were identical. They lived to kill.

They had killed many . . . *before*. Before was the time before now. They had swooped down on a mass of smoothskins and feasted well. The others had gone off somewhere now, but this Bredi had been left behind with a few like itself to stand guard. If any softskins happened by, the guards would be rewarded for their service by having the feast all to themselves.

Wistfully the Bredi waited, fantasizing in its cloudy mind about tasty morsels. Salty eyes. Fat breasts. Tender livers.

Instinct made it look up.

Vision blurred briefly as its slit pupils adjusted to distance.

Two softskins approaching. Yes. No? One had a skin that did not look soft.

The concept baffled the Bredi. A thing must be one or the other. It had no mental capacity to understand exceptions.

Then the breeze blowing down from the mountains brought an unmistakable scent to the Bredi, who licked its scaly lips at the fragrance of flesh. The second being, at least, was edible.

Dropping to all fours, the saurian Bredi slunk toward the two figures. Meanwhile the other Bredi guards began to emerge from their posts around the perimeter of the palisade, drawn by the odor of live meat.

When Caeled and Gwynne saw the first Bredi they rushed forward together without bothering to confer.

Something rustled in the bushes clustered at the foot of the palisade. As she reached the nearest clump of shrubbery Gwynne's massive morningstar swept through the air and disappeared among the leaves. There was a thud, a howl, then the weapon emerged dripping blood from its spiked head.

A Bredi leaped onto the Stone Warrior's back, talons raking her leather jerkin. She tried to dislodge the creature but it clung tenaciously with legs and even its tail, which it wrapped around her waist. The jaws opened beside Gwynne's neck.

A veined frill lifted along the saurian's spine as the poison sacs on either side of its mouth prepared to pump their venom.

But before the jaws could close, a metal hand seized the frill and ripped it from the creature's body to lay bare the backbone beneath. The Bredi gave an agonized squeal that broke off abruptly when Caeled chopped its spinal cord in two. As it slumped to the ground its comrades rushed to the attack.

With morningstar and silver hand Caeled and the Stone Warrior battled back to back for a second time.

They had killed two more Bredi when the remaining three hesitated as if becoming aware for the first time that they were in danger. But after a moment's pause broken only by the sound of harsh breathing, they lunged forward again. An arcing sweep of the morningstar knocked one aside. The other two appeared to think Caeled the easier target and went for him in unison.

Within moments, the pair of saurians lay on the ground. One still twitched spasmodically as the other died with a nauseous belching of internal gasses.

Caeled and the Stone Warrior looked at one another. "Well done," they said simultaneously; then laughed.

The sound of her own laughter took Gwynne by surprise. She could not remember the last time she laughed.

With her foot she nudged the twitching body, turning it over. The thing was obviously dead, its movements the mindless discharge of energy. "Some sort of big lizard," she commented, "but not like any lizard I ever saw before."

"In Baddalaur there were creatures like apes and wolves and werebeasts as well," Caeled told her. "But these . . . " he crouched to study the one that had belched gas. "These are perfect fighting machines."

"Not so perfect," Gwynne pointed out. "We killed them." She laid down the morningstar and stretched, with an effort, trying to ease her perpetual discomfort.

Caeled cast a glance toward the Bredi Gwynne had knocked to one side. The thing lay on its belly a few paces away, revealing scales like armor plate running the length of its back. The Stone Warrior's weapon had struck the saurian on the side of the head, slamming against a thick skull studded with small horny protuberances.

With grudging admiration Caeled remarked, "It wouldn't take much to make creatures like these invincible."

The Stone Warrior replied, "Perhaps. But right now we had better see if they have left anyone alive inside."

Cautiously, she and Caeled eased through the gaping gateway. What they found confirmed Caeled's suspicions. There were no living beings, only uneaten offal that lay like refuse from a slaughterhouse upon the bloody earth.

When they were certain none of the townspeople remained alive, Caeled gave Gwynne a weary smile. "Let's see if we can find a boat that will hold your weight and get out of here."

Flat yellow slit-pupilled eyes snapped open.

The Bredi tried to move, but there was no feeling below its neck. It lay and waited. There was nothing to do but wait.

Eventually — the creature had no real sense of time — the blood-eyed softskin came and bent over it. Inside its skull the Bredi tried to shrink away, but when the softskin only stared without touching it the Bredi relaxed slightly.

Terror attacked in full measure, however, when the creature realized the amber-haired female was somehow looking out of the male's crimson eyes.

Then there was pain; excruciating fire-wrapped knife-bladed pain! A crawling insect slithered inside its head, forcing it to remember, hissing insistent commands that dragged images into the forefront of its brain.

The stoneskin.
The softskin with the metal claw.
The boat, dipping low in the water.

The memories came bubbling up and were taken direct from the saurian mind. Their taking was painful, the Bredi tried to cringe, but its muscles would not respond.

When the blood-eyed one straightened up and walked away, at first there was only relief. The Bredi stared out with its warped vision, waiting.

After a long time the dog-rats and carrion-spiders came.

CHAPTER FORTY-FIVE

"Where are we?" Gwynne grunted as they hauled the boat out of the river and onto a bank of slippery red mud.

Caeled shook his head. "I'm not sure." He helped the Stone Warrior drag the wooden boat up the slope into a concealing clump of bushes. "I do know we've come south," he added, trying in spite of his weariness to visualize a map of the Nations he had studied in Baddalaur.

Baddalaur was situated high in the Spine, the range of mountains that ran the length of the Seven Nations. The land to the south of the College consisted of scrubby woodlands and abandoned farm sites for the most part, and was dotted with lakes and bisected by rivers. Still farther south, where the Spine gave way to rolling foothills, the Forest of Taesir sprawled across the country-side. The almost impenetrable blanket of trees was interrupted only by the Bretan Mountains bordering the Kingdom of Brethany.

Having been carried south by the current for most of the day, Caeled was certain they had travelled a consider-able distance. At one point they had taken a left-hand fork in the river and almost immediately found themselves swept into roiling rapids. The oars in the boat were useless against the power of the water, and the weight of the Stone Warrior unbalanced the craft. They could not even hear each other shout above the roar of the river as it foamed through a series of increasingly narrow gullies.

Caeled fully expected to die. Then, as the turbulence began to nauseate him, he almost hoped he would die. He clung to the edge of the boat and gritted his teeth.

Several times they were slammed against rocks in the riverbed, but instead of smashing to bits the boat was saved by its construction of willow wood and woven reeds. The materials absorbed the blow, allowing the vessel to shudder violently throughout its length but hold together.

As the light faded from the sky the torrent broadened into a gently flowing river. Weary beyond measure, Caeled halfheartedly picked up an oar again, then turned toward the Stone Warrior. "I'm sick of moving water," he said.

"And I."

With one accord they rowed toward the riverbank.

No sooner did they reach the shallows than Gwynne heaved herself out of the boat and dragged the craft, with a protesting Caeled still in it, to the shore.

"You had no need to do that," he said as he clambered out.

"I wanted to feel something solid under my feet."

"But . . . ah . . . you're very . . . heavy. When you walk you leave deep indentations in the earth. If the water had been deep, could you swim?"

Her green eyes glittered. "I doubt it very seriously."

"Or float?"

"Surely not."

"You would have drowned, then! I could not pull you out."

"No."

"And that did not frighten you?"

"No."

Caeled nodded to himself, absorbing the information. This woman had no fear of death. Her story must be interesting indeed.

They found themselves on a narrow strip of mossy

ground at the edge of woodland. Beyond the nearest trees
was no glimpse of light, only a melting into deeper
darkness.

Caeled said, "We must be close to the Forest of Taesir."

"How close?" Gwynne wanted to know as she stood
beside him, peering into the woods. She smelled of damp
stone and cold earth. "Taesir is near my homeland, for I
was born in Brethany. During cold winters the Gor Allta
sometimes came out of the forest to raid our outlying
villages."

Caeled had begun to shiver as the evening air chilled
his wet clothing. "I don't know exactly where we are," he
said regretfully. "If we could see a recognizable mountain
peak I might be able to tell you. Or tonight, if there are no
clouds and we can see the stars, perhaps I shall have a
better idea. I was taught in Baddalaur to find my way by
the stars." He broke off suddenly as a vivid memory of old
Nanri, patiently pointing out the various sentinels in the
sky, overwhelmed him with grief.

To distract himself he asked Gwynne, "Did you ever
see one of the Gor Allta? Is there really such a thing as an
ape werebeast?"

Gwynne stared somberly into the forest. "Oh they're
real enough. My father had a hunting lodge on the fringes
of the Brethan Mountains. I would have been ten —
eleven cycles — when we last stayed there. On that
occasion a band of Gor Allta got into the stables and killed
ten of our peris. The remaining two were so terrified they
injured themselves beyond saving and had to be put
down."

Caeled shrugged. "Could it have been something
else . . . mountain lion? Bear?"

"No," Gwynne said simply. She began to walk toward
the trees.

"Where are you going?"

When she had to turn her entire body to look at him,
Caeled realized she could not twist her head on her neck.

"Are you not hungry?" she asked.

To his embarrassment, Caeled's stomach promptly rumbled an audible reply.

The Stone Warrior turned back toward the woods.

Caeled followed the woman through the bush. She moved with what he considered surprising swiftness, now that he had been forced to consider how heavy she must be. She paralleled the riverbank until she discovered what she was looking for: a broad area of trampled mud where the forest animals came to the river's edge to drink.

"Stay here," she said firmly.

Caeled obeyed without question; she obviously knew what she was doing.

As he watched from the edge of the trees Gwynne walked down onto the muddy verge. Crouching on her haunches, tucking her arms tight against her body, she abruptly took on the appearance of an outcropping of weathered stone.

Caeled grinned with delight at the perfection of her camouflage. Even knowing she was there he could not see her.

While the Stone Warrior waited immobile at the watering area, he looked for a more comfortable — and less visible — place to wait with her. Reaching over his head, he caught one of the lower branches of a needlefern tree and hauled himself up amid the graceful foliage.

There was still enough lingering daylight to keep the needlefern from assuming its hunting posture, so it was safe enough. As Caeled settled on a sturdy branch with his back against the tree trunk, he recalled the last time he had climbed into a needlefern. That was the night Armadiel rescued him.

He owed his more recent rescue to the Stone Warrior. Thanks to her he was still alive and able to climb another needlefern.

In the green dusk of the tree Caeled wondered if it was

mere coincidence—or the hand of the gods.

The Seekers of the Way had not encouraged the practice of worshipping individual gods and goddesses. At Baddalaur they had taught that the spirit, the divine essence, existed within every man and woman. Many sought contact with that essence. Some came close. Only a few ever dared claim success, however.

Caeled's thoughts returned to the Seeker he knew best: Armadiel. With an effort he kept himself from recalling the last glimpse he had of the man in the wreckage of Baddalaur, and remembered instead the strength and dedication of his friend.

Aside from the fact that both had rescued Caeled, Armadiel and Gwynne seemed to have nothing in common. The Seeker had been a very human being, kind beneath his gruff exterior and gentle when he thought no one was looking. Gwynne was totally different. Caeled thought her as tough as her petrified skin, a warrior to her stony fingertips, with no feminine softness and very little left of normal humanity. He saw no similarities between her and Armadiel.

Taking advantage of the first quiet moment in that long and weary day, Caeled took the little bound book of his journal from its oilskin pouch and scribbled down his thoughts. But he was too tired to write much.

This day Baddalaur died.

This day I used my skills to kill.

The Duet have cruelly, callously destroyed the best of men.

I lost many friends today. Many I respected, a few were dear to me, two I loved.

But in destroying Baddalaur, the twins sowed the seeds of their own destruction, for the location of the Arcana was revealed to me.

Once I had nothing, then Baddalaur gave me a future. Now I dedicate my future to the destruction of the twins.

I have gained a companion of sorts, a strange fierce

woman who wears flesh of stone. We will travel together for a while, I think, although . . .

His writing was interrupted by a sudden movement below.

As Caeled watched from the tree a fawn, big-eyed, delicately striped from ears to puffball tail, stepped from the undergrowth almost directly in front of the Stone Warrior. The creature did not seem to see her at all, though its moist nostrils dilated and sniffed the air.

The Stone Warrior gave off no human scent.

The fawn took a hesitant step toward the water. Faster than the eye could follow, Gwynne's arm shot out and an unyielding hand closed on the little animal's neck.

Caeled heard the merciless breaking of bones.

No similarities between her and Armadiel at all, he thought as he jumped down from the needlefern.

Unwilling to light a fire as night closed around them, they ate the flesh raw, after first peeling back the skin and washing the meat in the river to clean it of blood.

Gwynne was almost invisible in the darkness, but Caeled could hear her teeth tearing meat from bone with enthusiasm matched only by his own.

It had been a long time since he last ate.

When the edge was off their hunger, Gwynne broke the silence by saying, "You mean to kill the twins."

"I am determined to destroy them," he replied.

Her voice was hard. "And I am determined that nothing will happen to them until they have restored me. Besides, Caeled Silverhand . . . if the Duet are as powerful as you say, how can you possibly expect to defeat them?"

Caeled started to answer, then hesitated.

In the ruins of Baddalaur it had seemed simple enough. He had the location of the Arcana in his hand; all he had to do was find the actual artifacts and turn their power against the twins.

But how?

His instruction was incomplete. Nanri could not have

told him exactly how to use the Arcana without revealing that he knew their location, which the wily old Scholar had not done until the end. When it was too late to tell him anything more.

And now even the Great Library that might have had instructions hidden somewhere in its myriad manuscripts was destroyed.

It was left to Caeled to discover, on his own, how to use the forces locked in the Arcana to reverse the process of chaos.

He felt as if a chill wind blew over him. His earlier shivering returned and he pinched his nostrils shut to stifle a sneeze. For some reason he did not want the Stone Warrior to think he was falling ill, showing weakness.

"We might be enemies," Gwynne said very softly.

"What? Why?" Caeled strained his eyes with the attempt to see her in the darkness but she was only a vague shape, like a stone outcropping. Cold and hard and unyielding. "Do you mean we could be enemies because I want to kill the Duet while you need them alive to heal you? That's no reason for us to oppose one another," he said to the silent stone. "Better if we be allies."

Gwynne made no reply.

He had seen her fight, had watched her dispatch the warriors of the Bred with arrogant ease. Suddenly he had little doubt she would do the same thing to him if she thought he stood in her way.

Caeled gathered himself in the darkness, tensing his muscles, flexing the joints in his metal hand.

"Allies," said Gwynne's voice directly in front of him.

Caeled's mouth went dry. He had not heard her move.

"Allies," she repeated. There was another silence. Then she asked, "Can you give me your reasons for wanting to kill the twins?"

She had a habit of being so blunt she took him by surprise. "Because . . . because the world must have order and discipline," he replied as he had been taught. "The Duet are out of control, they are destroying order and replacing it with chaos."

Gwynne gave a derisive snort. "That's no real reason. It comes from your head and not your gut. Tell me again: Why do you want to kill the twins?"

Caeled was glad of the darkness so the woman could not see the confusion on his face. He had been trained as the Spoken One until he accepted his destiny without thought, but he had never been questioned in this way. He started to repeat the statement about chaos and order, then stopped. Listened to the words in his mind.

Shook his head.

No, that was not the reason. Not if he was honest with himself.

In spite of all the high ideals and lofty aspirations he had learned at Baddalaur, he was motivated by something much more powerful. A gut reason.

It came down to a matter of personal vengeance, he thought grimly.

"Well?" Gwynne insisted.

"They killed my mother," Caeled replied in a voice stripped of emotion. He could not let himself feel. He was back in the room in Ward Point, watching the thing that had been his mother soaking into the straw of her pitiful bed.

"Did you love her very much . . . your mother?"

He took a long time before answering. "Yes."

Gwynne's breath hissed through her teeth. "I have worn this stone form for a long time, but I was not the only one to suffer. The Void that touched my skin and turned it hard took my family, my husband and children . . . and even snatched my baby from my back as I tried to flee.

"I was a long time coming to terms with what happened. Thinking it a horrible accident, a freak of nature, I was forced to accept my loss at last because you cannot endlessly rage against such things, they are mindless. So I decided to get on with my life and try to find a cure for my affliction.

"Instead I found you, only to have you tell me the twins are controlling the Voids deliberately. How do you suppose that makes me feel?"

Caeled had steeled himself against his pain, but he had no defense against hers. He could only close his eyes.

"We shall be allies," Gwynne continued. "Together we will hunt down the Duet, you and I, and avenge our loved ones. Perhaps if we have enough power we can force them to heal me before we destroy them. I assume you think you have sufficient power . . . so what is it?"

She was standing very close to him now. Caeled could smell her peculiar scent, could see her pale shape glimmering in the darkness. "The Arcana," he replied. "The combined forces of the Arcana are greater than the strength of the twins."

She dismissed his words with another derisive snort. "The Arcana is fable."

Caeled reached into his robe and produced the oilskin pouch from which he took Nanri's precious sheet of kenaf. In the morning, when there was sufficient light to study the sigils in detail, he would take time to decipher the Elder script the Scholar had so proudly used. It was in a strange way like a treat he was saving for himself. For now it was enough to hold the page in his silver fingers and run his fingers of flesh lightly, reverently, over its surface.

"You are wrong," he told Gwynne. His eyes blazed in the darkness. "The Arcana are real!"

CHAPTER FORTY-SIX

These are the Arcana.

The Staff and the Stone, the Cup and the Sword.

Such images are merely artificial constructs serving as physical manifestations of that which has no form in the tangible world. When they were brought into this world their creators gave them these cloaking forms. Could they be seen as they really are, the experience would shatter human minds.

Individually they are merely artifacts, but pair any two of them and an awesome force gathers. Bring all four together and the elements of earth and air, fire and water are brought into perfect harmony, setting up resonances sufficient to reshape worlds.

With just one pair of the Arcana the holder is enabled to traverse the thirty levels of the Aethyra in the company of those whose essence has long since abandoned the physical world.

Possessing but one pair of the Arcana, a person may assume any Aethyric form and wear it back into the physical world. Thus a man may take on the shape of a youth, a beast, a woman if he chooses.

But should he join two pairs together the pattern thus formed will stabilize the very fabric of the Aethyra, creating order out of chaos, bringing forth light from darkness, altering space and time.

Such is the power of the Arcana, and for this reason its four elements were separated after their construction.

The secrets of their location were hidden by the Elders.

Generations later men postulated the existence of the Arcana and undertook to search for its components. In time we know they found two: the Staff and the Stone.

The hiding place of the Cup and the Sword awaits discovery, but the possessor of the first two will have what he needs to find them.

The Staff and the Stone were secreted in the great and ancient city of Gor in the land of Taesir. The proudest of the Elders accompanied them to their resting place and subsequently devoted their lives to protecting and studying the Arcana.

But the power of one pair of the Arcana — a tiny power, a trickling power compared with that of the whole — altered the children of Gor. Imperceptibly at first, then with shocking changes, normal beings were transformed into the bestial creatures now known as the Gor Allta.

Their lineaments are vaguely similar to humankind but they are not human; they are atavisms. They are werebeasts.

They are legend.

And it is they who now guard the Staff and the Stone in the lost city of Gor in the Forests of Taesir.

translated and annotated by Nanri,
Scholar of Baddalaur

CHAPTER FORTY-SEVEN

Jocylyn swore softly as candle grease spattered onto the tattered chart. In the gloom scores of eyes watched the man seated at the small folding table; only a few of those eyes looked human.

"You're lost." The words were a high-pitched yap.

"I'm not," Jocylyn snapped. "I'm never lost."

A huge blond wolfhound rose on its hind legs and rested its forepaws on the table, regarding the chart with earnest, intelligent eyes. A child with identical brown eyes and white-gold hair stepped out of the shadows to put her hand on the animal's back. When the dog responded with a series of whines and growls the child nodded, then told Jocylyn in a high-pitched voice, "Madran says you should turn the chart the other way around."

In the shadows a dozen beings squealed and cackled their various versions of laughter.

Jocylyn's rueful grin revealed gold teeth gleaming in a mouth surrounded by thick beard. "Taking orders from a dog now," he grumbled, but he turned the chart around and squinted at it afresh. A forefinger with an exceedingly black nail tapped a pictogram of a tiny town. "We left Neer two days ago . . . " He followed a twisting track eastward until it diverged. "We came north along the Merchants Way . . . "

The dog rumbled deep in his shaggy chest. As the child began to translate she smiled in amusement, baring a mouthful of teeth more canine than human.

"Madran says you should have turned south to Brethany. The people there respect circuses."

Jocylyn nodded. "He may be right, Pup. But it's too late now." His finger touched the edge of the Forest of Taesir. "We're here. Somewhere." He folded up the chart. "Tomorrow, my friends. We've had a long day and we're all tired; we'll decide what to do tomorrow." He stood up, automatically ducking his head in the low wagon. "Secure everything for the night, draw the wagons into a circle. We camp here."

The dog whimpered, but before Pup could interpret Jocylyn held up one hand. "I know, I know, Madran disagrees. But Madran doesn't own this circus, I do. And unless Madran can buy me out he takes his orders from me. Understood?"

The dog growled once, then barked.

"Madran says he wouldn't want to take over this mangy circus," Pup announced.

Jocylyn shook his head as the dog and child disappeared into the night. One by one the others who had gathered in the Circus Master's wagon made their way outside, leaving Jocylyn alone.

The big man slumped into his sway-backed chair and picked up the chart again. Madran was right, of course. Coming east had been a mistake, coming north had been a disaster. Jocylyn's Circus of Wonders had made a good — though not spectacular — living on the west coast, travelling through Galloway, putting on a nightly show of magic and mystery. The beasts were always the best attraction: creatures from the four corners of the Nations, including Madran of the Madra Allta, a weredog and his almost-human daughter.

They had toured the Southlands a few cycles ago and enjoyed a great success . . . until the unfortunate incident with Sioraf that had forced them to leave Karfondal.

Ice-cold hands touched the sides of his cheeks and he jumped. "Sioraf! You startled me."

"You were thinking of Karfondal," the young woman said softly, her voice barely above a whisper.

"Why do you say that? As far as I know you can't read minds."

"I cannot," she agreed. Then she leaned forward, her rounded breasts pressing against the back of his head, and lifted his right hand off the chart. He had been tapping Karfondal with his index finger.

Sioraf walked around the table and sat down on the opposite stool, facing Jocylyn. Her eyes were a startlingly brilliant blue, but in the candlelight her pale face seemed disembodied, floating surrounded by a dark tumble of curls. She had developed a trick of keeping her lips drawn tightly over her teeth when she spoke. "I was not responsible for what happened in Karfondal."

Jocylyn reached out and squeezed her hands. "I know that, daughter. You must not think of it again."

"There's nothing stopping us going back," Sioraf replied. "We could retrace our steps and take the southern route. I simply won't appear as part of the circus. I can go about in disguise, I've done it often enough."

"We could do that."

"But we won't, I can tell from your voice. Why not?"

Jocylyn sighed. "Because the last promise I made your mother was that I would always care for our child. The gods know I broke every other promise I made her; I'm determined to keep that one."

"Then what will you do?"

"Turn back to Galloway, I suppose. We don't have much choice. Do you know how much we've made over the past twenty days? Nothing. The last three towns were a disaster."

"People around here are not interested in circuses or freak shows," said the pale girl.

"They're worse than not interested. I thought they were going to lynch us in that last wretched place. What is it they called us?"

"Bred," Sioraf replied bitterly. "They accused us of being the Bred." Even the sound of the name chilled her. "What about Barrow?" she asked quickly to change the subject.

The big man slumped in his chair. "I'm not sure. At first glance it would seem to be an obvious choice: a wealthy society, eager for entertainment and the more exotic the better. The Menagerie of the Seven Nations should be a great success with the children there: marsh lions, mantichores, merrow, dancing Simpan-sai . . . and even though we do bill them as savage and dangerous to give people a thrill, they're tame enough. Madran can control them in his human form and they all obey Pup."

"Yet you don't want to go to Barrow," Sioraf said, again reading his voice. "Why?"

"There are no circuses on the east coast any more," he pointed out. "And no travelling menageries either."

"Is that not good for us?"

"When I was a youth breaking into this business," Jocylyn reminisced, "there were a dozen shows like ours travelling along the coast. Each one had its own specialty. I remember the Circus Rufus travelled only with Clan Allta. It claimed to have at least one example of every werecreature in the Nations. Others like Shore and Manns preferred jugglers and tumblers and skydancers.

"Those were good times. We gathered at every Turn of the Cycle Festival to barter skills and personnel. That was how I met your mother, she was a star attraction with Micaela's Zoo — the biggest and certainly the most successful of the travelling circuses. They had some of the Clan Allta too — and a number of even more exotic performers. Micaela was a southern princess, or so the rumor went, who had run off to join a circus when she was still a child. I bought your mother in the morning and wed her in the afternoon. We shared the Communion of Blood for the first time that night." Jocylyn sighed, his eyes gazing past his daughter into some brighter world.

Sioraf coughed to recapture his attention. His thoughts were increasingly inclined to wander. Was it old age? Looking at him, it was difficult to decide how old he was. Fifty cycles? Sixty? But he had shared blood with a vampir, thus drastically slowing the human aging process.

Jocylyn's eyes refocussed on his daughter. "Where was I?"

"The disappearance of the circuses?"

"Aye. Well, now all those shows are gone. At the last Turn of the Cycle Festival no one came."

"How do you know . . . " Sioraf began, then forgot herself and grinned. Delicately curved, needle-sharp incisors gleamed. "So that's where you were!"

Jocylyn had gone off on his own for ten days last season. Looking for new attractions, he claimed. But he had brought none back.

"I heard rumors," the Circus Master said slowly, "that the circuses had been rounded up and closed down. It was whispered that the owners, the entertainers, the animals, even those of the Clan Allta had been thrown into the dungeons of Barrow at the order of the Duet."

Sioraf listened silently, her white hands folded on the edge of the table.

"Terrible things are said to be taking place in Barrow," he told her. "The twins are supposed to have created a bestiary of their own that would rival that of the finest circus."

"That's why you don't want us to go to Barrow, then. But if it's only a rumor . . . "

"I don't want to confirm it the hard way, daughter," Jocylyn said decisively.

There was a scratching outside, then Pup appeared in the doorway of the wagon. "Come quickly! Madran has scented intruders watching us from the trees."

Jocylyn shoved back his chair and stood up, reaching for his cloak and crossbow. He swiftly fitted a bolt to the weapon.

"Curse their eyes whoever they are. We may not have any business, but I won't have my troupe harassed . . . or worse," he swore. Holding the bow down by his side, he stepped out into the circle of wagons.

Sioraf followed him out but promptly melted into the shadows.

"Where are they?" Jocylyn whispered to Pup.

The huge shaggy dog pressed against her side and growled low in his throat.

"In the trees over there," Pup told the Circus Master. "Two of them. And neither are completely human," she added.

CHAPTER FORTY-EIGHT

Waves of scent had drawn them, the tang of sweaty human flesh mingled with the musky odors of beasts. Following the odors to their source, Caeled and Gwynne moved cautiously through the trees. It could be a village . . . or it could be a Bredi hunting party.

"It's a caravan of sorts," Caeled said over his shoulder as he lay flat on damp earth in the undergrowth, peering through a screen of diolyn leaves. "Eight wagons in a circle around a campfire," he further reported. "But I don't see any people, I wonder where they are."

Gwynne eased forward until she was crouched next to him. Her stony fingers parted leaves.

"Ah. It's a circus."

Caeled felt a leap of excitement. As a small boy he had once avidly followed a circus trundling down a nearby road, though he knew his mother would never have the price of admission. But he never forgot the thrill of seeing wagon after gaudy wagon carrying cages containing strange and exotic beasts. A beautiful darkhaired woman rode on the driver's seat of the lead wagon, and someone said she was the famous Princess Micaela.

With all his heart the little boy had longed to go with them. For seasons afterward he dreamed of running off to join a circus.

These shabby wagons, upon which only peeling flakes of paint remained, bore little resemblance to the glamorous procession that had lured him as a child.

"There's nothing for us here," Gwynne decided. "Let's move on."

Caeled scrambled to his feet and caught her arm. "Wait. If the Bred are hunting us, they will be looking for one or two individuals." He flashed a quick grin. "And you must admit we're fairly conspicuous on our own. But if we were to travel with a group . . . ?"

Gwynne glanced toward the circus again. "Your plan has merit, I suppose." But she sounded dubious.

At that moment a curious mix of human and beastfolk emerged from the largest wagon, chattering among themselves in a dozen different tongues. Foremost among them was a small blond girl accompanied by an enormous wolfhound with a coat the same white-gold as her hair.

Caeled and Gwynne froze into immobility.

The camp, which had seemed all but deserted, burst into raucous life. Two Simpan-sai, both recognizably female beneath their coarse fur, busied themselves building up the fire, using their long prehensile tails to carry more wood to the blaze. A squat bald man whose head and face were tattooed in the swirling patterns of the Island Peoples set a plank across two barrels to form a table, upon which he began to chop vegetables.

The thud of his knife brought a pair of marsh lions and their cubs out from one of the wagons. They gathered around the table, waiting for him to begin cutting up the meat which was brought to him by a mantichore.

Caeled had never seen a mantichore. His breath caught in his throat.

The little girl and the huge wolfhound gambolled around the camp, moving ever closer to the perimeter.

"It almost looks as if that big dog is deliberately patrolling the place," Caeled whispered to Gwynne.

"It might not be a good idea to come upon them unexpectedly at night," the Stone Warrior replied. "Perhaps we would get a warmer welcome if we wait for sunrise." As she spoke, her eyes were fixed on the child. The girl was about ten cycles, a little older than baby Derfyl would be if she had survived.

The warrior's granitic hands closed into fists, rock grinding rock. She had not allowed herself to think of her children for a long time. In the beginning the pain of their loss had been almost too much to bear, worse than Silan's death, more agonizing than the pain of petrifying flesh. The Snowscalds had comforted her; there were few women among them who had not lost a child, either stillborn or through disease. The mountains were a harsh environment — though paradoxically, far more healthy than the slums of Barrow or Karfondal where one in every five children failed to live through their first cycle.

But Gwynne had had her family, five healthy children as well as a loving husband. Her future had been assured. She and Silan expected to live to old age, watch their children find companions and have children of their own. Had not that always been the order of life?

Gwynne cherished a special memory from her early childhood, long before she was orphaned. During the latter days of every Cool Season, ten or twelve grandchildren would make the journey to her father's parents' villa on the coast to celebrate the Turn of the Cycle. There were games to play and races to run, and her grandmother always baked a large cake with carved seeds hidden in it, each purporting to predict some wonderful future for the finder.

And at night, when the stars came out, the grandparents spread blankets on the grass and they all lay on their backs and watched the magic of the sky.

She had wanted to create similar memories for her own children. That would never happen now. She felt the familiar sting at the back of her eyes, the burning at the base of her throat. But she knew she would not weep.

The little girl was close now, very close, eyes huge and liquid and of a surprising darkness for so fair a child. The enormous dog trotted beside her, sniffing the air.

When the dog gave a short sharp bark the girl stopped and looked at him as if he had spoken to her. Some message flashed between them, then girl and dog turned as one and ran across the camp to the largest caravan.

Gwynne's warrior instincts shouted a silent warning.

A bearded man lumbered down from the caravan with the child and the dog at his heels.

"He's carrying a weapon," muttered Caeled, tensing.

Gwynne strained for a better look. "Where?"

"It's concealed under his cloak, but I can tell by the way he walks that he has one."

The Stone Warrior said, "We had better get out of here, Caeled. This isn't a good idea after all."

"No, wait. He's just being cautious, what do you expect?"

The huge dog crowded close to the man. The little girl was clutching a fistful of skin and hair on the nape of the animal's neck. As they started toward the campfire the troupe gathered around it looked up, startled, then rapidly dispersed into their own wagons.

The man stopped almost directly in front of the place where Gwynne and Caeled crouched. The dog strained forward as if it would leap into the bushes and attack. Only the hand of the child seemed to hold it back.

The man slung aside his cloak to reveal a crossbow carried at his side. In one smooth move he raised the weapon and pointed it at the trees. "I know you're there." His was a trained voice, almost accentless. He sighted along the crossbow. "There are two of you; show yourselves at once."

The dog growled menacingly and crouched.

Caeled was inching backward when he smelled the musky odor of . . .

He rolled over as one of the female Simpan-sai landed on his chest, wrapping a tail tightly around his throat. Almost simultaneously the second creature appeared alongside and pinned his left arm to the ground.

Meanwhile a wraithlike figure flowed out of the trees to take a place beside his head. He caught one glimpse of a starkly beautiful young woman before she laid her hand across his face and pressed her long fingernails with the greatest delicacy against his eyes. Caeled froze, knowing that with the slightest movement she could blind him.

Gwynne was pulling her morningstar from her belt when a ponderous weight struck her shoulders and forced her to the ground, face down in mud. The incisors of a marsh lion touched the back of her neck but did not press down. She held still, though there was little damage the big cat could do to her. But it was not trying to hurt her.

It was merely holding her.

Torches flared. Humans and beasts appeared again, crowding forward for a look at the captives.

A high voice yapped, "It's all right, there are just the two of them."

Jocylyn stepped through the bushes and looked down at Caeled and Gwynne, with his crossbow at the ready. "What have we here? Spies? We don't like spies. Do you know what we do to spies? We feed them to our animals."

He waited to let that sink in, then made a gesture with his hand. Nothing happened. The blond-haired child yapped and the Simpan-sai released Caeled as the marsh lion backed away from Gwynne. Lastly Caeled felt the long fingernails lift from his trembling eyelids.

Gwynne levered herself to her feet. She hated being pinned to the earth like a tortoise on its back. "We are not spies!" she said hotly. "We were looking for employment."

"Come out in the open where I can get a good look at you," the man replied.

They followed him into the circle of firelight, where they were at once joined by his curious troupe. Ignoring Caeled, the bearded man looked the Stone Warrior up and down with professional interest, sucking on his teeth as he did so.

"My my, aren't you a sight. What is that, stone?"

"Near enough," Gwynne replied. "Feel it." She held out an arm.

Jocylyn attempted to pinch her flesh, then looked at her with renewed respect. Suddenly he swung his weapon so one end of the metal crossbow struck her forearm.

Sparks flew.

The motley audience squealed and jabbered.

The bearded man raised his eyebrows. "I am Jocylyn, owner of this circus," he told Gwynne, "and I usually hire my acts at the fairs. I don't expect to find them cowering in the woods."

"We were not cowering," she retorted angrily. "I told you, we seek work."

"Both of you? What does the young man do?" Jocylyn turned to Caeled. "You, strip down. Let's see if you have an interesting deformity."

"I'm not deformed," Caeled assured him. He had no intention of removing his clothes in front of these strangers.

"No? Then what use are you to me? It's freaks I need at the moment, like your stony friend here."

Gwynne spoke up. "Caeled has a metal hand that is incredibly powerful. Besides that he is strong, and skilled in fighting. And he can read."

Jocylyn lifted his heavy eyebrows still higher. "Read? Are you also versed in figures?"

"Yes."

"Let me see your hand."

Caeled stretched out his left hand. Jocylyn took it carefully, turning it to and fro in the light from the nearby campfire, examining its jointure with the wrist. "You've had this a long time."

"Many cycles."

Jocylyn bent over and pried a rock from the mud. He tossed it to Caeled. "Show me just how strong you are."

With his eyes fixed on the Circus Master's, Caeled closed his metal hand into a fist and crushed the rock to grit. He let the pulverized stone trickle through his fingers, then opened and displayed the empty hand.

The circus performers murmured; a couple applauded.

"I just might be able to find a place for both of you in my circus," Jocylyn said slowly, as if he still needed to be convinced.

But Caeled read the hungry look in his eyes and knew there was no doubt.

"A circus is like a family, however," Jocylyn said. He turned to gaze at the figures clustered around them. "My people here will have to approve you. What say you," he asked, "do we have room for a Woman of Stone and the Nations' Strongest Man?

The question was answered by grunts, barks, squeals of assent. One human woman shook her head and the mantichore said nothing.

Joclyn grinned. "That's settled, then. Now it's time for food; food and introductions. You know my name, I want to know yours, and all about you. You can tell me while you eat — I assume you are hungry?"

As Gwynne and Caeled were led away, Sioraf crouched beside Madran, the Madra Allta. Pup stood close to her father, listening intently to his whines. "Father smells blood on them, he says."

Sioraf's pointed tongue darted across her lips. She too had smelled the blood . . . and it had been a long time since she last fed.

Her eyes followed Caeled's back.

CHAPTER FORTY-NINE

Of the twenty-five men and women gathered in the Council Chamber, no more than five had served under the twins' father. Only their unswerving loyalty to the Duet had ensured their survival as they had watched friends and family disappear one by one, some accused of treachery, others succumbing to a series of mysterious illnesses, still others simply . . . gone.

The newer members of the Council had been hand-picked by the twins. None were from the Twelve Families, the noble class of Barrow. The newcomers included minor merchants, a circus owner whose circus had been disbanded, a couple of warriors who never made officer rank, several petty criminals and a prostitute from the wharves.

No one knew why such a curious mix had been selected for such high position. But in Los-Lorcan's time less than a third of the Council could be described as loyal to him. In his children's reign, the entire group was determinedly devoted.

"Baddalaur is no more," Lares announced to them with satisfaction as he strode around the room. He radiated an almost palpable energy. Earlier he had slain four men as part of an experiment aimed at freeing their life forces so that he could absorb them into himself.

Three had died quickly; the fourth had met a prolonged and agonizing death which had the effect of releasing a veritable torrent of power. To Lares' delight he had been able to draw almost all of this into himself before it dissipated. He could feel it now, sparking through his body, headier than wine.

The experiment would continue.

"A combination of Voids and the Bred have destroyed what might have proved a serious challenge to our rule," Sarel was saying. While her restless brother paced, she lounged at ease in a chair with the long silken sleeves of her gown dangling over the arms. "It was only a matter of time until those stiff-necked monks rebelled against us. Celibate old fools, they are better off dead. They had no appreciation of true creative energy."

She caught Lares' eye and gave him a radiant smile.

"Did anyone escape?" a wizened diamond merchant asked. His eyes flicked nervously from one twin to the other. He had not wanted this position, but no one refused the Duet. How he wished his natural volubility did not betray him at these meetings.

Lares paused. "Why?"

"I . . . I just wondered."

"None!"

"Our minions performed with gratifying efficiency," claimed Sarel. "Especially the saurian members of the Bred. We have been speaking to the Breeder about concentrating our program on this particular type and phasing out the more mammalian warriors."

"So now we must plan our next move," Lares snapped, moving away from the diamond merchant, much to that man's relief. "You all thought you were chosen randomly . . ."

"But you were not," Sarel concluded. "Each of you has had some particular experience of the Seven Nations and the regions that lie beyond. You, Nun," she went on, addressing the empty-eyed prostitute, "once sailed with the Island Corsairs and know every inch of coastline where their bases are hidden.

"Obrie," she said to a rat-faced forger, "you were once a

cartographer in Karfondal. You and Nun can provide us with the detailed maps we need."

Lares took up the commentary. "We intend to take our army into every corner of the Nations and beyond; we mean to extend the reign of the Duet to the ends of the earth. You have seen for yourselves the slow disintegration of the world we know. Crops are failing, plants are blighted and deformed, animals are losing their vigor. People everywhere are increasingly unhappy with their life and lot. All this we will change!"

He walked around to stand behind his sister and rest his hands on her shoulders. "Nothing can stand in our way," he predicted.

As the council members cheered their approval, a stray beam of sunlight slanting through a window flashed off a silver bracelet on the prostitute's arm.

Silver. Sarel's lips tightened over her teeth. When Lares' fingers bit into her shoulders she knew he was thinking the same thought.

Sarel reached up and placed her hands over her brother's. "It will be all right," she said softly, for his ears alone. "In a day, two at the most, I shall have the Silverhand. And he will be a long time dying."

CHAPTER FIFTY

Firelight gleamed on the Circus Master's gold teeth and the single gold ring in one of his ears as, smiling with satisfaction, he surveyed the ruins of his meal. He tilted the wooden bowl to his lips and swallowed what remained of the stew. When the last gobbet of cooling fat was gone, he set the bowl down and looked across at Caeled.

The young man had eaten less than half of the greasy stew, but the stony woman had devoured hers and then helped herself to Caeled's. Jocylyn wondered what could be the connection between the two. He had spent a lifetime watching people, and prided himself that one glance of a line of customers waiting to buy tickets was enough for him to read their characters. He could tell those willing to believe anything from the sceptics who must be convinced. He knew in a moment who had come to ooh and aah at the wild beasts and which ones would head straight for the freak show. Looking at a couple, he would make an infallible decision as to whether or not the man would be interested in slipping away to a little tent on the side to see something . . . unusual . . . without his wife.

But these two had so far baffled Jocylyn. Were they relatives? No, they were too aware of one another to be relatives. Lovers, then. No, they kept a subtle distance between themselves at all times and did not seek each other's eyes. They might have been strangers.

But they were not. Of that much he was certain.

Jocylyn leaned back, moving his head out of the light so they would not be aware he was watching them.

The woman was fascinating. Her peculiar hide did not repel him, he had once exhibited a woman with serpent's scales who brought in a lot of money. And hirsute females were common among circuses. But beneath the top layer of skin such women were the same as any other.

The one who called herself Gwynne, however, was different. Jocylyn wondered just how deep the petrification went. It did not appear to be superficial; he recalled the sparks he had struck from her arm, as if it were stone to the bone.

Yet she could move; her joints worked. She had some degree of lower facial mobility, and when she opened her mouth to eat he glimpsed normal pink tissues. What did she look like under her clothes? If he could get her to pose naked she might be a spectacular attraction indeed! The Living Statue. Sucking grease from his fingers, Jocylyn considered the possibilities with growing enthusiasm.

Then he turned his attention to Caeled.

The young man was easier to read and paradoxically, more of a mystery. The hand was a curious device. Beautifully crafted with skills beyond Jocylyn's comprehension, it was so integrated into Caeled's body that it had become a real part of him and hardly detracted from his overall appearance. A young man of eighteen or nineteen cycles, he could be the son of a wealthy merchant or even one of the minor nobility. His posture was proud, his flesh well-nourished, his eyes clear and confident.

But his flesh and blood hand had an unusual callous formation on the outer edge, and another between thumb and forefinger. Furthermore the muscling of his chest and arms suggested hard physical exertion.

Caeled's clothes were also at odds with the impression he gave. He was dressed like a peasant in a simple linen tunic and trousers, and coarsely made sandals. Jocylyn had no way of knowing these garments had been stolen for him by Gwynne, the clothing from a washing line and the sandals from a cottage doorstep.

The last puzzle involved Caeled's stillness. While the stone woman seemed to be constantly in motion, restlessly shifting her body as if she could never get comfortable, her young companion sat as still as stone. His dark eyes fixed on the dancing flames; no expression crossed his face. It was he who might have been a statue.

Was he a mystic of some sort? Jocylyn wondered.

Although he appeared to be lost in a trance, Caeled was fully aware of the Circus Master's scrutiny. He could feel the man's eyes roving over his face and form, just as he could smell the color of the firelight and taste the shape of the food he had eaten. The monks at Baddalaur had amplified his already keen senses and given him exercises to stimulate alternative pathways for them as part of his preparation for the day he was to become a Seeker.

Ignoring Jocylyn, he began directing his senses outward, seeking. A few paces away was the huge blond wolfhound. With an effort Caeled repressed a shudder. Something about the beast filled him with an inexplicable fear.

His questing senses moved on to linger, briefly, on the little girl who slumbered beside the great dog. Her head was pillowed trustingly on his shaggy side.

Beyond the rim of the firelight other members of the circus were preparing for the night. Caeled recognized the soft chatter of the Simpan-sai and the guttural cough of some big cat in a cage. Voices called to one another. A massively tattooed man strode naked past the campfire balancing a bucket of water on his head. A horse snorted on the picket line. Wagons creaked as their occupants moved around inside them.

But Caeled could not find the young woman.

He had caught only a glimpse of her before she

pressed her fingernails against his eyes. Afterwards there had been no opportunity to speak to her, and now he could not locate her at all.

He remembered her scent, though, a delicate ivory fragrance like white petals in moonlight.

"Who made your hand, young man?" Jocylyn asked abruptly.

Caeled raised his head, his mind still on Sioraf. "Nazariel the Senior Healer, in the Healing Chapel of Baddalaur."

"You're not serious!" Jocylyn was impressed. Perhaps the hand was Old Metal, then. Only the monks at Baddalaur had access to such lost arts. If the Circus Master's surmise was correct, Caeled was carrying a king's ransom on the end of his arm.

"Why did you need an artificial hand?"

"I was bitten by a Madra Allta. To save me from the werecurse, my hand was removed and this one created for me."

Jocylyn chuckled. "Hear that, Madran?" The huge blond wolfhound pricked its ears. "He'd rather chop off his hand than turn into a Madra Allta like you!"

The dog replied with a series of yips that sounded suspiciously like laughter.

Fighting back the ghost of an old nightmare, Caeled turned his head to gaze again at the dog. His stomach clenched into a knot.

In the moons after he lost his hand he had awakened many times, sweating and shaking, from a dream in which a weredog was slowly consuming his entire body.

"Madran is a born Madra Allta," the Circus Master said proudly. "He takes the canine form at night, but is powerful enough to assume human form by day. The child is his daughter, Pup, the offspring of a human mother. Pup translates for us when Madran is in his canine form."

Horrified but curiously fascinated, Caeled stared at the

pair of them. Father and daughter? Astonishing. But anything might happen in a world where natural order was breaking down.

He did not want to think about weredogs. "I saw a girl," he said to Jocylyn, trying to change the subject. "A very slender girl . . ."

And suddenly she was there. He heard her fragrance and smelled her beauty an instant before she appeared like a wraith behind the Circus Master.

In the firelight her eyes were the same astonishing blue Caeled remembered.

"My daughter Sioraf," said Jocylyn.

"Caeled Silverhand," the young man replied, holding her eyes with his. "And this is Gwynne." Without breaking contact he gestured toward the Stone Warrior.

Gwynne gave a noncommittal grunt.

So far, Jocylyn noted, she had vouchsafed no information about herself at all.

Could it be there was a price on her head? Their heads? Would taking them put his circus at risk?

Still looking at Sioraf, Caeled inquired, "Where are you going with the circus?"

"Karfondal," Jocylyn replied in a snap decision.

"I'd be quick about it if I were you. No menagerie is safe in this region. The Duet seized the last circus in Barrow not too long ago and . . . ah . . . dispersed it."

Jocylyn tensed. "Do you know the details? If you were in Baddalaur . . ."

Caeled interrupted before he could be questioned about Baddalaur. Perhaps it was not prudent to mention the College, or his connection with it. "I was on the road, it was just something I heard in passing. The travelling show of the Princess Micaela was confiscated by the Duet's guards and its personnel charged with sedition." He recalled the pain he had felt at the news. On that occasion too he had remembered his long ago glimpse of circus life, and wondered what turns his life might have taken if he had simply trotted off behind Micaela's wagons.

Jocylyn drew in his breath with a hiss. "Princess Micaela. That dear, intrepid woman. I don't believe for a moment that she would commit such a crime. What happened to her, do you know?"

"There was a rumor that she was tortured, but whatever happened, I do believe she was eventually made a member of the Council of Barrow. As for her company and her animals, no one will say for sure exactly what became of them."

"It looks as if yours may be the last circus in the Seven Nations," Gwynne drawled, finally breaking her silence. "The twins have eliminated all your competition. That might give you a new name for your troupe. How about 'The Last Circus'?"

Jocylyn stood up, belched, combed through his beard with his fingers. "I don't like the sound of it. Too final. Bad luck. And there's enough of that already.

"It's late and we're all tired. My daughter will find some blankets for you and you can sleep under one of the wagons for now. We'll talk some more tomorrow. I'm going to bed and I suggest you do the same."

The scent of ivory and moonlight woke Caeled. He lay still with his eyes closed, absorbing his surroundings through his senses.

She was close to him, no more than a few paces away. He could not hear the fibers of leather or taste the bitter tang of metal; she was not armed.

Caeled sat up in one smooth motion, startling Sioraf.

She sat cross-legged beside the smoldering remains of the fire. Only a light shift shielded her body from the night air, but she did not seem to notice the cold.

Wrapping a blanket around his shoulders, Caeled crawled out from under the wagon and went over to her. She watched in silence as he sat down beside her.

Without thinking, he reached into the embers with his metal hand and stirred them back to warm life.

"What are you?" Sioraf asked softly. Her lovely face was grave in the firelight.

Caeled shrugged. "A man . . . "

"A man with a silver hand. A man who's been to Baddalaur. And the woman? What of her?"

"I met her while on a journey and we agreed to travel together." It was not the whole truth, but it was the truth.

Her face was like a pale oval of moonlight. Her lips were very red. Caeled could not tear his eyes away.

"I smelled blood on you," Sioraf stated flatly.

Caeled knew he had washed thoroughly, not once but several times, since his last encounter with the Bred. Perhaps there was still blood on the Stone Warrior, though. It might have seeped into the fissures in her skin.

How could this young woman detect anything so subtle?

The safest lie, he recalled reading, was the one nearest the truth. "We were attacked by beasts in the mountains, some sort of huge lizard creatures. But how could you tell? You must have a fine sense of smell."

Sioraf's red lips curved into a smile of incredible sweetness that made Caeled's heart lurch. Then the smile widened, and he saw her needlelike incisors.

"I am a vampir," she said simply.

Only his training prevented him from reacting. He had read about vampiri in the library in Baddalaur, in texts describing them as long-extinct relicts of an Elder race.

Sioraf was not extinct. In that moment she seemed the most real being Caeled had ever seen.

"Some of the Elder races possessed the ability to pass blood from one body to another," Nanri had explained. "For that purpose they had special fangs. But they have been gone so long we have no need to concern ourselves with them. Vampiri are a forgotten curiosity, nothing more."

A vampir sat beside Caeled, smiling at him.

Suddenly he very much wished his old Master were there to see.

"Why are you smiling?"

"I was thinking of an old friend."

"A woman?" Sioraf asked quickly.

"No."

"Ah."

"An old man who once told me vampiri were extinct."

Sioraf's laughter bubbled up unbidden. "There is something about you, Caeled Silverhand. But my instincts warn me . . ."

"If you are a vampir, I am the one who should be cautious." Caeled was struggling to remember what he had read about vampiri. They had supplemented normal food with fresh blood in order to survive; it was one of the peculiarities of their race.

"I am not dangerous to you," Sioraf replied.

He wondered if he could believe her.

"But I fear you are to me. To us. To my father and our circus. Strange people who appear with no explanation have a way of bringing bad luck with them."

"That's the second time tonight someone has spoken of luck."

"We are performers and all performers are superstitious. We expect the worst because life teaches us to do so."

"My life has taught me the same," Caeled confided, "though I'm no performer."

"Then what do you do?"

He did not know how to answer. At last, and rather lamely, he said, "I study. I'm . . . a scholar."

"And you make a living that way? Just by studying?"

Sioraf sounded astonished, and now that he thought about it, Caeled realized why. Outside of the College he could not possibly support himself merely by being a scholar. At a loss for an answer, he shrugged. "I may do something else," he said vaguely.

When she got to her feet, her thin shift molded itself most disturbingly to her body. "I think I would prefer if you left us, you and your companion," Sioraf said. "I do not dislike your company, I just . . . something about you frightens me."

"Something about you frightens me," he responded with total honesty.

She gazed down at him with shadowed eyes. "If you remain and bring misfortune upon my father, I shall have to kill you." Drawing back her foot, Sioraf kicked the fire into a shower of sparks.

Caeled drew back hastily. When he looked up again, she was gone.

Later that night, Caeled dreamed.

A naked woman, pale, silver-skinned, nipples like dark coins on her high round breasts, came to him and crouched over him. He tried to wake up but the weight of her gaze pushed him back into drowsy helplessness. Taking his right hand, she pressed his palm to her breast. The skin was cool and smooth. His wondering fingers cupped the tender roundness, but she lifted them away and held the hand to her mouth.

He felt the touch of her lips on his palm. Then she bit into the soft pad at the base of his thumb with a bite so delicate he could hardly feel it, no more than the nip of a tiny insect.

Golden warmth flooded through his veins.

The dream faded. Caeled sank into a deep, untroubled sleep.

CHAPTER FIFTY-ONE

It came upon the spoor by accident.

It was scouring the forest, hunting. Twice recently it had killed: a female softskin bathing in a pool, then an aged male gathering roots. It had gulped down the tenderest morsels before pressing on, seeking that which was the true object of its hunt.

The two who had killed some of its fellows.

Thinking of their deed filled it with a cold heat that was not anger, but more cruel than anger. A targeted desire to rend and rake with claws, to savage and dismember.

The red eye had given it orders. The red eye had been connected in some way to the female with amber hair. Her essence shimmered through the red eye, a tangible haze that frightened the Bredi beyond bearing. Under her influence the red eye sent many of its kind along the riverbank, searching. Hunting the two softskins who had slain their fellows. They must be found and killed. Terrible things would be done to Bredi who failed.

Terrible things.

It cowered under the thought.

The Bredi knew it had failed in spite of the most diligent searching. It must return to take its punishment; there was no escape. The amber hair could find it anywhere.

It was slinking back the way it had come when its flaring nostrils detected a bitter odor.

Tracing the scent through the forest was easy. The

Bredi had been designed to differentiate between many smells and follow one to the exclusion of all else. Ponderous folds of flesh depending from its cheeks and jowls trapped scent rising from the earth and funnelled it to the eager nostrils.

As it followed the trail, it came upon the remains of a forest creature whose skull had been shattered. Part of it had been eaten by the two the Bredi sought; their smell lingered on what was left of the dead thing.

Tracking them deeper into the forest, the Bredi became aware, without curiosity, of other, stranger smells. Somewhere nearby were beasts it had never encountered.

But they did not matter.

Nothing mattered now but finding its prey and escaping the punishment of the red eye and the amber hair.

Lashing its muscular tail from side to side, the great saurian slithered down the forest path, grumbling deep in its throat with eagerness.

At dawn it came to a place of struggle where the two it sought had recently been. The earth was crushed and flattened, branches were snapped, leaves torn off.

But no blood had been spilled.

The Bredi paused and lifted its head. A slender forked tongue tasted the air.

Where were they?

Escaped? Or captured?

It had to find out. It moved forward again, through the trees.

Pup was dancing through the long grass at the edge of the forest with her face turned to the sky, waiting for the sun to come up. She loved catching the first rays of Nusas on her face. Then she would throw back her head and open her mouth and bay at the sun just as her father sometimes bayed at the moon.

It was one of her favorite games.

The wind was warm and damp this morning. She enjoyed its fresh sweetness as it flowed through the forest. Pup was tired of sea salt and desert sand, and she hated the stink of towns.

The forest was her favorite place.

Nusas peered over the rim of the earth to see who was waiting to greet him. Pup threw back her head and spread her arms wide, dancing in the long grass, inviting him to lift himself higher.

The Bredi attacked.

She managed a single scream before the huge lizard grabbed her.

It had anticipated an easy kill, but the small softskin moved with uncanny swiftness, responding not with the mindless panic of prey but with the fury of a predator. The child bared her teeth and emitted a deep growl such as no softskin should utter, and went for the saurian's eyes with clawing fingers.

The Bredi swung its massive head aside just in time. But it returned instantly to the attack, reaching for the child with scaly forearms.

Pup's second scream was so shrill it hurt the ears of the Bredi. The creature lunged forward, determined to bite off her head and stop the clamor. It saw her eyes glaze in fear . . . then, unbelievably, she smiled.

The Bredi never felt the blow that shattered its spine. As gray death descended, the last thing it saw was a shining silver hand reaching past it, toward the child.

CHAPTER FIFTY-TWO

"I've been with the circus all my life," Jocylyn said, cautiously turning the creature over with a mighty heave of his foot, "but I've never seen anything like this before." The Circus Master looked around at his assembled troupe. "Have any of you?"

The tattooed man knelt beside the dead Bredi, holding himself in readiness to leap up and run if it moved. When he was convinced it would never move again he closed his eyes for a moment. Tattooed eyes appeared on his eyelids, so he seemed to be still staring at the creature. With his two forefingers he tapped his closed eyelids.

Jocylyn understood the gesture. "Let me see no evil," the big man murmured. "What is it, Moi? You've seen such things before? Where, on the Islands?"

The tattooed man nodded. "On the Islands, yes. There were creatures like this, but they were small. Smaller than Pup." He looked up to smile at the child now cradled safely in the arms of a massively built man with hair as blond as her own.

"They are *fomori*," the tattooed man explained. "Flesh-eating lizards. On the Islands the bigger ones are sometimes trained as sentinels, like hounds. They are intelligent in their own way but inclined to be vicious. I've never seen one anywhere near the size of this thing, though." He touched the dead Bredi's face with a tentative finger. "And see here: the jaw is more developed than any normal lizard. And it has hands almost like a man's, except the thumb is curved and has a claw like a spur. I am baffled, Jocylyn," he concluded, standing up again and brushing his hands together as if to brush away the touch of the dead creature.

The Circus Master turned to Caeled. "You know what this is, though, don't you? I can see it in your eyes."

"One of the Bred," Caeled replied.

At the mention of the Bred several of the company drew in their breath sharply.

Caeled noticed, but went on. "The Bred are warriors developed by the Duet. This is just one of the many different forms they take, all horrible. They are strong, deadly, though not invincible. They can bleed and die and are susceptible to cold, though most seem impervious to heat. Some are almost blind in sunlight, but have excellent vision in the dark. Others exude an oily sweat that will burn. Most of them stink."

"What is it doing here?" Jocylyn demanded to know. His heavy eyebrows were drawn together over his nose into a ferocious scowl.

Gwynne stepped forward, allowing her stone elbow to brush Caeled's side as if by accident, but hard enough to hurt. Seeing this confirmed Jocylyn's suspicions. The creature had not come upon the camp by accident. These two were to blame for its presence and they knew it.

"The warriors of the Bred are all over the Nations now," Gwynne said calmly. "You might find them any-where; I narrowly avoided a large company of them in the mountains."

To Jocylyn's annoyance he could not tell if she was lying. The muscles of her lower face were apparently quite mobile, but those around her eyes had stiffened to an extent sufficient to prevent any involuntary, telltale twitches. She possessed a truly stony stare and one he could not read.

"Maybe this one was following you," he suggested.

The performers murmured among themselves.

"Maybe they brought it to us deliberately," said a female acrobat who doubled as cook for the circus. "I can't say as I like the look of either one of this pair, if you want my opinion."

Gwynne sidestepped, putting enough distance between herself and Caeled to allow her to use the morningstar without hitting him. The movement was swift and instinctive.

From her father's arms, Pup glanced meaningfully at the two Simpan-sai. Although no word was spoken, they turned and ran into the trees and scampered into the branches. Birds erupted squawking with alarm.

Before the Stone Warrior could do anything that might forever alienate them from the circus, Caeled said quickly, "The Bredi might have followed our track here, but more likely it was trailing you. Gwynne gives off no human scent, and I have long made it a habit to bathe twice a day. Your wagons, your beasts and performers, however, emit enough odors to draw a pack of wolves, never mind one of the Bred."

"Still," Jocylyn replied with a gold-toothed smile, "we could kill you just to be sure."

Caeled was not certain he was joking. "You could try," he said. The silver hand clenched as if it had a mind of its own.

A deep voice growled, "There's no need for that. I believe them."

"Madran," Jocylyn snapped, "stay out of this."

The big man carrying Pup stepped up beside the Circus Master. He stood a head taller than Jocylyn, and he moved with the assured muscularity of a superb athlete. Only a hint of his canine self showed in the jut of Madran's jaw and the angle of his cheekbones — and the shaggy blond hair drawn back and tied with a leather thong at the nape of his neck. Still carrying Pup in the crook of one arm, he put his other hand on Caeled's shoulder.

The young man flinched in spite of himself.

"This one saved Pup," boomed Madran's deep voice. "I am indebted to him."

"Well I don't owe him anything," whined the cook. "He's done nothing for me, and I think he's connected with that . . . that dead thing there in some way. People have accused us of being the Bred, you know. It's horrible. I don't want anything to do with any of them, and that includes these two!"

"Let Pup find out the truth," said Madran. "You know that no one has ever been able to make her believe a lie."

Caeled glanced at Gwynne. Her face was expressionless, her thoughts hidden behind a stone wall. If they were attacked she had already decided to kill Jocylyn and Madran first.

The Madra Allta still had his hand on Caeled's shoulder. "If you have told the truth, you have nothing to fear."

"I have told the truth," Caeled replied. He was agonizingly aware of the weredog's touch, and relieved when Madran stepped away from him and set his daughter on her feet.

Caeled bent his knees until his face was on a level with hers. "Give me your hands," the child said.

Caeled placed both flesh and metal on her outstretched palms. She stared down at them for a moment, then dropped the silver one and closed both her hands tightly around the other.

"Are you allied with the Bred in any way?" Madran asked above their heads.

Caeled looked into Pup's wide eyes and smiled. "No," he said.

She met his gaze with a luminous look that searched his soul. Then she turned toward Jocylyn. "He's telling the truth," she reported.

Madran growled, "That's good enough for me. What about you, Circus Master? Are you with us, or not?"

At that moment the two Simpan-sai ran up, chattering softly.

"There's no one in the trees and they don't see anyone else approaching," Pup translated.

"All right," Jocylyn conceded, trying to regain control of the situation. "Have it your way this time." Without Madran and Pup as his star attractions he did not have much of a draw and he knew it. "Strike camp."

Madran scooped up the limp body of the Bredi as if it weighed no more than Pup and slung it over his broad shoulder. "I'll dump this in the river." He glanced at Caeled, "Walk with me awhile."

Madran inhaled deeply as they stepped among the trees. "You're right, I can smell the camp. When you're part of it, you don't notice the smells."

Caeled remained silent, unsure how to respond. Merely being so close to a Madra Allta made him nervous, in spite of the man's apparent friendliness toward him.

"I meant what I said. You saved my daughter's life. I am indebted to you."

"I think you have already discharged your debt," Caeled replied. "Things could have turned nasty back there."

Madran nodded gravely. "They would have killed you to protect themselves. Circus folk are a clannish lot and suspicious of any outsider. They're all freaks . . . " He caught Caeled's smile and interpreted it correctly. "I am not a freak. I am a Madra Allta of the Clan Allta," he said proudly.

Then his tone changed, darkened. "But my daughter is a freak. I fell in love with a human woman . . . and she, may the gods be merciful to her spirit, fell in love with me." The big man ducked beneath a low branch. "We fled Amorica when our relationship became known. There are strict laws forbidding mating between an Allta and a human. But we loved each other, we had no patience with laws."

The river glinted through the trees. When they reached the bank, Madran dumped his burden unceremoniously, then scooped up mud and ground it deep into the fatal wound. "This will make it look as if the creature had a fatal fall," he told Caeled. "Perhaps from that cliff on the other side of the river."

Together the two of them rolled the big saurian into the water. Its white belly showed for a moment as it turned lazily on the current, then it was swept away.

Madran resumed talking as if he had never stopped. "There were good reasons for that law," he told Caeled. "I know it now; I know it every time I look at my daughter." There was a deep sadness in his voice that touched Caeled in spite of himself.

"But Pup is a beautiful little girl," he told Madran.

"Aye, she is. She is almost a true human. She cannot take the beast shape, though she wants to with all her heart, I know. She is forever caught between two forms of being; that is her tragedy."

"And your mate?" Caeled asked. "What of her, the human you loved?"

"Pup, my beautiful daughter, bit and clawed her way out of her mother's womb like a wild beast breaking out of a trap. My love died of her injury while making me promise to take good care of her killer." Madran's deep voice sank deeper until Caeled forgot what he was and felt only his pain.

Human and Madra Allta walked on together, each with his own thoughts.

They were halfway back to the camp when they heard the screams.

CHAPTER FIFTY-THREE

They discovered the body of one of the Simpan-sai first. Strangled with its own tail, it had been thrust into the bushes. Its sister lay curled into a ball close by, the small skull crushed.

Madran began to growl as they raced toward the camp, a guttural roar of accelerating menace. Glancing at him out of the corner of his eye, Caeled saw the features of his face rippling like clay softening in the sun. Coarse hair sprouted along the line of his cheekbones. His bared fangs gleamed.

A wounded Bredi warrior — as canine as the Madra Allta — staggered onto the trail before them. It cocked its shaggy head to look dully at Madran, as if wondering if he was one of its own kind. In that moment Madran lunged for its throat.

The Bredi died without a sound.

Caeled dragged Madran off the creature. For an instant the werebeast's eyes blazed irrationally. Then, as he recognized his companion, the savage light faded.

"Listen," Caeled commanded.

Madran's features were almost totally canine now, with a long blood-soaked muzzle, although he retained his human body. Like most of the true Allta, he could control the were-change. "I don't hear anything," he said in a rasping growl as he forced human words from a bestial throat.

"Neither do I, not now. That's what worries me."

Madran kicked the body of the Bredi out of his way. "There were thirty performers in the circus . . . "

"And Gwynne," Caeled reminded him.

They broke into a run again. They were at the outer perimeter of the camp when they found another dead Bredi dangling from the branches of a tree, turning slowly, a loop of vines knotted securely around its neck.

Caeled felt a hollowness in his belly. The forest was too quiet. The screams they had heard earlier — human screams — had carried a note of absolute terror. And they had ended too suddenly.

With preternaturally alert senses he sought a reassuring hum of insect life, a whisper of bird wings, any smell or feel or taste of normal activity. But the forest was as still as death.

"Madran, wait . . . " he warned.

Too late — the Madra Allta had already pushed apart the screen of leaves and branches and stepped out into the clearing where the caravans formed a circle around the smoldering campfire.

A groan of anguish was wrung from him.

The circus was devastated. After an appallingly brief battle bodies lay everywhere; few were intact.

The Bred were still crouched over their victims, feeding.

A score of heads raised to look at the Madra Allta. With a roar, he charged them. He killed two of the enemy before they could even get to their feet, ripping the throat from one and then hurling himself on the next without stopping for breath.

All control was lost to emotion as Madran flowed through his Allta shapes, alternately man and dog and terrifying amalgam, his form as fluid as tears and as savage as rage. When his jaws were not locked onto one of the Bredi, he flung back his head and filled the forest with howls of absolute despair.

Caeled had been about to follow him into the open

when a glimpse of movement among the trees to his left sent him into a battle crouch instead. His metal hand clenched into a fist.

Sioraf was standing half concealed among the trees, her eyes turned toward the scene in the clearing. In her right hand was a ripple-edged dagger. Her dark curls were wildly tangled, her clothing half ripped from her. Claw marks scored her throat and the upper part of her breasts.

No sooner did she appear than Gwynne materialized a few paces to the right as if rising from solid earth. Looking at Caeled, the Stone Warrior put a finger over her lips to signal silence.

She moved to Caeled's side. They watched together through a screen of leaves as Madran was being driven back and surrounded by the band of Bredi.

Gwynne abruptly turned away.

Caeled caught her arm. "Where are you going?" he whispered.

She pulled free. "While they're busy with him we can get away."

"But Madran . . . "

"Is as good as dead," Gwynne hissed, "and I don't want to join him. Those creatures have us seriously outnumbered."

"I'll not walk away and leave Madran."

"He is Madra Allta," replied Gwynne coldly. "A werebeast, nothing more. Let the Bred have him."

"Abandon him to them and you're no better than they are!"

They glared at each other as a silent battle of wills raged. Then Caeled, breathing hard to control his anger, turned back toward Madran.

Twelve of the saurian Bredi had penned the Madra Allta against the circus supply wagon. They were jabbing at him with spears and tridents, playing with him as cruelly as cats with a bird. Only Madran's reflexes kept them from impaling him, although he had already received a number of minor wounds. He continued to shape-shift, howling with a ravening rage that was terrifying to hear. In a hand which was sometimes a clawed paw he held a sickle torn from its holder on the side of the wagon. The curved blade dripped gore.

Caeled caught a whiff of copper and bitter herbs.

"What will you do?" asked a soft voice. "How can we fight so many?"

Sioraf stood beside him now. She seemed to radiate not human warmth, but an intense cold.

"Fire," Caeled replied with sudden inspiration. "If we could throw burning branches into their midst . . . "

"It might distract them long enough for Madran to escape!" Sioraf finished the thought for him.

"He doesn't want to escape," insisted the Stone Warrior. "Can't you see? The Allta blood lust grips him, he's out of control. He just wants to kill and kill."

"You cannot blame him," said Sioraf, pointing to a bundle of rags on the far side of the dying campfire.

After a moment Caeled recognized the bloodstained garments — and knew whose body they contained. "Pup," he whispered.

Sioraf nodded sadly. "Madran cannot rest while her killers live."

"I grieve with him," said Caeled. "So much pain, so much death. And now this child . . . "

"They are nothing to you!" Gwynne broke in, her voice hard. "They weren't even human. Think of yourself and forget about them, it's the only way to survive."

Caeled deliberately turned away from her, then darted from the concealment of the bushes. He kept his eyes averted from the pathetic bundle lying beyond the fire as he seized a smoldering branch and whipped it back and forth until it burst into flame again. Then he tossed the torch into the midst of the Bred.

The blazing brand struck one of the creatures full in

the face, igniting the oily sweat exuding from its pores. Flames raced the length of its body in an eyeblink. With a shrill screech, the burning saurian lumbered sideways, crashed into another Bredi, clutched at it, dragged it down. They collapsed together to die in flames.

Four Bredi left Madran and ran with surprising speed toward Caeled. He tossed another burning branch at them but it fell short. One of the creatures unexpectedly leaped the last two strides, landing on top of Caeled with a bone-jarring thud.

He managed to strike it once, delivering a blow with his metal hand that shattered the bones above its eyes and drove slivers into its brain. The dying Bredi pinned Caeled to the earth with its body. While he was struggling to free himself the others were upon him. He fought back as best he could, but felt them crowding over him; smelled their hate, heard their hunger. He was dimly aware that the rest of their party had come to join them, closing in for the kill.

So now it ends, Caeled told himself. So soon. . . .

The young man's lips twisted in a bitter smile. The Seekers were wrong. He was not the Spoken One after all . . .

Hot blood spattered across his face. He flinched automatically, closing his eyes so he would not see the face of death.

When he realized the weight had lifted from his chest he opened them again in surprise to find himself still alive.

A dead saurian lay beside him. Gwynne reached down and extended a hand to help him up. The bulbous end of her morningstar was clotted with blood and saurian scales, and as Caeled rose groggily to his feet he saw Sioraf wiping the edge of her dagger clean on what remained of her skirt.

There were eight remaining Bredi. Gwynne accounted

for three, fatally bashing them with her morningstar while they were unable to claw through her invulnerable hide. Madran, bleeding but still wild with rage, killed two more with fangs and sickle. Caeled cut down another two with single blows of the silver hand, using techniques Armadiel had taught him which he had never expected to need. Sioraf flowed up behind the last of the Bredi as it raised a lizardlike arm to strike Caeled from behind, and drove her long dagger through the armpit and into its heart.

Silence descended on the forest again, broken only by the harsh, ragged breathing of the living.

They looked at one another dazedly. Gwynne, who had moved her bulk with a warrior's speed at the height of the battle, was paying for it now. Her heart hammered as if it would burst, her lungs worked like bellows. But she hid her discomfort behind a stony expression.

With an effort, Madran stabilized his shifting form and ran to his dead child. What appeared to be a human man crouched over Pup, stroking the small body with a gentle, tentative hand. Then he threw back his head and emitted a howl of grief that was not human at all, a ululation that made the hair rise on the back of Caeled's neck and filled Sioraf's eyes with tears.

Only the Stone Warrior remained impassive.

At last the four survivors began burying their dead.

CHAPTER FIFTY-FOUR

"An entire troop!" Lares repeated with incredulous anger. He swept an arm along the shelf, hurling books and charts to the ground. "Twenty of the Bred!"

Sarel stood in front of her brother, forcing him to look into her eyes. Then she moved until her body was pressed against his, so he felt her nakedness through the diaphanous cloth of her gown. Her body was the comfort she offered him as she urged, "Be calm, my brother, calm. Whatever has happened, there is nothing we cannot handle."

Lares allowed his head to rest on his sister's shoulder. Frustration seethed and bubbled inside him. The Bred were meant to be invincible, the ultimate warriors. Many inferior early creations had been destroyed during the initial trials, but those were acceptable losses incurred in development. Suddenly losing twenty of the best, however . . .

"What happened?" Sarel wanted to know. She cupped her hand around the back of his skull and ran it soothingly downward, stroking his neck with circular motions of her thumb and forefinger.

"A raiding party was on the trail of the two who escaped from Baddalaur. They followed them downriver, close to the Forest of Taesir, but there they lost them. Scouts were sent into the fringes of the forest ahead of a troop of twenty of our best warriors.

"They all disappeared," he concluded bleakly.

"Could they have wandered into marshland and drowned?"

"There is none," Lares told her. "I sent Kichal himself in search of them and he brought me a detailed report of the area, but no living Bredi."

"And?" Sarel asked, although she could read the answer from the tension in her brother's body.

"Kichal found the remains of an encampment — a circus — and our troop. Their bodies had been mauled and chewed by animals, but he could see that weapons had done most of the killing. Weapons such as men carry."

"The same wounds as before?"

"The same. Except two Bredi were burned beyond recognition."

"The natural body oils of the saurian type burn easily," Sarel commented. "We shall have to speak to the Breeder about making modifications. What else did Kichal report?"

"There were piles of rocks scattered around the edge of the camp. Kichal had them pulled apart. They proved to be cairns over graves which contained humans and non-humans who must have been with the circus."

Lares paused. He wrapped his arms around his sister and squeezed her tightly. "You realize what this means?"

She nodded slowly. "Of course. The Bred are not invincible after all, and there are those who know that now." As she spoke an unwanted image of a silver hand drifted across her mind.

Lares felt her stiffen in his embrace. "What are we going to do?" he asked her.

"Find those who killed our Bred," Sarel said simply. "Find them and kill them."

"But how are we going to find them?"

"Through the Aethyra."

CHAPTER FIFTY-FIVE

They took shelter on a mud flat in the river. Huddled beneath the massive, drooping leaves of an abnormally large water-vine, they sat in silence and watched a driving rain whip the surface of the river to froth.

There was heavier rain higher in the mountains. A flood, perhaps. The water pouring downstream was brown and dirty beneath its crest of foam.

No one spoke. There was nothing to say. Only Gwynne eventually tried to sleep, but then her dreams were troubled. Her children came back to haunt her — though not her husband, never Silan. Collum, Marik, Nole, Bevan and baby Derfyl appeared in silent procession, their faces calm as death masks but their eyes accusing, as if she was to be blamed for having survived.

Then as she held her arms out to them they began to change. The childish foreheads became more sloping, the eyes narrowed to slits. Their horrified mother saw her children transmogrified into the Bred.

In her sleep the Stone Warrior twitched and moaned. One hand clenched into a fist, relaxed, clenched again. Behind her closed eyes her eyeballs rolled painfully, for their natural lubricity was gradually drying up as the relentless petrification process continued.

Within her skull, Gwynne's mind was also changing.

Desires altered, plans were reformed. Emotions faded to be replaced by new and stronger feelings.

Her loss became a stone in her heart, weighing more

heavily than any need for herself. The stone commanded.

She opened her eyes.

The expression in them had changed.

A decision was made.

She would slay the Duet. What good would it do her to force them to cure her strange disease? The children would still be lost to her, the grief would be as intense.

Only one thing might ease that pain. Avenging her dead.

Personally. Not Caeled, but the Stone Warrior must be the one to strike them down. Nothing less would suffice.

And for that she would need the Arcana.

She would allow Caeled to lead her to the Arcana, since he was the one with directions. Then she would demand he give the ancient tools of power to her. There was a chance he would refuse, of course. But if he did . . .

It would be unfortunate. But her need to avenge her family took precedence over everything else.

And Caeled was not as strong as she was. She could kill him if she must. Kill him without hesitation as what was left of her heart finally turned to stone.

Madran was not sitting upright but curled into a ball with arms and legs gathered against his body. Though he was awake he kept his eyes closed to shut out the view of the river. In the turbulent current an occasional tree limb spun past, looking like the upraised arm of a drowned figure.

Or a murdered figure.

No matter how hard he tried, Madran could not shut out the image of Pup seared on his brain.

At least she had died quickly; he had that small consolation. She could not possibly have survived her horrific injuries for more than a heartbeat.

But how terrible that brief moment must have been for her!

The big man ground his teeth together. His hands closed

convulsively, the nails piercing unnoticed the flesh of his palms.

The Bred had done terrible things to the child he had sworn to protect. Sworn, with all the superhuman devotion of which he was capable, to the only creature he had ever loved.

The Bred were controlled by the Duet.

They must be punished.

They *would* be punished.

Deep in his throat, the man who was not a man began to growl.

Sioraf had seen many dead in her short life. In childhood she had taken sustenance from the bodies of the dead who were to be found in the back streets of any large town. Their congealing blood was distasteful and unsatisfying, but at least it kept her alive. As she grew and her body ripened it became possible to entice living men — and women — and take what she needed from them. Hot sweet blood, flowing through the throat like velvet, bringing a glow to her pale flesh.

She had tried not to be greedy, taking only a little blood at a time. The bites of her tiny, needle-sharp teeth usually went unnoticed in the throes of passion. Then one night she had gone too far and taken too much from a plump merchant in Bhopal, only to have him die in her embrace.

She would never forget the curious mixture of fear and satisfaction she experienced, the sudden realization of the power she possessed.

After that there were other deaths, but they had little effect on her. They were simply the cost of her own survival. She was even able to look upon the ravaged body of her father and gauge with an experienced eye the depth of his wounds and the probable cause of death.

For the first time, her sense of detachment disturbed her. Was she becoming . . . so unhuman? What of the future? Would the Sioraf she knew fade away, leaving a monster behind?

Suddenly she, who had never been frightened, shivered with fear. Fear of herself.

There was another fear, also. Without the circus as protection, as camouflage, the life expectancy of her kind was limited. Sooner or later her identity would be discovered. Ordinary people would hunt her down. She was not immortal; vampiri could be slain and their deaths were usually horrible.

She needed protection such as Jocylyn had given her. Someone who loved her enough to give her a drink from his own warm veins when she could find no other prey. Someone strong and confident, who would not feel threatened by her existence but be willing to share.

From such a person she would never take enough to kill, not as long as he kept her safe. But to be willing to do that he would have to love her.

And who would love a vampir?

She turned her vividly blue eyes toward Caeled. Someone like him, perhaps; a man with a blemish of his own might be more tolerant of hers. He did not love her . . . yet. But Sioraf was an expert in making men love her.

Caeled stared into the river, using techniques he had been taught in Baddalaur to cleanse his mind of the scenes he had recently witnessed. But he could not build walls against the emotions of others. He was acutely conscious of Madran's pain. The Madra Allta's grief spread outward from him in concentric circles that seemed to penetrate Caeled's own flesh.

For many cycles he had believed the Allta nothing more than bestial brutes who lived only to kill and eat. Once he had actually accompanied Armadiel on a hunt through the mountains for a Madra Allta reported to be lurking along the trail leading to the Town. During three days' search they had found plenty of evidence of a large wild dog roaming the area, but no proof that it was a werebeast.

Caeled had been disappointed. He had wanted,

desperately, to find a Madra Allta and kill it with his silver hand, a nicely symmetrical vengeance. Though they never found the creature they sought, his desire for revenge had remained with him.

Until now.

When Caeled first met Madran he felt the old fear, the sick fear that welled up in the pit of his stomach and flooded his mouth with bile.

Then he had watched as Madran buried the body of his daughter. Until then he never knew that beasts could weep.

Now he hurt for the Madra Allta.

The sensation and its implications surprised him, but there were more immediate matters to consider. Decisions had to be made.

During the cycles he spent in Baddalaur he had been trained for one purpose: finding the Arcana and using them against the Duet. Reimposing order on a chaotic world. No one asked him if he desired this destiny, it was simply announced for him.

As time passed, however, he had begun to suspect the location of the Arcana might never be discovered. At first he felt disappointment, but as he grew older and the adventurous dreams of childhood faded he began actually looking forward to a placid existence as a Scholar. He would spend his days expanding his knowledge, losing himself in tales of the Elder Times. He would not even seek promotion to the brotherhood of Seekers. He told himself he had seen enough of the outside world.

He told himself a quiet life would be . . . comfortable.

Then chaos intervened.

Caeled's lips curved into an ironic smile. If the Bred had not attacked Baddalaur, if Nanri had not been slain, the secret location of the Arcana might never have been found and his life would have proceeded as he imagined.

Everything would have remained unchanged.

In order.

But now Caeled knew the location of two of the

Arcana. And when he found them, they would lead him to the other two.

His fingers stole to the leather pouch that carried the precious information. *The Staff and the Stone were secreted in the great and ancient city of Gor in the land of Taesir.*

The young man stroked the pouch, considering the tricks played by fate.

Was it fate that brought him to the edge of the Forest of Taesir?

Now there were decisions to be made. He could avoid his destiny and turn away, head south to Karfondal, or west into Galloway, or maybe east to the Barbarian Isles. But then what?

The Bred would remain, the Duet would remain, the Nations would sink into a chaotic abyss characterized by the dissolution of natural order. The plants, the very animals, were already giving evidence of a hideous regression. Everything humankind had built would be lost. The people would retreat further and further into ignorance and barbarism until they were less than human.

And the chaos would not be limited to the Seven Nations. Reports brought to Baddalaur had indicated that the world beyond was similarly caught up in a cycle of destruction. If the twins had access to the Aethyra and were working through it, their influence was boundless.

The young man shook his head. Such total, uncaring destruction was unacceptable. Pictures flashed through his mind: the horrors of the Voids, the stinking pools of filth that had been people, the rampaging Bredi warriors . . . there had to be an alternative future.

There would be, if he could defeat the Duet. His might be a futile attempt; the Arcana could be long gone, the twins could prove too powerful . . . but at least he could try. Must try.

Caeled smiled again, grimly.

Perhaps there was no escaping destiny after all.

CHAPTER FIFTY-SIX

"We're being watched," said Madran as he fell into step beside Caeled. "I feel eyes staring at the back of my neck."

"Ever since we entered the forest," Caeled affirmed.

"The Bred?"

The young man shook his head. "I don't think so. These smell . . . different. Almost human."

"Your nose is almost as keen as mine, apparently," said Madran with new respect. The big Madra Allta pulled his jerkin tighter around his shoulders and shivered, though it was not cold. His hand tightened on the hilt of the sickle he carried with him constantly now, still crusted with Bredi gore. "These are ancient forests. Who knows what survives in them?"

Caeled looked around with a sense of wonder. "The Heart of the World," he murmured.

Madran glanced sharply at him.

"The Heart of the World," Caeled repeated, "that's what the Forest of Taesir is called on the ancient maps and charts. The Elders ruled from the city of Gor. When their world died the city was lost and this mighty forest grew out of the ruins, nourished by the bodies of a million dead."

As far as the eye could see, nut-bearing goldwoods rose in their thousands, straight as spears. They sprouted no branches until they reached ten man-heights, at which point horizontal claw-like limbs encircled the boles of the trees. Like the bark, the pointed leaves were the color of old gold. Although the matted canopy they formed prevented much light from reaching the forest floor, an occasional slanting sunbeam shot a momentary radiance through the gloom.

Clustered around the roots of the trees were parasitic plants. Their thick tendrils climbed up the goldwoods, lacing the trunks with a clinging network of bruise-purple stems. On the largest trees these veins could be seen to pulse in a regular rhythm.

Sioraf darted away from her companions to stand in a sudden sunbeam. With her arms wide and head thrown back, she bathed in the light as if trying to draw the heat of distant Nusas into her cold vampir flesh.

She looks like a child, Caeled thought with surprise. A beautiful child, lost and alone and seeking comfort.

Madran brought his thoughts sharply back. "Are you sure you can find what you're seeking in this place?"

"No," Caeled replied, "I'm not at all sure. But I have to try."

"What will you do if your quest is successful?"

"Use the objects I find to destroy the twins."

"And what then?"

Caeled turned to look at him. "I don't know," he admitted. "I hadn't thought that far ahead."

Like a shadow, Sioraf slipped in next to Caeled. "Beasts in the trees," she whispered. "Many creatures."

The young man gazed into her luminous blue eyes. His dream of her was still startlingly vivid. "Are they human, Sioraf?"

Her lips parted; her nostrils flared. "Humankind . . . but not human," she replied, confirming Caeled's own impressions.

Gwynne, who was forging ahead of the trio, halted abruptly and raised her hand. In the green twilight of the forest her body appeared to be solid stone. As the others approached she knelt stiffly on the trail. "What do you see?" she asked over her shoulder.

Dropping down beside her, Caeled peered along the twisting pathway. "Nothing in particular. Trees, vines. What am I looking for?"

"What did they teach you in that college?" she snapped. "Tell him, Madran. I should think you noticed almost before I did."

The Madra Allta crouched beside Caeled and pointed at the ground with a long black fingernail. "Look at the pattern of leaves."

As Caeled examined the trail Sioraf leaned over them, frowning slightly. "It's just a fall of leaves covering the path," she said.

"Not quite," Madran replied. "Look behind you."

Caeled looked over his shoulder. "There are a lot less leaves on the track behind us," he observed. Turning again to the scattering of leaves before him, he realized they were not a random scattering, but a very thorough effort to cover . . . to cover. . . . He found a stone beside the path and tossed it onto the center of the trackway.

The rock broke through the covering of leaves and went on falling. An opening yawned in the trail, revealing a stake-lined pit cleverly camouflaged beneath the foliage.

Madran grinned, baring his canine incisors. "The hole was covered with a piece of leather, which in turn was covered with earth and leaves." He crept forward on all fours and gazed down into the pit. "Those stakes are newly sharpened. The wood is white and freshly cut."

The others clustered around him.

"Is this a man-trap?" Sioraf wondered.

"Not really," Madran told her. "It's too shallow." He stood up and stared off into the forest. "This trap was meant for smaller game. If we assume that the creatures in the trees built the pit . . . "

" . . . they are intelligent," Caeled finished for him. "And they eat meat."

Gwynne worked her stiff shoulders, muscles grinding

like old stone. "They're beginning to get on my nerves, whatever they are."

"They're close," said Sioraf.

"How close? How can you tell?"

The vampir sniffed. "I can smell warm blood." Her voice fell to a breathy whisper. "There's one in the tree beside you. It's in the branches directly above your head."

The Stone Warrior tensed. Then without warning she lunged for the tree, hitting it solidly with her shoulder. The massive blow sent a shudder through the goldwood. Some of its roots pulled loose from the soft earth.

The woman recoiled from the blow, sprawling on the ground while leaves and nuts began to rain down on her. As she lay on her back Gwynne raised her legs and drove her feet against the tree again and again. Wood creaked in protest. Then, with a slow grinding, the ancient tree tilted sideways. Roots erupted from the ground, clutching futilely at empty air as the big goldwood hung in space for a moment, then toppled. It crashed to earth with a thunder that echoed through the forest, crushing half a dozen smaller trees as it fell.

Only Madran heard the high-pitched scream that was swallowed in the tremendous noise.

"You fool!" Caeled raged, as Gwynne climbed slowly to her feet. "You've alerted everything in the forest that we're here."

"I assure you, they already knew." Brushing past Caeled, the Stone Warrior faced the vampir. "Can you smell blood now?"

"I smell meat," Sioraf replied. She pointed along the length of the fallen tree. "Down there."

As they approached the figure lying beneath the tree trunk, the forest burst into a cacophony of screeches and whistles and high-pitched ululations.

Madran squinted into the leafy canopy high above. "I've heard the Simpan-sai cry like that."

Caeled crouched by the body on the ground. Although

the face and shoulders were intact, the remainder of the body had been crushed by the falling tree. It was that of a young man not much older than himself. The eyes were glazing; light brown eyes in a finely modelled, handsome face.

As Caeled watched, the muscles of face and jaw began shifting beneath the skin, taking on a bestial appearance.

"Madran," Caeled called softly. "Look at this."

The Madra Allta leaned over his shoulder to watch the transformation.

The face was foreshortening. The eyes closed, sank into the skull. A mane of hair erupted from the scalp to encircle the features and conceal the thickening jaw.

"Allta . . .?" Gwynne said uncertainly.

Sioraf knelt by the man's head and touched one slim finger to the corner of the mouth, where a thread of blood was seeping into the beard. Raising her fingertip to her mouth, she licked it thoughtfully, closed her eyes, licked again. "Not human," she reported.

Suddenly the changes began reversing. The features of a beast melted back into the face of a handsome young man. Caeled and his companions glanced at one another in astonishment, but before they could comment another change took place and the bestial brow and jaw, the massive hair growth, reappeared.

"When a man who has become one of the Clan Allta dies, he returns to his human form," said Madran. "When a true Allta dies, however, he takes on his animal form. What we are seeing here seems to be a creature caught between both. A new sort of Allta."

"Is he dead yet?" Sioraf wanted to know.

"Almost. His dying is certainly upsetting the forest," commented Gwynne. "Just listen."

The shrieks and screeches had risen to an unbearable pitch. At the same time, a rain of missiles began to fall, hurled from the trees. Hard nuts struck the four companions from all sides. Sioraf yelped as one hit her cheekbone hard enough to raise a bruise. Another shattered on the Stone Warrior's skull.

"Now what?" cried Caeled, dodging. "This is your fault, Gwynne. Why did you have to knock down a tree?" He raised his arms to protect his face.

A nut pinged off his metal hand.

Gwynne told him, "Sometimes it's necessary to get a reaction. We could have walked all day with these things in the trees shadowing us, biding their time. Or we could do what we've done now: forced them into revealing themselves."

"Let's get out of here," said Madran as the pelting grew worse. He set off at a loping run. Caeled and Sioraf promptly followed.

But Gwynne lingered behind. A rain of nuts could not harm her.

She stepped close to a massive goldwood and peered upward until she caught sight of figures moving through the tree tops. Vaguely manlike, they slithered down the vines and clustered around the broken body on the ground. The Stone Warrior squinted, but her sight was not as clear as it once was and she found it difficult to make out details.

The dark figures clustered around the fallen tree communicated with high-pitched, chittering noises. They seemed to be making gestures of some sort. Then Gwynne heard a gasp followed by an aborted scream.

After that, silence. Until her ears detected the unmistakeable sounds of animals feeding.

Gwynne turned away; she knew now what haunted the upper levels of the trees.

She set off after Caeled, Madran and Sioraf, following their trail through the forest. Although she kept her eyes on the track, her ears were keenly aware of every sound around her, listening for the first hint of chittering and screeching that would warn she was being pursued.

When she reached a fork in the trail she paused. The

ground was firm and not easily footprinted, but she detected traces of Madran's heavy tread going off to the left, down toward a scummy pool half-hidden in undergrowth.

Following the trail, Gwynne discovered the footprints of Caeled, Sioraf and Madran in the soft mud at water's edge.

There the trail ended.

Gwynne found no footprints going away from the pond.

None at all.

CHAPTER FIFTY-SEVEN

Against a seething maelstrom of colors, the two white crows blazed with cold light.

Higher and higher through the levels of the Aethyra they rose on the Timewinds, soaring above the emotional outpourings, the dreams and nightmares of the World Below.

The twins could not remember the first time they had entered the Lower Realms, consciously visiting the dreamscapes lesser beings could only reach through sleep. The earliest memories of the Duet went back to their first few moons in the flesh. Certainly by their third cycle, they were accomplished enough to have explored all the lower levels of the Aethyra.

They were convinced, moreover, that they had visited the Middle Realms in the Time before Birth. Sarel in particular retained a vivid image of the Place of Old Memories. But unlike others who had access to the Aethyra, they had never attempted to retrace the Timewinds and watch themselves in the Time Before.

Sarel and Lares believed that only Time Now mattered. Always, Time Now.

As the cycles had passed and their strength increased, the desire to stretch their limits grew. Upon entering young adulthood they discovered the joys of sexual union. From this rapturous joining they learned to draw a special energy, allowing them to go higher and higher into the Aethyra until they gained access to the Realms of Power.

In that trackless landscape of audible color, of fragrant shapes, of sounds made tangible, they had learned to interpret what was happening in the World Below by observing the layers of the Aethyra. Every action in the World Below caused a reaction somewhere within the Thirty Realms Above.

The majority of events never penetrated above the lowest levels, where mundane feelings and experiences were reflected.

But the more intense passions — undiluted hatred, uncontrolled lust, deepest love — managed to percolate through to the Fifth Realm and sometimes beyond. Most magical exercises involved sufficient power to move still higher. When the twins began drawing power from the Realms to fuel the Voids, the ripples spread throughout the Aethyra, disturbing dreams, tainting emotions, distorting the shapes and colors of the dreamscape so that all who ventured within, even the innocent in their slumbers, were tormented.

So far the Duet had never attempted the highest five of the thirty levels. Those Realms were shadowy regions where moved huge shapes beyond the knowing of mortal ken. According to legend, the gods themselves inhabited the Highest Realms. The twins insisted they did not believe in any gods other than themselves. But even Sarel had not dared enter the uppermost levels. Yet.

Following the invisible tracery of power that shaped the topography of the lower Aethyra, they had flown westward toward Baddalaur, gradually climbing until the only landmarks were the explosions of color resulting from powerful emotions in the World Below.

Baddalaur was marked by a pustulous yellow smear permeating a number of layers of the Aethyra. The deaths of so many men with powerful minds, some of them long-time travellers in the Aethyra, had left an ugly stain on the dreamscape that might never disappear. The hideous echoes of death and pain would attract evil entities. Drawn by the foul discoloration, some would make their way into the World Below, giving the ruined College the reputation of being haunted. Many of the lesser forces — vile thoughts and malignant emotions made substantial in the Realm of the Unsubstantial — would remain in the Aethyra. But in the Aethyra, thoughts became words and words became flesh.

As the twins approached the extinct volcano which had housed the College, Lares' form changed from that of a white crow into a gleaming man-shape of polished jet. Onyx eyes regarded the ruins impassively. "Such a waste," he commented. "They should have joined us."

Sarel chose to assume a form of cut crystal, her brother's exact opposite. The female voice emanating from the sparkling facets said, "We gave them the choice, but Maseriel refused. If anyone is to blame, he is."

Lares replied, "He was an arrogant fool. He thought he would find a way to destroy us, probably because he wanted our power for himself. But he's dead now. They're all dead, the brotherhood who worshipped order."

Not quite all, Sarel thought. But she did not speak aloud. Acutely sensitive to her brother's emotions, she did not want to spoil his feeling of triumph.

Lares drifted lower, jet turning to jade. His masculine form softened, curved, became feminine. Sarel held herself apart, allowing him peace to formulate his thoughts.

Her brother's body shimmered, changed. She smiled to see that he was now her mirror image in every way.

"The ultimate compliment," she told him.

Together the now-identical pair examined the rents in the Aethyra which the Voids had created. In the Central Courtyard there was a swirl of invisible activity as the lowest of the layers attempted to heal itself.

To one side was a black hole, a pinprick in the fabric of the Aethyra which was all that remained of the largest of the Voids. Sarel noted its position; the hole would never close. If they ever again needed to create a Void in this region, it would be a simple matter to open the small hole and allow the dark energy they summoned to come flooding through.

In the beginning she and Lares had been forced to move the Voids from location to location through the Aethyra. Then they had discovered that, once activated and allowed to feed, the Voids never totally disappeared. The Aethyra above the dungeons in Barrow was speckled with tiny black holes. Sarel sometimes speculated on what might happen if they ever flowed together . . .

"Come to me."

Lares' voice drew her closer until they were almost one figure, not two. Sarel relaxed her own edges, letting herself flow into him. She knew it pleased him to have her thus, with no line of demarcation between them. Unable to tell where one left off and the other began.

"Look," Lares commanded with a voice that might have been hers, or his.

Two pair of eyes became one pair; stared; sought.

The Aethyra shuddered sickeningly.

After a moment of disorientation, Sarel realized they were seeing into the Realm of the Timewinds.

As if viewed through a haze of smoke, the scene below changed and took on life. Or the memory of life.

As the Duet watched, figures once again fought to the death. Bredi battled Seeker. Bursts of intense emotion exploded like flares, illuminating the scene with flashes of hot yellow and slashing red, pulsing moments of blue pain. Black blood lust, white light of death.

"Only the higher consciousness leaves a clear sign," Lares reminded his sister as the dull, muddy emotions of the Bredi warriors faded to nothingness. The more intense auras generated by the Seekers and Scholars remained as afterimages when the men themselves were dead, but eventually they too began to disappear, absorbed into the fabric of the Aethyra.

A burst of brilliance caught Sarel's attention. Delicately extricating herself from Lares, she traced pulsing prisms to a wounded Seeker in the doorway of a stone chamber, slashing the air with two swords. His image was so powerful it dimmed his opponent's to nothing, so he appeared to be fighting empty space.

A line of blood slashed his forehead, a savage wound opened on his torso. He turned his head and called, mouth opening and closing.

Sarel slipped farther from her brother, following the sound waves. As she moved into the stone chamber she recognized an anomaly in the Realm of the Timewinds. This level of transparent colors was bisected by an opaque white cone. The cone was a dead consciousness, but one powerful enough to sustain its integrity even in death.

Sarel's curiosity quickened, leading her on toward the rear of the chamber.

She saw him then.

The Silverhand.

A very young man, his emotions incandescent, crouched over the body of a dead Scholar. The white cone was emanating from the corpse.

Around them, the air crackled.

Enough light was cast by the white cone to illuminate the dead face. The lips were not moving, nor were words discernible, but Sarel felt their vibrations and knew that the Scholar was somehow speaking to the young man who bent over him.

The Silverhand rose, crossed the chamber, bent, picked up something. He held a slipper; tore it apart. Sarel glimpsed a flat rectangular shape.

"Brother?" she called silently to Lares.

In an instant, she felt him with her. His warmth was at her back, his breath on her cheek. "Watch closely," he advised. "Do not lose sight of him whatever happens."

Sarel stared at the face of the young man with the silver hand, but there was no need to memorize his features. She would never forget them.

The Realm shifted; the Timewinds blew. Lares and Sarel followed the Silverhand as he was blown along time's pathway. There were glimpses of the young man each time his emotions flared . . .

. . . fighting a Bredi . . .

. . . falling down a well . . .

. . . seized by a stone hand . . .

. . . more battling against the Bred . . .

Then for a while, nothing.

"Where is he?" Sarel gritted. "How can he suppress his emotions so we cannot find him?"

But the search was fruitless until the Duet turned southward on the Aethyra. Above the forest where the troop of the Bred had been lost, they caught glimpses of a familiar aura.

"Silverhand!" Lares cried. "Down there!"

But he was not alone. Mingled with his consciousness were traces from human and non-humans, a bewildering assortment of life forms. The familiar, angry hues of battle and killing.

In the Realm of the Timewinds a Madra Allta threw back his head and emitted a howl of such human grief that the colors surged through five layers of the Aethyra.

Then the auras faded. From the Aethyra, the twins sought to find them again but without emotions intense enough to mark their location, the Silverhand and his companions vanished.

Later, much later, lying in one another's arms in the bedchamber in the Imperial Palace in Barrow, the Duet reviewed their experience.

"The Silverhand is like a blight upon the rose," Sarel said angrily. "For many cycles he has been our enemy."

"Was he Maseriel's tool?" Lares wondered. "The Hieromonach's weapon?"

"You remember that night . . . ?"

She felt Lares' nod as he recalled the night the silverhanded boy invaded their sanctuary.

"In the Realm of the Timewinds I saw the dead Scholar communicate with him," Sarel continued. "He told the Silverhand where to find something, and while I watched, he . . ."

"Such power!" Lares interrupted, unable to control himself. "Imagine a mere Scholar holding the spirit to the body like that, after death! He must have been in terrible pain, tugged this way and that way, yet his will power was incredibly strong."

"Strong enough to pass a message to the Silverhand," Sarel continued.

"What was it?"

"I could not tell for certain because the object gave off no emanations in the Aethyra. But by reflected light, it appeared to be a page with writing on it."

"A book?"

"Just a single sheet. But obviously terribly important."

"Important enough for the Scholar to delay his dying," Lares said. "What could possibly be that important in Baddalaur?"

Sarel gasped.

"The Arcana!" they exclaimed simultaneously.

Before dawn, while the terrified people of Barrow cowered behind bolted doors the largest army of the Bred ever assembled was marching through the city's deserted streets, on its way to the Forest of Taesir.

CHAPTER FIFTY-EIGHT

A high-pitched squeal brought Caeled suddenly awake. The squeal was cut short by the snap of brittle bones. He opened his eyes in time to see the convulsively kicking hindquarters of a dog-rat disappearing into the maw of a massive wolfhound.

An old memory came flooding back — bloody fangs and snapping bones! He leaped to his feet with a cry of terror.

The dog's shape lost cohesion, flowed into that of a big man with shaggy white-blond hair.

Caeled took a deep breath to calm his racing heart. For one moment he had been a boy again, attacked in a swamp by a Madra Allta. He was a boy no longer yet the terror could still reach across the cycles and clutch him by the throat when he was least prepared. His left hand closed into a fist.

"What happened to us?" he asked hoarsely. His lips felt numb. "I remember . . . a sudden prickling on the back of my neck, a feeling of danger . . . I crouched, ready to fight . . . then . . . then it's all blank. I must have lost consciousness."

"I think we ran into a dense pocket of marsh gas by that pool," Madran replied. A thread of blood dribbled from the corner of his mouth and he wiped it away unthinkingly. He was accustomed to people being afraid of him but the young man's reaction was more, much more. "I sensed danger just as you did," he told Caeled. "It was all around me and I tried to change into my Allta shape, but everything began to swim before my eyes. I saw Sioraf fall; I tried to get to you— it felt like something grabbed me. I fought back but there was a roaring in my ears and a buzzing in my head . . . then I passed out too, I suppose."

"What about Gwynne?"

"The stone woman isn't with us. The last time I remember seeing her is when those creatures in the trees began pelting us with nuts."

"Sioraf?"

"Still sleeping, but she seems to be all right."

"Where are we?"

"In a dungeon, that's all I can say for certain. A dungeon full of rats," Madran added unnecessarily, licking his lips.

Sioraf lay a few paces beyond the Madra Allta. She slept on her side with her head pillowed on her arm. In the dim light she might have been any lovely young woman.

Caeled crouched over her. Her breathing was harsh, ragged; perhaps an effect of the marsh gas. He pressed his fingers to her throat.

Where he expected to find a pulse, none beat. Her skin was cold.

Gripping her wrist, he tried again.

No throb of life there either.

When he lifted her eyelid with his thumb, he was horrified to discover that her eyes had rolled back in her head. Blank orbs like white marbles stared at him.

"If I couldn't hear her breathing I would think she was dead," he told Madran in a puzzled voice.

"Vampiri are not quite like humankind," replied the Allta. Taking Caeled's right hand, he pressed it between Sioraf's breasts. "A vampir's heart is larger than a human's and many chambered. Situated here, in the center of the chest, it is well-protected behind the ribs and a bony plate peculiar to their race."

Now Caeled detected the steady beat of Sioraf's heart. He was also suddenly, acutely aware of the softness of her breasts. He drew back his hand and turned his face away to hide his burning cheeks. He had never touched a woman in that way before. "Have you any idea where we are?" he asked Madran to cover his confusion.

"Well, it was late afternoon when we encountered the gas. When I woke up it was as dark in here as the inside of a rock. Then suddenly light blazed through those slits near the ceiling, as if torches had been lit in the passage outside. So it must be night now. That means not enough time has passed for us to have been carried very far. We must still be close to our original location, whatever that was."

The Allta's reasoning impressed Caeled. Aside from his eating habits, Madran was proving to be a valuable companion.

The young man closed his eyes to concentrate on the charts he had studied at Baddalaur. After a moment he could see the maps as clearly as if they were spread out in front of him, but he recognized no landmarks.

Because there were none, he realized with dismay.

There were no roads or settlements shown on any map depicting Taesir. The forest had an evil reputation; its vast reaches were usually illustrated as an undifferentiated mass of vegetation.

They could be almost anyplace within it.

"If we are in a dungeon," he told Madran, "it is beneath some castle I've never heard of. I don't recall any castles in the Forest of Taesir."

"Well, there must be one," the Madra Allta replied, "because we're under it. Could it be some remnant of the Elder Days?"

"Possibly. Though I would have expected to see it on a map, the Elder sites are . . . were . . . clearly identified."

"Unless this one wasn't meant to be found," suggested Madran.

"That's it!" Caeled reached out with his right hand to feel the damp wall of their cell. Old stone, cold stone, the blocks perfectly fitted together without benefit of mortar. His questing palm moved along the wall to a square door coated with dust and grime. When he brushed away some of the dirt, metal rivets gleamed.

Caeled turned to meet Madran's eyes. "This is Elder work, all right," he said triumphantly.

Such is the power of the Arcana . . . the secrets of their location were hidden by the Elders . . . the Staff and the Stone were secreted in the great and ancient city of Gor in the land of Taesir.

Madran's brown eyes gleamed. "Could this be the place you're searching for?"

Caeled hesitated. "I don't think so."

"Why not?"

"Because we've come to it too quickly."

"Does everything have to be difficult? Perhaps the gods were guiding you. The gods expect us to be slavishly devoted to them while they use us for idle amusement and laugh at jokes we cannot understand. You and me and Sioraf — and that stone woman of yours, wherever she is — we are all picked up and thrown down at the whim of beings mightier than ourselves."

"But I have a destiny!"

Madran barked a laugh. "Destiny? What do you mean by that?"

Three days ago Caeled had been in Baddalaur; its influence was strong in his mind. "The ordered pattern of my life," he said stiffly.

Madran laughed again, a harsh and mirthless sound. "Ordered pattern? If you think back honestly, I wager you'll find yourself in this dungeon as the end result of countless unrelated incidents, cycle after cycle. Things you didn't expect, things that happened to you without any particular reason, they just happened. It's the same for all of us. Step by step our reactions to disorder in our lives brought us to this particular situation, but purely by accident. That isn't destiny. It's the gods, playing with us," the Allta concluded bitterly. "Watching to see what we do."

Caeled clenched his fists. "I refuse to accept that my life is shaped by . . . by accident and chaos! The Order is dedicated to the eradication of chaos and we . . . we . . . "

Unexpectedly, the grief and strain of the last few days rolled over the young man, exacting their toll. The strength to argue drained out of him. His shoulders slumped and he buried his face in his hands.

"Everything seems to be falling apart," he said in a muffled voice. "What I thought was permanent and true has been swept away. The Order is . . . "

"The Order is no more," Madran reminded him. "You told us yourself, Baddalaur is destroyed. Chaos reigns."

Chaos reigns. The words seemed to echo in Caeled's head.

Chaos. Random chance. The unforeseen and uncontrollable.

The enemy.

The training so deeply instilled in him fought its way to the surface. Slowly, he lifted his head. The lines of his body grew taut; his jaw set in a grim line. "Not yet," he vowed. "Not while I'm alive."

There was a stirring in the shadows. Wraithlike, Sioraf arose and came toward them. Caeled felt the cold radiating from her before she put her hand on his arm. "Someone's just outside," she warned in her husky whisper. "Someone's at the door."

CHAPTER FIFTY-NINE

Huddled beneath an exceptionally massive goldwood, Gwynne cursed the pelting rain. She could not feel its moisture on her skin, but the weather was making her bad mood worse. Gloom encased her like bitter fog.

The rain had begun before sunset as a mist that first gathered in the upper reaches of the trees, then gradually strengthened until it beat through the leaves, drenching the forest floor. It sounded like the tattoo of a thousand drums and reverberated within the Stone Warrior's skull until she wanted to scream.

Gwynne slammed her fist into the tree trunk in frustration. Whatever chance she had of finding the others had vanished with nightfall and the storm.

She had spent considerable time circling the pool, searching in vain for their footprints. She could not believe they had simply vanished into thin air . . . or walked into the tree-fringed pool and never come out again.

Whatever happened to them must have been almost instantaneous, she decided; otherwise there would surely be signs of a struggle. None of the three would have surrendered easily.

When the first drops of moisture fell, Gwynne's search had grown more desperate. Rain could wash away footprints — if there were any. But as the drizzle turned into a deluge, she had at last found a clue.

On the earth at the base of some goldwoods she

discovered torn shreds of fiber. With an effort, she tilted her head back and looked up. Dangling from a branch over her head was the broken end of a vine.

The other end of the vine was part of the network in the trees.

Bending over in spite of the protestations of her increasingly stiff body, Gwynne walked another slow circle around the pool with her gaze fixed on the ground, then widened her track into an outward spiral. East of the pool she found a second scattering of torn fibers with a single spear-shaped gold leaf tangled among them: a leaf from the high canopy of the forest.

Gwynne crouched and picked up the leaf in clumsy fingers. It was fresh, with sap still oozing from its stem and tiny blue aphids scurrying along its underside.

With a grunt of satisfaction the Stone Warrior looked up. Her eyes sought the dense mat of leaves far above. *Vanished into thin air after all,* she told herself. *Carried into the treetops by those cannibalistic creatures we saw earlier.*

But how did they succeed in overpowering the three?

She would continue the search as long as she could, but she began to despair of finding the missing trio alive.

If Caeled is dead, she thought glumly, *the secret of the Arcana is gone with him.*

Her body felt stiffer with every step she took.

Suddenly she caught a whiff of an acrid odor strong enough to survive the rain. The foul effluvium made her gag and would have brought tears to her eyes if she were still capable of tears. Staring hard at the pool, she thought she detected a shimmering disturbance in the air above it.

Marsh gas.

Now she knew what had happened to Caeled and the others. She had reason to be thankful for her altered state; without her stone skin and changing metabolism she would probably be lying unconscious at the water's edge.

But she would not have suffered quite the same fate as her companions.

In the high mountains of the Spine, Gwynne had once led a rescue party into a collapsed mine shaft in search of four Snowscalds who had been seeking purple gems to use for trade with the Gallowan merchants. When the rescue party broke through the barrier of stone and mud, they discovered the bodies of the women huddled together.

Gas trapped in the mine had killed them. When found, their bones were being gnawed by rats.

The Stone Warrior smiled grimly at the memory. She had little to fear from the creatures in the trees; anything that tried to feed off her would find itself toothless.

She had followed the trail of broken fibers until night closed in and the storm grew violent. Then a leaden exhaustion overtook her. There was no point in trying to go farther in the darkness, so she had taken shelter among the half-exposed roots of an incredibly large goldwood. Its canopy of leaves seemed to be turning most of the rain.

Gwynne awoke from a nightmare in which she was trapped beneath a fallen tree while a creature with blazing eyes tore at the few remaining fleshy parts of her body — her mouth, tongue, eyes, her genitals . . .

At first she thought it was still raining. Then, as the fragments of nightmare dispersed, she realized she was hearing the sound of leaves dripping. The storm itself had stopped.

But the night remained, lightless and filled with danger.

She need not fear carnivores but she was far from safe. Her senses were dimming and her joints were threatening to lock. She would not be able to survive in this form much longer.

Alone in the darkness, Gwynne faced her worst nightmare.

The last remnants of humanity would be lost to her;

she would become a living statue. Deaf, dumb, blind, trapped in an immobile body . . . but still aware, still sentient. Somehow she knew her brain would continue to live in its prison of stone.

At times like this she allowed herself to plot the one infallible escape. She knew enough herbalism to concoct a poison that would be deadly even to her.

But not yet; not while there was a chance Caeled still lived. She needed him to find the Arcana, but, alone in the dark, she could admit to herself that she cared what happened to him as well. She had lost so much and so many. The young man from Baddalaur was her last contact with humanity.

With her back braced against the tree trunk the Stone Warrior shifted position, trying in vain to make herself comfortable. At least it was fairly dry among the roots of the immense goldwood.

A brilliant red glow flashed somewhere deeper in the forest.

Gwynne's eyes opened wide.

The red light was joined by another, then another. Soon beams of blue and yellow and gold could be glimpsed through the trees.

Marsh lights?

Gwynne had heard of pockets of marsh gas igniting spontaneously, luring unwary travellers to their doom in deadly bogs.

But these lights were too strong, too steady. And aside from the pool now far behind her, this was not marshy land, but a forest.

Gwynne squinted, cursing silently. Her eyesight seemed to have grown worse since she lay down. Gazing toward the lights head-on, she could see little more than a colored blur. By turning her head, however, she found her peripheral vision was still clear. From the corner of her eye she could just glimpse distant shapes silhouetted against the lights . . .

. . . shapes like buildings . . .

She heaved herself to her feet and tried to run.

Instead she fell into a nightmare of icy water and semiliquid mud. The storm had turned solid earth into a viscous sea. She sank deeper with every step, fighting to pull her feet free as the mire sucked at them. Her weight worked against her. In places she sank to her knees, then to her hips.

Earlier she had contemplated ending her life, but faced with the possibility of drowning alone in mud she fought to survive. Somehow she dragged herself free and went on, floundering, swearing, splashing, too stubborn to give up.

Eventually the ground grew firmer. The Stone Warrior clambered up a long incline and collapsed blindly at the top, where she lay listening to the thud of her overtaxed heart.

No wonder the cannibal creatures kept to the trees. Only the fact that she had been sleeping pressed against a huge goldwood had kept her from being swallowed up before she knew what was happening. The roots of the great tree must absorb enough moisture to keep the ground in its immediate vicinity relatively solid.

She realized why she had seen no large animals on the forest floor. If rain turned the earth of Teasir to a semiliquid, the environment was too inhospitable for the likes of wolves and striped bears.

Too inhospitable for humankind as well, Gwynne thought sourly. She could not stay where she was. Wearily levering her torso upward, she raised her head.

And found herself gazing down at a city.

Nestled in the cup of the valley below was a vast stone citadel containing numerous stepped layers of flat-roofed apartments interspersed with clusters of bulbous domes. These domes surmounted what appeared to be public buildings, fronting on paved plazas. Small domes sprouted from some of the larger ones like a form of exotic vegetation.

The city was a blaze of light. Light glowed from every window, while vast beams of color shone from apertures in the largest domes.

Gwynne stared in astonishment.

Even her dimming senses could detect the hum of activity the skirl of discordant music.

Bending over as best she could to keep from being seen by any sentries, the Stone Warrior crept down the incline and approached the walls that curved to embrace the city. Only when she stood below them did she realize how high they were. The flawlessly fitted stones were immense; the skills that shaped them had vanished with the Elders.

Gwynne had been educated in her youth and received an additional, more practical education riding with the Snowscalds. She considered herself far more knowledge-able than many. But she had never suspected there might be, anywhere, an intact Elder city.

A city that was obviously inhabited!

Following the walls around to the left, she came upon the middens. Huge pits were sunk in the ground, their contents still reeking in spite of the long slow process of liquification.

Gwynne paused to recall what she had once studied about the construction techniques of the Elders. Had they not built their cities with elaborate sewage systems for carrying dissolved waste to the nearest river?

The Stone Warrior was turning away from the nearest pit when her foot struck something that rang like a hollow gourd. It rolled, rattling, out of the shadows. She stooped as quickly as she could to pick it up before anyone heard.

In her hand was a human skull.

A few shreds of flesh still clung to the bone.

Gwynne examined the skull with curiosity. It had been broken open deliberately: a gaping but clean-edged hole in the crown was too neat to be accidental. Putting the skull down, she groped in the shadows and found another one. When she held it to the light it too had a precise hole in the top.

Somewhere nearby were beasts with a taste for human flesh.

Beasts with enough intelligence to drill holes in the top of the skull to extract the brain . . . a prized delicacy, no doubt.

Stone or not, Gwynne suddenly felt queasy.

CHAPTER SIXTY

Locks grated and the door slid back with a metallic, grinding sound. Light blazed into the dungeon chamber. Then a shadow danced across the floor and wavered up the wall.

Madran and Caeled moved apart, giving each other room to fight if necessary.

Sioraf gathered herself into a narrow column with hands palm outward and claws curved.

"I am Bochar." The voice was light and unaccented, the voice of a youth who had not reached full manhood. He touched the wall beside the door. Strips in the ceiling flared brightly, washing the room in shadowless light. Sioraf hissed like a startled cat.

"I am Bochar," the newcomer repeated.

He was beautiful: tall and long-boned, with finely modelled, almost feminine features, though the breadth of his shoulders and the line of his jaw were unmistakably male. Unblemished skin was several shades darker than his fair hair, which he wore pulled back from his face and knotted at the back of his neck. His clothing consisted of an elaborately wrapped and folded rectangle of white fabric that covered his torso but left his arms and legs bare.

"I am Bochar," he announced a third time as he looked from Caeled to Madra. His eyes slid past Sioraf as if she were not there.

"I am Caeled. This is Madran . . . and Sioraf."

With a smile Bochar acknowledged the two males but continued to ignore their female companion. "I have been sent to welcome you to the City," he told them.

"What happened to us?" Caeled wanted to know. "One moment we were in the forest, then the next thing we knew . . ."

"I understand you were overcome by the noxious exudations of one of the dead pools to be found in the forest. You were lucky; if you had remained there any longer you would have died."

"How did we get here?"

"Fortunately, some of the People were passing and saw your plight," Bochar answered smoothly. "They brought you to the City."

"They saved us? Then why were we locked up?" Sioraf asked.

As if she had not spoken, Bochar put a hand under Caeled's elbow and began to guide him toward the door. "I have come to escort you to a banquet in your honor. We do not get many visitors in this part of the forest."

"We were lost," Madran interjected. "Creatures in the trees were tracking us and we ran from them."

Bochar bowed his head. "We are familiar with those creatures. Their domain is the day and during daylight the entire forest is theirs. But at night they disappear so we are free to enjoy the City again." He gave Caeled's arm a gentle tug. "Come with me now. The celebration awaits, can you not hear the music?"

The chillness of Sioraf touched Caeled's other arm, the one with the silver hand. "Be wary," she whispered in his ear. "He is not as he seems."

"None of us are," Caeled murmured. But he told Bochar, "We shall be with you in a moment. Just wait outside for us, will you?"

The youth hesitated, obviously unwilling. But he could not refuse the request without seeming impolite, so he bowed and left the chamber.

No sooner had the door slid shut behind Bochar — though it had not, Caeled noted with relief, been locked — than Sioraf said, "He does not look at me nor respond to anything I say."

"So I noticed." He glanced toward Madran. "Have you any idea why?"

The big man shrugged. "I've heard of societies where women are considered little better than beasts. Sioraf may be invisible to him, according to his code. But she's right. Be wary." His nostrils twitched. "Something doesn't smell right."

They found Bochar waiting for them in the corridor. The walls, floor and ceiling of the passageway were sheathed in Old Metal. The sheer extravagance took their breath away. Due to its rarity a small cube of Old Metal was worth a king's ransom, yet here the material was lavished on every surface.

Strips of milky light ran the length of the corridor, though in places the lights were dead, leaving pools of shadow. In places too the floor was broken, revealing discolored pipes beneath. Elsewhere panels of metal had fallen off the walls to expose the rough stone.

"This way," Bochar urged. "The others are waiting for you." He set off down the passageway, beckoning them to follow him.

Caeled took note of the youth's unusual way of walking. He moved fluidly, but with a peculiar rolling of his shoulders and a tendency to slide his feet rather than lift them. His head was thrust forward in a way that marred his graceful physique.

"What is this place?" Caeled inquired as he followed him.

"The City."

"Has it a name?"

"The City." Bochar looked back by swivelling his head on his neck without turning his body. The effect was unsettling.

Sioraf's fingers tightened painfully on Caeled's arm.

"Just the City?" Caeled persisted.

"Why should we call it anything else? We know what it is."

Making an abrupt right hand turn, Bochar led them up a steep flight of metal stairs. Some of the steps were missing, revealing an understructure of rusting cogs and wheels.

"This place is very old," Caeled observed, his voice echoing. "With so much metal . . . it has to be one of the Elder cities."

Again Bochar turned his head at an unnatural angle. "This is *the* City. There are no other cities."

"What about Sarafantis? Or Engless? Or Lowstone?"

"There are no other cities," Bochar repeated irritably, his politeness slipping.

"Let it be," Madran advised in a low voice.

Caeled changed the subject. "Do the beasts in the trees trouble you?"

Bochar's backward smile was chilling. "Never."

At the top of the stairs a second person was waiting for them, a tall, regal woman who bore a strong resemblance to Bochar, although she seemed somewhat older. She was dressed identically. As they came up to her she turned without a word and walked off down another corridor.

Her gait was identical to that of Bochar.

The youth shepherded his charges along in her wake.

"Where are we going?" Madran asked him.

"I told you — to the feast in your honor. You will tell us of your experiences in the world beyond Taesir. We should like to hear some new stories."

"And then?" Sioraf demanded. "After the feast, what then?"

Bochar paid no attention.

Caeled said in a firm voice, "We want to know what will happen after the feast."

"After?"

"Yes."

"It will be dawn."

"I know that. But what happens then?"

"Why, we sleep, of course. The beasts come out during the day, so we sleep."

A third figure stepped out of the shadows: male, older than Bochar, with fair hair tarnished by time. Otherwise his resemblance to Bochar and the woman was marked.

He fell into step beside them without saying anything.

"They carry no weapons," Sioraf whispered to Caeled, "and wear no ornaments. What sort of people are they?"

"They don't smell like people at all, not to me," Madran muttered. But before he could say more, their forward progress was interrupted by what looked like a blank wall.

The older man struck the wall sharply with the palm of his hand.

A seam opened down the center. The two halves of the wall slid back with a grating noise, revealing a chamber beyond.

The room was crowded with the inhabitants of the City. They had been making animated conversation and listening to harsh, discordant sounds played on battered instruments by a group at the far end of the chamber, but the noise ceased abruptly when Bochar appeared with his party. Heads turned as Caeled, Madran and Sioraf were ushered into the room. Making a cursory count, Caeled estimated there must be at least two hundred people there . . . each one looking very much like all the others.

But it was the room that took Caeled's breath away. The chamber was enormous. A huge dome served as a ceiling, fitted with transparent glass. Had the glass been clean, it would have been almost invisible. But it was smeared and speckled with bird droppings and some of the panes were broken.

The floor was scarred, red-veined marble, gritty underfoot. Marble walls were stained with smoke and streaked with mud. There was an unpleasant, musky odor caused by so many bodies crowded together.

The crowd parted. Bochar led the way through their ranks to a huge, horseshoe-shaped table laid out with a mismatched selection of plates and utensils.

In solitary splendor, an elderly man occupied a high-backed chair at the head of the table, facing the empty space in the center. Bochar guided his guests through the opening opposite, so they stood within the ring.

Madran felt his hackles rising. Sioraf was even paler than usual.

Caeled appeared to be relaxed, drawing deep, slow breaths.

The inhabitants of the City crowded around the table now, saying nothing, not touching the plates or cutlery. Just standing. Watching.

The silence was oppressive.

Bochar stopped before the man in the chair. With an air of deference he relieved Madran of his sickle and Sioraf of her knife and laid them on the table. "You need no weapons here," he murmured. Then he bowed deeply, folding at the waist, his every gesture submissive. When he straightened he said to Caeled, "This is Panasen, First Citizen of the City."

The young man stepped forward and nodded politely, but with no trace of submission. "I am Caeled Silverhand, and these are my friends, Sioraf and Madran."

The man in the chair might have been Bochar's grandfather. His age was hard to assess, though his forehead was heavily lined and deep grooves ran from his nostrils to the corners of his mouth. His eyes were very bright, however, as he looked from one to the other.

"An Allta and a human," the old man said. Then his lip curled with contempt. "And a cursed one, a vampir. I never thought to see their like again."

"There are not many left in the Nations," Caeled replied. He kept his voice calm.

Panasen said, "There will be one less, soon."

Sioraf moved closer to Caeled. He found himself putting a protective arm around her shoulders. They were slim shoulders, cold. Trembling. "Do not threaten my friend," he said in the same quiet tone.

"Not a threat. Simply a foretelling."

"I thought we were your guests. Is this how the people of the City treat guests?"

Panasen raised expressive eyebrows. "Guests?"

"Bochar told us there was to be a feast in our honor."

"Oh, there is," the old man assured him. "But in the City of Gor . . . you are the feast." He brought his hands together like a thunderclap. "Butcher them!"

CHAPTER SIXTY-ONE

The gates were unlocked and ajar, the hinges rusted open. Timber planks were rotted and stained with fungus.

Keeping to the shadows, Gwynne scrutinized the entrance to the city. What sort of people left their gates open like this in a forest famed for its dangers? Only those who were absolutely confident of their own strength. Or those who were totally foolish — and fools never survived. Gwynne slowly turned to look back toward the trees. Why did the creatures in the trees not raid the city?

Grunting with the effort, she crouched and ran her hand across the earth in front of the gate. Unmarked. No grooves left by cart wheels, no wagon ruts . . . no tracks of any kind. Perhaps this particular gateway was unused?

But if so, why was it open?

She flattened herself as best she could against the wall and sidled around one of the open gates until she stood with her back pressed to the rusted hinge. Then she took a cautious step more and peered inside.

The streets were deserted. Spiky rollerweeds had piled in the corners; rotting leaves carpeted the ground.

Yet lights burned in almost every window. And she could hear voices, many voices. They seemed to be coming from one of the large domes.

Holding her morningstar at the ready, Gwynne stepped through the gate. She expected at the least a challenge from an unseen guard, but there was nothing. No doors opened, no light poured out into the street.

Two quick strides brought her to the nearest window. Rubbing her hand across the grimy glass to clear it, she peered inside. The interior was an empty shell, filthy and long abandoned. A milky light poured from a strip set into the ceiling.

The next building was also empty. Its light strip was pulling loose from the ceiling at one end but still managed to cast a white glow over the forlorn interior. A few bits of broken furniture were the only occupants.

The third building was almost in darkness, the bright milky light within having faded to a dull, faintly pulsing ochre.

The Stone Warrior moved swiftly down the streets, checking buildings at random, occasionally climbing up stone steps to a higher level and finding the apartments abandoned there as well. Most of them were lit, however, with the peculiar strips of cold fire. In some places it burned brightly, in others it seemed to be dying, fading from white to a sullen yellow.

She was not unfamiliar with deserted towns. The Snowscalds told weird tales about the Ghost City in the High Spine. Within impenetrable, glasslike walls, lights came on and off of their own accord and sometimes music and voices drifted on the wind. The Ghost City was one of the minor wonders of the Western Coast and had long been a source of income for the Scalds, who demanded tribute from curious visitors who wanted to wander around its walls and speculate on what might lie within.

As Gwynne continued her exploration, the voices she was hearing grew louder. The streets widened into avenues lined with huge containers that had once held trees or ornamental shrubs. Along these avenues the deserted apartments still bore traces of vividly colored paint, flaking now like patches of dead skin.

The buildings were increasingly large and elaborate. Many had door and window frames of metal, and on some, traces of engraving could be seen. Once these streets and avenues had been paved with what appeared to be one seamless sheet of a stonelike substance, but now the paving was cracked and fissured. Viney tendrils burst through these openings and crawled across the streets, choking them with dense, unhealthy foliage.

Square apertures along the edges of the streets indicated an underground drainage system, but the metal grills over them were clogged with dead vegetation and filth.

Gwynne rounded a corner and stopped abruptly. Across a broad plaza, a high-domed building blazed with light. A thread of spiral stairs could be seen winding around the outside of the dome, climbing to its top where some sort of platform stood. Through broken windows came the sound of human voices mingled with dissonant noise that might have been intended for music.

Moving cautiously, Gwynne circled the building looking for a way in. The dome was set in what had once been a carefully tended parkland but was now an overgrown tangle of bushes and vines. Paved walkways leading from the plaza ended in impenetrable screens of thorn.

The only entrance she found was a narrow path crudely hacked through the undergrowth. She was about to follow it when a new sound reached her ears. Above the chatter and discordant music from inside she heard something primal, animalistic. Nearby, but not emanating from the dome.

The Stone Warrior froze in a fighting stance.

Was it an animal?

But she had seen no animals since entering the city. Not even dog-rats or flying devils.

The sounds she was hearing were definitely animal in nature, however. Leaving the dome, she set about tracking them to their source.

Within the ruined park was a small circular structure walled with broken trellises. The roof had long since collapsed to be replaced by a great vine that stretched from one supporting pillar to another, concealing what-ever was making the noises inside.

Gwynne pushed the leafy screen aside and looked in.

As she did so, she recognized the sounds.

Her teeth flashed in a rare smile.

Light from the dome revealed two figures lying coupled together, their bodies moving rhythmically. The sounds they made were moans and shrieks of passion, and for a moment Gwynne felt a surge of envy.

On the morning before the Void took him, Silan had made love to her.

There had been no one else since. Nor was there likely to be, thought the Stone Warrior. Not now. Not ever again.

She was swept with sudden uncontrollable rage.

Heedless of everything but the fury boiling through her, Gwynne battered her way through splintering trellises and into the ruined structure. The couple separated with a shout and lay staring at her.

Light poured in through the opening Gwynne had torn. She could see the pair very clearly now. They were young, fair, beautiful, with unblemished skins flushed by lovemaking.

Their faces were almost identical.

Perhaps they were siblings. Such unions were no longer unheard of; the Duet themselves were reputed to have such a relationship.

As they lay on the ground and stared at Gwynne the couple made no effort to cover their nakedness. They did not even seem repelled by her appearance. Their gaze was vacuous, uncomprehending.

"Can you understand me?"

The male nodded.

"I am looking for a man with a hand of silver." She held up her left hand and closed it into a fist. "And a big man with thick blond hair, and a pale skinned, brown-haired woman. Have you seen them?"

Suddenly the female smiled, revealing tiny white teeth like a row of seeds. "They were brought for the feast." Her voice was clear and pure.

"Brought where?"

"From the forest to the City."

"Where in the City?"

They stared at her blankly.

She jerked her head toward the domed building. "In there?"

The female nodded.

"Why?" Gwynne asked. "Who brought them here?"

"The Treeselves," said the woman. Her eyes were opaque, devoid of curiosity.

Gwynne was frustrated by their attitude. Were they drunk, or drugged? "Why?" she repeated.

"For the Cityselves."

"The Treeselves brought three people from the forest to the Cityselves?"

Another nod.

"And the Cityselves are holding a feast in their honor?"

The man frowned as if suddenly understanding. "Holding a feast!" he cried. Ignoring the Stone Warrior, he caught the woman's hand and pulled her to her feet. He was tugging her toward the opening when Gwynne stepped in front of them, blocking their way.

They gazed at her as if surprised to find she was still there.

"I want you to take me to my friends," she said firmly.

The man frowned and tried to shove past her. "We must go," he insisted, "or the best parts will be taken."

The sound of voices and music emanating from the dome stopped suddenly.

The male became almost frantic. "Now! We must go now or they will be all gone!"

A horrible suspicion struck the Stone Warrior.

"Who will be all gone?"

"The three strangers," the female said. She giggled

incongruously. "The fresh meat the Treeselves brought. One of them is young and tender. One is an Allta, they say. I've never tasted Allta meat before . . . "

She licked her lips; her red, moist lips.

Gwynne's stone hands seized their two heads and slammed their skulls together. She beat one against the other until bone shattered and pulpy brain matter exploded over her. Then she dropped the bodies and strode over them on her way out.

She did not feel the vines; when she reached the barrier of thorns she did not feel them either. She was only aware of the bitter taste in her mouth.

Cannibals.

CHAPTER SIXTY-TWO

Caeled's metal hand shot out, clamping around Bochar's slender neck. He pulled the young man back against his body like a shield. "I'll kill him," Caeled promised.

He kept his eyes on Panasen but allowed his other senses to sweep the room, alert to the slightest reaction.

It was Sioraf who moved first. She darted forward and grabbed for her knife and Madran's sickle. The old man moved more swiftly than Caeled would have thought possible. He seized the sickle before Sioraf could reach it and swung it toward her, hooking the front of her blouse. He gave a jerk and she stumbled forward. Panasen freed the blade and swung it again, this time hooking it behind the vampir's neck. The sharp blade tore her skin but there was no blood. He pulled, inexorably forcing Sioraf to clamber onto the table and then down beside him.

"Let her go!" Caeled cried. He tightened his grip on Bochar's neck. In the absolute silence that gripped the room, the sound of crushing cartilage was clearly audible.

Breath rasped in Bochar's damaged throat. He began to thrash wildly. But Caeled continued to hold Bochar in spite of all the more slightly built man could do to tear himself free.

Panasen's expression never changed. He did not even look at Bochar. "I will let her go," he said coldly, "after you and the Allta prostrate yourselves on the ground before me."

"Let her go now! Prove you are to be trusted, then we

will bow down to you." Caeled was playing for time, aware of Madran stealthily moving around behind him. Perhaps together . . .

Panasen said, "I do not want this vampir. Their flesh is foul and their blood brings madness. They are anathema to the Cityselves. So do not doubt my word, I shall be quite happy to release her . . . "

"And then cook us!" Madran barked.

The old man's laugh was a phlegmy cough. "We do not cook our meat."

Madran was just behind Caeled now. Out of the corner of his mouth he asked the Allta, "Can you reach him in beast form?"

Madran growled a negative. "The change is swift but not that swift; he'd kill her before I could get to him."

"Then what can we do?" the young man whispered urgently.

"Surrender, fight or walk away," Madran told him. "But decide in a hurry, they're getting restless."

Caeled risked a quick glance around. The Cityselves were drawing nearer; some had vaulted over the table. Many were armed with clubs or rocks which they must have brought with them, as if expecting this.

"Shall I make your decision for you?" Panasen inquired almost pleasantly. In one lithe movement he grabbed Sioraf's knife from the table and tossed it to Bochar.

Caeled's grip tightened spasmodically as Bochar snatched at the weapon. There was a brief but desperate struggle between them before the youth collapsed with a gurgle . . . and Caeled discovered that Bochar had driven Sioraf's knife into his own heart.

Panasen laughed as if it were all a show being staged for his amusement. The Cityselves closed in. Caeled struck out at the nearest man, driving his right fist with all his trained skill into the center of the breastbone. The blow should have killed the man. Instead it only stunned him for a moment; he staggered, flailed his arms, then kept on coming.

At the same time a gray-haired woman threw herself onto her hands and knees and locked her teeth on Caeled's calf muscle. With a roar of pain, Caeled whirled and struck downward with his metal fist. He felt her skull cave in.

The first man he had hit swung a wild blow that missed Caeled completely just as a young couple leaped at him in unison from the tabletop. He dropped to the ground and rolled, striking upward with fists and feet.

His blows found their targets. Breath whooshed out of the pair and they collapsed together, whimpering.

Meanwhile Madran surrendered himself to the change. Within moments his face became a bestial mask. The Cityselves drew back but he hurled himself at the nearest and began tearing out throats.

Caeled vaulted across the table just as Panasen calmly drew the sickle blade across Sioraf's throat, opening a gaping wound. She shuddered; her eyes rolled up in her head.

She was still in the act of falling when Caeled's metal fist struck at Panasen's face. Only the old man's extraordinary speed saved him. Caeled's fist punched through the back of his chair as Panasen dodged sideways. He tried to draw back his arm for another blow, only to find it caught fast.

Suddenly Panasen was pressing the sickle against Caeled's own throat. "Your flesh will taste very sweet," he said.

"Why didn't they kill us?" Caeled wondered aloud.

"I think they're saving us for something special," Madran replied as together they lowered the limp body of Sioraf onto the floor of their cell. Madran's forearms were bloody and one eye was swollen shut. His body was battered, hair torn out in great clumps, bite marks everywhere. The big Madra Allta had savaged and been savaged.

"We underestimated those creatures," he told Caeled.

"Forget them for the moment," said the young man as he bent over the unconscious girl. "What about Sioraf?"

With tentative fingers he touched the hideous wound in her neck.

"We all went for the throat . . . back there . . . " Madran mused. But Caeled was not listening.

"Sioraf?" he whispered. "Can you hear me?"

There was no response.

Madran licked the palm of his hand and held it before her face. "I can't feel any breath." Then he pressed his ear between her breasts and listened.

"Well?" Caeled asked impatiently. He reached forward to put his hand where the Allta's head had just lain, but Madran drew him away.

"I think her heart's still beating, Caeled, but it's better not to disturb her. Vampiri heal themselves."

"Even when they're as badly wounded as she is?"

Madran took a long second look at Sioraf's torn neck. He realized there was not enough blood oozing from the wound, even for a vampir.

He said as much to Caeled, adding, "If she doesn't get some sustenance soon she will die."

"Sustenance?"

"Blood," the Allta replied bluntly.

Caeled felt instinctive repulsion. He had been raised on legends of the blood drinkers, the stealers of life, who crept into houses in the dead of night to drink the blood from newborn infants. Everyone knew that vampiri could infect others with their foul disease. When a vampir made a Get, they had total control over it, and when the Get made itself a Get, then the original vampir controlled both of them.

Through such methods, it was claimed, vampiri sought to regain the great power they had once exerted in the Elder Times.

They were not so numerous now, but still the objects of fear and loathing. The idea of exchanging blood with one — whether giving or receiving — made Caeled's stomach turn over.

As if reading his mind, Madran told him, "No one would blame you for refusing. But I cannot give Sioraf my blood; I'm an Allta. The fluid that sustains me would be poison to her. Only human blood can help her." The big man paused. "If you do give her your blood, no one need ever know."

"I would know," Caeled said grimly.

An image flitted unbidden through his mind: Sioraf, dancing in a sunbeam.

He swallowed hard and began rolling up his sleeve. His right sleeve. "Will you do it for me?"

"I've nothing to open the vein with."

"Claw it open with your nails if you must. Do it quickly, before I change my mind."

Caeled briefly closed his eyes as the Allta tore into his wrist. Accepting without flinching was the most courageous act of his life.

"Hold your arm here now," Madran commanded, moving Caeled's arm over her mouth. Warm blood dripped between the vampir's slightly parted lips. "Now above her throat . . . " Caeled's blood flowed into the open wound.

Sioraf convulsed. Her mouth worked violently and she made sounds as if gasping for air. Her eyes opened very wide, with the look of a terrified child.

Then as Caeled watched incredulously, the torn flesh of her throat began to come together. Between one breath and the next the wound closed, leaving only a thin pink line to scar her pale skin. Then even that faded.

She closed her eyes but her lips continued to work, sucking air.

Madran shifted Caeled's arm back to her mouth. She fastened on it voraciously. Caeled tried to pull away but Madran held him in place. "Be still now. She must feed."

"She'll drain me dry!"

"She cannot, she's too weak. Besides, she could never draw all your life's blood from that one vein."

"You seem to know a lot about vampiri, Madran."

The big man chuckled. "You pick up quite a bit of unusual knowledge in a lifetime spent with circuses."

Sioraf's deep blue eyes flickered open once more. The whites were stained by scores of tiny ruptured blood vessels. Lifting her hands, she pressed Caeled's arm to her mouth and suckled it hungrily.

Madran kept a close watch on how much she was taking. Soon he pulled Caeled's arm away. "Lick your wound to stop the bleeding," he suggested.

Caeled looked down at the vampir. She was beauti-ful . . . but her lips were red with his blood.

He turned away, sickened.

He felt . . . sullied. Yet the experience had not been unpleasant. The touch of the vampir's lips against his skin was curiously exciting. He knew he would think about it . . . later.

Cradling his right arm against his chest, he asked Madran, "What do you expect will happen now?"

"I expect I'll sleep," the Allta replied. "If you'll let me. And I suggest you do the same. Whatever happens, we're all going to need our strength."

"I wish I knew why they didn't kill us."

As he curled up on the floor, Madran replied, "Don't worry about it, Silverhand. They will."

Within moments he was snoring.

Unable to follow his example, Caeled leaned against the cell door, resting his forehead on its coolness. In a burst of frustration he hammered the door with his met-al fist. The sound boomed hollowly. To have come so far . . .

Icy fingers stroked his cheek. Sioraf flowed around him until she stood between his body and the door. She was as pale as ever but she had wiped her lips clean, he was relieved to see.

When she smiled at Caeled, she was careful to keep her teeth covered.

"I owe you my life," she said in her feathery voice.

"Don't thank me yet. Madran believes they're going to kill us any time now."

"But we are not dead yet. You were, you said, trained in Baddalaur. The wisest men in all the Nations studied in Baddalaur. So were you not taught to think while you were there?"

"What do you mean?" She was so close to him now Caeled could smell the blood still on her breath. "What should I be thinking about — dying? Being torn apart and eaten by those . . . those. . . . At least you don't have to worry about that, they won't eat you, according to Panasen."

"No, they won't eat me. Those creatures retain the ancient fear of my kind. I suspect they mean to follow the old ways. They will cut me into pieces while I still live, then burn the pieces and pound the ashes to dust. If they are very skilful they might keep me alive for days by cutting just a little bit at a time."

Caeled reached past her and pounded the door again in a frenzy. The sound echoed through the ruined building like a bell, solemn and sonorous.

CHAPTER SIXTY-THREE

Kichal, Commander of the Bred, stood at the edge of the Forest of Taesir with his arms folded across his chest. When he turned his head his red eyes reflected the campfires of the enormous Bred army. Shadows caused by the leaping flames turned his face into a grotesque mask in which two fiery eyes blazed.

He thought he heard a bell tolling and strained to listen.

Kichal was waiting.

The Bred had refused to enter the ancient forest. The army comprised fifty companies, almost the entire Bred stock. They were primarily of the saurian type which the Breeder was now developing at a monstrously accelerated rate in hundreds of breeding stalls to keep up with the demands of the Duet, but there were also mammalian types which had shown particular tracking skills, creatures that bore a vague resemblance to bears and wolves.

At late afternoon they had first sighted the forest. The trouble began immediately as a ripple of disquiet spread through the ranks. The saurians ceased to swarm forward, crushing everything in their path, and began a nervous, side-to-side skittering their officers could not control. The mammalians halted and huddled together with others of their kind, darting frightened glances in the direction of the trees.

Even the fine peri which Sarel had given Kichal reared and bucked, embarrassing him in front of his officers as he sought in vain to bring the animal under control. At last he had to dismount and lead it by the reins.

At the edge of the forest, the stalled army milled around uncertainly. They forgot the discipline which had been painstakingly drilled into them. In the confusion scores of fights broke out, saurian turning on mammalian in mindless savagery. Fifty Bredi were killed and another thirty so badly injured they were of no further use. Kichal had ordered them destroyed.

Then he personally stalked through the ranks, using his metal-tipped flail and terrifying presence to enforce order. Some of the Bredi snarled at him and a few challenged him with fang and claw, but in time they sullenly submitted.

When they were quiet he pulled them back a distance from the forest. Almost immediately a dramatic change came over them as they reverted to their inbred obedience. The ranks reformed; the warriors docilely awaited his commands.

As an experiment he sent his two most trusted scouts — one a huge saurian and the other an immense bearlike creature — toward the forest. They advanced shoulder to shoulder and had reached the skirting undergrowth before they slowed, stopped; then turned on each other like total strangers venting an ancient animosity.

As Kichal watched, they tore each other apart.

He had not repeated the experiment.

Even now, standing as close as he dared to the edge of the forest, Kichal felt . . . *strange.* Uncertain. Images flashed through his mind, haunting images. Faces: a woman, a child, the woman lying in a street, murder in the child's eyes. He felt . . .

Images of a woman, old, gray-haired, an old man, and four others seated around a wooden table. A family at supper, breaking bread, drinking wine, laughing, talking. The faces were so familiar . . . so familiar. Kichal felt . . .

He felt the communion with Sarel.

She flowed into his mind, flooding him with such overpowering sensation that he almost fell to his knees in worship. He could *feel* her creamy skin, smell the perfume of her flesh, hear the silken glide of her hair across her shoulders. His vision swam. Patterns danced erratically across his eyeballs. When they settled, Sarel was settled inside him: the ultimate communion.

"The Bred will not enter the forest. It is almost as if they cannot." He said the words aloud although he knew Sarel could read his thoughts.

"Show me." Her voice was rich and warm, employing the same tone she had used when she commanded him to love her.

Kichal concentrated on the events of the afternoon: the disintegration of order throughout the ranks, the spontaneous fights, the deaths of the two scouts.

"In proximity to the Forest of Taesir, Bredi seem to revert to their animal natures," he reported. "If I should succeed in forcing them into the forest, we will lose them altogether."

Kichal shuddered and gasped as Sarel abruptly abandoned him, leaving him empty, hollow. Alone.

Into his emptiness the faces returned. Familiar faces, one very like his own except it was much younger. Fragments of comprehension suddenly slotted together and for an instant — a single heartbeat — he hovered on the edge of understanding. Then the moment fled and Kichal turned away from the trees, red eyes blazing.

"Nothing," Lares said finally, sinking through the layers of the Aethyra to hover just above the Forest of Taesir. Its colors were a uniform dull yellow-green.

Sarel flickered into her crystal shape beside him. "Look again, brother," she urged. "What do you see?"

Lares concentrated on the ancient forest, his own form shifting as he looked. To the far right he eventually discovered the tiny sparks that were the Bred, with an occasional brighter aura surrounding one of the human officers.

But to his left, there was nothing.

Nothing.

"No living creatures," he reported.

"No birds or beasts, no humankind or Alltas," Sarel concluded. "Yet there must be something there. Something extraordinary."

"I've passed over this forest a hundred times and never noticed anything unusual about it," Lares told her.

"But The Bred refuse to go into it . . . and Kichal was very troubled. Keep trying, help me solve the mystery."

Lares' form shifted again as he directed his concentration elsewhere. He was jet, he was jade; he lost substance altogether so that only a voice could be heard saying to his sister, "Look in the very heart of the forest. Do you notice anything peculiar?"

Sarel joined in his intense concentration. From the Aethyra she was able to make out an endless expanse of goldwoods wrapped with parasitic vines, but in their center . . . in their very center . . .

She could not see into the center. No matter what effort she made with the eyes of her Aethyral form, she found herself looking at an insubstantial blur.

"I think something's blocking us," she said irritably. "What could possibly have enough power to . . ." Her breath hissed. "The Arcana!"

Lares' form abruptly solidified. "Yes! Of course, the Arcana! That's why the Bredi are reverting to type. The Arcana must be in the Forest of Taesir; its power is negating ours." He reached for Sarel. "Come, we have work to do."

"You have a plan?"

"We are going to send the mightiest Void of all into the forest, into the very heart of darkness!"

CHAPTER SIXTY-FOUR

Cacophony awakened them.

Shrieks and howls rang through the dungeons, bringing Caeled and Madran to their feet at once. Sioraf groaned in a troubled sleep but did not wake. Caeled pressed an ear to the metal door, trying to find out what was going on outside. Madran stood in the center of the cell with his head cocked to one side and his moist brown eyes intent.

"There are beasts out there," Caeled reported. "Those aren't human voices."

"The creatures from the trees," Madran agreed.

"Do you think they've attacked this place?"

Madran's nostrils flared. "I don't think they've attacked, actually — I don't hear anyone screaming, and that racket doesn't resemble war cries."

"Bochar said the creatures in the trees claimed the forest during the day," Caeled recalled. "That must include this city as well. But if the . . . what do they call themselves, the Cityselves? . . . if they surrender the city to the creatures, where do they go until night falls again?"

"Probably lock themselves down here in the dungeons," Madran guessed. "It's the safest place." The big Allta cocked his head to the other side. "The noise is fading."

The last whoops died away and silence fell once more. Overhead the milky light flickered, then sputtered to a dull yellow glow. "They've gone," Madran said. "Now what?"

"If it is dawn, then the Cityselves have retired for the

rest of the day. We can wait here for them to come for us or we can try to escape. But to do that . . . " Caeled tapped the door with a metal knuckle. "This door is solid; even my hand can't break through here."

Madran reminded him, "When Bochar took us to that domed chamber, the old man put his hand to the wall and something opened."

Caeled promptly pressed the palm of his hand against the wall beside the door, but nothing happened.

"Strange," said Madran. "It worked for Bochar's friend."

Caeled frowned. "I'm not sure Bochar and the others know what they're doing," he told the Allta, "any more than we do. I think they're imitating some ancient ritual they don't really understand."

"An Elder ritual? *Is* this Gor, then?"

"I have no doubt of it now." Caeled tapped the metal door frame with his knuckles, listened, tapped again. "There's something here . . . "

Madran stepped closer. "It sounds hollow."

Caeled took one careful pace back from the door and planted his feet firmly. Locking both hands into fists, thumb atop the index finger, he drew a series of deep breaths. Do not punch at the object, punch through it, beyond it, he could hear Armadiel's patient voice explaining.

Sometimes, when he realized that the Seeker and all the others were gone, he felt desperately alone.

But he did not feel so alone with Madran beside him and Sioraf sleeping nearby.

He inhaled once more, then rammed his fists forward as he exhaled.

The strip of metal doorframe crumpled.

He struck it again. With his third blow it broke apart and pulled loose from the wall.

A spark crackled in the opening. Peering in, Caeled saw something that looked like metal worms twisting up through the wall. He started to reach in with his right hand and touch one when Madran caught his arm. "Wait. Elder buildings have magical wards. I worked for a while with an Island circus whose owner lost all his eyesight when he tried to take apart an Elder artifact someone sold him. Metal worms that looked like those spat fire into his eyes and blinded him."

Caeled lifted his left hand, flexing the fingers. "This isn't so vulnerable," he said. Reaching into the hole, he wrapped his silvery index finger around one of the worms and pulled.

Lightning hurled him against the wall on the far side of the cell. Fire danced from his fingertips; smoke curled from his clothing.

The air stank of old magic, scorched and metallic.

The explosion woke Sioraf. In one swift bound she was crouched beside Caeled, her blue eyes wide with concern. "You must touch your hand to metal," she told him, "to allow the magic to drain from your body. My father taught me that," she added.

Getting unsteadily to his feet, Caeled staggered to the door. With his silver hand he reached toward the Elder metal. A blue spark as vivid as Sioraf's eyes leaped from his fingertips to the door.

It grated open.

Caeled stared down at his hand. The silver was streaked and blackened.

The Madra Allta bared his teeth in a smile. "Useful, that metal hand," he observed.

"So I've discovered," replied Caeled. "At first I hated it. Every time I looked at it I was reminded of the past; bitter memories. Now I never think about it, it's become part of my body. In the last few days it's saved my life more than once."

"Everything has its purpose," Madran told him. "Even a dog's tail." He grinned and winked one bright brown eye.

Caeled was startled to realize he had actually begun to like the big Allta though he had lost his hand to a similar weredog.

Looking at Madran, he was torn between fear and fondness . . . as with Sioraf.

She stepped out into the metal corridor and drew a deep, questing breath. "I can smell blood." Sioraf pointed. "This way."

"Maybe the Cityselves are holding other wounded prisoners," Caeled suggested.

Madran looked dubious. "I doubt if they keep prisoners alive — for long."

They followed Sioraf down the corridor in the opposite direction to the one Bochar had led them. This stretch of passageway was in deep shadow for most of its length because the majority of lights in the ceiling had died. They passed a number of metal doors that seemed to be locked or rusted shut.

But eventually they came to a section of corridor where one white light still burned, and a door was very slightly ajar.

Finger bones like desperate claws protruded through the gap.

Caeled put an eye to the opening. He could dimly make out four skeletons in a small room. Three, an adult and two small children, were huddled together, while a second adult skeleton lay with its dead fingers jammed in the doorway. When Caeled touched the bones they crumbled into powder.

A thin cylinder of metal foil fell from the disintegrating fingers.

Caeled's heart was thundering as he carefully unrolled the foil. He had seen its like in Baddalaur: it was the kenaf of the ancients.

Sioraf pressed close to his side. "What do you suppose happened here?"

"There is no odor of death," Madran commented. "Whatever it was, it happened a very long time ago."

"Very long indeed," Caeled murmured as he began deciphering script from the ancient past. How Nanri would have thrilled to this discovery!

As Caeled read a lump rose in his throat. "These were Elders," he said, glancing back at the skeletons with a sense of wonder although they were human in form, unremarkable. But knowing who they had been invested them with glamor. "They were trapped in this room when the power went," he read slowly, stumbling over the archaic writing. "The door opened just a crack, then locked in that position. In the days that followed no one came. Before they could starve to death, the man forced himself to strangle his wife and children. Then he died an agonizing death, without food or drink, accompanied only by the decaying bodies of those he loved."

Caeled's eyes filled with tears.

With one slim finger Sioraf lifted a single drop of moisture from his cheek. She carried it to her lips and tasted it curiously. "Why do you weep?"

Caeled merely shook his head.

"They are long dead, their pain is over," Sioraf told him.

"I feel for them anyway. I can imagine what it must have been like for them — for him especially."

"Ah, you are just being human," the vampir said in a dismissive voice. She turned abruptly and continued down the corridor.

"Why is she angry with me?" Caeled asked Madran as they followed her.

"She isn't angry. She's envious. Of your humanity."

Caeled was surprised by the Allta's insight. He was, he realized, continually expecting Madran to act like a beast. But he was not a beast, or not entirely.

"Are you envious of my humanity?" Caeled wanted to know.

"Not in the slightest," was the honest reply. "I would hate to be trapped in one frail form with just one set of senses."

They found much fresher bodies at the end of the hall, in a domed room where another white light still survived. Metal floors and walls amplified the light to blinding. Caeled had to squint to be able to look at the naked man and woman laid side by side on a long table.

Their youthful bodies were perfectly shaped, but their heads had been crushed beyond recognition.

"Gwynne," Caeled said with conviction. "This is her work."

Madran bent over the ruin of the woman's skull and sniffed. "You're right; her odor is on them. Like stone dust, almost. But not quite. Unmistakable, anyway."

"Here!" cried Sioraf, following a trail of spattered blood across the floor. The drops ceased at a blank wall.

Caeled joined the vampir. He was about to tap on the wall when once more Madran stopped him. "Be careful until you know what's on the other side."

"I do know," insisted Sioraf. "Blood. I am never mistaken about blood."

Madran's nostrils quivered. "Nor I about meat. I think there's meat on the other side of this wall. But how do we get to it? This is the last room on the corridor."

Caeled thought back again to the previous day, and the old man opening a similar wall. But . . . he had not pressed his hand against the wall, Caeled suddenly recalled. He had slapped it. Sharply.

Yes!

Imitating the gesture, Caeled gave the blank surface a smart slap with his right hand.

Nothing happened. He moved down a little and tried again. There was a sound of something ponderous and rusty creaking within the wall, then a seam opened down the middle.

The three recoiled from the stench.

The room beyond was an abattoir, its walls and floor unspeakably stained. Suppurating sacks leaked foul liquids. A torso that might have been human dangled from a hook set in the ceiling.

Spreadeagled on a metal table were the gnawed remains of another body. The stomach cavity was open, organs and entrails missing, and the neck ended in a ragged stump, but from the knife buried in the chest Caeled recognized what had once been the beautiful youth known as Bochar.

"This is where they prepare the meat for the feast," Madran said. Unconsciously, the Allta drooled.

Caeled felt his gorge rise in disgust.

Sioraf paused beside Bochar's body and ran one index finger through the congealed blood pooled on the table. She tasted it, then spat. "Bitter! Unlike any blood I ever . . . " Catching the look of revulsion on Caeled's face, she said testily, "I am what I am. Do not judge me. Humans have habits that are disgusting to me; I just don't comment on them."

"What habits?" he asked in surprise.

"Never mind."

At the back of the abattoir was a narrow doorway leading into yet another corridor, low-ceilinged, darker, filthier. After a moment's hesitation, the trio entered. The way was littered with piles of excreta, rotting meat, and refuse so old it had disintegrated into a foul-smelling mud. Caeled pinched his nostrils shut to keep from smelling the fetid air. Breathing through his mouth, he muttered, "Whatever they are, they live like animals."

"They live like humans," Madran retorted with icy scorn. "Animals would be cleaner."

They continued through a maze of corridors. The few remaining lights in the ceiling cast a leprous yellow glow. Somewhere in the distance water dripped incessantly.

Caeled's skin had begun to prickle and burn.

They came to a metal door halfway retracted into the wall. Followed by Madran, Caeled entered warily, allowing his eyes a few moments to accustom themselves to the gloom.

Then he saw a woman . . . with a fur blanket twisted around herself?

He shook his head in disbelief. He was looking at a dead human female lying wrapped in the arms of an equally dead beast.

The creature resembled a Simpan-sai, but was bigger, the hair coarser, the features brutish. He formed an appalling contrast to the woman, who was as beautiful and delicately-featured as Bochar and his kin.

The air was heavy with musk. Scratches and bite marks scored the woman's breasts.

At his shoulder Madran growled something and Caeled had a sudden image of the Allta mating with a human.

Obscurely embarrassed, he backed out of the room.

"So now we know," Madran said when they were in the corridor again. "They've mated with the beasts in the trees. It's a perfect relationship; the beasts guard this place during the day, and the humans, as Bochar said, reclaim it at night. It's a partnership."

It's disgusting, thought Caeled, but he could not say so. Not to Madran, who had loved his human woman.

Sioraf, ahead of them as usual, called again and they hurried to join her. She stood in the doorway of a large chamber where the lights still burned. "I've found Panasen," she announced.

Her eyes were gleaming.

The air in the room was thick with the cloying smell of sweet wine. Tossed on the pallet of straw that served as a bed were Sioraf's knife and Madran's sickle.

The First Citizen lay sprawled insensate across a metal desk. He was quite drunk.

Caeled rubbed furiously at his prickling flesh while Madran crossed the room in two loping strides to snatch up the sickle and knife.

That was when Caeled noticed the spear casually propped against the wall in the corner.

A slender metal shaft ended in a triangular head, its center ornamented with a disc of what appeared to be crystal, though surely crystal was too fragile to be used in a weapon. Hanging beside the spear was a small shield fashioned of greenish-gray stone studded with bosses incised in Elder script. The bosses were connected by a delicate metal tracery encircling a precisely shaped hole in the center.

Caeled stared at the artifacts in amazement.

He had never seen the Arcana before, yet he knew — instinctively and beyond question — that he was looking upon two of the most powerful objects in the world.

Yet here they were in Panasen's chamber. And there was dried blood crusted on the head of the Spear.

Suddenly Madran clamped his hands over his ears. He grimaced in pain. "That whine!" he cried. "That high-pitched whine!"

Caeled heard no whine, but his flesh was itching as if thousands of insects were crawling over the surface of his skin.

He clawed at himself with desperate fingers. "It's the Arcana," he managed to gasp. "The power of the Arcana!"

Madran took his hands from his ears. The sound only he could hear made him wince. "What did you say?"

"I said, it's the Arcana. I can't believe we've found them but here they are. The Spear and the Stone."

Ignoring his itching, Caeled touched the shaft of the Spear with reverent fingers. At once a great surge of power flowed through him . . .

And at that moment the beasts attacked.

Scores of hairy Treeselves burst through the doorway and swarmed over the trio, battering them in a frenzy. Caeled went down under a rain of blows, hearing Sioraf's scream and Madran's roar. Something hammered his forehead. His last thought before losing consciousness was to acknowledge the awful irony: he had found the Arcana only to lose them again. To have come so close . . .

So close . . .

CHAPTER SIXTY-FIVE

Their lovemaking built to a crescendo of tightly controlled passion. At the zenith of ecstasy, consciousness melded and fused. In that instant — that single instant — two truly became one.

A pulse of incredible power thundered through the layers of the Aethyra, tearing holes in the fabric of time and space.

A black spark ignited. In its core a cancerous red light blossomed . . . and grew.

In the Aethyra above the Forest of Taesir, the Void grew.

Her fist had been raised, about to pound through the glass, when the Stone Warrior realized the bloody corpse being torn apart by the people within did not belong to Caeled. They were ripping open the belly of a more slightly built young man, with battered but still-beautiful features.

As she stared through one of the few remaining panes of glass, Gwynne had watched identically beautiful, blank-faced people rend one of their own.

One of the men, older than the others, pushed his way forward. The blood-smeared crowd parted to make way for him with curious cringing postures. Crouching over the torn corpse, the old man lifted something . . . the curved blade of a sickle briefly caught the light.

Gwynne knew that sickle. The last time she saw it, Madran had been carrying it.

She leaned forward, straining to see better and cursing her disintegrating eyesight.

In the chest of the corpse on the floor was a knife with a handle that looked suspiciously like the distinctive, leather-wrapped handle of Sioraf's ripple-edged knife.

So they were here. Could they still be alive?

As the Stone Warrior watched, the old man below used his sickle to slice the head from the dead body, then broke open the top of the skull and began to feed.

Cannibal.

Other cannibals crowded close with gleaming, jealous eyes, lusting after the delicacy the old man was devouring.

Beautiful cannibals.

Eaters of Flesh.

The Stone Warrior gave a grunt of revulsion.

When Gwynne was a small child, the children's nurse in her parents' house had used the Eaters of Flesh as a threat to force her young charges to obey. The Eaters of Flesh, she claimed, were pirates from the World's Edge who provisioned themselves for long sea voyages with prisoners whom they put to work on shipboard, then ultimately ate.

They particularly favored children, the nurse related. "Tenderer," was her explanation as she pinched a childish arm.

The child-Gwynne had often wakened screaming from nightmares in which corsairs climbed in through her bedroom window to capture and eat her.

Once cannibalism had been virtually unknown in the Nations. But by the time she rode with the Snowscalds, there were an increasing number of stories about outlying villages where people turned cannibal when their livestock died of unnamed diseases and their crops failed.

There was a time when men would rather starve than eat their fellows, but like so many other taboos, this one had lost its power to terrify. The world was sinking into a morass of savagery where kill or be killed seemed the only remaining law.

Gwynne was not horrified by the eating habits of Madran, whom she did not consider human. As for Sioraf, the vampiri were a law unto themselves.

But for humankind like herself — as she once had been — to turn cannibal, dismayed her as Caeled had been dismayed by the Madra Allta. Some things were too terrible.

Caeled. His face flashed through her mind; his strong features, his clear dark eyes bright with intelligence. Not long ago she had calmly considered killing him if need be to gain her own ends. Now she was worried about him. Somehow he seemed the last remnant of something that had once been fine and clean, humankind as the gods intended them to be.

But where was he?

The cannibals inside must know.

Her every instinct was to turn away and leave them to their repulsive feast, to push through the barrier of thorns embracing the dome and go as far and as fast as she could from this place.

But she must stay. She must find Caeled.

Stepping back from the window into the shadows, she watched the feast proceed. Men and women as beautiful as the others carried in great lumps of skinned meat, haunches and shoulders and racks of ribs, which they dumped unceremoniously on the table and even on the floor. The crowd attacked in a feeding frenzy. Some raw vegetables were provided, but for the most part the feasters dined on raw meat.

Gwynne was thankful she could not see clearly enough to tell if the bloody meat had originally come from animals or humans.

The men and women fought over choice morsels, cramming the food into their mouths with both hands. When they had eaten their fill they openly relieved themselves on the floor, then rutted enthusiastically or curled up and slept against the wall.

It had been a long time since anything had so moved the Stone Warrior to anger other than her own plight. But now she found herself trembling with rage. These debased creatures . . . she who longed to regain her humanity was appalled at those who seemed so content to throw off humanity altogether and become worse than beasts.

The Stone Warrior turned to look back through the tangled vegetation toward the small round hut where she had left two corpses. She had killed them without compunction . . . like an animal. What did that make her? she asked herself for the first time.

She had always been strong; circumstances had made her so. This foul affliction that covered her skin had made her cold and uncaring as well, but now she faced the fact that it was costing her the very things she prized most about humanity, the tenderness and love her family had engendered in her.

Silan! she cried silently. My boys!

Baby Derfyl. What infant would snuggle in her stony arms now?

Resolve returned in a rush. She would become a woman again, she must.

And to do that she had to find Caeled, the Arcana, the twins . . .

When dawn paled the sky and the chamber abruptly emptied, Gwynne stepped through a broken pane and into the domed room. She would find Caeled, or his corpse. And she would wipe these cannibals from the earth before she left.

She came to him as he lay wide-eyed on his pallet, staring up at the sky. Red streaks of light stained the east and were reflected in his eyes.

Since Kichal entered the service of the Duet, he had never experienced the need to sleep.

"Only the weak sleep," Sarel whispered approvingly,

bending down to him. "And you are strong, so strong. I have made you so."

Kichal groaned with a mixture of pleasure and pain, agony nullified by rapture. Closing his eyes, he felt as if a naked human female lay the length of him, although he knew Sarel only visited him in her Aethyral form.

Soft fingers seemed to touch his face, tracing the line of his jaw. "Do you dream, Kichal? Do you still dream?" she asked curiously.

"Yes. No. I don't know, I don't remember. There are times when I see images, but I'm not sure if these are my own memories or real dreams. The line between what is and what might be is lost."

"When you have power," Sarel replied, "absolute power, there is no line. Everything is attainable. Now rise up, Kichal, and prepare your army. When the sun rises, a Void will devour the forest to clear a way for them. It will be the most powerful Void we have ever created, far larger than the one that destroyed Baddalaur. When the Void has done its work you can release the Bred. Order them to hunt. Any living thing they find is theirs. And when you have scoured this place, when it is purified, Lares and I will come. Prepare the way."

"It will be done." Kichal shuddered as the woman left him. He opened his eyes and sat up. When he rubbed his hand across his cheeks, he discovered that he was weeping blood. Again.

CHAPTER SIXTY-SIX

"Just you!" A smiling Cityself whose exquisite features were marred by an eye the color of alabaster, separated Caeled from the others using the jawbone of an enormous carnivore as a prod.

Caeled glanced back toward Madran and Sioraf. All three of them had been bound with red-veined vines when they were brought from their cell. They had lain there for a lengthy but indeterminate time, recovering from the battering they had received from the Treeselves.

Now the trio were surrounded by armed Cityselves. Smiling with no warmth or meaning behind the expression, the people carried an assortment of stone, bone, and crude wooden weapons which they brandished from time to time.

Light from the interior of the dome washed over Caeled and his companions as they were herded through an opening in the thorn bushes and out into the night. Stars shone high above. A faint glow in the east heralded the false dawn.

Caeled shouldered past the walleyed man to rejoin Madran and Sioraf, then fixed his unblinking gaze on the crowd surrounding them. The Cityselves were curiously unable to meet his eyes for long. They fell back a few paces, giving him space in which to say his good-byes.

"Now it ends," Caeled told his companions. His voice was low with regret.

Madran bared his teeth. "Not yet it doesn't. We're still breathing."

"You could escape," Caeled told the Madra Allta. "You could were-change and make a run for it. They might be so startled you could break through their circle and get out of this place."

The big man shook his head. "No."

"Why not? Don't you want to live?"

"Of course I want to live. But it isn't in me to leave those I . . . " Madran's jaws snapped shut.

He pressed close to Caeled's shoulder until shaggy pale mane mingled with coarse black locks. "I won't go yet," he said. "I imagine it will only be you and Panasen atop the dome. If Sioraf and I can distract them, it might give you a chance."

"But you are two, and they are many," Caeled protested.

"I am a Madra Allta . . . "

"And I am vampir," Sioraf whispered. She rested her head on Caeled's other shoulder. "Give me some of your blood, give me some of your strength, and I will show them the power of the vampir."

Without hesitation, Caeled exposed his neck to her fangs. "Take it."

Madran used his bulk to shield them from the eyes of the Cityselves. "Hurry," he urged, "before they get too suspicious."

The vampir's bite was a feather touch, cool but sensuous. It sent an erotic tingling through Caeled's body. He felt a powerful sexual arousal as her pointed tongue began to lap with the greatest delicacy at the tiny wound she had opened in his neck. She was cold but he was warm; he was hot; he was vibrantly alive even though blood was seeping from him. Exhilaration ran through his veins like tiny bubbles. He was swept with a heady sense of invulnerability.

He wanted to laugh out loud.

Sioraf withdrew her mouth from his neck. Then before he could respond, she kissed him on the mouth.

❖   ❖   ❖

The taste of his own blood was salty and metallic on her lips but the breath she breathed into his nostrils was, briefly, warm.

"Enough wasting time! The First Citizen is waiting above." The man with the jawbone strode forward. His eyes roamed over Caeled's body appraisingly. "Lot of meat on you," he commented. "Go. The stairs are that way." They pushed through dense shrubbery.

The metal stairway spiralled around the outside of the huge dome. Although the steps and rails seemed solid enough, the brackets affixing them to the structure had rusted so the stairway creaked with every step.

Caeled lifted his head and looked up. The stars were beginning to fade. Already the purple of the sky was giving way to violet.

Would he live long enough, he wondered, to greet Nusas one last time?

As a student in Baddalaur — could that have been only a few days ago? — one of his greatest pleasures had been to stand in the doorway of his cell and watch the sun rise over the rim of the extinct volcano.

The jawbone prodded his spine. Caeled swayed. He had been too long without food. Madran had eaten a dog-rat, and Sioraf had taken strength from his blood, but Caeled himself had nothing to sustain him but his own will.

"Hurry. Soon it will be dawn."

When Caeled paused to glance over his shoulder he was surprised to discover how high they had climbed. "I'm in no rush," he told his guard.

"Soon it will be dawn," the white-eyed man repeated in a tense voice.

"What happens then?"

"Then the Treeselves come," the guard replied. "If we have not fed before they arrive, they will eat you themselves." He jabbed Caeled again with his prod.

"I'd hate to deprive you of your meal," the young man responded sarcastically. He resumed climbing.

As he followed the spiral stairs around the great dome he was surreptitiously testing his bonds. Before the vines were twisted around his body he had drawn in a huge breath and held it, so that when he expelled all the air in his lungs his bindings would be loose. His wrists had been tightly lashed together, with particular attention paid to his metal hand, but the fingernail on his metal thumb had by now almost severed the vine twisted around his right hand.

"Hurry!" the Cityself urged, prodding him again.

Caeled looked to the east. Most of the stars had vanished, only the brightest remained. Then while he was watching they suddenly shimmered as if a gauze veil had been drawn across them.

He was almost at the top of the dome now. When he looked down he could make out something of the original outline of the city. Once it must have been very beautiful. An array of interlocking circles were joined by swirling spirals. There was something hauntingly familiar about the design . . .

Caeled stopped so abruptly the jawbone dug into his spine.

The city of Gor had been laid out in the same pattern that once covered the floor of the Central Courtyard in Baddalaur.

Although most of the pattern was now obscured by vines and thorn bushes, or marred with collapsed buildings and broken paving, there was no mistake. As he gazed down in wonder, Caeled recalled how he used to feel when he stood on the volcano's rim and gazed down at the pattern in the courtyard far below; the sense that he could fall into the spiral and continue falling, on and on forever.

In ancient folklore the spiral meant eternity.

Caeled stepped onto the small circular platform atop the dome and prepared to meet his death.

✧ ✧ ✧

Life flowed out of the Aethyra. The pulsing spark grew, drawing energy from the Realms. Formed from the intense, cojoined sexual energy of the Duet, it was now feeding on the life force that sustained the Aethyra, altering it, turning life into the antithesis of life, a deadly spiral of death and annihilation.

The Void grew, spinning down through the violated layers of the Aethyra.

Panasen touched Caeled's throat with the tip of the triangular Spearhead. "You should be honored," he said. "Only the best are brought here." Around his neck, Caeled observed, the Stone hung like a shield from leather cords. The strengthening light revealed tiny colored beads amid its engraved bosses and wire tracery.

Caeled tried to back away from the point of the Spear. But the circular platform was less than one long pace across, and featureless save for a metal spike jutting from its center.

"Your death will be painless," Panasen promised as he glanced toward the east in anticipation. "When the sun rises, in that moment before the Cityselves retire and the Treeselves arrive, I will kill you and make a feast of your soft brains." His mouth gaped in a parody of a smile that displayed toothless gums. "I can show you no greater honor."

"But I am not honored," Caeled yelled at him. He did not know he could be heard below, but if Madran and Sioraf were going to try something, they had better do it now. "Where is the honor," he shouted, "in being killed and eaten like an animal, by an animal!"

Panasen's grip tightened on the Spear. "I'll overlook your ignorance because you do not know us. You do not know our history. Ours is a great race. We can trace our lineage to the ancients, we are of Elder blood."

Caeled spat. "You lie. The Elders were a proud and noble people."

Panasen replied, "When the gods moved upon the face of the earth, and there was light and the world ended, the City was one of the few places that survived. Beneath its domes in chambers of metal and stone our forefathers listened to the gods bellow above them. Only the Artifacts kept them safe from the gods' rage." He lifted the Spear slightly and with his other hand touched the Stone on his chest. "The Shaft and the Badge worked their magic. Our race survived."

"To become cannibals. Abominations."

"We survived!" Panasen cried. "Our ancestors ate whatever they had to in order to survive! And we live because of their courage; we carry on the glorious traditions of our forefathers."

The shining face of Nusas peered over the Rim of the World.

The Spear and Stone came to glittering, blazing life.

And Panasen lunged.

CHAPTER SIXTY-SEVEN

Madran changed. In the instant before the first beam of sunlight lanced the sky, his form altered. Muscles rippled into new configurations, sinews knotted, bones ground together. The planes and angles of his face altered to reveal the wolfhound within.

As his body changed, his bonds fell away from the new shape.

It took a single heartbeat.

The Madra Allta threw back his head and howled.

Before the transformation was complete, however, Madran froze the process so he was part man and part beast, combining the strengths of both. Canine claws slashed at the nearest Cityself, tearing his shoulder. A man's fist crashed into another and sent him reeling backward to be impaled upon the wall of thorns.

Another of the Cityselves rushed to the attack only to have Sioraf appear before him. She too was transformed, her beauty lost in a terrifying visage. The skin of her face pulled taut, revealing the skull beneath. A lifted lip bared vampiric fangs. Her red and pointed tongue thrust forward, hideously suggestive. The Cityself hesitated, appalled. Sioraf attacked with long-nailed hands hooked into claws and tore through his chest as if it were butter, pulling out the beating heart.

Instead of running away at the sight, however, the other Cityselves closed in . . . and began to change.

✦   ✦   ✦

Desperation lending him strength, Caeled burst his weakened bonds. Cycles of training in Baddalaur came into play as he tilted his body and allowed the head of the Spear to slide harmlessly past his chest. Throwing himself down, he lashed out with his feet and kicked Panasen's legs from under him. The First Citizen fell with a crash onto the metal platform.

The Spear rolled out of his hands.

Caeled twisted to one side as the walleyed Cityself, with the jawbone still in his hands, lunged for him . . . then stopped in midstride as sunlight touched his face.

The Cityself changed.

His features sagged and softened into a new shape. Brow jutted; mouth widened; nose flattened. Coarse hair sprouted.

Cityself became Treeself.

With a howl the brute threw itself on Caeled. Long arms wrapped around him with inhuman strength as savage teeth snapped close to his face. The sickening breath of a carnivore washed over him.

Caeled managed to thrust his metal hand into the creature's gaping mouth. He closed his fingers on its lower jaw while he braced his other hand against its breastbone. Then with all the strength he possessed, he twisted.

The jaw was torn from the Treeself. The brute's scream shrilled beyond human hearing. Caeled allowed it to stagger blindly away and tumble over the edge of the platform.

Before the body hit the ground far below, Caeled was reaching for the Spear. Panasen got to it first.

Then Panasen . . . changed.

With the coming of day, the Cityselves became Treeselves. Hundreds of large apes crowded in on the vampir and the Madra Allta. Madran was swift and savage, a human brain calculating every bestial movement, but a blow that would have eviscerated a man only ripped through the flesh of his enemies' muscular bellies.

Revitalized by Caeled's blood, Sioraf was fighting with equal speed and skill if not strength. But the pair were hopelessly outnumbered.

Blows rained down on them from all sides. The Treeselves seized stones, branches, whatever came to hand that could be used to club and destroy. Werebeast and vampir were harder to injure than humankind, but it was obvious that even their abilities would not be enough to save them for long.

As she stumbled back, Sioraf cast a last despairing glance upward, hoping to see Caeled atop the dome.

Then a figure battered its way through the thorns to join the fight.

Gwynne lifted her morningstar in both hands, laughing at the blows that thudded harmlessly off her stony hide. Then, screaming the battle cry of the Snowscalds, she hurled herself into the midst of the Treeselves.

Panasen lunged forward with the Spear, driving Caeled back.

"Which is the beast form, human? This or the Cityselves?" Coming from his Treeself body, Panasen's voice was a shrill screech. "Once we were human, but we became greater than mere man. We became the Gor Allta. Ape and human, cleverest of all the werebeasts."

Caeled danced lightly to his left. He was trying to maneuver Panasen around to face the sun. "Legend has it that the Arcana changed you," he said. "Generation after generation the power of the Arcana worked on you, turning you into monsters. Now you live in filth no animal would tolerate, in the ruins of former glory."

With a roar of fury Panasen leaped forward. Caeled brushed the head of the Spear aside with his metal hand. At the moment of contact a spark jumped from his fingers to the Spearhead, causing a shock to run along his arm.

The head of the Spear began to pulse with a rhythmic glow.

The Gor Allta that had been Panasen swung the Spear in a broad arc. Caeled dropped to one knee, punching his silver fist into Panasen's belly. But the Gor Allta's muscular body absorbed the blow.

Panasen staggered but did not drop the Spear.

Driven to the very edge of the platform, he blinked into the rising sun, uttered a despairing cry and hurled the Spear at Caeled.

Nusas blinded him so that he missed. Caeled's metal hand closed on the shaft in midair, catching and holding.

He reversed the Spear in one smooth motion and drove the head deep into one of the Gor Allta's eyes, passing into the brain behind. There was not even time for a cry of pain.

The body tumbled sideways and fell. Caeled was still clutching the Spear, but the Stone hung from its leather thongs around the dead neck.

Panasen's body slid over the edge of the platform; then the angle of incline sent it tumbling down.

Caeled made a grab for it, but too late.

He could only watch helplessly as the dead Gor Allta went slithering down the glassy curve of the dome, painting the surface with its blood. As Caeled started to run down the stairs, a flicker of movement at the corner of his vision arrested his attention.

He turned and looked up.

Nusas no longer claimed the sky.

Overhead the air was rippling visibly around a circular black cloud. The cloud was spinning and falling, growing larger with every moment. And the sound it was making . . .

. . . the sound . . .

. . . was terrifying familiar.

Ward Point.

Baddalaur.

The White Scream, the voice of the Void.

Panasen's body struck the ground directly in front of Sioraf, spattering her with gore. As she jumped back, startled, a female Treeself attacked her. She fought off the female, feeling her strength ebb as she did so. She was wounded; she was losing precious blood.

Sioraf turned back to the body of Panasen.

She recognized the round stone shield, now throbbing with fiery pinpoints of light. In spite of her desperate situation, Sioraf smiled with satisfaction at the death of the First Citizen of Gor.

When she stooped to touch the body her fingertips brushed the shield.

At the moment of contact between her fingers and the Stone, Sioraf's body convulsed. The vampiric cast was stripped from her features, leaving a young and beautiful woman.

Her eyes rolled back in her head and she fell unconscious across Panasen's body.

With a yowl of triumph a Treeself leapt onto her still form, but Gwynne's morningstar promptly crushed life from the creature.

The Void descended, growing, sucking life out of the atmosphere. Trees and bushes withered beneath its shadow. As it drew closer to the forest it began to uproot the trees and pull them into its vortex. Ancient goldwoods groaned in their dying. Parasitic veins ruptured to leak a crimson ichor.

At the edge of the Forest of Taesir, Kichal released the Bred.

The Stone Warrior was drenched with blood, almost unrecognizable. Madran's fur was clotted with gore. But when Caeled reached the foot of the stairs and saw them, he thought they had never looked better.

He had no time to greet them, however. A Treeself bounded toward him. With a smooth turn of his wrist he impaled the creature on the point of the Spear, then saw its crystal ornamentation blaze even more brightly.

Caeled shouted at Gwynne, "There's a Void coming!"

The Stone Warrior flung one hand to her mouth. "We have to get out of here!" she cried. Mention of the Void stripped her of courage.

Madran stooped to lift the unconscious Sioraf from Panasen's corpse, and as he did so, Caeled reached forward with the Spear to prod the Stone free of the ruined body. He accidentally thrust the Spearhead into the hole in the center of the Stone. When he raised the Spear the Stone slid down the shaft . . . and locked into place with an audible click.

The fireball that engulfed Caeled lasted less than a heartbeat, but it sent the surviving Treeselves screaming away.

When Madran and Gwynne could see again, they discovered to their amazement that Caeled was . . . undestroyed. But different.

He still held the Spear in his left fist. Blue snakes of light ran hissing along the shaft from the Spearhead to wrap around his silver hand.

The face belonged to Caeled, but the posture had changed. He seemed taller, broader. The look in his eyes was that of someone gazing into far distances.

When his gaze swung around to Gwynne and Madran, however, his expression was very gentle.

He spread his arms. "Come to me."

The Void descended.

CHAPTER SIXTY-EIGHT

The Void had devoured the ancient forest, creating a swath of utter devastation in which ragged stumps of ancient trees jutted up from a soupy mire, soil was stripped down to bedrock, stone was ground to powder. Then, unsated, it swirled over the outskirts of the city, scouring the ancient walls of Gor. They ran like liquid and flowed upward into the Void in long glutinuous strands.

Whirling on, the Void swept up the few surviving Gor Allta, warping them through their dual selves — human and beast — before absorbing them into its core, where their terrified screams gave way to an even more terrible silence.

Then it touched the dome.

The remaining glass exploded into slivers, but before the slivers reached the ground they turned to liquid, then to sand.

The Void moved on while what remained of the dome collapsed inward, its metal skeleton crumbling into tiny brown flakes.

As he held the Spear aloft in his left hand, Caeled *saw* a barrier of cool blue light around himself and his companions. Gwynne and Madran huddled close to him, with Sioraf in the Allta's arms.

The Void rolled over them.

The world became silent, terrible.

In the heart of the Void there was nothing the five senses could identify, neither darkness nor light, heat nor cold. No sound, no sensation.

Yet the Void was not empty. It was brimming with a stupifying emotional desolation.

Madran screamed but there was no sound. Gwynne shut her eyes, then opened them again only to discover that it made no difference.

Blue light flared around them, suddenly visible, encircling them in an azure bubble.

Within the bubble, Caeled laughed.

He laughed as he might have done when he was a boy, playing at heroic games where he always won. Where triumph was sure and sweet. He laughed as if there was nothing in the world to fear.

The first moment he touched the Spear he had felt intimations of its power. Wondrous possibilities had shimmered at the edge of his consciousness, fragments of knowledge, incomplete mosiacs, unfinished friezes. Then, when the Stone had locked in place on the shaft of the Spear, he felt his mind expand to encompass endless vistas, and for an instant — a single instant — he had almost known *everything*.

Pain blossomed in his head. He felt as if his skull were being ripped apart. But suddenly he knew what he had to do. The necessary fragments of wisdom came together in his brain. Yet even as he was assimilating their message, the rest of his newfound knowledge was fading away like the remnants of a dream.

He had no time to mourn the loss, he must destroy the destroyer!

With the knowledge he retained, creating a shield of power was simplicity itself.

So was destroying the Void.

Caeled sent his questing consciousness into the core of emptiness, where the fire of lust that gave birth to the Void still burned. He traced its glow back along a pathway of passion . . .

And suddenly he was a small boy again, bursting uninvited into his mother's bedchamber, gazing with shocked eyes at a scene he could not understand.

But that was another place, another time. He was not seeing his mother and one of her lovers writhing upon the bed now — he was looking at Sarel and Lares, the dark heart of the Void.

His left hand reached out and a bolt of blue fire sparked from his fingertips to lash across the woman's naked back, blistering her pale skin. She leaped off the man with a shriek of agony; whirled around; saw Caeled.

"Silverhand!" Sarel screamed.

Caeled struck at the twins again. Blue lightning sizzled through the air to Lares, knocking him from the bed. He fell with a crash to the stone flags, all his weight landing on one bent knee and shattering the kneecap. A moment later his temple struck the corner of the bedstead, knocking him unconscious.

The sudden sundering of the Duet broke their connection with the Void.

Without a center it rapidly lost cohesion. A ravening tentacle whirled off on its own to feed upon the nearest life forms — which happened to be the army of the Bred, marching across the ground the Void had so recently swept clean.

In the instant before they were swallowed up, the disciplined troops turned into savage beasts. They had no time to attack each other; the White Scream rang through their heads and they were no more.

But the Void had taken its final victims. Spinning out of control, it began to collapse.

An explosion of warped light bathed the Aethyra in acid fire. The atmosphere roiled with turbulence; thunder boomed in the distance.

The White Scream faded to a sigh as the great Void dissipated. In its wake only a fresh, clean wind blew across the land.

Slowly, Sarel crawled from the bed to crouch over her unconscious brother. Her skin was scored with blisters and the long weal of burnt flesh on her back would leave a terrible scar, but she felt none of this, all her suffering was for Lares. She had not imagined anything could injure him. Everything else was forgotten as she pressed her mouth to his and poured her breath into him.

When she felt him stir at last, she raised her head, only to find herself confronting the shadowy form of a tall young man wreathed in blue fire; a young man whose grave eyes studied her as if reading the secrets of her soul.

They stared at each other for a timeless moment in which the only sound either heard was the clean wind blowing.

"We will meet again," she swore, gasping, "and next time I will kill you, Silverhand!"

"We will meet again," Caeled promised grimly.

EPILOGUE

A riddle, is it not?

Out of the ashes of the Forest of Taesir, a new forest is growing. I saw the first green shoots pushing through the gray ash as we walked away.

The City of Gor is gone, and in its place a lake now shimmers. A lovely lake of green glass.

The Gor Allta are no more, and the Bred were almost totally destroyed by the Void the Duet made.

A paradox. Out of evil, good can come.

I have taken the first steps upon the road of my destiny. When exactly did I start out on this road? When we destroyed the Gor? Or was it when I met my companions whose help has brought me this far? Did my journey begin with the destruction of Baddalaur, or even earlier, on that terrible day in Ward Point when my childhood ended? And my life began again.

This much I know: my destiny is to restore order to this chaotic world. My teachers taught me that there must be order; the survival of humankind depends upon it.

I owe it to my teachers, to Nanri and Armadiel and the others, to carry out their precepts. I must find the remaining two Arcana, destroy the Duet and make the world as it should be. This is my destiny . . . and I have learned now that a man cannot escape his destiny.

The Spear and the Stone have gifted me with knowledge and partial understanding. And if but two of the Arcana can do this, what then will the Sword and the Cup make of me?

Once I have the four together — will I still be a man?
—from the Journal of Caeled Silverhand